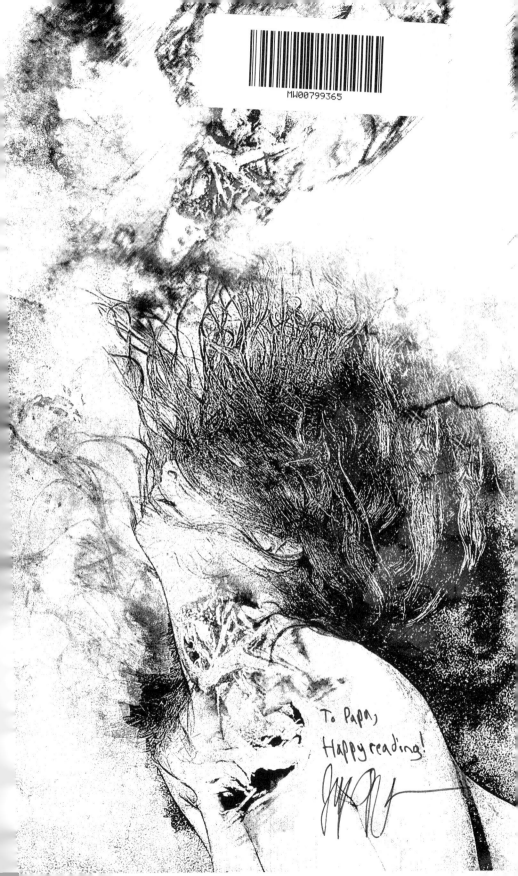

To Papa,

Happy reading!

ALSO BY RANDY CHANDLER

EDITOR:
Stiff Things: The Splatterporn Anthology

NOVELS AND COLLECTIONS:
Bad Juju
Daemon of the Dark Wood
Devils, Death & Dark Wonders
Dime Detective
Duet for the Devil (with t. winter-damon)
Hellz Bellz

EDITED BY CHERYL MULLENAX

Stiff Things: The Splatterporn Anthology
Vile Things: Extreme Deviations of Horror
Sick Things: Extreme Creature Anthology
The Death Panel: Murder, Mayhem and Madness
Necro Files: Two Decades of Extreme Horror
Deadcore: 4 Hardcore Zombie Novellas
Deadlines: Horror and Dark Fiction

YEAR'S BEST HARDCORE HORROR

VOLUME 2

EDITORS:

RANDY CHANDLER

CHERYL MULLENAX

WWW.COMETPRESS.US

First Comet Press Trade Paperback Edition
June 2017

Year's Best Hardcore Horror Volume 2 copyright © 2017
by Randy Chandler and Cheryl Mullenax
All Rights Reserved.

This edition copyright © 2017
by Comet Press
All Rights Reserved.

Cover and interior by Inkubus Design www.inkubusdesign.com

ISBN 13: 978-1-936964-62-8

Visit Comet Press on the web at: www.cometpress.us
facebook.com/cometpress
twitter.com/cometpress

Copyrights Continued on page 338

WWW.COMETPRESS.US

Diabolically dedicated to all the hardcore and extreme publishers, editors, and authors.

CONTENTS

ELEPHANTINE EXTREMES

INTRODUCTION BY RANDY CHANDLER & CHERYL MULLENAX

EXTREME HORROR. You know it when you see it, right? The hard stuff. Be it extreme in theme or with gore galore, you know *hardcore.* It's the explicitly graphic stuff its creators delight in showing you after ripping your eyelids off, right before slamming your naked face into the disgusting goo.

It's the "gushy stuff," as a prolific living-legend once called it.

Hardcore comes in many shapes and guises. It may be torture porn, body horror, erotic splatterporn, or virtually any sort of horror tale imaginable, from low-keyed but no less disturbing psychological horror to the hardest prurient pervo stuff laid bare simply for shock value. Of course the best hardcore is more than the gore on the floor, the needle in the eye, or the deadly instrument hitting the vital organ. Much more, and that's why a precise and satisfying definition is not easy to come by.

Remember the parable of the blind men and the elephant? A small group of blind men are asked to feel a different part of an elephant's anatomy and then recount what they think an elephant is. Naturally each has a different idea of what the thing is. The guy who touches the tail thinks it's like a rope, the one who touches the trunk thinks the thing is like a tree branch, the dude who touches a leg believes the elephant is like a great pillar, the one who fingers the ear thinks of a big fan, and so on. The allegory is used to illustrate various abstract concepts having to do with subjective experience, truth and the nature of reality.

Okay. Now give this ancient folktale a hardcore horror twist and *boom!* The elephant suddenly goes wild and unleashes an avalanche of very loose poop on the blind man holding his tail, grabs another up with his trunk and smashes him into the ground and then impales another with a deadly tusk. Finally the creature stomps away, trampling another man as he goes. The lucky few that survive the elephant's mad rampage still cannot agree on the precise nature of the awesome power they've just experienced but they can agree that it was nasty, brutal and horrific. Not to mention malodorous as hell.

Ask any number of horror readers to define hardcore horror and you'd probably get just as many definitions, even though they have all "seen the elephant."

What we're getting at here is that the stories in the pages ahead might be said to represent various parts of horror's extremities. Yes, there *will* be blood. Lots of it. Gore galore and plenty of the aforementioned gushy stuff. But you'll also find tales less graphic but with hardcore *attitudes* or extreme themes, transgressive stories you're not sure you should be reading, stories showing you things you shouldn't see.

Recently we asked a group of horror writers to define hardcore horror, Wrath James White came up with what we think is the best response: "Hardcore horror epitomizes the axiom 'Show. Don't tell.' It does not leave the sex and violence to the reader's imagination. It shows the reader what's in the writer's imagination. No ideas, themes, plots, or images are taboo. It is born of the taboo. Awww, hell. Let me just write it."

As if we could stop him, even if we wanted to—which we don't. Write on, Mr. White. Write on.

The stories and poems within these pages represent the best hardcore horror of 2016. They are, in fact, the best we could find. It's not possible to read everything published but of all we did read, this is the bloody cream of the creepy crop.

Now a word of warning before we turn you loose. You will find no "safe spaces" here. If you are easily offended or of delicate sensibilities, you'd best not enter. If you do forge ahead, you **will** *see the elephant.* Pray the elephant doesn't see you.

Cheryl Mullenax & Randy Chandler
January 13, 2017

55 WAYS I'D PREFER NOT TO DIE

MICHAEL A. ARNZEN

From *555 Vol 2: This Head, These Limbs*
Editor: Joseph Bouthiette Jr.
Publisher: Carrion Blue

ESCALATOR

The teeth munch my left foot just as I step onto the escalator, the steel chewing my ankle. I struggle, but no one notices as I am swallowed by the sinking steps at the bottom. I flip into a topsy-turvy mall where organic items shop for people stuck in the rotator like a shooting gallery.

CHAINSAW

Unlike most killers, chainsaw murderers don't care much about the clean-up afterward. That's why they use a sloppy lopper in the first place—they love a bloody good mess. I can appreciate that, and I don't fear losing a limb. It's just a terrible way to find out I forgot to booster my tetanus shot.

RUN OVER

There's a difference between being "run over" and "hit by a car." Run over is what happens when your body folds under the bumper and is torn apart by the automobile's undercarriage—your brains smeared on the exhaust system and flesh spit out like mud from spun tires. It's the next car that hits you.

TASER

Don't tase me, Bro! Don't tase me, Sis! Don't tase me, Mom. Don't tase me, Pap. Don't tase me, Grandpap. Don't tase me, Grammygoo. Don't tase me, Uncle Charlie. Don't tase me, Auntie Sue. Don't tase me, Buddy. Don't tase me, Boss. Don't tase me, Mister President. Don't tase me, God. God! Don't tase me!

AMUSEMENT PARK RIDE #1: THE SWINGER

The Swinger spins and our playground seats catch wind, angling sideways as we accelerate too fast for such weak fabric and chain.

"STOP!" I cry.

The carny obeys, and the sudden stop sends all the swings twisting into each other, wringing the rusty metal and children off the ride like crud from a bloody mop.

ENNUI

I hate the kissy face I make when I say "ennui." I trim my lips off with a nearby razor. "Enn-eee," I say. Still too French. I slice out my tongue,

slippery as a fish in my sloppy mouth bowl of blood. "Uhnnn . . ."
Nope—your turn, teeth.

I smile at my gory mirror face: "Eeee!"

CHEERLEADER PYRAMID ACCIDENT

I probably deserved it when the pyramid of sweaty cheerleaders
toppled upon me, crushing my rib-cage in a flurry of bone and
scrunchies and tartan up-skirts—so many plastic pom-
poms pummeling my face and crushing my throat from the
weight—a mass of perky prettiness screaming in that way that is sort
of still cheering.

BURIED ALIVE

The intrepid beach comber lazily waves his metal detector until it beeps
so loudly he tosses his headphones.

He brushes sand and exposes my skull.

My jaws, full of tokens: a tiny top hat. A small Scottish Terrier. A
baby battleship. Dice.

A sand-scratched monocle rests above an orbital fracture.

Me, buried beneath the Boardwalk.

SINUS ALLERGIES

I'm writing, trying to shut out the springtime sounds of neighborhood
weed whackers. The murder scene I'm describing requires concentrated
research. In it, my murderer is carving up a face, scooping flesh and
peeling back bones to layout the sinus cavity. It's a Rorschach blot of
bloody snot.

I sneeze on my mirror and continue.

AMUSEMENT PARK RIDE #2: ROLLER COASTER

When the roller coaster plunges, people always throw their arms up
above them like they are making jazz hands in the face of oblivion, while
everyone else clutches the guard bar. Not me. I choke the throat of the
person in front of me and bottle up their scream to make a human air bag.

EMERGENCY BROADCAST SYSTEM

We're blasting the concert on TV, dancing oblivious, when that obnoxious
Emergency Broadcast Signal takes over my surround sound equipment.
Hella loud. At such volume, we clutch our ears in pain.

A staticky voice reassures: "This has only been a test . . . If this had

been a real emergency . . . well . . ."
My speakers explode, killing us all.

DARTS

Not only does he draw a dartboard on my face, but he colors in the numbered wedges with black and red sharpies. He measures the official position, ticks the line on the ground, and throws. I laugh when he misses, but not just because of that. He uses juggling cleavers for darts, so why bother?

DIRTY DIAPERS

I leap from the hospital roof, landing in a steaming dumpster marked BIOHAZARD. The bin brims with diapers; they splash when they catch my fall.

Lacquered in shit, I clamber through a plastic haze of stinky diapers, only to slip and lacerate an artery on a scalpel sticking out of a bloody baby bearing one.

MER-DUR

My sinking like a stone to the bottom of the sea is experienced in shock-waves. First, I'm shocked that mermaids actually exist! The next shocker occurs when I see their beautiful heads swarm with spark-flashing electric eels. These eels shock me with 650 volts. But it's the Mer-Medusa's gaze that ultimately turns me to stone.

AMUSEMENT PARK RIDE #3: FERRIS WHEEL

I trip as I'm climbing into the Ferris Wheel cart, but nobody notices. My left foot catches between the brushed aluminum floorboards, but nobody sees. I complain that I'm stuck but nobody responds. Each cart bumps me in the head as it passes, but no one pays heed. The carny pushes the accelerator and smiles.

GRAPEFRUIT SPOON

It's such an evil device, this grapefruit spoon. Half-knife, half-scoop, it slides between my lips as easily as a fresh cut Ruby Red. I probe around the scalloped edges with my tongue and slurp it right off the spoon in the process. It's hard to distinguish between pink fruit and red muscle— both taste bitter.

THE RACK

I always wondered if the arms or the legs would give out first if I ever found myself stretched on The Rack.

I'd have bet on the arms.

But it's a draw: one leg pops from my pelvis in sync with my left arm. The torturer stretches me into a disco pose, awaiting the tie-breaker.

A THOUSAND CUTS

Wait, Mr. Executioner! The State specifically sentenced me to lingchi. Death by a thousand cuts. That's one thousand. By my count you're at 999. Only one remains! You haven't touched my genitals yet, and I thank you for creatively avoiding them, but with these scars I'll never date again, so, balls away! Not—my—throat!

FAST FOOD

"Let me read your order back to you: One Happy Time Meal, with double meat, shredded lettuce, Zika skeeter proboscises, onions, rusty staples, poisoned rat droppings, fried peyote, pickled private parts, extra scab, phlegm, and gun barrel-fried bacon on a demon seed bun dusted with cremated clown ash. Is that correct?"

Almost. Hold the gun.

AMUSEMENT PARK RIDE #4: CAROUSEL

I am strung up to the rafters of the carousel ride. All the shiny king's horses eyeball me with porcelain glares, some raising hooves like they want to ask a question. But I know they're actually rearing to kick me as the carousel starts to spin, taking the stool out from underfoot in the process.

PINOCCHIOTOMY

The EMT says he has to perform an emergency Pinocchiotomy. He pulls out a long pair of iron pincers—medieval-looking, like something out of the Black Forest.

"Hold on! What is that?"

"Bone extractor," he says. "Your skeleton is all wood, right?"

"Of course not!"

He eyeballs my face. "Liar!"

He starts with the nose.

ALIEN PROBE

I writhe naked as they lift my legs with pincers. A telescoping robotic prod moves into position, like some insanely large rectal thermometer. It spits out a squirmy bit—a twitching green stalk with an eye. I hesitate, but let go, shitting in its face—releasing the fusion grenade I've snuck into the alien nest.

PAPERWORK

The boss told me to digitize our insurance company archives. I gave him my middle digit instead. I could burn all that garbage, none the wiser.

I scanned enough to keep up appearances, then struck a match. Flames spread. Heat rose as I cackled. Then the scanner exploded in a fireball of glass and shrapnel.

KNIVES

I confessed I never liked her cooking. So for dinner my wife serves up revenge. It is cold. And metallic.

She uses the fancy silverware to dish it out. Surgical slices and painful pricks.

For her final course: I swallow a dessert made of magnets and she tosses blades over her shoulder, like wedding bouquets.

AMUSEMENT PARK RIDE #5: THE VORTEX

The Vortex spins so fast they drop the floor and everyone is held against the cylindrical wall by centrifugal force and we laugh at each other defying gravity until the machine gun turrets drop in the center of the room, spinning and shooting and the ride doesn't stop until the blood rises to our feet.

MORPHSUIT

It's tight, but I love how unrecognizable I become in my gold morphsuit. The fabric clings to my flesh, but you don't even know what color I am inside. When I remove my costume it sticks and peels my skin right off with it, and though the pain is unbearable, I grin, finally, permanently, unrecognizable.

OFFICE BUILDING

A rumble above, like God's coughing, and we instinctively look up, bearing our necks, opening our mouths, squinting over noses. But when your office building collapses above you, you're lucky if you get to enjoy a moment of sky before you drown in all that falling furniture, that flurry of floorboards, that frenzy of friends.

SEAHORSES

Seahorses are the zombified torsos of retired ancient Roman centurion stallions that were dismembered and given an ocean burial. I know this because a troop of them ganged together and head-butted me into unconsciousness before they chewed off my limbs. Now I am a seahuman. I ride the nightmares, galloping the seven seas for brains.

ARCHERY

I am found five hundred and fifty-five years into the future, skeleton impaled to a petrified tree by a high tech arrow amazingly engineered to take down a mutant grizzly bear in just one shot! But there aren't any bears anymore so no one understands these relics of war: my empty skull, this godforsaken arrow.

AMUSEMENT PARK RIDE #6: THE HAUNTED HOUSE

The Haunted House ride is for babies: a carriage tour of plastic cut-outs—creatures that slowly spring out and weakly scream at you in the dark.

But I'm locked in the cart. It never stops. On the fiftieth tour, I cry for help from the people in line, but they just glare at me, bored.

FATE

My mystic draws the final card of my tarot spread . . . and gasps.

I expected the Death card, but it's the Hanging Man.

I drop my head in relief.

She reads the cards. "There's a traitor in your life . . ."

And then the assassin above lets go of his rope and falls, katana swinging toward my neck.

FIRE

Any last words?

"I get 'dust to dust.' Our cells are living dust. And dead skin is even floating in the dust. But what's with 'ashes to ashes'? Who's made up of ashes? Not even this cigarette. Sure, there's cremation. But shouldn't we say 'dust to ash'? Or 'creme to creme'? Or . . ."

Ready . . . Aim . . . Fire!

GIANT MUTANT TICKS

Ticks are lazy. They loiter in brush, hopping a ride if they're lucky, and burying their head in their dinner plate. But giant mutant ticks are different. They bloat so big that they eventually grow appendages on their back larger than yours, and after you're drained they carry you to the bus stop and wait.

POLITICAL ANIMALS

I am being trampled to death by elephants chasing—and being chased back by—donkeys.

In this sick circus, an Uncle Sam clown directs me to a red lever.
That lever decides which beast lives.
I crawl amid the tumult. Grab it. Pull . . .
But voted for neither.
A trap door opens and I am hung.

AMUSEMENT PARK RIDE #7: TUNNEL OF LOVE

The neon sign above the cavernous ride entrance reads Tunnel of Love. Pink light laps the waves around our boat as I hug my lover closer, hoping she'll kiss me inside.

The sign splashes into the water, electrifying the moat.
We sizzle and spasm in shock—and in the air between us, we swap spit.

LEAF PILE

What a tall pile of leaves! I must dive in! The fluffy crackle of it all is exhilarating. There's nothing on Earth like leaves tussling in a feathery plume, browning the air above while I tumble in red flannel and oak. But this red is blood. A steel rake fingers my spine. Help! I've fallen.

SPACKLE

I have drums of spackle in my shop. So when I accidentally shot my hand with a nail gun, I was thankful. I plugged the bloody hole with so much I could feel the grit crunching between my knuckles. But when I later pulled the pink plug, I fainted and painted the floor with blood.

INSOMNIA

I rolled my tired eyes beneath their lids and turned to cliché: counting sheep. One by one, the fuzzy balls of yarn happily hopped a fence. I think I was put to sleep around five hundred and fifty-five, because then, en masse, the herd attacked, smothering me beneath a gigantic, writhing pillow of living wool.

BONES

The femur is the most painful bone, of course, but size doesn't matter. Any bone with girth could be used as a club, sure, but even a knuckle could be sharpened to shiv. But it's not about pain. It's about the embarrassment of being boned to death by another man. Especially your wife's paramour's pelvis.

AMUSEMENT PARK RIDE #8: LOG FLUME

It feels like milling around aimlessly in 1950s kitsch at first, but soon the cool and chaotic splashing is pleasant as the flume picks up speed. Channels of water propel our hollow log up a tall slope to the finale: a dead-dropping splashdown before an awaiting logging saw that mists the audience with our blood.

ASPHYXIATION

My murderer shoves a retail bag over my head, tied off with a zip cord. My mouth sucks only plastic—no air. He lets me lumber around the room, struggling for breath, seeking escape. It's a bag from Target. The bullseye logo is over my face; through it I see a shadow aiming a gun.

DRILL

The driller killer really means business, wearing his construction cap, goggles, apron, and gloves. He has me secured, spread-eagled atop a large, laminated U.S. map on the floor. He surgically drills his holes and places tiny wooden lattices above each wound. He dances action figures under the spurting red geysers of my blood, crying "Oil!"

DIABETES

The needle disposal bin above the paper towels is brimming with hypos. Disgusting. How many diabetics are in this casino?

A stall bursts open. A haggard man approaches, needles porcupining from both fists.

I direct him to the overstuffed bin.

"Sugar!" he shouts, knocking me down, jabbing them in and sucking out my blood. "Sugar!"

SUET CAKE

I'm in a drugged stupor when my neighbor submerges me in her bathtub brimming with lard. She empties sacks of seed over my chest, weighting me down in the muck. I awaken in her backyard, frozen solid in a block of hardened fat. A starling lands. It considers my eyes the entire time it pecks.

AMUSEMENT PARK RIDE #9: BUMPER CARS

I am climbing out of my cart when I'm gently bumped, and trip out onto the concrete. An oncoming cluster bumps chaotically against one another, dimly reminding me of TV commercials for "scrubbing bubbles"—when one cracks my skull, and another smears my brains under his rubbery carriage like foamy bird shit beneath a squeegee.

CAFFEINE

What the glorious fuck do you mean you won't sell me another extra-large caramel mocha triple shot latte? I demand to talk to your manager! What?! You're the manager? The only thing you've managed to do is fuck up everything I've ordered all day. WHAT?! You think I'm gonna overdose on caffeine? You can't overdo . . .

AUDIOBOOK

It takes a minute for me to realize those high beams ahead are actually on my side of the interstate—and then I'm sailing through a shower of glass, another, my head finally slamming another man's dashboard. A nearby speaker still plays an audiobook. It's some self-help crap, about attaining a better life through hypnosis.

VIRGIN SACRIFICE

We both have pierced noses and tattoos, but the tribal chieftain is not my friend.

"I'm not a virgin!" I cry from the volcano's rim.

"Dunka-punka!" he shouts.

His gobbledygook sounds almost . . . British.

"I'm male! Doesn't that matter?"

"DUNKA-PUNKA!"

Tribesmen push me closer to lava. I'm sweating.

Cockney? "Dunk a punker?"

They push me over.

BRAIN TUMOR

My brain had become impregnated with too many fruitful ideas. Time grew them tumorous, nestled together like a bunch of green bananas lining the inside of my skull. When the time was ripe to birth, I pushed and my brains squirted out of my eyes and ears. But somehow, nothing came out of my mouth.

AMUSEMENT PARK RIDE #10: THE TILT-A-WHIRL

"Listen, son. The whole Earth is a Tilt-a-Whirl, swinging all drunk around a wobbly axis while simultaneously looping in orbit around a fireball and the whole universe is nothing but an amusement park run by an insane carny called 'God' . . . so I do this because I love you," he shouted as he pushed me out.

PACK OF WOLVES

The thing about being murdered by a pack of wolves is realizing that the first wolf's jugular bite really was all it took. After that, it's not "murder" anymore as much as it's embarrassing. Why struggle now? Worse than murder is the massacre of your dignity; you're nothing more than sloppy seconds and lucky leftovers.

CORKSCREW

I wink at my gorgeous lover and show off my corkscrew skills by twisting the bottle, not the screw. She squirms in her seat like she's the bottle and I'm the screw. I blush, slipping, and the bottle's neck cracks off as I twist, screwing into my wrist. Blood decants.

She drinks it later, anyway.

LAUGHTER

I love laughing, but I don't want to die laughing, my chortles echoing in the lonely execution chamber as I cackle at my joke about the guard's expert "baton handling" right when the warden turns the switch and my diaphragm twitches, still laughing the air in and out of my wheezing, boiling brown lung tissue.

SWEAT

I am trapped in a giant tank full of sweat. The gathered perspiration of who knows how many people. I float with just a thin sliver of air between the surface and the lid. I wonder: Where'd all this sweat come from? Then I realize, treading heavily: my own sweat will soon top it off.

AMUSEMENT PARK RIDE #11: BOUNCY HOUSEY

I climb into the Inflatable House of Usher just as some kid cuts our anchor. Wind carries us swiftly over a cliff. We tumble—a knife spinning among us—like bones in a dice cup. The house hisses. Children scream. Lacquered in their blood I slicker around, laughing, living it up all the way down.

AUTHOR'S STORY NOTE

#56: Michael Arnzen died trying to write something pithy in just 55 words about the motivation behind "55 Ways I'd Prefer not to Die"—something about beating the reaper at his own game by imagining alternative endings to his own demise—and how this was what all horror fiction is always about—but instead created the most autobiographical thing he'd ever written: his obituary. Unfortunately, it was the extra 20 words that killed him.

AMERICAN GODS, AMERICAN MONSTERS

JOSÉ CRUZ

From *Hybrid Moments: A Literary Tribute to the Misfits*
Editors: MP Johnson and Sam Richard
Publisher: Weirdpunk Books

"My consuming lust was to experience their bodies. I viewed them as objects, as strangers. It is hard for me to believe a human being could have done what I've done."
—Jeffrey Dahmer

"To a new world of gods and monsters!"
—*Bride of Frankenstein* (1935)

THE EDITOR IS DRIVING A BATTERED Impala down a haunted stretch of Florida backroad on a late afternoon in October. The scrapbook rides shotgun.

A raw-gold sun blisters the windshield and gives illumination to the refuse of a roadbound life: fast food wrappers balled into knots; sweat-sogged cigarette packs, most half-full; amber-bottled stimulants illegally obtained; a scuffed thermos containing traces of brown water from a restroom tap, gas station coffee, lighter fluid masquerading as whiskey. The fumes from the tailpipe have taken on an ominous shade, and the engine hacks noisily in the hot, heavy air.

The Editor isn't in any better shape. He hasn't been for some time. The scarlet rings under his eyes were ironed into the flesh years before from too many sleepless nights spent cobbling together a shit-can magazine at the cluttered kitchen table of his Atlanta duplex. The sallow paunch that bulges against his nicotine-starched shirt has been nurtured through a lifetime of microwaveable dinners eaten alone. There is more hair in his beard than his scalp; both are healthily peppered with gray.

The Editor is a sad man in a dying car pulling through the steaming Florida countryland on a late afternoon in October, thinking that for perhaps the first time in his long, unfulfilling life, he has finally come to the gates of transcendence. The key to the gates rides shotgun.

The Editor is chasing a ghost.

HER name is Marilyn. Marilyn. Prescott. Ford. Beauty queen. Wife. Mother.

Murderess.

Even in this age of information, biographical data is scarce, with one paperback from the Cottonmouth Crime line—*Little Miss Sunshine*, Sid Haberchak, "The Unsolved Mystery of Florida's Beautiful

Butcher-Witch"—purporting to tell the whole story: late-night rehears-als at the demand of a cruel stage mother, taking lumps from Orange County johns, midnight visits to unlisted clinics. The Editor thinks that ninety-five percent of the book is precisely bullshit, an attempt to rationalize the boogeyman, give it a reason for what it did. But Marilyn's motives, like so much else about her, still remain unknown, the source of breathless speculation.

She was crowned St. Cloud's "Miss Citrus of 1956" at the age of twenty-four. Hazy photographs of the event contain an undeniable kitsch factor—chorus girls in rotund orange costumes, an emcee in Brylcreem and bow tie—but Marilyn had been a vision amidst the trailer park Madonnas that surrounded her: marble skin and healthy curves, hair a sensuous wave, luminescent eyes that could've given Barbara Steele a run for her money, her perfect teeth like fangs, devouring time and space for those who found themselves caught in the magnetic pull of her smile.

There was one surviving color photo from the pageant; the Editor had had to pay triple figures for it on the Forum. Its greatest revelation was that Ford's pageant dress had actually been cherry-red. On the body of an inferior specimen, the shade would have looked incredibly gauche, slutty, but on Marilyn the fabric was subsumed into her anatomy, a gor-geous outpouring of the all-American blood that flowed within her. The Editor had pasted this picture to the very first page of the scrapbook.

Ford had an abbreviated film career following her pageant days, mostly nudie-cuties and splatter flicks made by H.G. Lewis and the verminous fly-by-night hacks who circulated through the independent scene. The sex pictures were fairly standard stuff for the day, but the later turn of events in her life gave Ford's appearances in the horror films an irrepressible, perverse chill. There was an uncanny dissonance in watch-ing a known killer play the role of victim, massaging pointed breasts with electric-red paint as the shadow of a leering psycho swallowed up her beautiful eyes. Unlike with other "actresses," seeing Marilyn naked did nothing to take away from her ethereal sensuality. If anything, her nude form only moved her deeper into the realm of enigma.

When she married a car salesman with political aspirations in 1960, the pageants and the drive-in films ground to a stop. Ford assumed the role of housewife, a part, albeit humble, that she seemed to happily play. An archived feature from the *St. Cloud Herald* covering her husband's gambit for mayoral election included a few photos of the family at home. Here, the salesman grinning from a plastic-wrapped floral couch, Marilyn tucked under his arm. There, the couple's five-year-old daughter beaming in mid-leap as she demonstrated her expert jump-roping skills, parents looking on in approval.

Marilyn had traded in the silk gown and sash of her glory day for a sundress and apron, and though motherhood had marked her face with a few extra wrinkles and blemishes, her beauty was just as tactile as it had been before. But the Editor felt there was something different about her in these later shots, a calcification of the spirit made manifest in her appearance. Looking at these photos, the Editor thought that he could have reached out and removed Marilyn's face as cleanly as if it were a mask.

And of course, that's exactly what it was.

DAN and Patty Kessler were enjoying spiked lemonade in the dim of their Florida room when they heard the sound of weeping drifting from their neighbors' backyard. Concern bubbling with tipsy adventure, the couple decided to investigate. This was August 13th 1965, the night it all happened.

It was on entering the sprawling, manicured yard that they found Marilyn and the remains of her family. Her husband lay twisted in a checkered sheet, cold and bleeding out from a dozen crying wounds delivered by an ax that had fallen nearby. His face had been mutilated, the lips slit upward into a Glasgow smile. Charred meat sizzled quietly on the smoldering grill. Somewhere in the darkened house, the Righteous Brothers were wailing into the shadows.

Marilyn sat gripping a straight razor, eyes running with black tears, hands gleaming in the orange dusk. She had performed the same operation on herself, and she would periodically choke on the tears that leaked through the open cuts in her face. She managed to utter only a single lament between sobs: "It should've been harder . . . It should've been harder."

Dan rushed into the house to call an ambulance while Patty watched Marilyn from a respectable distance. She followed Marilyn when she rose suddenly and trudged to the tall fence that bordered the woods, watching with barely-contained repulsion as her traumatized neighbor began rocking herself slowly underneath the shade of a pepper tree.

Patty was a schoolteacher by profession; she tried coaxing Marilyn back to the house as if calling in one of her students from recess. Stopping, Marilyn turned and gazed up into the buoyant entrails of Spanish moss that hung from the cracked limbs overhead. Her scars scissored open, wide. "Baby," she cooed. *"Baaaaby."*

When Patty saw the thing in the tree, she screamed.

Dan raced outside, but by the time he stumbled to the back of the yard Patty had fainted and Marilyn was gone, a single scarlet handprint left on the fence in her wake. He quickly determined the source of his wife's terror and ran back into the house.

When the police arrived ten minutes later, they cut through the jump rope cord and brought the girl's body down from the tree.

THE Editor remembers a time when he was a boy watching the *Friday Nite Movie* while his mother was busy washing sheets at the hospital. It was the first time that he saw Boris Karloff, his favorite actor, here gazing longingly at the polished skull he held aloft in the moldering crypt of the crackling television set. "I love dead," the Creature intoned. "Hate living."

It was the first philosophical thought the Editor had ever heard and felt that he understood, and he, in turn, felt that he was understood. There was a strange beauty to the death depicted in those hoary old films, in the stillness, in the enshrining. The monsters would become his nightly companions from then on—Dracula holding slaves under his lustrous stare, the Wolf Man trawling misty seas for fresh throats—and he would revel in the exploits of these brilliant machines of destruction.

He was fourteen when he found the books in his mother's closet. They lay akimbo on the top shelf, tucked away like familial skeletons. The musty cream pages between the black hardbound covers were transcribed with a new unholy lexicon, names full of mystery and dread import: the Zodiac, the Angels of Death, the Candy Man, the Night Stalker. These were new monsters, ghouls and vampires in Halloween costumes of hardbitten flesh stalking the bustling veins and lonely arteries of America's urban and country heartland alike. If Karloff had given the Editor his first taste of philosophy, the books were to become his religious texts, their passages inspiring equal parts awe and horror. He would pore over them at his altar of mothball-incense, learning of the men and women who lived as the bestial gods of old, gruesome to behold, free to take life as they saw fit.

Though the pictures of their grinning masks terrified him, the Editor found that he could never look away, not even from behind the drawn blinds of his fingers. He'd toss the books back onto the shelf before his mother came home, disgusted by what he'd read, disgusted by himself, but every night he would bring them down again and read the same passages till his eyes grew heavy with experience. They were brilliant machines of destruction, these new gods, and they were everywhere.

One time his mother came home early from a night out she'd insisted she deserved. A giantess in crimson, funk of nickel beer hot on her breath, she'd dragged him out of the closet, her knee a stone in his gut as she bent him over and rocked him with wild, flailing slaps on his ass. He was blind to the pain, too overwhelmed with surprise and shame to fight back. Afterward he'd just lain on the cold floor and wept, a flagellated priest spilled across the church steps, the glowering mask of the Sex Beast singing him to his rest.

THE girl had been killed like her father: axe cleave to the skull, mouth torn open with the razor. She'd been strung up to a branch at the top of the tree. Neither of the Kesslers had seen her at first due to the mass of Spanish moss covering the body. When Patty had looked up, all she saw was the whites of the girl's eyes and her new red grin. In later interviews she confessed that face would come to her every night before she went to sleep.

Marilyn couldn't be found. Considering the faint traces that were left of her former life, it seemed plausible to think that she had never existed in the first place. She had merely been a whispered rumor, a fantasy. A ghost.

The Osceola County Police felt differently about the matter. The sheriff was convinced that Marilyn was in hiding—with whom he couldn't say, as she had no immediate family or close friends—and suggested that she would be seeking out cosmetic surgery to mend her telltale scars. A statewide search was instigated. News anchors grimly intoned the crimes to stunned households. Curfews were rigidly observed. Bloodhounds bayed fear-wild in the night and parents sat up late in the smoky stillness of their dens, wondering aloud to each other where God ran off to during that little girl's last moments.

Nothing came from any of it.

After three weeks, no trace of Ford could be found anywhere in the miles of swamp and scrubland that lay on either side of her home. The sheriff grunted a few vague oaths at the press meetings, and the public gradually turned their attention to crashing planes and immolated demonstrators for their reminders of mortality. Just as she had been for her entire life outside of one unsullied moment upon a stage in St. Cloud, Marilyn Ford was cast aside and promptly forgotten.

Six years later, the murders began.

THE Editor passes a bizarre sign as he takes the exit from the highway: a giant, gaily-colored clown holding a little suited man in its lap. The circle of inverted 9s carved into the clown's extended hand can't be the mile marker, but there's no other indication on the road that he can see.

He pulls into a dilapidated service station. An insidious droning of flies issues from the open cavern of the faded barn that squats behind the station. He heads towards the service building, eager to relieve himself. A low voice scrapes the air.

"You have to use ever' part a the animal. Can't waste nothin'. Injuns knew that. Used it all. House, food, tools, everythin'. They were smart, them Injuns." The man on the porch seems to have materialized from thin air. A rocking chair cradles him as he contemplates his mud-splattered boots.

"Nothin' to be done 'bout that smell though. That smell . . . that's just part a the job." The man peers up at the Editor from under the brim of a hunting cap and smiles, flashing crooked teeth. A faint breeze stirs the wind chimes hanging over the man's head and the Editor sees that they're too white, their music too dull, to be only metal.

The Impala's wheels are spinning through dust and pulling the Editor away from the station in the next second. His pants are stale with urine. He pays no mind to it, only drives, glancing in the rearview just long enough to see the split alabaster statue swinging from its ankles inside the mouth of the barn. A peal of distant thunder cracks open a metal cask in the air, blue ozone surging with rusting blood.

The Editor knows he is close.

THE first one was found in his car. An officer passing a lover's lane at Lake Alfred on a muggy night in '72 noticed that one vehicle didn't speed off at the sight of his cruiser's lights. The officer knocked on the driver's side door expecting to catch a pair of fumbling high school lovers *in flagrante.* He shone his flashlight in the window and instead saw the jack o' lantern face of a corpse staring out at him. Backup was promptly called.

The victim was lashed by his wrists to the steering wheel with his own unknotted tie. All other articles of clothing had been taken. His abdomen had suffered incisions of varying depth, his mouth carved open. The car was redolent with the damp smells of fear and sex. There was only one indication of the killer's presence: a single bloody handprint left on the passenger seat. When tested, the fingerprints were discovered to be those of one Marilyn Prescott Ford.

The ghost of St. Cloud had returned.

Three more bodies were discovered in as many counties within the week. A homeless woman stuffed into a storm drain, a security guard caught in a department store's revolving doors, a shoeless teenager propped against a McDonald's dumpster. All of them kissed by razors, all of them smiling their benedictions.

The sheriff, noticeably aged, proved less vociferous at the next press conference and shortly afterward took an early retirement. It was rumored he moved to Arizona to become a reptile handler and then emptied his skull out with a snub-nosed pistol on the night of his 61st birthday. Neither story was ever confirmed.

And then the murders stopped. For one week, residents of central Florida kept to their houses, leaving only for emergencies, before the pendulous cloud of terror evaporated as quickly as one of the region's erratic thunderstorms. The swiftness of the crimes provoked questions as to their legitimacy. There was talk that they'd been politically motivated, a means of booting out the sheriff by resurrecting the coldest case from his checkered career. Marilyn's *modus operandi* was a matter of public record and local legend, easily duplicated by any enterprising saboteur. And the fingerprints? Surely those could be copied.

Improbable, but it was all easier to believe than the notion that a missing, insane pageant queen resurfaced half a decade later in the next county over to strike out at random strangers. No, better to swallow the other theory, or the truth, as it came to be accepted by all concerned. Better to let the matter rest, and pray that this would be the end of it.

THE Editor began *Carnage Nation* during college, covertly making copies of the B&W zine on the library's Xerox, tucking them under dormitory doors and windshield wipers by cover of dark. Issues frequently made their way into campus wastebins, but occasionally he would glimpse a burnout or a meatheaded jock hovering over his carefully reproduced portraits of the Manson family at play and the child-killers of the Weimar Republic. Word of mouth seeped into the cultural bedrock, and after two years the Editor began receiving mailed requests for subscriptions, all of them with return addresses to anonymous PO boxes. That was all right. He could understand his readers' desire for secrecy; the zine's masthead identified him simply as "Editor." He wouldn't feel the sense of distant **camaraderie** he'd gotten from those letters again until he joined the Forum.

The Forum was an online community dedicated to highlighting what their manifesto called "public works of the esoteric." The sub-group that the Editor participated in was named "De Mortuis." It consisted of roughly a dozen steady members who commented on the pieces published by the group's lead moderator, the RiverMan. There were galleries dedicated to Hollywood autopsies, fatal highway collisions, and animal maulings, among others, with one folder specifically devoted to the mugshots that haunted the Editor's adolescence and pictures of all the grimy leavings from their crime scenes. *Carnage Nation* was a pamphlet of doodles compared to the splendor of those morbid collages.

The Editor felt a special kinship with the Forum members that couldn't be shared with anyone else. His dirty secret was everyone's dirty secret. They were all identified only by usernames: TripleH83, Giggling_Granny, Heckler Skelter. But even under the auspices of a pseudonym, the Forum allowed the Editor to be himself, to drop all pretense and give sway to his charnel fascinations. There was a shared knowledge among them all that they were society's misfits, the select few who dared to look death in the face and find something worth loving.

He suddenly remembers the woman from Glenn's Tavern, the only real connection he'd made outside of the Forum in that time. She'd been sweet, and drunk, a little heavy, but he was no looker, and she didn't mind it when he came too quickly, so they tried again, and it was good, but then the next morning she left with boozy apologies, breath just like his mother's, knocked over the folder of glossies for the next issue, saw them pour across the floor, and screamed, not looking at him, just running out the front door half-naked and screaming, the brown ruptured skulls on the floor screaming with her—*no*—he wouldn't think of it, not again, just pack it away, swallow it down—

Forget it.

That's when he'd heard of Marilyn again. The RiverMan packed the message board with personal theories supported by evidence that the Editor thought only a law enforcement officer or experienced hacker could obtain. The RiverMan claimed that Marilyn was responsible not only for the killings in '72, but also a host of others scattered throughout the state. The Editor found the very concept preposterous, fuel added to the campfire balladry that Ford's life had become.

That was before he saw the pictures. Murky, unprofessional shots of bodies black with rot tied to trees, laid across flaking railroad tracks, tucked in their own beds. 1981, 1988, 1995, 2002. Every one of them smiling.

Scans of crime scene and autopsy reports were laid out in the River-Man's dissertations. Included in them was one note that had made the Editor feel the weight of his mother's stony knee again. "Handprint in victim's blood noted on windowsill of bedroom," it read. "Submitted to lab for testing. Pathology found that prints—"

Here it appeared as if a section of the report had been whited out. The following line of text read: "Results inconclusive."

"Ever wanted to know how to get rid of a ghost?" the RiverMan asked. "Just deny that it exists."

A SQUAT figure stands on the road's shoulder, thumb hitched. The sun that frames him is liquid flame, a final protest against the coming night. The Editor sees the man's face for a split second—arched eyebrows, pursed lips—and as the car zooms past he hears the barking of many dogs, though there are none to be seen.

It will be dark soon. The Editor knows he will have to find lodging for the night. He can't risk being awoken by another state trooper. Too many questions. Just looking at the inside of the car they'd know he was up to no good, though not for any of the reasons they'd suspect.

Appearing as if a heavenly beacon, a blue-lit sign on the horizon: LAST RESORT. VACANCIES.

A little rest for the night, then the mission could resume. He would be out before dawn's first light and arrive at his destination by early evening. After that . . .

After that, who could say?

The Editor turns into the parking lot, and the invisible hounds resume their chorus.

HIS madness insinuated itself slowly.

It started just as a trickling of thoughts and incidents permeating his daily routine—a clothing catalog featuring a red dress, a serpent of Spanish moss lying across the sidewalk—but after a month of visiting the Forum, the Editor began actively seeking more information, trolling newspaper archives at the library, printing message board posts, contacting anyone still alive who might have ever spoken to Marilyn Ford. He felt as if he'd been told that something was missing from his life and, now aware, was driven by the need to find it again.

An old photo album he'd taken from the hospice room where his mother finally died of cancer was emptied of family members he never met or knew and replaced with the growing pile of material that he was accumulating based on Ford's life. He sent a private message to the RiverMan, asking him if he had anything else that could help him in his search.

He received no reply, but two weeks later a package arrived at his door marked "ATTN: EDITOR." Inside was a cache of photos taken of each of the known crime scenes and several other locations: iridescent seaside piers, bus stops, little league fields. The Editor remembered them as the sites of Ford's other alleged killings from the RiverMan's threads. They were stabbed through with a pinned message: "Look them up."

Following the penciled dates and names written on the back of the photos, the Editor discovered that these were in fact the locations of several homicides. The newspaper write-ups he found online were all decidedly terse, referring to the victims simply as having been in "stabbing incidents," the police commenting that they were probably "a drug deal gone wrong" or "attempted robbery." There was something elusive about it all, a quiet insistence that everything was as it appeared on the surface.

The Editor knew subconsciously that the thoughts he was beginning to have were intrinsically paranoid. But how could he possibly avoid the conspiracy when it was all laid out so plainly before him?

WRINKLED, road-sore, the Editor slumps down the concrete walk towards the ice machine. The keeper of the Last Resort didn't ask any questions when he rang for a room, hardly glanced up from her cooling coffee as he wrote his name in the registry.

A door creaks open to his left and slams shut just as he glances over, severing the hoarse laughter coming from within. He looks towards the parking lot and confirms his suspicion. His is the only car there.

He heaves back the lid on the ice machine and stares into its roasted depths. A few inches of water sit at the bottom, the dark corpses of spiders gliding across its scummy surface in slow pirouettes. He watches them dance for a few seconds more before heading back to the room.

The place is serviceable for the night. He'd only noticed one cockroach upon entering earlier, and the scrim of dust coating the oak-paneled walls wasn't too thick. But as he opens the door and turns the switch on to the room's twin lamps, their yellow light gleams off the surface of a stark mural on the ceiling that wasn't there before.

The Editor recognizes the image by the colors before he processes its full scope: the sensuous hair, the white devouring smile. It is the color photo of Marilyn from the Miss Citrus pageant blown to fit the expanse of the ceiling. On impulse, he rushes to the bed and pulls the scrapbook out from under the mattress to make sure that his copy is still there.

It is.

The two shots are identical save for the black inverted crosses that have been spray-painted over the eyes of the mural. He notices a line of text scrawled across the bottom. He lies across the bed to make out the message. A single question blazes down at him in burning fuchsia: WHO ARE YOU?

The Editor reads it aloud, lets the question hang suspended in the air. If one were to hear it, they couldn't be sure who it was that was really asking.

THE scrapbook began to fill up and take weight, its pages adorned with a clumsy assemblage of highlighted articles, magnified photos, hastily-scribbled notes from twilit interviews conducted in whispers over the phone. Packages from the RiverMan arrived with regularity. One envelope contained shots of slabbed cadavers from various morgues, their rushed quality indicative of secret photography. Toe tags showed they were the victims from the sites in the RiverMan's earlier photos. All the corpses were flayed with razor scars, some even eyeless, but all of them bore the gruesomely beatific Glasgow smile like a dark wax seal. There could be no doubt about any of it now. Marilyn Ford lived.

He began ignoring anything else that came through the mail that wasn't from the RiverMan, and the disconnected telephone was soon tossed onto the collection of past-due bills and eviction notices piling on the kitchen floor.

There was a pattern emerging in the evidence, slowly and gradually. He could see it now. The supposedly random murders in '72 actually showed a geographical progression towards the south, a fact reinforced by the material supplied by the RiverMan. The crooked trail of bodies cut a path leading all the way from the rolling hills of Winter Haven to the historic avenues of Fort Myers. Marilyn seemed to be following the clarion call of wild forces back to a point of origin, like the gods of myth returning to their crowned kingdom atop Olympus. But where was she trying to go, and what home could possibly be waiting for her?

Inside the RiverMan's last package was a torn, underlined passage from a volume entitled *The Diabolist's Contagion*. The writing of the unnamed author was cryptic, the page shattered with mildew:

"For where else might the world turn upon the brink of destruction but the birth canal of its first sin, the swamp from where man was formed in the image of his Father with the Red Blade? It is not to the dust we must return, but to the broken black waters of our creation."

Suddenly, it all became quite clear. There wasn't much time left. Using the last bit of his meager savings, the Editor bought the first clunker he spotted on a used car lot and was soaring south on I-95 before the landlord of the duplex and the policeman accompanying him even arrived at the front door.

THE Editor steers the Impala to the edge of the marshy wood just as the radiator sends its last gasping vapors into the air. His fists shake on the wheel. Bloody rapids roar through his brain. He has made it: the blessed empire, the Promised Land . . .

The Everglades.

A million and a half acres of restored wilderness spread across the state's lower jaw like a primal scar. Even with a history of excessive human tampering, the land retains a remote, sacred quality. It is here in this fetid bestiary that he knows he will find her. His ghost; his witch; his messiah.

The night envelops him in a damp stranglehold as he steps out of the car. Flesh tingling, he hurtles forward, crashes through the hardwood hummock. He is well out of the national park's range. There is no well-stamped path or wooden walkway for him to follow here, only the devouring magnetism pulling him ahead, dictating his course.

Fat mosquitoes swarm in droves, greedily feasting on his exposed skin as he pushes aside the thick, cloying vegetation. He crushes the scrapbook against his chest and runs as fast as his aching legs can carry him across the squelching earth. Sweat pours down his face, soaks the shirt to his back. His breath comes out in short, ragged bursts. A scalding dagger begins to turn in his chest.

Not now. For God's sake, not now.

The fingers gripping the scrapbook are starting to numb when he sees a dazzle of flame behind a stand of slash pine. The ceremonial odor of woodsmoke spurs him on, and when he emerges from the brush into the sawgrass prairie on the other side he witnesses the scene before him in all its black majesty.

A massive bonfire serves as fierce sun to the swamp's dank universe. Its dancing light gleams off the ebony bones of the hearses that encircle it, their yawning trunks spilling forth desiccated caskets. Their occupants are now scattered amidst the group of revelers present, cradled in the arms of a dancer, pinned in the tall grass underneath the weight of a passionate lover. Howls of ecstasy and cries of shame rend the air. Sharp-beaked owls battle over tawny ropes of muscle. The movements of the revelers are jagged and ungainly. Through the glare of the fire the Editor sees what clothing they wear, if any, is shredded and burnt, marked with wounds long dried and scabbed, now festering. Underneath the heady odor of spilled blood and brackish water, he detects another smell. It is the unmistakable perfume of rot.

A hand grasps his shoulder. He turns and stares into the face of a hollow-cheeked old man. The man's other hand is being held by a young girl in plaid dress and knee-high socks. She wears no shoes, stares blankly into the roaring fire. The circuit of scorch marks on the man's scalp is complemented by the necklace of dirty fingerprints worn by his escort.

"Do not fear," the old man whispers to him. "I am Jesus Christ, and I am here to deliver you unto salvation."

He guides the Editor around the bonfire, past the corpulent transvestite hugging his new pair of still-warm breasts to his chest, past the hooded executioner carving his sign into the back of a man shrieking from his bonds.

"Some of them are not satisfied with the cadavers," the old man explains. "They require a more dangerous kind of game. Old habits are hard to abandon, even after all this time. Isn't that right, Gracie?" He shakes the girl's hand but she doesn't respond. The old man's smile fades as he looks back to the Editor. "She cannot speak because I took her tongue. I cut it out of her little mouth with a knife and fried it and ate it all up. Now her voice belongs to me."

The girl turns and regards the Editor with her vacant gaze, parts her lips as if to cry out and reveals only a tiny darkness. Head rushing, the Editor stumbles away from them, dropping the scrapbook. He reaches to pick it up, and a stinging arc in his side sends him to his knees. Panting, he grasps feebly after the book. The gentle touch lights on his shoulder again.

"You've been asking yourself the same question your entire life. Are we gods, or monsters? As if the two were any different. My Father was the greatest monster of them all. He stabbed holy needles into my groin and used them to pin me to the cross. He took what He wanted, like He took that tight little Mary. And then He begat me, His little bastard monster, only to kill me. But look at your art, your paintings, your myths. All the great gods devour their young."

The Editor tries to escape his companion's grip but, seeing the old man's drawn face, follows his gaze out to the prairie ahead. They look upon a great and sweeping void. It is still the prairie in appearance, but there is a coldness teasing the edges of his heart, a thermonuclear charge of pain and longing irradiating all sense of the familiar. In whispering grass and stagnant water he sees gray twists of human carrion rising up from the mud, giving vent to unheeded torments with supplicating hands and gaping maw. The sound they make is the sound of mothers crying over closed caskets, of screaming husbands grown fat on stifled rage at the thought of their ravaged wives, of electronic static drowning out the wild pleas for help that come from the courtyard, the alley, the room down the hall. It is a sound that both fills and empties the air.

It all washes over him in a ceaseless wave, but the Editor is only vaguely disturbed to find that it leaves no mark. Soon even the teasing cold at his heart is gone. The revelers' bonfire keeps him comfortably warm. He looks back to the prairie and watches a vision make its way towards him.

She walks among the rows in the distance, a bloodshot membrane twitching forward at an unnatural pace, a symphony of color: red shroud, white fang, golden eye, a withered lightning bolt in her hair the only concession to time. Tumbles of paper blow across the prairie, catching in snags of dead grass. He realizes that they are MISSING posters, prom queens and store managers and vacationing retirees grinning from old family photos, each one curling with flame as she trods upon them, their ashen deaths eliciting another eruption of cries from the choir of gray phantoms. She comes upon the three of them like a dark angel gracing the manger. Her mouth is a gnawed, unwavering scar; her gimlet eyes and the old man speak for her.

"You and your fellows have done well so far," the old man croaks. "But it still falls short. There's only so much power to be found in your cinema, your novelties, your ceaseless recycling of crimes long shorn of their heat. It isn't enough. To your generation we remain nothing but fairy tales." He spits the last two words.

"What we need is someone to take up the call, to spread the word of our good works." His palsied claw digs deeper into the Editor's skin, drawing blood, but the kneeled man does not flinch. "We need the world to know that we are not history. We need it to know that we live." The old man shakes with unchecked hunger. "We need its *fear*."

A dry wind sweeps across the prairie, blowing smoke and bits of stubborn anatomy from the bonfire. The revelers surround them now, their stench monstrous, black smiles crowned with maggots. The Editor feels a great weight shift inside of him, a leviathan passing under the vessel of his soul. The vision moves for the first time since favoring him with her presence. The straight razor in her hand catches the light.

He can hear the smile in the old man's words. "What we need . . . is a prophet."

The Editor feels the steel blade work its way into his mouth, stab into his gums.

The old man leans in close, rank breath curdling his ear. "We've made the call. Will you answer; will you open the door?"

In that moment a kaleidoscopic reel of images flickers across the Editor's memory: black and white TV demons; scripture in the closet; virgin mother's lashing; pillaged copies of *Carnage Nation*; the nonbeliever running from his room; photos whispering darkroom promises, loving him, holding him . . .

A single tear whispers across the Editor's cheek. He closes his eyes, and nods.

There is no pain in the marking. His body buckles with orgasm as the razor spreads him open. The heat from the fire surges through the slits of his new mouth; he smiles as warm wine flows down his chin, spatters his chest. He cups his hand to it, strains the blood onto his head, a scarlet baptism.

The Editor picks the scrapbook up from the ground, marking the paperboard cover with a gory handprint. It is as fitting a talisman as any for this new Bible.

The revelers coo and hum as the Editor walks through their moldering ranks, a priest amongst lepers. Blessings pass from his wet lips to their bowed heads. He holds the scrapbook aloft and an ugly cheer rises up from the congregation. She is at his side now, smiling her approval, the razor glimmering red under the cloudy moon.

The little girl steps alongside the old man, her eyes two charcoal smears. Though tongueless, she makes an idiot whimper that the Editor recognizes. He knows all too well the sound of cries for mother going unanswered, and he suddenly despises her for her weakness. The old man beams at him from across the fire; his jubilant grin is runny with slick juices.

In the distance, skeletal hands pound on drumheads of taut skin. The revelers take up their knives, their cudgels, their barbwire garrotes and turn back to the victims by the fire. They advance slowly, savoring every step. The victims try dragging themselves to the safety of the woods, moaning quietly. The Editor can't help laughing to himself. He knows they will not get away. None of them will.

The Editor will not record the names of the victims. Their lives are unimportant, and history has never favored the conquered. Turning to a fresh page, he prepares to write down his testament in blood. A requiem of screams shudders from the throat of the prairie as the new gods raise their weapons. The Editor watches what comes next.

He does not look away.

AUTHOR'S STORY NOTE

This story was written in response to a call for submissions to MP Johnson's and Sam Richard's second tribute anthology from Weirdpunk Books, *Hybrid Moments*. It gave me the opportunity to reunite with the music of the Misfits and listen to the songs as closely as I did during my first exposure to them. I shuffled through their discography trying to find the track that would serve as the main inspiration for my piece. I was surprised when songs that I initially thought would instantly jog a story in my head, songs like "Last Caress" or "Ghouls Night Out," only left me with dim impressions. Nothing concrete, nothing that I could see shaping into a narrative.

It was with some further surprise that I found myself tuning into "American Nightmare," the final track on the band's *Legacy of Brutality* album, and seeing the pieces starting to lock into Tetris formations in my head. For starters, I just liked that phrase: American nightmare. White picket fences mounted in grounds soaked with blood. Very Lynchian. While the serial killer is by no means an American invention, the cult of the serial killer is something that has always seemed to me to be a homegrown movement. We can't seem to get enough of them; just seeing that phrase on the cover of *People Magazine* the other week made its potency all too clear. It still has taboo-power, is still mythic. What does our fascination with murderers say about us? And where might it lead if we were to follow it? If you listen to the lyrics of Danzig's rockabilly murder ballad, you might have an idea. Those three inverted nines don't lie.

MOTHER'S NATURE

STEPHANIE ELRICK

From *Cthulhusattva: Tales of the Black Gnosis*
Editor: Scott R Jones
Publisher: Martian Migraine Press

THE MAN IN THE LIMOUSINE wore a white Egyptian cotton shirt. It was the first clean thing I'd seen in a home saturated with slaughter and mud. No one came near my Uncle's farm, not if they could help it, hence the reason I'd sat amongst the shattered parts of man and beast for so long. Pain was a chord that hummed through the air there, the bellowing of the animals heard for miles around.

When he came, all was silent except for the soft purr of the engine as it approached. Generations of butchery had made my family more inbred than the cattle, now their limbs mingled indiscriminately with the livestock's. No one else had heard the screams, mine or theirs; of that I was certain.

He emerged from the backseat with a cool, fluid grace. Black sun-kissed skin and wide burnished eyes. The menthol freshness of the vehicle's interior hit me even from a distance, a synthetic tang that stung my nostrils and made me raise my gaze from the pattern I was tracing in the dust. Entrails squelched underneath designer shoes yet he seemed indifferent to the scene. I'd never seen anyone so beautiful. Spotless. Immaculate. He seemed to gleam. Lifting my taut little body up with long strong arms he placed me in the car. I curled like a clenched fist into its viscid leather and slept for the first time in days.

IT'S difficult to remember exactly what happened after leaving the farm. I have flashes of remembering, things that collide and combine in gusts of red and green, moments resistant to coherence. We traveled for days, or hours, and when I woke I was in a doll-filled room that smelt like antiseptic. Clamping my chin he pushed green mush past my lips and the mess I made resisting irritated him. He scrubbed at the stains on my chest 'til my skin was red raw and I wailed like a baby. He never spoke a word. Trauma ricocheted through my system still and I fought like a cat held in a bucket. I'd resigned myself to death days earlier, so eating seemed like a meaningless task, another invasion of my will.

I do remember that he bathed me, holding me down in a high backed copper tub 'til I stopped struggling and calmed down. He cared for my body and quieted my chattering mind in all the practical ways a person can. Eventually his silent resilience put me at ease. I let him scrub away the years of neglect.

Finally sitting still, resigned not to kick or bite anymore, I noticed that I was bleeding, heavily, not from a wound but from my womb. I watched the haemoglobin snaking from my body, mingling delicately with the fresh clean water. How much finer it was than the lurid splatters that streaked the barn. None of us were squeamish, my cousins included, but when they'd seen my Uncle splayed open like an autopsy, wriggling in Its grip, they'd bolted like heifers.

I roughly pushed my fingers inside the soft mounds of my labia, deliberately not thinking of their blood but my own. He continued to wash the gore from my hair as aspic strands of jellyfish tendrils hung from my fingers. All that blood, all that death, and nobody had survived but me.

WHEN I slept that night I wove a patchwork of dreams. My mother came to me, covered in mildew and smiling through a mouthful of foam. She'd been sharpening her fingertips with a whetstone and grit and I marveled at her cleverness, eagerly doing the same. We sat in silence, honing our bones to pointed pins, threading our hands with muscle stripped from her thighs. Overhead the sky was dying, brown oil slicks spreading across its surface. Time to start again. She promised me that nothing ever goes to waste and we stitched oceans to oceans as the clouds dropped like bombs. Floundering monsters opened heavy lids, then clambered on the land like babies learning to walk, dragging blankets of crimson waves behind them. Every gill-less thing that ever was suffocated under that mantle and we sat patiently, watching them sink, our fingers twitching in anticipation.

THE next time I woke he took me to his workshop, a large room with small windows high above my head, covered with collages of animals and people. A sink and metal table stood in the corner with various knives and tools nailed to the wall, above piles of uncut leather. Jars of murky embalmed things filled long shelves. A velvet curtain separated the studio from a shop, dimly lit and full of golden oval mirrors. A distinct white circle with arrows spiked from its perimeter was painted on the floor and adorned the window that overlooked a busy street, idyllically flanked by oak trees. Mannequins stood in rows with stuffed animal heads perched on willowy plastic necks. Clothing hung from their gaunt physiques at dramatic angles, garnished with pearlescent gemstones. The shop felt more like a museum than a boutique.

"Do you know what this is?" he asked, taking my hand and ignoring my flinches as he ran it over a coat.

I shook my head, as startled by his question as the sudden grip of his hand.

"It's crocodile skin, difficult to work with but highly rewarding. It's incredibly thick and tricky to stitch, has to be done by hand. Do you know what this is?" He moved my hand to a white trim. My ignorance embarrassed me.

"The pelt of an Arctic Wolf, so soft! The wolf itself does not keep it so well."

"What about this?" He smirked. This new material was rubbery, cold, like the sticky seats of the car. I winced as specks of blood welled on my fingertips.

He chuckled. "You will learn little lamb. You like animals, don't you. We can make such beautiful things from their gifts, nothing should ever go to waste. Would you like to learn?"

I paused, overwhelmed by my sudden lesson.

"You're not stupid," he said, grabbing me again by the chin. "So, choose. You understand better than most the cycle of creation and destruction. The farm taught you things, didn't it? Nature is as brutal as she is beautiful." He paused thoughtfully, moving closer. "Sentimentality is a curse that animals do not suffer."

He released his grip and I nodded complicity to save face. Some kind of agreement had been struck.

At first I wondered if he'd force himself upon me; my Uncle and cousins had taught me well what man and beast desired most. But he never approached. He was only concerned with his work. As my trust grew, so did my lust. I was a woman now, with churning hormones and smoldering dreams, and we spent long nights alone in our candlelit studio. I grew possessive.

I wanted to impress him, show him what a seamstress and artist I had become through his instruction. If the sculpting of flesh was the only way to do that then I vowed to surpass all his expectations. As well as skinning and cleaning the creatures that shifty men in blacked out vans delivered weekly, I began to preserve and bleach their bones, creating sculptures of delicate complexity. From a sparrow I made a tiny crescent moon, fixed to a pin he could wear on his lapel. From a horse's jawbone I carved a knife handle engraved with hieroglyphs from his most treasured book. When I had time to spare I practiced taxidermy, fashioning exotic chimera to present as gifts. With a paltry remark he might acknowledge my needlework or comment on the plausibility of the synthesis, yet I knew he was pleased as the shop filled with my experiments and even the customers remarked on my art. He would smile obliquely when asked if they were his and my pride swelled at the suggestion.

My training passed with the dizzy swiftness of a blossoming romance. I devoured books about evolution and discovered tomes exploring the rituals of zoolatry. We skinned and preserved all kinds of species and I watched him turn each into extravagant attire to be draped on human forms. He was an artist and a perfectionist, suturing skin into glorious amalgams. Clients came from all over the globe to buy his hybrid couture, and price was never a concern.

We had special customers too, ones who didn't seek our garments and mostly came at night. These fidgety bundles, barely preened and unable to articulate above grunts and nods, would wait until the shop was empty before being lead through a trap door to the 'fitting rooms' in the basement. Some emerged, eyes bright and skin glowing after a few hours, some after a number of days. Some I never saw leave.

I was never forbidden to enter the basement yet I was never invited either. In the early days I was eager not to displease, but of course it wasn't long before I found myself locking the shop and pulling back the heavy bulk of the trapdoor. He'd been down there for longer than usual, almost three days, with a drip of a woman not much older than myself. What kept him from our work for so long? I stared below, there was no sign of him or anyone else.

A phosphorous glow poured from the opening and I squinted in its caustic light. A long narrow corridor stretched to either side and the air down there was thick and hot. It smelt of sweat and shit, the same dank musk as the farm pens. Static shivered through the air, fondling the hairs on my scalp and my arms. A humid waft brushed my cheeks and on it travelled the groans of bovine beasts. I froze. My guts twisted, my senses pricked. Other muffled noises came from the corridor. Scratches, slaps, the sloshing of fluid. Cracking and panting and spontaneous laughter rose in soft crescendos before fading back into muffled whimpering. My temples throbbed, matching some unseen pendulum, and I moved down the steps, pulling the trapdoor closed behind me.

I walked for what could have been a mile on a floor lined with cracked stones and broken mosaics. The ground sloped up, as if I was climbing to the top of a hill, yet I never seemed to reach a peak or start descending. Tiny doors lined the corridor, the same pointed circle painted in a rusty brown above every one. They were so small that even I would have to crawl through them, with padlocks bigger than my hands.

The slapping and sucking intensified and a garish yellow light leaked from their tiny keyholes. Sometimes a frame would lurch as I passed, as if someone was throwing their weight against it from inside. I stopped, studying a pinkish fluid leaking under one threshold. The puddle smelt of brine and bleach and hissed quietly as it slid. I tried to peek through the keyhole, no bigger than my fingernail, but it was futile. A wet smack preceded a shuddering groan, then something like water spattering on a metal roof fell for minutes. Something gurgled, like water flowing down a drain. Who was in there, and was he inside too? Was he bathing that woman in the same way he had bathed me? Pride smoldered white hot.

"So you have found your way to the Emporium, little lamb?" he purred whilst exiting a door down the hall.

I stammered, and could summon no words, my jealousy hanging like a dead weight from my neck.

"You needed to know what was happening down here. A natural response. I was wondering how long it would take you." He smiled, putting a key in his pocket and wiping his hands on a lace handkerchief. "And you're ready now." Holding out his hand he lifted me from the floor. "This is the Flesh Emporium, where the most exciting parts of our work happens." For the first time since we'd met he took my arm like an equal and we strolled down the corridor as if walking through a park.

"Down here we cater to fantasies more juicy than vanity. We let explorers run wild, let them learn that boundaries are much more amenable than reason allows. Skin is malleable, a semi-permeable membrane, resilient. It stretches, absorbs, regrows, it can be refashioned. Flesh is a canvas at best. Would you like to see?" He paused at a door. I nodded, not wanting to show my unease. I bent down, ready to enter, then instantly backed away.

A skinless person, a woman or man, had been stripped to their muscle and was cradled in the grip of a hovering creature. Still alive, their eyes were wide and their mouth gasped madly for breath. Their skin hung just behind them, not torn or damaged, obviously carefully removed, and their body lay glistening like a newborn in its clutch. Arachnid arms of white jointed bone protruded from the creature's mass and it picked decisively at their flesh, humming scales of insectoid trills from a mouth jumbled with fangs. The thing had no eyes, and an exposed spine extending into a disjointed tail that thrashed from side to side. It dribbled in delight as it pulled the person apart, gelatinous salvia trickling from mandibles that burnt holes into the body, which twitched in response. Both victim and inflictor were absorbed in the work.

"When we use pain creatively we awaken sides of ourselves long since denied. Humans are gifted in destruction, yet they rarely use it to evolve.

They slaughter indiscriminately, they rape what sustains them, they feast on all things and yet it does not enrich them. You understand, don't you, little lamb? You know how order is birthed from chaos. Look in here . . ."

He opened another door to my left and beckoned me forward. Inside, what looked like immense starfish were stuck to the walls, transparent spines on their backs filling with blood, like ticks. They pumped and ground their bodies obscenely and I noticed human shapes underneath. Hands and feet stuck out at all angles, fingertips flexing with each undulation.

"Are they eating them?" I whispered.

"Sometimes. If they want. It depends on what else there is to offer. These creatures have needs, they don't always desire the same thing. Some people come here to wear the flesh of others, to leave refined, reformed and redesigned. Some wish to be garments for the Old Ones; I treat them in the same way I treat our animal friends upstairs. Some simply beg to be obliterated, pushed to the edges of madness and then crushed into stardust. I open doors to those who delight in doing just that. Everything is consensual, everyone has a choice." He paused, watching me closely, as if waiting for a response.

"What do you choose, little lamb?"

I turned away as one of the twitching hands fell to the floor, shriveled and bloodless, leaving only a twisted stump of a wrist. My trembling voice disgusted me.

"I don't know."

"You have a gift, deep within you. A knowledge that far outweighs these dabblers. We are one, under the skin, the creators and the destroyers. You know this."

Electricity crackled in my sinuses and nausea swelled.

"I need to breathe," I mumbled.

"Do you? I'm not sure if you do. Let it happen," he soothed. "You are its Mistress, its lover. It's only energy, pure energy, waiting to be birthed into the world. We *are* One."

I bit my lip, trying to startle myself back to full awareness, but blackness closed in and my body went limp.

I AWOKE on the stone floor of a windowless room, the coolness of the rock soothed my throbbing head and I remained still for a long time. Sitting up, I saw shapes scrawled all over the walls, a tiny door closed in the corner. I was inside a chamber.

He sat in the corner on a low wooden stool, removing his jacket and waistcoat, folding them neatly in a pile on the floor. Then he stood, removing his trousers and shoes until obsidian skin was all I could see. I'd dreamt of this for so long, yet now I felt like a child, timid and trembling, exposed and unsure.

He began to speak, his usual honeyed tones replaced by a cloying rasp. He sounded like he was drowning. I concentrated harder as guttural growls rose from his chest, felt blood rush to my groin. I trusted it instinctively, the rhythm of this visceral language, and as he flared with a blaze like uncorrupted starlight I could do nothing but draw closer to the flame.

The air smelled of wet soil and copper and his flesh began to simmer, slick and reflective. He gripped my mouth, nails embedding into my gums, lifting me up to his full height. As his incantation swelled the pores of the atmosphere yawned open, dripping jade secretions onto the floor, and our gazes locked as a spinning void of space rippled between us. I saw my fragile form, dangling jagged-boned and fretful, through his eyes. I was a weakened shell, a mess of shivering meat, brutalized and subliminally bruised by the shocks I had endured. This body was deformed, owned by its fear, bent and broken into intolerable angles and if it must be destined to perish then I welcomed destruction by his hand.

Thin black fissures formed on his face, splitting down his forehead and up the slope of his chin. Two more trailed across his cheeks until six met in the center of his nose, then the whole façade split apart. Writhing triangles of rubbery flesh wriggled free as his head became a star covered in puckered suction cups, a blinding light pouring from a cat's eye slit in its center.

He moved my hand to the center of his chest, digging my fingernails into the tissue and ripping it away. He wanted to be stripped. I pulled the skin from his sternum, tearing his torso too, freeing the squirming innards eager to be released. My fingers slashed and grasped, growing slippery from his fluids until his new shape writhed around us, a mandala of twisting tendrils with tiny hooks at each end. They whipped and whirled against me, flaying skin from my bones. Now we were entangled, a mesh of limbs and meat. Everything shuddered ice cold.

Pain as pervasive as I'd ever known sharpened me into a lightning rod. I'd never felt so alive as I did in that second, weightless and naked in his monstrous grip. My body, a crossbow of agony, fired arrows into the dark heart of oblivion. Tentacles surged seeking secret crevices, tugging clumps of gristle systematically from my innards, jagged hunks of raw emotion that I'd let fester and cling to my organs. Guilt, shame, doubt, hesitance, jealousy, fear—he pulled them all from my body and tossed them like scraps to the void.

I saw us in that room, a conjoined mass of matter churning in a spherical cocoon. I saw all the rooms, saw the thrusting, slipping, dripping things feasting on each other and roving through the labyrinth of a dark communal mind. We all saw it, felt it all. Our minds hooked into a consciousness only versed in pain and obliteration.

I saw that night. Saw my Uncle's pelvis stabbing and jabbing and pushing its way into me. Semen and blood and fear in my mouth and the searing pain of a thousand similar conquests reverberating up my spine. Faces blurred and smeared indistinct until She appeared, enveloping all attention.

I saw her birth. A white hot spear shooting from my body, blazing from my third eye to my neck down my back and exploding from the void of my crotch. She was a hulk of clotted hurt, staggering forwards to the source of her pain, an eyeless wound of a face split open revealing row upon row of bloody, shattered teeth. With harpy claws she tore at her hair, capillary networks fanning like wings from her back. She hurled my Uncle's body against the floor, impaling him with a tongue suddenly stretched into a spike. Then she screamed, a vile gargling shriek that spat hunks of meat onto his petrified face. My voice, her voice, giving form to every wretched thing that ever suffered without consent. His flesh flew away from the impact of her sorrow and the farm became a maelstrom of ripping, twisting, unforgiving energy. Everything flew apart: the barn, the cows, the dogs, the pigs, my Uncle, my cousins. Me. Everything exploded with the sincerity of her pain.

I felt his body judder from the weight of her presence. Now every ounce of will he had was forced into me. I shattered like a nebula, spewing razor shards of light across the Universe. Every string of my psyche and all the dark communes sang that we were one.

We were One.

We

Are

One

It took a long time to rebuild myself after he left me in that room. Not as long as the first time, I'm sure, but then it's hard to recall. At first my awareness hung in a sentient mist, fused gently to every particle of air around it and nothing more.

There was a strange satisfaction to that state, light and clean, holding nothing but the weight of air and moisture. I suppose it was inevitable that my ego would prevail, that the idea of my own importance would infiltrate space and I'd start to flourish. The simplicity couldn't last; evolution is an obstinate beast. At the farm I'd believed it was over, that I'd finally found a sanctuary in the stillness, away from the nightmare life I'd known. But something had murmured me back together then, and this time I murmured to myself, willing that kernel of being to dream of a deeper purpose, something slipping past my consciousness as fluid and persuasive as the tide.

I nurtured my seed, focused on the multiplying of cells, and knitted myself slowly whole with the needle of my will. Since my initiation I remembered much more than my mortal self ever could and I'd lots of time to recall in that suspended loop. The more I remembered the denser I became until disparate particles starting bumping together, creating the friction and warmth needed to condense. I became a puddle, a plasma pool of poetic potential, and from this embryonic water, mixed with our blood, I pulled myself up, forcing bones to calcify and organs to grow. My heart began to pump, and I developed, curled in a bud of becoming, held in the palm of the Old Ones.

I remembered what They remembered, I dreamt their bloody dreams. I saw the apocalyptic ends of a thousand worlds and felt them, rebuilding and rejuvenating in their fathomless nests. How many times had they risen from their slumber? Resurrected from eons of sleep to crown the world's madness. The desperate soul of Nature summoned them time and time again and they rose to vanquish her foes, lest she break under their demands. They had ripped the world asunder, drowned it in floods, feasted on its children, scorched it with flaming rocks. Afterwards, it was forced to grow again, and they retreated, to observe from the tattered edges of reality. Gaia's shadow, her lovers, harbingers of the New Dawn.

Now I know with absolute certainty that when the time comes I will be there, open hearted and wide as the sky, as their Priestess and their Guide and an Architect of the Flesh. I will pluck up the fragments discarded in their wake, lick the wounds of the broken, and teach them the wonder of destruction. New humanity will be my masterpiece, my most inspired work of art.

Without the skin, we are One.

AUTHOR'S STORY NOTE

"Mother's Nature" is a twisted coming of age, a tale of physical and mental dissolution and transcendence through the eyes of an unnamed girl. Discovered by an exotic stranger her innate talents are cultivated by an eccentric tutorage in sculpture, fashion and taxidermy. Under his watchful gaze she transitions between a child, woman and artist, unaware that a deeper shift is taking place. As her empowerment swells, sex, death and sanity conjoin, proving that reality is only skin deep and revealing Nature's true face.

The story is influenced in parts by the Lovecraft Mythos and the works of Caitlin R. Kiernan, obliterating the duality of good and evil and reveling in the joy of monstrous desire. It was written in Autumn/Winter 2015 in Manchester and Morocco and first appeared in Martian Migraine Press's *Cthulhusattvas—Tales of the Black Gnosis,* May 2016. It was as much of a rite of passage for its author as it was for the character herself.

THE CONTRACT
PAOLO DI ORAZIO

From *The Monster, The Bad And The Ugly*
Editor: Jodi Renée Lester
Publisher: Kipple Officina Libraria

I DREAMT OF THAT HAIR AGAIN.
The worst nightmare was to fall asleep fearing that the vision was going to haunt me, devouring my heart and brain.
And so it was, yet again.

LONG pubic hair, thick and coarse, overflowed from beneath the pillow like worms to assault my face. My eyes rolled back, so that I could see a trembling sickle of light on the world as the black threads tried to force my mouth open. At the same time, I could hear my mother calling me to the table. I tried to get up, coughing and spitting hair, even after freeing myself from that living tangle. *You bitch!* I yelled at my mother, without knowing why. She seized me by the neck and pushed my face against the plate, forcing me to eat another handful of hair, that damn hair, my dark meal. I had nowhere to run. They hadn't stayed in bed or on the floor where I had spat them. They piled up and chased me. Those obscene curls climbed back into my mouth, and from the dark heart of that bramble they found their way back to my nostrils, diffusing a scent of tanned leather, of a wet animal. I coughed, but in the end it was all pointless. Again they went inside my mouth, entangling my tongue, my teeth, attempting to flee down my throat, inhaled by my breathing. There wasn't a filthier torture I could imagine. The cocoon slipped down my throat. That raven clump got stuck behind my palate, almost as if it wanted to climb back up my nose, and my stomach jumped in painful convulsion. Swallowing the clump was the only thing I could do to avoid choking. The effort to not vomit and hold that thing inside was so violent that it abruptly ended my dream.

I OPENED my eyes, trying to catch my breath.
In the darkness, slightly weakened by the dim light that filtered through the closed window, I saw the sooty shadow of my mother on the door. She looked at me, perfectly still.
Without talking.
Without breathing.
I closed my eyes, expecting the worst.
But nothing happened.

THE next morning while sitting at my desk, I still felt as if my throat was burning, after that horrible dream.

A test. The essay topic said, "Describe your vision of world politics and then, in more detail, the national political scene here in Italy." I wasn't sure the teacher would have liked what I was going to write. With my mom, we had often discussed politics in a rather contemptuous way. I didn't know how to proceed; I wanted to favorably impress the board. My pen slowed down, tangled by modesty and the fear of a bad grade. I knew that in order to get a good grade at that Catholic institute, I needed to align my views to those of my teachers. I had serious problems, and my thoughts would not pour freely onto the paper. I had to lie. In the end, it was just a bargain, really. I had to renounce a part of me, exchange a lie as if it were currency, in order to obtain the product I craved: promotion. Time went by quickly. The silence was so tense I could hear someone's leather shoes creaking, pens dancing across sheets of paper, even the nervous sizzling of fingers passing through the hair of someone lost for words.

"Excuse me, Miss Jones. Tomase smells bad."

"Tomase?"

"Yes, he really stinks. Can I move my desk?"

They were speaking in hushed tones, my friend and the teacher, but I could clearly hear them. They looked at me and then turned back around, possibly hoping that I had not heard them.

Do I really smell? I asked myself, while looking at them as they moved the desk.

The other pupils were immediately attracted by the movement. After having assessed the situation, the students sitting next to me quickly moved their desks, too.

Then it's true. I do smell.

As soon as they resumed writing, I looked at the soles of my shoes: I had not stepped in shit. I sniffed my armpits, but they actually smelled nice. I stuck the pen down my pants and then smelled the tip: My ass was not dirty.

Angered, I wrote without thinking. The cowardly behaviour of my classmates had humiliated me. I found myself in the middle of an empty circle, a sort of island of shame. The teacher and the external examiner kept staring at me: It seemed obvious that my smell annoyed them, too; they were patrolling between the rows of desks, walking slowly so as not to break the silence, but never approaching the empty atoll. They kept their distance, making my blood boil with contempt and rush to my head.

I didn't have the courage to open my bag and eat my snack during my ten-minute break; when the time to hand in the test struck, I left the classroom as quickly as I could, without even putting my things in order.

I left with the dictionary under my arm, without looking back, chased by the looks and by that damn stench that I alone could not smell.

THAT day, the sun blinded me.

The bus that was supposed to take me home missed the stop, even though I had called for it, and sped away, leaving me stranded. I walked all the way home under the one o'clock sun. It was the best choice: I avoided the risk of infecting passengers with my mysterious stench.

I was crying, and my tears reflected the light. The road ahead was long. At one point I had to drag my school bag like a dead weight; the burden seemed to grow with each step. I kept drying the snot coming down my nose and wiping the sweat off my forehead. Mostly, I thought about my stench. I must have smelled terrible, but why?

A scooter with two guys raced alongside, raising a great cloud of dust. The one sitting behind turned. They were laughing at me. I could not understand.

No, I really could not understand.

I entered the garden of the house, closed the gate behind me, and ran to my mother who was waiting for me at the door.

"Mom."

"Come, my love."

I hugged her tight. I had missed her a lot.

"You're late."

"Sorry, Mom, I missed the bus."

"You should have waited for the next one."

"I was alone there at the stop."

"Come on, let's go inside. Your lunch is ready. You must tell me how the test went," she said, leaving me there with a kiss.

I heard a voice calling me from the garden, but I remained on the threshold. Oh, no.

"Tomase, I'm here."

I did not want to, but was forced to turn.

Luckily, my mom had already gone inside when I saw the fairy standing on the lawn; she looked at me with a finger in her mouth.

She was back. Damn it.

"Tomase," she repeated, sucking her finger. "Hello."

That small blonde creature, who every now and then visited our garden, was back. I did not know where she came from. She spied on us and did strange things when I was alone. She hid in the midst of the dwarf pines; she had hidden there so as not to be seen by my mother. "Come, come see what's under my dress, come and play," she said.

"No, I must go, I'm late for lunch."

"Come on."

"I can't, really."

My mother called again, but I wanted to find out what the fairy meant to do.

She giggled, and then made up her mind. Looking at me with her pure smile, she slowly lifted her dress, revealing her knees, legs, and belly. Her skin showed bruises, burns, and long surgical scars that looked like horrible red caterpillars.

"Oh, sure you can," she insisted.

I just stood there paralyzed. She wanted me to look at all costs, and I couldn't help but obey.

She bit the trim of her dress, lifting it up to her pubis, and then she touched her pussy with her fingers. She opened her legs, blushing for the effort, and sprayed on the grass a river of pee and a brown rope. I couldn't swallow or move. I felt as if the hair spider I had swallowed in my dream was climbing up my throat.

The fairy opened her mouth and the dress fell off her dirty, naked body. "Here," she said. "Wait." She bent over and picked up the feces, holding them between her fingers. She ate entire mouthfuls of the stuff, and what was left she spread on her body, on her neck, until she finally licked the palms of her hands and her filthy fingers. As she showed me that disgusting stuff she laughed. Then she walked toward me. "You have some, too."

I backed away, leaving my bag at the base of the stairs. The fairy quickly walked through the grass to give me that warm gift. I walked into the house and closed the door just in time. She stopped outside the door; I could hear her panting. I stood there listening, waiting for her to go, until my mother called me for the last time.

Mom was cooking. She chopped and threw the ingredients in the pot. "Tell me, honey, how did the exam go?"

"It went well, Mom."

"Was it the essay today?"

"Yes."

"And what was it about?"

"Politics, Mom."

"And what did you write, honey?"

"In the end, I wrote what we always say, Mom."

"And what is that, honey?"

"That politics is the intestine of evil, which only serves to digest the spirit of the people."

"Well done, honey. And do you actually believe it?"

"Yes, Mom. Politics is a bloodsucker."

"Exactly. Did you really write that in your essay?"

"Yes. I had started by writing something different, but then I had to put down what I actually thought. I'm afraid I'm going to fail the year, Mom."

"Don't you worry. Do you like the lasagna?"

"Yes, Mom. It's really good."

"Thanks. Eat it all. I made it just for you."

The fairy was standing outside the window, watching us, listening to us with her smeared face. I did not want to look at her, I wanted to eat but in that condition I could only chew a few forkfuls. I watched her no matter what, even though I was trying to look at my mother, who was bent over the stove. The fairy stood there staring at me, licking her lips. I just couldn't swallow; knowing she was out there with her face covered in shit filled me with a sense of disgust. I made an incredible effort to finish my plate, but every time I put the pasta in my mouth, my gaze fell on that brown face. I spat out the food twice. I had the urge to vomit but I forced myself to eat: I did not want my mother to scold me. In the meantime, the fairy was signing letters of the alphabet: *y o u a r e a n a s s h o l e*. She was harassing me, and I did not know why. I threw the fork at her and she disappeared.

"I'm full, Mom," I muttered.

"That's all right."

"Can I go out to the garden?"

"Sure, honey, go ahead. I'll join you in a few minutes. Are you up to eating some fruit together in the sun?"

"Great idea, I love fruit."

I OPENED the door and looked out.

The fairy was gone, finally.

My schoolbag sat at the bottom of the steps. I tried to lift it up to put away the books, but it weighed a ton. In the effort, I tore the seams of the strap.

I opened the bag and found it full of shit.

I WAS afraid to talk to my mother; I knew she would never believe the story of the fairy. School was over; I could throw the smelly stuff in the dumpster. The sun was burning. Green and blue flies were beginning to cloud the patio while Mom was in the kitchen washing the dishes.

I dragged the school bag full of excrement outside the gate. I walked toward the bins without ever looking back at her. While dragging the bag, in my head I imagined it shape-shifting. Another nightmare similar to that of the hair, the difference this time was that I was awake. I had the strange idea that the bag, in friction with the ground, had turned into a severed head. It felt like I was carrying a head that rolled and bounced, following the rhythm of my footsteps. It couldn't be a new trick of the fairy, but even the strap with which I pulled the head gave off the stench of dried meat. That day, everything had a bad smell. I thought that this was a descending wind of death, overheated by the angry womb of summer.

I dragged that dead thing, my bag, along the dirt pathway that ran around my house, almost all the way to the paved road that then led onto Appian Road. I finally saw the garbage cans at the crossroads. I threw open the metal mouth of the box and handed the load to that oven of flies. Then I ran toward the gate of the house and stopped to catch my breath as soon as I was far enough from the dumpster. I turned to make sure that the bag was not trying to escape. Carrying that weight and running to safety had put heaviness in my chest. The chirping of the cicadas and the smell of pine resin and fir trees around the Circeo comforted me, soothing my heart.

I crouched down to rest, and some drops of sweat fell to the ground between my feet. I was alone. The area where I lived with Mother was still dotted with construction sites; our house was the only inhabited island in the middle of a village of incomplete structures that died before being built. In the eerie silence of still cranes, bulldozers, concrete mixers, and concrete skeletons, inside the dumpster where I had thrown that absurd load, something began to crawl amid the trash, rubbing against the plastic. The buzzing of flies went up and down in intensity like a gasp, until I began to feel observed by the blind windows of the buildings under construction. In the toothless, eyeless heads made of brick, I had already heard the howling night wind, imagining that its cold voice was coming from the throat of a hidden spirit among the dark foundations.

Now that voice was absent. But the fairy was standing at the end of the street, looking at me from a distance. Although I could not see her eyes distinctly, I knew she was staring at me. That was her place: the clutter, unfinished and abandoned. The girl just stood there, planning a new attack, for sure.

A noise came from the dumpster, something hard being crushed and chewed by a powerful jaw. I pushed open the gate and rushed to fasten it carefully, before taking refuge in the house, with my heart in my throat, sweaty hands, and a deadly need to pee.

THE following day we went to Terracina to do some shopping, following another dream of hair and choking; a feeling that stuck in my throat the entire day. Before going out shopping, my mom always asked me what I wanted, to try and make all my wishes come true. So she did this time also, but the memory of that dream lingered on, scratching my throat.

"Honey, what should we bring back home?" she asked, holding the steering wheel with her stretched arms. Our orange Fiat 127 darted about on the scorching asphalt under the sun.

"A lot of fruit, Mom."

"Sure. I also want to buy you something to read, a new swimming suit, a small rubber boat to play with in the water, some new CDs, maybe some colors and paper to draw on, some films to watch together, and a new TV, too. What do you think?"

"Oh, Mom. I think that would be great."

"OK, honey. I'd like to eat out and go for a walk, pizza and then ice cream. Up to it?"

"Sure, Mom. But it's not my birthday."

"I know," she replied. She changed gear, making the engine roar. "And some clothes, too? We could buy some new clothes, perhaps two or three pairs of Adidas. We could go to the mall and then to the supermarket."

"Mom, I'm super happy!"

"That's what I'm here for. Your wishes are mine, Tomase."

She changed gear again and the car gained speed. We passed a tractor trailer full of dirt at one hundred and forty kilometers an hour. We were driving the wrong way. "Don't worry," my mom said.

The truck honked its horn in a sign of protest. But we were already ahead by several meters.

The truck abruptly steered to the left, leaning to the side: The cars that were passing at that moment were forced into the opposite lane, the ones behind crashed into them. It was a disaster.

"Mom," I shouted. "Had we not . . ."

"I know," she interrupted me.

ALL the things my mom had promised to buy were loaded into our 127: toys, clothes, a big TV. That day she was tireless. She never took off her sunglasses. She didn't say much, but she always smiled.

"Here you go, ma'am," the newsagent outside the mall said.

"Here, Tomase," Mom said, handing me a pile of comic books.

"Ma'am, don't forget these," the man behind the counter said as he picked more comics from the shelves, handing them over to my mom. She kept giving me comics. By now, I literally had *kilos* of them.

"Thanks, Mom."

"Goodbye," she said to the newsagent.

He looked at her, after a puff on his cigar, and said, "Goodbye."

At the supermarket, pretty much the same thing happened.

The cart filled up in just a few minutes. The day seemed endless. The sounds seemed muffled, part of another dimension. I was living through that morning with the carelessness of an afternoon doze. Less than an hour after the road accident that we had miraculously avoided, I had the distinct impression that life was floating around me in the albumen of a transparent egg. I found myself on the point of asking my mother if I was breathing. The feeling of not being me, *really* began to take shape. The nightmares, the strange events and meetings with the fairy did not seem like nonsensical, unrelated episodes. Suddenly, following my mother, among the shelves full of food and other products, I began to think of something that was condensing and consolidating into a strange disease.

We were not alone at Terracina's supermarket.

Whenever my mother filled the cart with fruit, canned goods, jams, cheeses, butter, bread, and packaged meat, enough to feed an army, the fairy returned to make an appearance. I was sure I saw her standing in the refrigerator, making fun of me from behind the door, under the white and blue light; she was crying, desperate, lying in the ice cream fridge; she put her fingers in her nose and then stuck green stuff on baskets of bread; she spat into the bottles of milk. She was everywhere, spreading her tiny crap in every department. I followed her in spite of myself, horrified, unable to tell my mom.

Finally we finished the tour. The cashier scanned all our items, took out her own wallet, and placed the amount my mother should have paid in the cash register. Then she handed us the receipt, put everything into four plastic bags, and said, "Come back whenever you want, ma'am, for more great offers."

On the beach, the sun hurt my eyes. I stayed under the beach umbrella so as not to get sunburned, while my mother lay on the sand without shedding a drop of sweat. She approached a stranger and started talking to him. He wore sneakers, sunglasses, and a bathing suit. His body showed strong muscles under smooth skin. As I looked, it occurred to me that from the newsstand to the supermarket, and then at the pizzeria and ice cream place, my mother had never pulled out one euro to pay. I tried to remember, but I could not recall if it had happened in the past. Suddenly, I realized that I had never seen her handle money, either in the house or outside.

Looking at the man, who spoke with her while the wind confused the words, I was certain that reality had somehow gone off track. I did not feel in danger. I was in a safe and secure place, despite the nightmares and the blonde fairy.

The stranger, squatting on the ground, temporarily stopped paying attention to my mother to lay eyes on me. He opened his mouth, but he had no teeth.

AFTER the beach, we went to the solarium. My mother wanted to give me a great day.

"Thanks for everything, Mom."

"You're my love. And, you've also been promoted."

"How do you know? The results won't be announced until next week," I said in astonishment. We were sitting in the sauna. We were alone, almost in the dark. I could barely see my mother, wrapped in a large towel. The white towel reflected a dim light on her face; in the semi-darkness, that small ray of light barely showed her profile.

One of the beauticians came in and gave us a black telephone. "Ma'am, it's for you. Christ, it's so hot in here. Keep it down."

My mother seized the phone that the girl, fleeing the boiling room, was about to drop to the floor.

Mom set the phone on her lap and grabbed the receiver. She said nothing, and I could only see the wet sparkle of her eyes in the dark.

She stretched out her arm, handing over the receiver: "It's your school's secretary."

The warm, wrinkled voice of an elderly person, with whom I had never spoken, told me that I had been promoted with honors. She suggested that I enroll in a particular school famed for its excellence, and then choose law school and later political science. She said I could have a bright career, become a man of power, guided by a friend of hers who would inspire in me an interest in physics and other subjects that I had never heard of. Before saying goodbye, she added, chuckling: "By the way, dear Tomase, your essay gave everyone the shivers."

Before the secretary hung up, I realized I had not memorized much of what he had told me. In the incredibly hot temperature of the sauna, I felt lost, and asked myself whether that voice actually belonged to a man or a woman.

As I sat leafing through a fashion magazine, the ambiguous tone of the voice that had spoken to me on the phone manifested itself as a persistent, mysterious fog. It became part of that bubble, which I was now more convinced than ever I was slipping into and away from the old world.

I had been promoted; I was no longer a child. In less than sixty days I would start high school. I was going to project myself into a new life beyond imagination. My mother was generously rewarding me in that long, hot day of changes.

I was about to become a man, although everything I had lived through during those last few hours seemed illogical and unreal.

I LEAFED through the magazine without any interest.

My mother was having her hair washed; I waited on the bench while the other ladies, in front of me, wore the helmet dryers on their heads. Those plastic helmets were heat robots, and I just looked at them in amazement. They looked like alien mouths that were cooking the brains of those unfortunate women.

I looked for a moment at my mother, sitting by the sinks where the two hairdressers were washing the customers' hair. She was talking to them, holding the hand of the customer by her side; whose chin had been forced down, the hot water spraying in her face and up her nose. The victim tried to free herself, kicking and stomping on the ground, her face smoking. But the more the woman squirmed, the more she choked on water that ended up in her lungs. My mother laughed along with the hairdresser, and it seemed to me that they continued to talk about shoes and elegant dates, even when the assassin turned off the water and covered the dead customer with a black cloth.

WE went home and I fell asleep on the couch, without eating dinner.

Again I dreamed of the fairy and of the bramble of hair. But this time it was she who regurgitated them. I saw her in the living room, bent over, vomiting hair with a gasp, almost a desperate scream. She spat the huge black spider out, along with foamy saliva that, as always, began to chase me.

I woke up just in time, my heart pounding.

Could it be that the hair thrown up by the fairy represented the water in the lungs of the woman who had been murdered at the hairdresser's? But the idea vanished in the dull phlegm of sunset.

My mother was not at home.

From the backyard I heard the rushing of water pouring into the fountain. I thought it was my mother, busy with laundry. I went out. It was dusk and the sky was red and bruised. I called my mother, circling the house. In the fountain, the jet of steaming water ran freely into the empty tub. I had a dizzy spell.

I grabbed the knob to turn off the faucet, burning my hand. I tried again with a cloth wrapped around my hand, while hot water kept splashing on me, burning my skin. My attempt was in vain, the knob turned without shutting off the tap. I left it running and decided to go downstairs to the cellar. Surely my mother was already trying to close the water mains and switch off the boiler.

I ventured down the stairs leading to the foundation of the house. The noise of the boiler was deafening; it was working at full capacity, building up a worrying pressure. It was very strange; there was no need to use heaters in summer.

The basement was divided into many rooms, some had white concrete walls, and others bare brick walls traversed by cables, pipes and knobs, meters and wires, niches and low empty corridors that stretched into the darkness. I found a few items that I had forgotten: the tricycle, the cradle, boxes of old strategy games, an electric train, scale models, and toy bricks. Below the ceiling, from which hung a light filtered through opaque glass, an impressive array of furniture loomed. The presence of these objects was somehow inexplicable. The humidity increased, covering my back and the hair on my forehead with tiny beads of water. I wondered how those big pieces of furniture could have been transported down there: a marble table, a wardrobe with five doors, a canopy bed, and a dresser. All were too large to pass through the doors or the narrow walls of the stairs. Then it struck me: Could it be that our house had been built around them? I noticed a huge metal trunk sticking out from under a pile of boxes, broken chairs, lampshades, rolled up mattresses, bundles of clothes tied with old strings. Everything seemed out of place, deformed by the low light and the din of the boiler. I called my mother, but got no answer.

The heart of the house was over my head. I felt submerged in a world reigned by stale air, where no one could have survived for more than an hour.

After reaching the boiler room, I looked at the red glow emanating from the lights of the machine and the burner cap.

The noise and heat were unbearable. Just then I saw my mother sitting on the boiler.

Planted on the ground and as big as our car, with the cylindrical stomach of a kettle resting on four legs, the machine worked relentlessly. The loading and discharge pipes, smooth and grooved, stretching all around, climbed the walls like wet, throbbing tentacles before disappearing somewhere in the darkness. The valves, pressure gauges, counters, radiators, springs, turbines, and heaters dotted the body of the machine: They looked like eyes and ears, fingers, periscopes and pipes. At its base, the boiler trod on an iron jaw, an open box of wires, filaments, electrical coils, transformers, buttons, valves, levers and latches, digits, serial numbers, numeric symbols, all covered in grease and dust. The machine was breathing, its vitality pulsing through red, green, and yellow lights, and puffs of steam. The walls enclosing it were veiled by its sweat, which fed black mold.

I could not understand the presence of my mother in that room. She had not seen or heard me arriving because of the fierce roar of the boiler. It was not clear to me what she was doing. She was completely naked, riding the boiler with her legs spread open, straddling the cylindrical top. She was letting the machine flay and burn her legs and calves. The smell of melted flesh was suffocating, pungent, and revolting. Her fat fried on the back of the boiler, producing foam in the spots where my mother stoically remained seated, sliding back and forth. I threw up on the floor, both from the stench and because I was beginning to understand. A bundle of tubes sticking out of the boiler went up and up toward the ceiling, bending along the top. Some conduits branched into fan-shaped formations, penetrating the concrete and the house. From the center of this sunburst, a dark, shiny tube, as thick as an arm, crept between my mother's legs, into a bloody hole whose greed shocked me. The slit between her legs was like the spider hairs that had often haunted me in my dreams: In an instant, the nightmare became horribly similar to the obscene feeding of the hole that swallowed, spat, and swallowed the heat pipe of the machine.

The human fat that fried on the boiler casing congealed in patches on the ceiling and then dripped down the back of my mother, who slid on the black tube, allowing herself to be possessed, faster and faster.

The scream of the machine and that of my mother were no longer two distinct sounds, but only one symphony of torment.

When I had the strength to move toward one side of the boiler, I saw the dark outline of my mother mottled by a red beam of light. Her throat stuck out of her mouth, pulsing at the rhythm with which the black pipe impaled her. Her trachea flexed in and out of the oral cavity, showing gleaming white grooves and dripping saliva. Her arms were welded to the cylindrical case of the boiler, which reminded me of the connecting rods of a locomotive.

I wished that my mother would stop, see me, and feel ashamed. But everything led me to believe that nothing and nobody could have dissuaded her from that moment.

I involuntarily walked two steps forward to find out what lay between the boiler and the wall. Perhaps, by circling the machine, my mother would see me and stop.

Once I got to the front of the boiler I noticed that the red light did not reach that dark space. There was nothing but a filthy darkness in the area. I just stood there, mesmerized by that void, until I thought I could see the reflection of a black eye, a stupid blank eye that slowly opened and shut. Then I saw a pointy snout with horse-like teeth facing my mother, and large horns that scraped the floor. Gasping, I finally took a better look at the beast lying inside the boiler, its iron lung.

Retracing my steps, now on the verge of suffocating, I discovered that the embrace between my mother and the machine, in a forest of rivulets of flesh and melted skin, tubes and pipes, gauges, welds, nuts and bolts that mingled with ribs, muscles, arteries, nerves, limbs, and joints, was a kind of infernal bull, half robot and half animal.

I RAN away, desperate for air.

But I found the fairy blocking my path toward the exit. I did not want to go back, where my mother and the fire beast were making those sinful moans. I tried to detour around her, one side and then the other, but the little girl was as fast as me. She walked toward me, forcing me to enter a small niche lit by a dim cone of light that filtered through the glass ceiling bricks.

"What do you want from me? What?" I yelled in her face, my shoulders against the wall.

She lowered her cute face, still smeared with shit.

Between her feet lay her own corpse.

I had never seen a corpse before.

I did not believe in ghosts.

The body lying on the ground was identical to the one in front of me.

"What do you want from me?" I asked again in tears.

"Just a caress," she whispered over the roar of the boiler. I believe that's exactly what she said. "Please," she begged, taking my face in her hands.

No, she was not a ghost. On that cold, filthy ground stood both her corpse and her double, holding my hand. She opened my fist, kissed the palm of my hand with her eyes half-closed, and led me to gently touch her cheek, pushing her hair aside.

My heart was beating fast, but I wasn't afraid.

She held my hand against her face, and then put her forefinger and middle finger into her mouth, wetting them with saliva. Without giving me time to react, her fingers flashed and pierced my eyes.

A flash of pain drove deep down into my brain making me fall to my knees.

I fell. She held me by the arm. Her fingers were an electric plug that electrocuted me to death.

In the midst of the convulsing flames of my eyes, a vivid scene showed itself between her fingers.

IT's the middle of the night; I see everything through the window of my bedroom that faces the house garden. The gate opens, letting in a large, long black car, which proceeds slowly along the cobbled drive that leads to the veranda. The headlights emanate a strong light that envelops my mother, who's patiently waiting. The car's engine turns off, leaving the headlights on. Three men dressed in black get out. One hastens to open the left rear door. My mother approaches the figure who's about to leave the car. A man cloaked in red gets out, a cardinal or someone similar. He greets my mother with a kiss.

"Now that we are standing face to face, we are finally ready to settle our account," he murmurs. Then he bends back into the car, leading the fairy out by the hand. Yes, the fairy. "Once every three moons," he whispers, holding the little girl by her shoulders, "You allow us to stay here, granting us the exclusive right to operate evil, until the day of the covenant." The cardinal receives no answer: He hands over the girl to my mother, before bowing and getting back into the car. The escorts look around, do not see me, and the car leaves. The engine is silent.

Mom closes the gate, and then leads the girl down to the basement.

In the bowels of the foundation, my mother breaks the arms and legs of the fairy. She kisses her on the mouth, sucking in her spirit, a tangle

of hair that she then spits on the ground in the dark.
Then she sacrifices the girl on the voluptuous pipes of the boiler.
The young and virgin flesh dies.

"For every soul that is not given back to the Creator, the celestial armies
have one less angel to fight the devil," the fairy said, freeing my eyes
from her fingers.

I remained on the ground, blinded.

"Your mother will receive other pure souls to subtract from the
kingdom of Heaven, and you will have to learn to love the family," she
whispered again, vanishing amid sparks of pain.

I cried a lot. The tears did not want to stop; my suffering widened
to form a flat, oily sea.

In my eyes, all that remained was a painful buzzing and a frantic pulse
of needles, and nothing else. My sight was back. I saw something moving
amid a slow smoke of tears, lit by the dawn. I had cried the whole night.

"Stop being sad, now," my mother said as she stood in front of me,
dressed in her red bathrobe.

"Who is my father, Mom?" I asked her.

"I am, honey," she answered, frowning in shock. "Keep me hidden,
Tomase," she said firmly. "And you will be the happiest man on earth,"
she promised.

"Forever."

AUTHOR'S STORY NOTE

When I started writing "The Contract" I already had in mind a bunch of
strong and clear visions. The monster, the location (a real seaside place I
went on vacation during my childhood—60 miles South of Rome), the
little girl in the yard, the bush of hairs in mouth.

The main inspiration, all over my whole writing production in years,
is always focused on *Rosemary's Baby* (the movie), both atmosphere and
plot, Carpenter's *The Thing's* metamorphosis and Hans Rudi Giger's
byomechanics. So, in this short story I wanted strongly a very-classic
faced background-main character. The *evil* looks heavily like the eldest
representation of the Devil, better known as the Antichrist, but giving it
(or him) the deadly body-horror mix between flesh and machine, iron,
bones and steam, and finally hiding him inside the most natural place

we know: a simple house. I love to search at first for ideas for tormenting my characters, so that weirdly painful solutions themselves often give me the logical sense of the story I'm gonna tell.

Maybe I am just a romantic guy, at last. I love those immortal American horror stories in EC, Warren and Marvel Comics (translated in Italy in early 70's from *Dracula Lives, Creepy, Tales From The Crypt, Strange Tales, The Unexpected, House of Secrets,* and so on—every one a supercult to me), short stories in which never there is a way out, never salvation, never a Hollywoodian happy ending for the main characters. The common Good and Evil fight always ends in a bad (and ironical) solution, either you'll see blood or not, making the villain friendly to readers, and victims the target of readers' natural ancestral wildness.

OWNERSHIP
WRATH JAMES WHITE

From *Into Painfreak: A Journey of Decadence and Debauchery*
Editor: Gerard Houarner
Publisher: Necro Publications

L ORD WHISKED THE SCALPEL through her flesh in deft, rapid strokes, carving forgotten runes and symbols, more from instinct than memory, as Miyu continued to moan, and scream, and masturbate with her one free hand. In his intricate designs, he used the welts and cuts caused by the whip, the bleeding avulsions left by the reed-thin rattan cane he'd lashed her ass and thighs with, slicing and cutting with the scalpel to connect wound to wound. Soon, the tapestry of bleeding lines formed hieroglyphics in languages that were ancient when mankind was new.

Miyu's eyes were glazed, far away, sparkling like Christmas lights as adrenaline and endorphins coursed through her. She never once attempted to free her other wrist or her ankles from the leather restraints. She was enjoying the endorphins too much, the euphoric waves of dopamine flooding through her bloodstream.

"Ooooh, yes. Don't stop, big man. Hurt me! Hurt me!"

Miyu loved the high she got from pain. The sweet intoxicating nectar of agony. She was enjoying all of this . . . until she wasn't.

It was some type of twisted mercy that made Lord bow down between Miyu's muscular thighs and lick her engorged clitoris, sucking it, flicking it rapidly with his tongue until she began to tremble with the first tremors of a tremendous orgasm, adding an avalanche of her juices to the blood soaking the red satin bed sheet. Lord sucked her tender labia, eased his tongue deep inside her to lick the inner walls of her sex, fucking her with his tongue as she continued to convulse in ecstasy. He knew these few orgasms, no matter how delicious, would be small payment for the agony to come, but it was all he had to offer.

"You will be my doorway," Lord said, as he traded the scalpel for a large bowie knife, plunging it to the hilt in Miyu's sopping wet vagina, seizing the hilt with both and hands and ripping the blade violently upwards, slicing her open from her sex to her stomach. She'd had no time to scream. Lord wasn't sure she would have anyway. He wasn't certain she could even distinguish her own murder from the salacious agonies he'd given her for the last couple hours.

Blood sprayed everywhere, raining down upon them like rainwater, a meaty red deluge pouring from the yawning maw gaping in Miyu's lower torso as Lord sawed his way up through her sternum and cracked open her ribcage. He reached into her chest with both of his gigantic hands to pry her apart and open the door.

"I told you bitches I'd be back," Lord said, smiling triumphantly as he stood, stepped both feet into Miyu's vandalized corpse, and descended the stairs into Painfreak.

3 HOURS earlier.
"Because she is mine."

It was really that simple. Sophia was his slave, his submissive, his slut, and that made her his responsibility, and she was in danger, even if she was too deep into sub-frenzy, too busy chasing that next endorphin rush, to know it. She was in way over her head.

Lord stalked through the streets of Las Vegas like a great, black, tidal wave. An irresistible force, kicking in doors, twisting arms, and breaking jaws, looking for his submissive. He was looking for the hell-spawned nightclub/dungeon that had swallowed up his property somewhere in San Francisco and spit her out here.

He'd spent enough time at Painfreak in his twenty-plus years in the S&M and bondage scene to be familiar with its rhythms. It would be here. He knew it. And no matter what it took, he would find it.

Las Vegas had fallen to ruin since the recession. The people here were broken. They had lost their homes, their jobs, and their marriages. Desperation and despair permeated the atmosphere all around like a sweaty film of existential malaise. Even the tourists that still trickled in came like vampires to suck what life remained from its desiccated carcass, or snuggle beside it in its grave and wait to be picked clean by the local scavengers.

It cried out for extreme distraction, a screaming orgasmic escape from reality, and the normal disease-ridden street whores weren't enough to satiate its thirst for debauchery. The swinger's clubs could not appease its hunger for excess. The bars and casinos could not suck its soul out fast enough. Even the local dungeons and BDSM groups, now packed with sadists and masochists eager to exchange their pain for another's, to torture themselves and others into forgetfulness and absolution, struggled to keep up with the growing influx of deviants, and faltered as their members demanded increasingly violent and prurient diversions, straining and bursting the limits of safe, sane, and legal. The City of Sin was starving for sex and violence on a plateau far beyond its typical mass-produced, vaudevillian iniquities. The starving hole in the pit of this city was a siren call for Painfreak.

Lord searched in the old seedy part of Las Vegas Blvd, where the peep shows and strip clubs with ten-dollar lap dances and twenty-dollar blowjobs still proliferated. Empty crack vials, condoms, and heroin balloons competed for space on the sidewalk with cigarette butts and broken glass. You could get married, drunk, high, pick up a prostitute, or gamble away your life's savings all on the same beer-stained street. Hallow-eyed addicts, and worn and wounded whores shuffled zombie-like, squinting and scowling in the early a.m. sunlight, like ghouls startled to find themselves caught outside their graves at sunrise. Their hunger urged them forward, not satisfied by whatever sins they'd indulged in the night.

Lord was not a fan of sunlight either. The dark suited him better. His midnight complexion blended in with the evening shadows and he felt himself one of them. The night was an extension of his being. But the club would be more dangerous after dark. Painfreak was a nocturnal predator that slept during the day. At night, it harvested pain and innocence, devoured souls, much as Lord did. But Lord considered himself the hero in this story.

He'd taken many lives, broken many more hearts. But it had all been consensual. He gave the lost and lonely what they desired, and sometimes agony and death was what they wanted most. Who was he to deny anyone the lusts of their darkest hearts? The more he tried to convince himself he was different than the club's owners and infernal occupants, the less dissimilar they both seemed. But the fact that Sophia's fate would be no less agonizing with him than inside Painfreak was a secondary consideration. The point was that she wore his color, his wolf's head brand on her inner thigh.

She's mine, and she has the book!

The Stratosphere Hotel loomed overhead, casting its long shadow over the twilight streets while the morning sun slowly chased back all other shadows. Lord walked among the damned. Their ravenous eyes crawled over his ebon flesh, searching for some morsel of generosity. Money. Sex. Conversation. A simple smile. He had none to spare.

Even well into his forties, Lord was still an impressive figure. His six-foot-six, 230+lb body was still lean and hard with muscles bulging beneath his leather trench coat. The only signs of his age were the two inch-wide streaks of white in his goatee, and an overall hardening of his face and eyes. His gaze held a cold wisdom that old warriors acquired after years of sustained battle. As if his very soul had grown callouses to protect itself.

Lord was shirtless beneath the black leather trench coat. Even in January it was sixty degrees in Vegas, though the strong wind dropped the relative temperature another twenty degrees. His coat flapped in back of him like raven's wings. Between the two slabs of black granite that formed his pectoral muscles hung a simple silver chain adorned with a dried rattlesnake head. He had accumulated a few scars over the years, some from battle, some from violent, primal sex. A lightening bolt of keloidal tissue ran from beneath his right eye down his cheek, neck, chest, to just above his right nipple. That had been a fun night. Lord absentmindedly traced the scar with his fingertip, remembering the dominatrix who'd given it to him. She had cut him, then he had cut her, and then he had cut her some more, and some more, until they'd ended the evening fucking in a pool of blood while her husband watched, masturbating while suspended from the ceiling from metal hooks. She had been a succulent morsel who'd soon bowed before him and become his slave—as had her cuckolded spouse.

Sophia, on the other hand, had been an innocent—comparatively. She was no virgin, but she was a virgin to the pleasure of pain. She was new to the world of deviant sex. Her experiences had been limited to the positions commonly found in internet porn. But she had wanted more.

She'd been haunting San Francisco's bondage and kink clubs. The ones South of Market and in the Tenderloin district, trying everything with everyone, from rope play and predicament bondage to whips, floggers, paddles, and knife, electrical, and fire play. Every night she was with a different Dom or Master, until Lord took notice of her, and brought her into his fold. Lord introduced her to salacious agonies she'd never imagined herself capable of, and she'd gobbled up every torment he'd subjected her lovely flesh to, then begged him for more. She was a pain-slut, an endorphin junkie, and she was going to get herself killed, and worse. Much, much worse. It wasn't just that she'd gone to Painfreak without him. She'd taken the book with her, *The Book of A Thousand Sins*, and Lord knew exactly what she intended to do with it.

Lord found what he was looking for on Industrial Avenue, a block down from the self-proclaimed "World's Largest Strip Club," adjacent to an old furniture warehouse. It was a large nondescript structure of gray stucco and stone with blacked out windows. The place looked no different than the other buildings in the area, deliberately innocuous. The exterior changed from city to city, but the interior was always the same, updated every so often to keep up with style trends, but essentially unchanging. Lord could smell the blood, the semen, the hellfire. It singed his nose hairs and fired something deep within him that only came out during intense scenes, when he let the animal inside take prey. It awakened the dark, violent, predator inside. This was the place. Painfreak.

A ten-foot high chain-link fence surrounded the building. There was barbed wire on top that looked brand new, giving the place a secretive, forbidding appearance, yet the front gate stood open for anyone to walk in. *Because it knows very few would. And those few were more than enough to keep the club alive.*

Lord pondered the fact that he repeatedly anthropomorphized the club, ascribed a will and a motive to it, along with appetites and desires. It was how he'd always thought of it . . . a living thing within whose entrails they indulged and celebrated their lusts. The people who worked there were merely parasites riding it like ticks. The regular members, like Lord himself, enjoyed a more symbiotic relationship. It fed their passions and perversions, and it, in turn, fatted itself off their dark sexual energies. The tourists, however, they were merely snacks, hors d'oeuvers for the beast that was Painfreak.

The club was the true monster. It was Lord's rival for Sophia. Not any one of its patrons or employees, but all of them, the collective whole. And if any of them got in his way, he would not hesitate to make them casualties . . . even if he was not entirely sure how to accomplish such a feat when it came to the club's more Luciferian denizens. The ones who lorded over the lower chambers of Painfreak. If she was down there, getting her out would be—challenging.

Several cars were still in the parking lot, though there were no other signs of activity within or without the building. Lord walked around to the back and found a red door beside the loading bay with a small black placard, no bigger than a business card, just above the doorbell on the left that read "Painfreak." He rang the doorbell.

A skinny Asian man with Fu Manchu facial hair and a notoriously sour disposition, cracked open the door. He squinted against the morning sun and snarled in disdain, as if he took sunlight as a personal insult.

"We're not open yet. You know better than to come here during the day."

"Make an exception. I need to see someone," Lord said, pushing the door open. He could have been more diplomatic, but he'd been here often enough to know sweet-talk would get him nowhere.

A big bald guy with tribal tattoos mixed with traditional American tattoos covering much of his muscular bulk, stepped forward with his arms folded across his chest, barring Lord's way. The man filled the entire doorway from frame to frame, even when he turned sideways. It was a mystery how he managed to get in and out of the tiny door. He must come in through the loading dock, Lord thought. The man resembled an old wrestler from the mid-eighties who'd called himself "The One-Man Gang." He'd been one of Hulk Hogan's many nemeses.

"Okay, what can I give you to let me pass? You know, besides an ass-kicking."

The man smirked, amused by Lord's threat, but not the least bit concerned.

"Just turn back around and come back tonight, Sir," the hulking bald man said.

"Do you know who I am? What I am?"

The Asian man stepped up and poked Lord in the chest.

"Yes. We know exactly what you are. The rules still apply to you. Come back tonight or get banned for life."

Lord looked past the skinny Asian guy, and appraised the big bald guy behind him. The guy was as much fat as muscle. Built like a power lifter, big arms, big chest, and shoulders, equally big belly. Lord believed he could take him, but was far from positive. None of the employees at Painfreak were exactly what they appeared to be. And if he failed, he would be banned from the club, and there would go any possibility of rescuing Sophia. Even if he fought his way past the two doormen, there were others inside he would have to best, and they would get more difficult the deeper he ventured. Eventually, he would be stopped—permanently. Caution was definitely the better part of valor.

Lord stepped closer to the big, bald guy, locking eyes with him, trying to see into the man's spirit and take his measure. The big man's eyes were black pools of obsidian that reflected nothing back. Were it not for the circle of white around the man's irises, he would have thought he was staring into hollow pits. Whatever the man was, he wasn't human, not anymore, if he ever was. Lord was the same height as him, and just as broad, though easily a hundred pounds lighter. Every fiber in his being wanted to test himself against the big guy, alpha male to alpha male. He wanted to see if the man had any guts, and what they looked and felt like.

"Fine. I'll be back. Believe me. I'll be back."

"Wise choice," the Asian man said.

The big guy only snickered again.

Lord turned and walked away, feeling wretched for not accepting the challenge, even though he knew he had made the wisest choice. It wasn't what his heart wanted. His soul called out for combat and death. But he knew there was another way. Painfreak had its followers, fans, and acolytes, but so did Lord. He took out his cellphone and sent out a group text. Hundred's of submissives of every race and gender, most unknown to each other, in dungeons and bedrooms all over the country, and all over the world, shuddered in fear or squealed with excitement as Lord's text was received. He had been planning this moment for more than a decade. Now, the time had come to transcend. There were other ways to enter Painfreak besides the front door, ways he didn't even know if those two assholes were aware of. All Lord needed was a sacrifice . . . a big one.

"TALK of the Desert" was about the seediest stripclub/peepshow on the Las Vegas strip or in all of Las Vegas for that matter. Most of the women who worked there were prostitutes, drunks, crackheads, and meth addicts. Both of the bouncers were high on painkillers and juiced up on testosterone and human growth hormone. One was a large Samoan with dreadlocks a thick beard and a neck the size of most people's waists. He looked like he could bench-press a dump truck. His friend was a big white guy with the face of Jim Carey and the body of Lou Ferrigno. Lord kept an eye on both of them as he scoured the club for just the right kind of whore. He was looking for bruises, welts, burns, cuts, rope burns, anything that might suggest the predilection for pain.

The place was so dimly lit, it was difficult to discern the features of the naked women slithering between the tables, eyes unfocused and sparkling with amphetamines. They were pale silhouettes, illuminated briefly by roving spotlights and flickering disco balls. That was undoubtedly by design. In the red and blue strobe lights, they did not look nearly as unappetizing as they no doubt did in full light. In the darkness, they were reduced to tits, thighs, hips, and asses. Those were the only parts that mattered to the average customers anyway. From the features Lord could make out, it would be a blessing not to see more of their faces.

Lord found the darkest corner, just beyond the flicker of the strobelights and the glow from the dim bulbs behind the bar. Immediately, like hungry piranha, strippers from several different parts of the room began to slink toward him.

"Wanna dance?" Asked a slender bleached blonde woman with perfectly round fake breasts that sat up on her chest like scoops of ice cream. Her face was a maze of wrinkles, and her lips were swollen with collagen. But other than the damage her plastic surgeon had done to her, there were no other visible bruises or marks.

"No," Lord replied, turning to look at the next woman, a Hispanic woman with big, floppy, tits, wide hips, and a thick waist, hair dyed with streaks of burgundy. She smiled revealing a mouth full of crooked and rotting teeth.

"You wanna dance?"

Again, Lord inspected her for signs of masochistic tendencies, and again, other than a swollen jaw, probably the result of a poor choice in domestic partners, he found nothing. Lord waved her away.

A muscular Asian woman came next. She was just over five and a half feet tall and had the arms and shoulders of a boxer or mixed-martial artist, the thick muscular legs of a gymnast, and the beginnings of a six-pack. She was built like a warrior, like she was hardening her body for battle. Her face was lean and angular, manly, with an oversized jaw and forehead, obviously the result of too many testosterone injections. Even naked, breasts and vagina fully exposed, she could easily have been mistaken for a male to female transsexual, just not a very convincing one. A man transitioning to a woman would have undoubtedly taken greater care to appear more feminine. Even when she began to sway her chiseled torso to the music, grinding her muscular ass in the air, she still gave off a distinctly masculine air.

What caught Lord's eye, however, was the micro-branding of an Aztec sun on her upper thigh, the intricate Kanji symbols carved on her chest, arms, and stomach in delicate thin lines, obviously the work of a steady hand and a scalpel, the seven silver rings pierced through her labia, and the whip marks on her back. On her neck she wore a rolled steel choker, a collar. Someone owned this powerful beast of a woman, or at least thought they did.

"Sit with me," Lord said before she could entreat him to pay for a lap dance.

"Do you want a—"

"I said, sit!" Lord growled, pointing to the empty seat beside him. The Asian woman dutifully complied, slipping soundlessly into the chair. The other strippers who'd been headed toward his table turned away to find other prey.

"What is your name?"

"My name is Jade."

"No. Not the name you use to get twenty dollar tips from desperate Asiaphiles. What is your real name?"

"My name is Miyu."

"Japanese?"

"Yes."

"But no accent?"

"Born right here in Las Vegas. My parents moved here from LA. But I can do a Japanese accent if that's what gets you off."

Lord reached out and traced one of the Kanji symbols above her left breast with his fingertip. Then did the same with the sun burned onto her thigh.

"This. This is what gets me off. Tell me where you got them."

"Are you going to buy a lap dance?"

"No. No, I'm not. But I might just take you with me to Painfreak tonight if you can convince me you're ready for that level of—intensity."

Miyu smiled. Then leaned in to whisper into Lord's ear.

"Do you think you can break me, big man?"

"Oh, I know I can. The question is, will you enjoy it? Or is cell-popping and light blood-play the furthest your limits stretch?"

Miyu laughed again.

"You do say all the right words, don't you big man? If I was into guys, I'd be all over you."

"Oh, men may not be your preference, but this wouldn't be the first time you've played with a man. I'm sure I won't be the first man to bring you to orgasm either—or subspace. But, I will be the best. I will be the one you remember when you are old and feeble, breathing through a respirator, counting down the seconds to oblivion. This night, will stand out from all the rest. You may forget the sound of your mother's voice, what dress you wore to the prom, your grandmother's face, the name of the first girl you finger-fucked, but I promise you, you will remember every detail of this evening as if it were yesterday. You will masturbate to these memories for the next fifty years—if you live that long."

"You think much of yourself."

"I know my strengths and weaknesses."

"And what are your weaknesses?"

"My greatest strength, is in hiding my weaknesses."

"Touché," Miyu said. "Painfreak, huh?"

"Heard of it?" He asked.

"Rumors."

"Ready to see the reality?"

Miyu smiled coyly and nodded.

"I think I am, big man. Give me a few minutes to get changed."

The two of them stood and Miyu scurried off to a hidden room behind the DJ booth. Lord stood, watching the carnival of flesh parading through the flickering lights. A curvaceous, pockmarked woman with stretch marks on her flopping breasts, and dimpled blue-veined thighs gyrated on stage to a hammering techno beat. Lord closed his eyes and inhaled the powerful fragrance of sweat, sex, perfume, alcohol, amphetamines, and infection. They all smelled like prey. From the bouncer glaring at him from the front door, to the waifish, raven-haired, barely-legal bartender, to the woman with the pendulous breasts cavorting on stage. He wanted to consume them all, to fuck them to death, make them scream, cry, orgasm, and perish in agony.

"Okay, I'm ready," Miyu said, curling her hard body around Lord's tree-trunk arm and hugging it tight.

"We'll see."

They walked out the door together into the harsh glare of the sun.

"It doesn't open for a few hours. How about we go to your place and get acquainted in the meantime?"

"How do I know you're not some kind of serial sex killer who picks up girls at strip clubs and rapes and murders them?"

"Well, you don't really. Do you?"

Miyu laughed.

"You really suck at instilling confidence in a woman, you know that, big man?"

Lord smiled, but did not reply.

"Okay, I'll trust you. Just promise me you'll at least make me cum a few times before you torture and kill me?"

"How about I make you cum a few times while I torture and kill you?" Lord said, while letting the smile slip from his face. Miyu laughed.

"It's a deal. Let's go. My place is just about two miles from here. I hope you can fit in my little KIA Soul, big man."

"I'll manage."

In just a few short minutes they arrived at Miyu's apartment building. Lord was feeling anxious. It would still be several hours before the club opened. He needed something to relax him and take the edge off.

"Show me your toys," he said moments after walking into her apartment.

"Damn. You really aren't much for small talk are you?"

"We talked enough at the club, don't you think? Let's see what you're into."

Miyu's smile broadened. She bounded into her bedroom and began rummaging through her closet, returning with a large rolling suitcase.

"I've got a lot of stuff," she said.

"So, I see."

Lord walked over to the suitcase and crouched down before it. He unzipped it and began pulling out various instruments of torture and pleasure. He held up a spiked truncheon, shaking it in the air to test its heft. It appeared to have been weighted at the end for added impact.

"So, what are your hard limits?"

"I'm not into water-sports or skat, and no anal."

"I'm afraid I must insist on fucking you in your ass. You have worked quite hard with all those squats you must do in the gym to make your ass a muscular marvel. It would greatly disappoint me if you were to deny me that pleasure."

Lord held up a stainless steel butt plug with a base shaped like a wolf's head.

"Do you always carry butt plugs around with you?" Miyu quipped.

"Yes. I do. Disrobe and bend over."

"We aren't done negotiating," Miyu protested.

"Oh, we'll pick right up where we left off. After you do what I say. This is non-negotiable."

Miyu folded her arms across her chest and stood there tapping her foot. Lord stood and stared down at her, towering more than a foot above her. He slowly reached out and wrapped a hand around her throat. Miyu did not resist, raising her head slightly to allow him a better grip. Lord tightened his grip, squeezing her windpipe shut and applying pressure to her carotid artery. Miyu made a soft choking sound then wheezed, gasping for air. The sound of her choking put steel in Lord's erection. As Lord squeezed tighter, Miyu's hands went to her throat, her eyes widened and she began to visibly panic. He pulled her closer to him, staring deep into her eyes. He kissed her softly on her lips then let go of her throat and grabbed her by the shoulders, spinning her around so her back was pressed tight against his hard abdominal muscles, the back of her head buried between his pecs. He reached around and seized her by the throat again, this time with slightly less force, not choking her, just squeezing firmly. With his other hand, he rubbed her breasts. His hardened manhood throbbed against her.

"Need I repeat myself?" Lord asked.

"No, Sir," Miyu said.

Lord took a single step back from her, and Miyu obediently dropped her pants and bent over, grumbling under her breath. Her ass was one big, round, muscle, the powerful, oversized gluteus maximus of a sprinter. First Lord lubed his thumb with saliva and slid it into her rectum, fucking her tight little asshole with it while she grunted and hissed, gritting her teeth against the uncomfortable invasion. When her sphincter finally relaxed and opened up for him, Lord withdrew his thumb and replaced it with the wolf's head butt-plug.

"That's much better," he said, admiring his handiwork. "Now, remove the rest of your clothes and lie down."

Miyu stood and pulled off her shirt and bra. She glared at him angrily, even as she complied.

"You're an asshole. You know that, big man?"

"You like it. You're not even into guys, but you like pain and humiliation. Every bit of that turned you on. You are dripping all down your thighs. That's what makes me sexy to you. Not my body or my cock. Just knowing that I will hurt you, and humble you, that I will dominate you like you have never been dominated before."

Lord drew back a hand and slapped her to the floor. Miyu dropped onto her belly, and Lord placed a boot on her neck.

"Are you more comfortable down there on the floor? Look at me, Miyu."

Miyu's lip was split and bleeding, but when she looked up at Lord, her eyes were cloudy with lust.

"Tell me everything you want me to do to you. And I want you to masturbate while you tell me. What are you into?"

"I want you to flog me with the heavy flogger, as hard as you can. Really put your back into. All your strength, like you were driving railroad spikes. That's what gets me into subspace. Then, once the endorphins are flowing, I want to be whipped and caned up and down my back, ass, and thighs, until I'm bruised and bloody. Then I want you to cut me. After that, if you want to fuck me, you can. I won't care anymore at that point. You can rape my asshole all you like if that's what does it for you, big man."

Lord nodded. Then reached down and picked up Miyu, placing her on her feet and bending her over the bed.

"I think I'll start with the bullwhip," Lord said, reaching back down into Miyu's toy bag and removing a five-foot, red and black, paracord bullwhip.

"Ooooh! Yes, Daddy! Make me bleed!"

And so he did.

It took a moment to orient himself. The smell of sex, incense, blood, and candles was the first thing Lord was aware of. He had made it. He was inside Painfreak. The floors were all tiled in a red and black volcanic rock. The walls covered in black satin. Black, red, and white candles were everywhere. And so were the bodies. Some were still grunting, sucking, licking, and thrusting, fucking unselfconsciously in every corner of every room. Most were chafed and bleeding, sloughing off skin from the relentless friction of flesh abrading flesh, unable to stop themselves, lost in prisons of ecstasy. Others were still "playing" branding, cutting, beating, and burning each other with various devices, some Lord recognized, many more he didn't. The inferno was continuously reinventing itself. It would take an eternity to catalog all the devices of pleasure and torture that could be found in the club. For every two or three people that were still either fucking or playing, Lord counted half a dozen more lying still, dead or exhausted. It had been a good night at Painfreak. Soon the staff would come to drag the dead ones down to the lower chambers. None of the others would even notice it when it happened. The removal of bodies was done as casually and unceremoniously as a waiter clearing tables for the next guest.

The few people not entwined in the flesh of others, stared suspiciously at Lord as he passed from room to room. These were the regulars. Some were staff. Some had once been patrons of the club who'd themselves been carted down below after a night of overindulgence. Lord was ready to kill them all again if he had to. He had to find Sophia. She was his property, and this club could not have her.

It took what Lord estimated to be a full hour to reach the main ballroom. The cavernous room was decorated like a medieval torture chamber. The walls were covered in black crushed velvet instead of satin. The floors were black granite streaked with silver and white veins. Wrought iron chairs, cocktail tables, and fixtures, along with the black candles flickering from several dozen wrought iron candelabras gave the place a carefully cultivated medieval, almost satanic, appearance. This room, no matter how often they changed it, always seemed familiar to Lord.

Here, the staff had already done their work and cleared out the deceased. All that remained were a few lonely souls, waking from a night of debauchery as if from a dream. X-shaped Saint Andrew's crosses lined the walls. A huge inverted crucifix took center stage. Lord immediately recognized the woman chained to it. Sophia. Though her back was to him, he could see the tattoo on her neck, his brand on her thigh. It was her.

Sophia was being flogged mercilessly by a large, naked, full-figured woman in thigh-high leather boots. Her body was full and succulent, all smooth thick curves without a single stretch mark, wrinkle, or roll, like the body of a voluptuous teenager. Her skin was completely white, as if she'd been drained bloodless, and totally unblemished. Not a scar or a freckle. Her breasts were large and did not droop even slightly. He could tell they were real by the way they flopped and jiggled as she swung the heavy flogger, but each time they bounced they would return to their perch high on her chest. She had thick opulent hips and thighs, and a perfectly round ass that was easily twice the size of Miyu's. Her arms and shoulders, however, were knotted with hard muscle that bulged with power and effort as she beat Sophia bloody.

With each "Thwack!" of the flogger, blood splattered and flesh tore. Lord stepped closer and could see that the flogger had twenty or thirty, three-foot-long falls made of thick alligator skin, and a dozen or so made of barbed wire. The woman wielding the flogger turned her head slightly as Lord approached the crucifix, providing him a view of her profile. A coy smile played across her lips and Lord stumbled. He knew this woman.

"Hello, Lord. It looks like you lost something. Does this belong to you?"

She held the *Book of A Thousand Sins*, pointing with it at Sophia whose back, ass, and thighs looked like bleeding hamburger. Sophia's head was rolled to the side, and as Lord stepped closer, he could see that her face had been removed, the skin peeled completely off so that he was looking at raw pink muscle and white cartilage and bone. Her pupils were dilated, eyes fixed heavenward as if in a religious rapture. Without lips, she appeared to be smiling insanely. She was convulsing, in shock from the pain and blood loss. Lord was impressed.

"Mistress Anja."

"I am flattered that you remember me."

"What are you doing here?"

"You mean why aren't I burning in hell? The same reason you aren't."

"I'm not dead."

"And when has that ever mattered? The inferno is all around us, all the time, every second of everyday. Life *is* hell. You know that as well as I do. No, you aren't getting sodomized by a horde of demons right now because of this book. This book that you stole from me."

Lord shrugged. "You didn't need it anymore. You were dead, remember?"

"No. I was very much alive. I descended into the inferno bodily. Alive and screaming. As will you."

Lord laughed.

"Nope. Ain't gonna happen, sweetheart. I'm not afraid of your demons. They can't touch me."

"You mean they couldn't. But you don't have the book anymore now do you?"

Lord shook his head and let out an exasperated sigh as malformed, vaguely human shadows slipped into the room and began to coalesce into nightmarish parodies of humanity. Demons. They wore flesh draped over their infernal souls like costumes. Meat suits adorned with animal horns, antlers, scales, claws, fangs grafted into their flesh to make themselves more lethal and hideous. Some had a multitude of limbs. Some had more than one head, often one human and one animal. Most had sex organs from different species hanging between their thighs, often of both sexes. They had designed themselves to be mockeries of creation. Their very appearance was blasphemous. Lord had seen them many times before. Yet this was the first time he had no fear of them. He turned his back to them, and smiled malevolently at Anja. Her own smug, triumphant expression faltered.

"Anja, you never understood who and what I was. I don't need the book anymore. I'm so much more than that now. You always wanted to be an arch demon, to sit at the right hand of Satan and rule over hell. Am I right? Better to rule in hell than be a slave in heaven, right? You knew you were destined for inferno, so you thought the book would give you a leg up on the competition and grant you an honored place in hell. How'd that work out for you?"

"Splendidly!" Anja said, turning to face him. She was gorgeous. Hell had definitely changed her for the better. She looked fifteen years younger than she had when Lord tossed her into the pit.

"Me? My aspirations were much grander. I wanted to be a god."

The demons began to shrink away. Howling and shrieking in mortal anguish. Some exploded like hard-boiled eggs in a microwave. Others burst into flames. The rest fled, still screaming in agony.

"What the fuck is going on in here?" It was the bouncer, the big guy. He started heading toward Lord, then abruptly stopped and shuffled backwards with his hands held up in surrender. The Asian guy who worked the door with him was nowhere around. Obviously, he was wiser than he appeared. Anja was still looking around confused.

"What the fuck did you do?" She said.

Lord held out his arms, expanding, growing, filling the room with his essence until every shadow, in every darkened corner, was him.

"I have transcended, my dear Anja. Human faith, it is a powerful thing. When focused, it can make Gods of men. Such is how deities are born. Six hundred souls all sacrificed to me, on my command. It only took one text. Even your Satan has not accomplished such a feat in more than a millennium. You wanted what was mine? You wanted to own me? Now, I own this entire place. Painfreak, and everything in it, is mine!"

Anja trembled, she moaned, stricken with fear. Black tears wept from her eyes, as her very soul cowered and submitted. Lord stepped forward and reached out for her, seized her by the throat, and lifted her off the floor. "Including you," he said.

"I am your god now, Anja. I always have been. You have always been my property, even when you thought you were free, when you thought you were the dominant one. You have always belonged to me. Worship me."

He dropped her to the floor. She fell limply like a discarded Raggedy Ann. Sobbing and trembling she crawled forward on her hands and knees, then reached out and kissed Lord's feet as he towered above her, grown to the size of a titan. His smallest toe was now as large as her entire head. Keeping her head bowed, she held up the blood-drenched flogger to him.

"Yes, Lord. I am yours. Do with me what you will. Punish me."

Lord lifted the flogger from her hands. It was like a child's toy in his hands. He tossed it aside. Instead, he freed his cock from his pants. His massive organ bobbed in the air above her head.

"Rise and worship!" Lord commanded, and Anja sat up and took her deity's cock in her hands, and eased it slowly down her throat as it continued to thicken and lengthen. Soon, it filled her throat, clogging her windpipe as it continued to expand and grow.

"Uuuurrrlgh!"

Anja clawed at her throat, raked her nails over Lord's thighs and testicles as he began fucking her throat with a cock that was now nearly as long as she was and half as wide. Her neck ruptured, splitting like a banana peel. Blood poured from her nose and ears as his cock pulverized organs and battered her intestines. She shuddered and convulsed, dangling from the end of his impossibly large organ like a spent condom. He tossed her aside and picked up the book of sins from where it lay beside the inverted crucifix—beside Sophia's corpse. Kicking Anja aside, Lord wrenched Sophia free of her shackles and gathered her in his arms. He stroked her hair tenderly, then knelt down and put his lips to hers breathing life back into her. She blinked several times, looking around in a panic.

"It's okay, Sophia. Your Lord is here. You are safe."

It was almost dark again. Almost time for the club to reopen for a whole new crowd of deviants and sinners. They would come for sex, for pain, for ecstasy and death. The curious. The desperate. The deranged and debauched. And they would all bow to their new Lord.

THE HALLOWFIEND REMEMBERS

JEREMY THOMPSON

From *Sanitarium Magazine*, Issue #41
Editor: Barry Skelhorn
Publisher: Sanitarium Press

THE FIRST RECOLLECTION: AGE SIXTEEN, that unforgettable All Hallows' Eve. Nestled in a Ford Tourneo's rearward seat between two brawny accomplices, he fingers an aluminum bat, spray-painted Day-Glo orange. His sweatshirt and sweatpants match that fluorescent shade, as does his skeleton mask. As a matter of fact, scrutinizing the eight individuals filling the minibus, one would be hard-pressed to distinguish one from the other.

And when the mucky vehicle screeches to a standstill—on a desolate street, where skeletal trees grope toward fog stars, and it seems that every deity has been blinded—the group bursts nightward, whooping and howling. Down come their clubs, again and again, obliterating the intoxicated plead-murmurs of a homeless encampment, shattering glass, staining frayed sleeping bags crimson.

Piling back into the Tourneo, treacherously giggling, they exchange congratulations.

"Man, did you see . . . one of 'em was a woman," the Hallowfiend's younger self gasps. "Ya know, we probably should've abducted her."

Silence meets the declaration, as it is too ludicrous to respond to. After all, how does one kidnap a corpse?

THE second recollection: age seven, an earlier All Hallows'. Having ditched the neighborhood family he'd accompanied on their trick-or-treating trek, the Hallowfiend's childhood self ascends a paved hill, one slow step at a time. His weighted-down pillowcase makes his arms ache. Sweat clouds his corpse paint, and stench soaks his reaper hood. Silver-streaking the sidewalk, his cheap plastic scythe drags behind him.

Rightward, he sees parallel streets teeming with ghouls, bats, arachnids and goblins—frozen upon green lawnscapes, string-tethered to overhangs—with masquerading families parading from household to household, spewing the customary catchphrase in exchange for sugared confections.

Leftward, he spies only shadowy underbrush: shrubs and saplings, wherein sting-insects lurk. Soon, the vegetation will be slaughtered, the site paved over to birth additional neighborhoods, resembling those rightward residences glimpsed in a mirrorscape. Perhaps aware of this factoid, the shrubs seem to whisper, until screaming, a young unicorn bursts out from their depths.

Upon closer inspection, the unicorn is actually a costumed human: a young female wearing a coral fleece onesie. Her hoof slippers are muddy. Integrating with downflowing lacrimae, snot slides from her nostrils. Her face ripples as she moans, "Where's my mommy?"

Shrugging, the Hallowfiend's childhood self continues on his way.

Reaching the cul-de-sac of his latest foster family, he takes one last look at the moon. For him, it reveals its true countenance: a fanged jack-o'-lantern, ethereal radiance spilling through its sharp features. Smiling, the boy enters the residence.

He sprints to his bedroom, to toss the pillowcase into the closet before his faux family can spot its widening gore blotch.

THE third recollection: infancy, his first Halloween. Contentedly gurgling, he lies on the sidewalk, staring up into the night sky, from which rain just ceased plummeting.

Suddenly, a strawberry-costumed female looms over him, her flaccid, friendly features overwritten with concern.

"Oh my!" she exclaims, crouching to lift him. "Somebody left you alone in a puddle. Who would do such a thing?"

As her fingers brush his midsection, the better to heft him, a thunderous crack sounds, and the woman topples over. Where her friendly face was, flesh tendrils flank a shattered-bone cavity. Hair clumps and cerebral chunks curl into a pulpy grin as she settles.

A younger woman materializes, gripping a revolver. Under her felt cowboy hat and purple domino mask, she chews her lower lip bloody. Passing the firearm to her correspondingly costumed husband, she tenderly scoops the Hallowfiend's infant self into her arms.

The couple's soaked ebon locks hang down to their shoulders, resembling spider legs layered in olive oil. Their glittering oculi strain from their sockets, as they bustle their way into a battered Saab.

As the man places one trembling hand on the steering wheel, and with his other keys the engine to life, the woman reclines in the passenger seat, her undernourished arms a child cage.

"Quick, before the pigs come," she implores.

Tittering, her husband complies.

Accelerating down a street of smirking pumpkins, they see no neighbors emerge from their homes. Mutilated, arranged in otherworldly tableaus, all are too busy decomposing.

"Ya know, covered in bitch blood, our boy resembles a lil' devil, doesn't he?" the woman remarks, finger-tracing pagan symbols on the child's crimson forehead.

"His first costume," her husband agrees.

IN the candy apple room decades later, wherein flame gutters from ebon candles, beneath rows of frozen latex faces, a guidance counselor cavorts. Snickers bars squelch beneath his footfalls. Fog machine vapor hangs heavy. Mummy moans and graveyard winds sound from hidden speakers.

Disclosing three recollections as he skins a fresh All Saints' Eve victim, peeling back the boy's dermis and subcutaneous tissues to unveil a wet-gleaming ribcage, he then asks the pain-delirious young fellow a question:

"At which point did I become the Hallowfiend?"

AUTHOR'S STORY NOTE

"The Hallowfiend Remembers" was written in homage to slasher film franchise villains, whose gory exploits defined many late-night movie marathons throughout my childhood. Wide-eyed, my kid self watched Jason, Michael, Pinhead, Freddy and others stalk and slaughter youthful jocks, dweebs and bimbos, and return in sequels to start the cycle again.

Realizing that their undying bloodlusts rarely permitted such evildoers to indulge in nostalgia, I decided to turn my serial killer contemplative. Primarily drawing inspiration from my favorite holiday, as well as the John Carpenter franchise that bears its name, I scripted snapshots of a madman's lifetime, to be recounted by the villain himself to his current victim.

"The Hallowfiend Remembers" appeared in the 41st issue of *Sanitarium Magazine*, which was edited by Barry Skelhorn. Prior to its selection for this *Year's Best* collection, I hadn't received much feedback on the tale, aside from someone snidely asking, "What's wrong with you?" Ergo, I am equally honored and relieved to see it in this anthology.

Initially, the Hallowfiend was intended for only a one-and-done short. He persisted in my mental recesses nonetheless, demanding more prose flesh to wear, more souls for the pumpkin. I found myself pondering the shape of his future. Arriving upon it, I was astounded by that destiny.

Currently, I am writing a novel wherein the Hallowfiend returns to embark on a grand journey, staying true to his own evil nature all the while. Perhaps I should be worried by the ease with which I crawl into the character's perspective.

THE FIELD
MARVIN BROWN

From *Insomnia & Obsession Magazine #5*
Editor: Bob Pope
Publisher: Rawketsock Design

I

'LL NEVER AGAIN SEE THE FIELD the way I did the first time it seduced me from the deserted highway taking me home and guiding me into a long cold night of its despair. You can only see such a thing that way once in your lifetime; the rest is ever-shifting approximations.

Make no mistake, I still see the field. Its improbable existence remains the thinnest of threads snaking along and slicing into the breathing coils of my mind, leaving micro-cuts since the day I walked into that fallow field, until the final time I looked upon it.

II

I'm on the trip home from college. It's a holiday weekend, Halloween, but that isn't why I'm heading back to New Haven. A convenient excuse, since I'm going home to change the scenery—and interrupt the pain.

I-95 North keeps serving up patchwork asphalt and my rickety Focus never gets tired of eating it. The Focus' Bluetooth system lends my smartphone the car's speakers. I love this sound system. My custom speakers are the best thing about my eight-year-old Ford. Clo thought so too. She loved blasting Taylor Swift. I let that shit fly because I loved her, because I was addicted.

I'm a recovering romantaholic. I've been on the wagon for three weeks. During the first week of our breakup I manned up and refused to call, care or cry. But by Week Two I'd already begun touching myself while thinking about Clo and stared at her number on my iPhone with my thumb dangling over the dial button. Later, I found myself blasting Taylor Swift cuts everywhere I drove. Three weeks in I knew it was time to hit open road and put some space between myself and my addiction.

I like to think of night as a blanket flung upward, me underneath waiting for its darkness to softly descend. Under this cover I think of things to pass time and keep my mind from Clo. My momma's Sunday morning bacon and grits. The Ethics final, still weeks away, but already a block of ice in the pit of my gut. I think of how man made these hard roads on top of dirt ones and somehow put them everywhere. The last thing I'm thinking before seeing the phantom billboard: how many human beings had it taken to paint these never-ending solid and dotted lines down this highway?

The car stereo cuts out and sudden silence jolts me. I look up from the road, drawn in by a beautiful glowing wall of fog. It's in a field a quarter-mile ahead. First I think it's some high-concept ad campaign. The billboard has to be translucent; I swear through it I make out a rusting silo and dilapidated barn. This is some slick advertising: a smoky, incandescent giant rectangle rising above redundant dark acres of farmland. The closer I get, the more impossible it seems. It's made of swirling fog that never breaches it edges and is backlit by some unknown source.

It takes a while to find an access road to the field I think contains the billboard, me inching the Focus along the berm with my high beams on. I find the road. The music kicks back on, louder than I remember setting it. Silencing it, I navigate a path along alternating green and dormant plots.

I rationalize that I happened to find one of those farms tricked up for Halloween. Like cornfields cut into mazes, acres of unharvested crops used as haunted playlands for thrill seekers, where in one corner you can find a permanently parked old school bus promising doom to those who enter. I've gone far enough off the road to muffle sounds of highway traffic; it's quiet enough to hear pebbles on the dirt path pinging against the undercarriage of the Focus and popping beneath its tires. The road ends at a field where ungainly stalks of grass, black to my vision, sway against a gray sky draining of light.

Walking into a spot of field lit by headlights, my pre-law mind tells myself not to go any farther, lest I contaminate a possible crime scene. But whatever brought me here, pulls me onward, the tangle of crabgrass slowing my stride. My eyes adjust to night that's deepening with every step. The field has been left to tend to itself and has chosen a state of anarchy. I hear and feel but cannot see night critters and insects tearing around the geography. The moon eventually helps steer me to a clearing. I step into it and see for the first time the crops of this field.

Infants.

Rows and rows of unclothed human infants. More than I can count. More than I can see. The field is alive with them. Dark, oily, naked, squirming. Some are crying, some seem nonplussed, their limbs jiggling silently. Uncountable pairs of white eyeballs float in an ocean of black grass.

The sight wobbles my knees and my mind. I pull the cellphone from my pocket, fumbling it. I call for help. Reception is weak, but I reach a dispatcher. Screaming the situation into the phone, I'm asked four times to verify what I'm seeing. I'm pressed for a location, an address; I do my best to guide them here. I wait. I am afraid to move. I am afraid of what these children might think of me if I abandon them.

Near me there is movement. I spin to see a woman walking out of the field. Haggard in moonlight, she looks *through* me until I motion toward her. It takes her by surprise.

"Do you see this?" I ask. "I called for help."

"They won't come," she replies. "No one wants to find this place."

I'm realizing how chilly the night's become, how much colder it must be for the children. Without hesitating I reach down and pick up an infant, shuffling to hold it correctly. Cocoa skin. Thick but tiny lips. Quiet. On the side of its face is a birthmark made attractive by symmetry: a deep-purple moth. I quickly carry the cold, soft child to the warmth of the Focus. By the time I get there the woman from the field is gone.

I lay the child on the passenger's side and pump up the heat. Over the fan I hear hissing from the back seat. I've made a terrible mistake. I shouldn't have taken this child from the field. Something moves in the back, rocking the car. My heart's bouncing against my ribs as I reach for the door handle. A smell drifts from the back as my vision tilts and bends. A crooked hand with seven fingers reaches out from the darkness, over the headrest, to take me and the child. I lose consciousness.

I AWAKE in my car parked on the I-95 berm as a semi blasts by. The child is gone and I feel hungover. I have all my body parts, and the car still has gas, so I tear out of here with an uneasy feeling that something from the field remains with me. I do a U-turn and drive to a motel I remember passing fifteen miles back, never once daring to look in the backseat. After checking in I commandeer beers from a Circle K across the street from this No Tell Motel.

After showering and finishing a liver and onion sandwich, I sit on an unwashed bedcover jonesing to call Clo. God, I miss her in all her blond-haired blue-eyed perfection. First meeting her I thought her only flaw was her really thin nose. On our first real date she smiled and was rendered perfect; she smiled and was redeemed of my private criticism. I was mistaken to not understand she was made to smile. The smile curled her lips and slightly widened her nose, making her perfect. The smile is the thing. Now my finger hovers over the Chloe Stine thumbnail photo on my phone. A field of demon babies seems like a good enough excuse to call her.

A pounding on my door pulls my thoughts from Clo. The door rattles in its frame. This craptastic motel doesn't have an eyehole in the door, so I take a chance and open it.

A terrified girl stands at the threshold. A caramel-skinned cutie.

"Please, help me," she says. "Three white guys. I think they mean to harm me."

"What?"

She is trembling. "I'm sorry to bother you. I don't know what to do."

"Where are they?" I ask.

"They followed me around the mall up in Brookfield, then I think they've been following me down the freeway. I lost them, but I think they're gonna find me."

There's something familiar about her. I wonder if I've seen her on campus.

"Can I come in?" She's pushing into the room.

"No!" I push her back to the door. She looks hurt. "I'm sorry," I explain. "I'm a little thrown off here. I'll walk with you to the office. We'll put in a report. Or call someone . . ."

She's scanning the hall outside the room, her wide eyes rolling everywhere at once.

"Let me get my shoes on," I tell her. "Stay here." When I come back she's gone. I stand where she stood, looking around for a few minutes. Back in my room I replay the incident, but before long I hear a muted scream. Down the hall. I get that tilting, bending feeling again. I hear more low screams near the stairs. The cement walkway to the stairwell wobbles. My breathing is loud and distorted in the lightless staircase. The screams draw me down the stairs, edging me onto the lower-level walkway, then three doors down. One. Two. Three. The screaming has stopped. The third door is cracked open. Don't go in, I tell myself. Myself doesn't listen to me. I widen the door with my foot and step into the room as an unlapsed Catholic crossing myself and counting rosary in my mind.

Oh, God!

The room should be lit dull yellow, but the bare bulb hanging by a wire and the walls sprayed red with blood gives the place a crimson glow. Blood is in places it can only get to by being flung there. The swinging light pulls and pushes shadows around this horror show. The girl is the room; she is all over it. Parts of her on the floor, fragments soaking and staining the dingy carpet. The smell is awful. Nothing I've ever smelled before, but I'm sure will hang in my nostrils like visual memory.

A name defiling her in death is scrawled in ink on the wall over the blood-soiled bed. Among the carnage I eventually find her head, beneath its ear is a birthmark. Like an insect. A purple moth. I give up my liver and onion sandwich in two stomach-twisting blasts, a meal forever linked to this motel room, never to be eaten again.

III

Omarion Cake's blood runs through the streets of Cincinnati. As Ohio's district attorney I'm helping to clean up the spill. The who and wherefores always end up being distilled down to the same cluster of newspaper headlines:

UNARMED BLACK TEEN SHOT TO DEATH BY POLICE OFFICERS

I step into my eighth-floor corner office awaited by the Haves: a Hamilton County commissioner, the county sheriff, the mayor and my ADA. The Have Nots, Cake's family, civil rights hawks, beleaguered protestors—locals and out-of-towners—will get a separate meeting, one to encourage calm and patience and tease the prospects of accountability and justice.

Cake's sordid history with the demon weed marijuana and a juvenile record that was never expunged has already inflamed both sides.

"Second fatal altercation in this city in eight months. Fourth death by cop in two years. Election year for the mayor," I'm told.

We hunch around my beautiful polished oak desk like we're varsity starters in a huddle. And we're a multicultural lot: the sheriff and my ADA are white; the commish is Hispanic; the mayor's black, like me. There always has to be sides, and one side has to win. The mayor looks to me. Everyone knows whose call this is.

"It's all of us, or it's a no-go," he says. "You understand?"

I'm a learned man. I understand. My power is divisible by 3: privilege of my occupation, privilege of my income, privilege of my gender. Having pocketsful of privileges takes the edge off, but it's never been fun, only ball-breaking relationship-sacrificing work to get here. If the adage says my race works twice as hard to be seen as half as good by white folks, well, I work five times as hard to be seen as superior. But now Omarion Cake, fatherless and flunking out of his last-chance high school, in death holds a power equal mine.

My momma, God rest her soul, lived to see my success, if not my disgrace. Do I hold ill will toward a 15-year-old unarmed black boy whose amber-colored eyes were blown out from a gunshot to the back of the head? Fifteen-year-old Mr. Cake, who never met me, could never conceive how hard I worked in high school and law school and in life, now holds in his cold, dead 15-year-old hands my future.

"I understand," I say.

IV

It should have been nearly impossible to find the field again. No phantom billboard to guide me this time. In truth I've been here in reflective thought so many times over the years I wonder if I ever left this place. Its expanse and contours have outlasted my fluency with catechism, my parents, two marriages and a child.

I was a smart-ass college student when I found it, a retired jurist as I return to it, a life looking over my shoulders in between. I am an old black man, aided by cane, with a heart subsisting on super-pills and jumpstarts from a pacemaker.

I twist myself out of my car and hobble down the dirt road to a place as faint and familiar as my childhood scars. The field seems larger, with more rows of ebony babies than years before. Of course there are more.

Kneeling to the closest child, I reach out to touch his tiny big toe. He is a 49-year-old Texas man wrapped in a chain and dragged for three miles by a pickup truck. To my left I press my palm to a child's cool indigo forehead. She is a stripper who committed suicide months after being gang-raped at a bachelor party. I stumble deeper into the field and take a plumb-size fist in my hands. He is shot at age seventeen for playing his hip hop music too loud in a car in Florida. I rub the smooth, heaving caramel chest of a baby boy. He is strangled by a police officer while being arrested for selling cigarettes outside a beauty supply store in New York. I brush away cradle cap flakes from a tiny little head. She is nineteen and shot in the face on the porch of a Detroit man whose help she is seeking after crashing her car. The next is a boy who drowns with his mother after she jumps from a slave ship with him tightly in her arms. The next is a victim of a drive-by shooting. And then, a 12-year-old Alabama girl with seven fingers on each hand is sold to a pedophile slave owner. And then, a young man is lynched along with two others at a public hanging. A girl is blown up with her friends in their church's basement.

My arthritic fingers dig into hard, dry dirt until softer soil beneath clumps under my fingernails. I won't seek out the half-dozen I know. I scan the darkened field, but I won't look too hard or too long. I won't find the baby with honey-colored eyes who never knew his father and didn't make it through high school. I have to believe these last ten years have been lived by me in the best ways I could. I like to think that after I reached the pinnacle of my professional career—a state supreme court judge—I reached the pinnacle of my compassion. I get dizzy and lose balance. I collapse to my stomach, pinning my cane beneath me.

Despite the soft grass my ancient bones wail. I roll onto my back and look skyward to a soaring crow, or a bat, wondering if the scope of this field can be seen from up there.

A field of weeping tar.

The tank's on empty. I yearn to believe there is more ahead for me. But my future, once somewhere down a ceaseless winding road, is finally before me, on a path narrowed from vast crisscrossing highways and avenues to a single dirt road to this place, ending at a plot of land that beckons us each. I was damn fool enough to stop pretending not to see it and drove right up to it.

There was a time when I was so sure that man could make the span of roads endless, that lead anywhere and everywhere. I know surely that man makes hard roads that eventually run out at the end of the world. And this field. Man makes this field too.

AUTHOR'S STORY NOTE

I do my best thinking in my car while I'm driving alone.

After being asked to contribute a Halloween-themed story to a magazine I decide I'll construct it around a road trip. My idea is to create a chilling tale that basically takes place within the car. Quickly the story veers off the main road, as they often do, and takes me down another path. It isn't simply about the journey anymore, it's about the destination. I think about all these anonymous fields whipping pass the car window and my story gains bones.

This is a season of political strife and social unrest, and these concerns worm their way into the tale. My story gains blood.

Finally, the story can't be read, it has to be *told*. Once I establish a first-person voice, my story gains flesh.

The rest, I guess, is just driving right up to the field.

A FACE IN THE CROWD

TIM WAGGONER

From *44 Lies by 22 Liars*
Editor: Eric Beebe
Publisher: Post Mortem Press

S HE CAN'T BREATHE, CAN'T MOVE. She's surrounded by other people, all of them naked, just as she is, all of them packed so tightly together that she can't tell where their bodies end and hers begins. Her heart pounds and sweat beads on her skin. She wonders what would happen if her heart gave out and she died like this. Would her body go limp and eventually slip to the grated floor? Or would she remain upright, held in place by the still-living bodies of those pressed against her? It's how everyone here sleeps, after all. If she does die, she wonders if anyone will notice. *Probably not until I start to stink*, she decides.

Everyone can't inhale and exhale at the same time. There's simply not enough room for people's chests to all expand at once. They have to alternate. As one starts to breathe out, another breathes in. You have to relax and let it happen. Empty your mind, not think of anything, for even the slightest distraction can disrupt your part in the rhythm, and when you fall out of sync, it affects everyone else. Great ripples of uneven breathing spread outward in all directions, resulting in thousands, maybe millions of people gasping and panicking, pressing uselessly against one another as their bodies seek escape. The woman has experienced these mass panics before, and she's determined not to be the cause of another.

She closes her eyes—not much to see anyway, other than the back of the head in front of her—and does her best to think of nothing. Her panic subsides, and she's once again able to take shallow breaths. She can't draw in much air, but it's enough to steady her nerves.

After a while, she opens her eyes, gazes upon the short black hair belonging to the man in front of her. The tip of her nose touches his neck, her breasts press against his back, and her pubis is jammed to his buttocks. There's nothing remotely sexual about any of this, at least not to her.

She can turn her head from side to side, but she doesn't like to. The people in the crowd aren't arranged in neat, orderly lines. To her left is an old man, and when she turns his way, she sees his ear, which is liver-spotted and has a tuft of white hair growing out of it. To her right, another woman faces her. Whenever she looks at the other woman, the woman smiles and tries to talk. But the other woman long ago forgot how to make words, and all that comes out of her mouth are inarticulate grunts and moans. So mostly she keeps her gaze fixed on the black hair in front of her. After all this time, she's gotten used to it, and sometimes she imagines she's gazing into a starless night sky, or that she's in a cave deep beneath the surface of the earth, a place so far down that no light has ever reached there. And in that cave she's wonderfully, blessedly alone.

One thing she hasn't gotten used to is the smell. At certain intervals, a rain of thin gruel falls from above. It lasts only a few moments, and people have to do their best to tilt their heads back, catch what they can in their mouths, and swallow it down before the rain ends. The residue coats everyone's skin, and it leaves a sour smell like spoiled milk. People piss and shit, too, and what little they excrete falls through the grate below. But no one can clean themselves afterward, which adds to the smell. Thousands of stinking bodies, thousands *upon* thousands, create an unbearably thick miasma so rank that she can only bear to breathe through her mouth.

She spends her waking hours listening, waiting—for the *sound*. She has no way to accurately gauge the passage of time, so she doesn't know how often it comes, and she can't remember the last time she heard it. But now, over the susurration of thousands of people breathing, she thinks . . . Yes, she hears it! The others do too, and their muscles grow tense, and their breathing becomes erratic with excitement. It's *time*.

A metallic sound, a chink-chink-chink-chink, as of ratcheting machinery. Soft at first, but growing louder—and closer—with each passing second. There's a shadowy dim light in this place, and as she looks up, she can make out the hazy forms of objects descending from above. Three-pronged claws dangling from chains, dozens of them, and as they draw closer, the prongs slowly spread open. *Please*, she thinks. *Please, please, please . . .*

The claws stop for an instant, teasing almost, and then plunge the final few feet. Prongs fasten on heads, necks, shoulders, needle tips piercing flesh, digging deep. Blood flows, people scream, and then the claws retract, pulling their prizes from the crowd, lifting them up into the shadows, and away. Blood drips for a few moments, falling like warm red rain, and then it stops.

For a short time, there's a bit of space to breathe, even move, but it doesn't last long. Soon they are pressed close together again, packed tight once more, and that's when the sobbing begins.

The woman sobs too. She was not taken. But the woman next to her was, the one that could no longer talk. The lucky bitch. She caught a glimpse of the other woman's face as she was lifted away, and although she was screaming in agony, she was smiling, too. Someday the woman left behind hopes to know that pain, that bliss. *Next time,* she tells herself, as tears slide down her cheeks.

Next time.

AUTHOR'S STORY NOTE

When I write horror, I don't make distinctions between different types. "Quiet," "weird," "hardcore," "psychological," "surreal," etc. are all different colors on my palette, and I use them whenever I need them. Horror should never be safe—for either readers or writers—and if you limit yourself to one technique in a story, readers quickly figure out that this is a "quiet" story or an "extreme" story, and whatever happens from that point on is expected. But if you mix things up and blend different techniques in your horror fiction, readers are kept off balance. They can't anticipate what will happen next, which puts readers in the same position as your characters, and what could be less safe than that? That's what I tried to do with "A Face in the Crowd," and hopefully, I succeeded.

REDUX

ALEXANDRA RENWICK

From *Murder Mayhem Short Stories (Gothic Fantasy)*
Publisher: Flame Tree Publishing

WINNIE RAISED HERSELF UP on one elbow and squinted in the direction of her bedroom doorway. The room was so dark it was like staring at a sheet of solid tar. The sound came again, a whisper of fabric followed by a nearly inaudible intake of breath. She saw a silhouette move, personsized, personshaped, a darker patch of darkness, and her still half asleep brain struggled to make sense of what was happening. She fumbled with the lamp, clicked it on, saw the person standing in the doorway, and though she began to ask *Peter, is that you?* with all the confusion, the lack of comprehension, the slow lickings of the dawning understanding of danger, her lips barely compressed into the first letter of his name before he raised the gun he held and shot her twice in the center of the chest.

WINNIE raised herself up on one elbow and squinted in the direction of her bedroom doorway, dislodging the book she'd fallen asleep reading. It slid off the vintage satin coverlet to the floor with a crash.

She reached down to rescue the book, to smooth its fresh-bent pages and close it properly, when an odd sensation of extra stillness made her pause.

She glanced again at the doorway leading to the hall. Had something flickered there, in the blackness? She clicked the bedside lamp on and squinted at the pitch-dark rectangle of the open door.

"Hello?" she called out, her voice sounding feeble, wobbly. She felt instantly foolish. Stupid. Embarrassed, even alone with no one to witness her being all squirrelly and girly and scared.

Shaking her head, she got up to head for the bathroom. She stepped into her slippers—puffy ridiculous moonfaced panda slippers, a gift from her mother last Christmas—and grabbed her garish pink and purple chrysanthemum kimono off its hook by the door, shrugging into it more from habit than a need for warmth or modesty in the empty house. As soon as she stepped into the hallway a hammer smashed into her left temple.

With a soft startled cry she fell sideways, knocking a framed picture off the wall. Glass crunched and tinkled as she crawled over it. Her head felt hot, but the alarm bells going off in her brain drowned out any immediate sensation of pain. Warm sticky wetness trickled into her left ear. Her palms trailed red smears on the wall as she pulled herself upright and turned to see her neighbor Peter standing with a bloody hammer in his hand. Weak light spilled from her bedroom, casting his face half in shadow. A weirdly rounded cap perched on his short blonde hair, like a compact bike helmet with a too-thin strap running under his chin. There was not an ounce of any emotion she could understand or even recognize as he lifted his arm again to send the hammer crashing down into her skull.

Winnie raised herself up on one elbow and squinted in the direction of her bedroom doorway. Had something woken her? She'd been dreaming about her mother. Her mother turning into a goldfish the size of a city bus and swimming down the street, obeying traffic laws with other vehicles half her size.

Shit, it must be late. Winnie rolled to the far edge of the bed—a bed too big, now she and Liz had split for good—and grabbed her phone off what used to be Liz's nightstand. 2:22 a.m. A nice solid number, but way too early to wake up.

Rustling in the hallway. Not her imagination.

Silent, phone in hand, she slithered off the coverlet onto the floor. Her naked skin hardly made a whisper on the vintage satin. She pressed the cold flat glass face of the phone hard between her breasts, trying to cover any lights it might emit, hoping she could keep it from making inadvertent sounds. She thought she heard breathing in the hallway just outside her bedroom door—not labored breathing, but tight, irregular, excited but as though the breather fought to keep it under control.

With some wriggling Winnie managed to squeeze mostly under the bed. It was disgusting under there, grittily colonized with dust creatures the size of kittens—neither she nor Liz had been vacuum-under-the-bed types. Even in the dark she could see the lower legs of someone entering the room. The person attached to the legs approached the bed, not seeming particularly stealthful and certainly without the hesitancy Winnie would expect of anyone unaccustomed to navigating her bedroom at night without light. Whoever it was even sidestepped her ridiculous slippers where they lay as they'd fallen when she'd kicked them off going to bed, one humped up onto the other's back as though intending to populate her room with plush moonfaced panda babies.

She held her breath as the person stood beside the bed. Her heart beat too fast, slamming against the flat face of her phone, the sound reverberating so loudly she was sure it echoed up into the room, giving her away.

"Winnie? Where are you?"

Winnie's heart skipped its next beat as she recognized the voice. Peter, from next door. Why the hell would he be in her room in the middle of the night? Had softhearted Liz extended him an open-ended invitation to drop in that she'd neglected to mention? Or maybe Winnie herself had once made some offhand neighborly comment about him being welcome anytime—something no sane person would take so literally? Maybe he was in trouble, hurt or bleeding from some freak kitchen accident, desperate for his only nearby neighbor to drive him to the hospital. A dozen implausible notions scrambled to present themselves as plausible scenarios, to explain away the intense weirdness of a neighbor she barely knew being her in her bedroom uninvited after two in the morning.

The fabric of his trousers made a whisking sound as he knelt to peer under the bed. His bland-handsome face was a pale splotch swimming in darkness. His head looked strangely over-rounded, misshapen as though he wore a fitted lumpy hat.

"There you are," he said. "That's a first."

Trapped. Winnie felt trapped, without enough room for her lungs to expand, to breathe the dust-choked air. Cold wood floorboards pressed hard against her naked spine. She felt flushed all over, simultaneous ice and heat, fear and the flight urge competing, suffocating her, adding to the confusion of *what the hell was happening.*

He reached under the bed as though to drag her out and she squirmed out the other side, not even enough room to roll, her skin scraping along the dust-gritted floor. It was a relief to stand. The relief hit her like a betrayal, a false promise of improved circumstances. Nothing was improved.

Peter straightened to regard her from across the rumpled bed. He stood between Winnie and the door. Her brain raced, sketching a hasty plan, something to do with leaping onto the bed, launching past him in the darkness, dashing down the hall, running naked out into the night toward the vague safety of *away.* She and Peter were the sole residents of this particular cul-de-sac, but the builder had never gotten around to connecting streetlights, so perhaps the cover of darkness would help her. Could she make it to the next cluster of occupied homes some distance down the main road, naked and barefoot? Buying her very own house had seemed a dream-come-true at the time, getting in at the ground floor, so to speak, with a developer desperate to sell units in an unestablished neighborhood at the ass-end of town. But then she'd gotten Liz, and a small but nice house near enough to the woods that they saw deer in the evenings, more birds than they could count . . . even a persistent coyote, leggy and lonesome and—she'd observed with a tinge of guilt—clearly displaced by the suburban encroachment on his natural habitat. No noisy neighbors to shatter the peace out here; only one quiet, corporate-drone sort of guy, Peter, who kept to himself, rarely spoke, never brought home friends. Mostly he seemed to hole up in his garage and fiddle with expensive tools, inscrutably tinkering on unrecognizable projects like any number of random suburban yuppie-type dudes. Winnie and Liz had tried to create a circle of friendly proximity and always waved, said hello when appropriate, were careful to respect the neat hedgerow dividing their pie-wedge yards, but privately referred to him as Khakipants.

The windowsill Winnie had backed up against dug into the flesh of her upper thigh. More half-baked plans and thoughts scrambled for attention in her brain (*open window, tear through screen? fall from second storey? survive fall?*) when Peter stepped back and flipped the overhead light switch.

Blinking against the sharp stab of sudden brightness, Winnie said, "Peter, I don't know what you're doing here but you have to leave now. I've already called 911." She hadn't. Shit, shit, she hadn't. Everything was happening so fast. She fumbled with her phone—unlock! unlock!—and wildly started thumbing for the keypad.

Her vision had adjusted quickly enough that she saw him shrug. "Doesn't matter," he said. "I'll finish up and travel back before they get here. I'd wanted to try this tonight, you know, for strangling . . ." Tangled in the fingers of his left hand was a loop of strong soft cord, an unmistakable garrote which he crumpled in his fist and shoved in his pocket. ". . . But I always bring a gun just in case."

Her lips barely compressed into the first letter of his name before he raised the gun he held and shot her twice in the center of the chest.

Flat on her back in the gap between bed and wall, Winnie watched the ceiling turning red—or was something in her eyes? Her chest felt heavy, as though her heart had turned to lead and now weighed her down, pressing her to the hard wood floor. She dimly understood the wet gurgling as herself, sucking breath through the mess of her shredded lungs. All thoughts of rescue, of Liz, of rage, even of fear left Winnie's brain like air from a burst balloon. The sole remaining thing, the one thought burning away all the rest in the final moment, was *why?*

"Peter, why?" The words wheezed from her, bubbling and nearly unrecognizable even to her own ears. He walked around the end of the bed to stand over her, to lean down with a look of polite inquiry on his innocuous, unremarkable features.

"To test my chronofluxic resonator." He tapped the thin plastic shell of the small helmet he wore, laced with braided wires visibly embedded with dozens of old-fashioned computer chips. "I needed to do something irrevocable. Something, you know, *important.* Something the world would notice. Had to make sure everything worked before I take it public. That was why, the first time."

The ceiling was all red now. Peter's face, hovering above, was washed in pink. Her chest hurt, but not so bad as it had a few moments earlier. She tried to speak but the words ended as a ragged cough. She tried again. Again Peter leaned over to hear her, tilting his head with that same impersonal politeness one might use with an elderly stranger.

"How . . . many?" Winnie burbled. Warm trails ran from the corners of her mouth. "How many times?"

Peter smiled. It was the first recognizable emotion to come into his face, reach all the way to his eyes. He nudged the end of the gun gently against her left temple.

"This is number twelve," he said, and pulled the trigger.

WINNIE raised herself on one elbow and squinted in the direction of her bedroom doorway. Groggy, mind thick with sleep, she reached for her phone lying on what used to be Liz's nightstand. 2:20 a.m. A nice solid number, but way too early to wake up.

She'd been dreaming Liz was trying to tell her some urgent thing, trying to wake her, though it wasn't Liz but her mother, and then it wasn't her mother but her eighth-grade French teacher. *Rise and shine, lazybones,* her mother had chimed in that maternal singsong she'd often used to get Winnie ready for school; *Attention, mademoiselle!* Madame Giroux had snapped; *Wake up, Winnie!* Liz had shouted. *Wake the fuck up!*

Winnie rolled out of bed, shoved her feet into her slippers. She was awake, she might as well use the bathroom; it was one of her mother's dearest and most firmly held beliefs that the font of all nightmares was a sleeper's need to urinate.

With one hand she grabbed her garish pink and purple chrysanthemum kimono off its hook by the door, shrugging into it more from habit than anything else. She was about to step into the hall when something made her freeze. Not a sound, not a movement—a disturbance in the silence? Winnie pressed back against the wall behind the door and strained to listen to the inky nighttime darkness. Her heart thudded against the flat square face of the phone she still clutched, now in one fist, pressed hard against her chest as she listened to the quiet.

The unmistakable sound of someone walking up the stairs. Not Liz, who'd moved back east, leaving Winnie heartbroken and three thousand miles away. Not her mother, whose arthritis these days prevented her from driving, much less from tackling even the most forgiving staircase without a fistful of painkillers. No one else came to Winnie's mind as anyone who might have any claim to be in her home in the middle of the night. So when the intruder—taller than she was, a masculine frame—stepped into the open doorway, Winnie slammed the door into him with as much force as she could.

The door ricocheted off the collision with his solid body with more force than Winnie had anticipated, slamming her back against the wall. The intruder staggered to his feet and lunged, striking wildly in her direction with something sharp enough to slice the loose fabric off her kimono sleeve at the first pass. The second pass missed her face by an inch, notching her earlobe, and the third bit deep into the flesh of her left forearm, bared of its sleeve, before tugging free.

A bellow of rage erupted from deep in Winnie's chest as though it had amassed and been waiting, surprising her, infusing her with unexpected strength as she tackled him. They fell into the hallway, she landing heavily on top. His surprised grunt was enough for her to recognize her neighbor Peter.

"Stop!" he cried. "You'll damage my prototype!"

Hot blood rained from her sliced ear down as she raised her right fist and let it fall onto his face. Her injured arm pressed against his throat. Her thumb, sticky-slick, slid across the screen of the phone still clutched in her left hand, activating the torch function. Hard white light flooded his face, blinding them both. In the afterimage snapshot fused to her retinas she saw why he hadn't dislodged her immediately: he was trying to protect some strange hat he wore made of plastic and braided wire, twisting to keep her blows from striking it.

She ground her injured arm harder against his throat, wishing she'd paid closer attention to that stupid Wreal Wrestling reality show Liz liked—would he really pass out this way? She bellowed again, bearing down, fist tight over the illuminated phone. Red drops and smears looked like fake blood under the harsh mechanical light, like stage blood, like gory theater.

Her other fist fell again toward his baffling headwear. He managed to deflect the blow while keeping grip on his bloodstained knife, a wicked dagger-point item she imagined was designed to gut deer like those for which she and Liz used to leave buckets of water in the yard on hot summer days. The skin over Winnie's knuckles parted as she was forced to make a glancing punch at his jaw rather than in the middle of his face where she'd aimed. The strap holding his helmet snapped. The contraption skittered across the wood floor.

With renewed vigor he threw Winnie off. Her phone went flying from her hand, its blinding light spinning crazily down the hall, throwing shadows, making everything dance in the strobe effect. Peter scrambled to retrieve his helmet. Fueled by an engulfing rage beyond her surface understanding, Winnie lunged after him. Some internal scale tipped inside her, stuttered into being like a flame ignited by flint. Not even the urge to run could overpower her urge to stop him from doing it again.

Even as she swiped at him, missed, hooked her fingers in his jacket pocket instead, the query scampered across Winnie's forebrain: *again?* Stop him from doing what, *again?*

A loud ripping came as Peter's pocket tore free, spilling its contents into her hand.

The gun was cold. Winnie had never held a gun, never pointed one, never wanted to.

In the faint electroluminescent wash from the phone down the hall, Winnie struggled to her feet. The metal of the gun was so cold it burned her fingers. She watched Peter retrieve his helmet, clamp it with one hand down over his short blond hair—pink hair at his temple, with her blood smeared across. There was nothing in the expression of his face she could recognize.

"How did you know I was coming? Was it the chronometric reverb?" he said, not to her so much as to himself, musing aloud.

Winnie was shaking. She gripped the gun in both fists, pointing it at him, hoping she held it properly, wondering how to retrieve her phone and dial 911 without letting him overpower her, wondering if she could last long enough for help to arrive without passing out from the pain in her arm, her hand, the side of her head, the dozen other shallow cuts leaking her blood and turning the wood floor sticky. Her teeth chattered so hard, it was a struggle to force words out: "What have you done to me?"

He glanced up as though startled to see her standing there. He made a dismissive gesture. "There was a small possibility repeated actions would set up a kind of pre-verberation. A precursive echo, if you like." His fingers fiddled with the braided wires dangling from his headwear, trying to press them up back under the plastic, twiddling things back into place. "Don't worry. I'll tinker a little more, find a different chronometral fold to access. I'll adjust the parameters and you won't know a thing next time."

"Next time?"

She recognized something suffuse his expression then. It wasn't guilt, exactly. Closer to a rueful admission of weakness.

"Unforeseen variable—I didn't know I'd like it so much," he said. At her blank stare he added the words her mind filled in, words she'd dismissed in some last ditch effort to keep any semblance of feeling sane. "I didn't know I'd like it so much, killing someone. You. Killing you. Over and over, every way I can think of. Night after night."

The sheepish look on his face shifted to triumph as his fingers found the right wire, shoved the right chip back into its slot. The contraption on his head flickered, humming with power, coming alive. Two blue lights blinked at Winnie like two mischievous eyes, sparkling and mirthful. *Next time*, they seemed to promise. *See you next time.*

He surprised her, leaping, slamming into her chest so the gun was crushed between them. She'd forgotten the red-slick knife still in the grip of his off-hand, the hand not clamped over the crazy helmet. She felt the blade where he held it to her ribs, pushing aside the open kimono, but her attention kept riveted on the mocking blue lights blinking, turning his pinkened hair purple as they made ready to engage at his command. *Next time*, they winked at Winnie: *next time.*

As his blade parted the flesh between her ribs she twisted. Her arm sprang free of their slick and awkward embrace. The arm with the hand holding the gun.

His knife pressed deeper. Winnie's skin parted like ripe cheese. The helmet lights blinked faster. Peter began to feel less substantial in her grip. In a moment she would be dead with his knife in her heart and he, if she understood him, if she believed him, would be gone. The lights would win, would see her next time.

Reverberation from the gunshot tore through her injured arm. The knife slipped from her chest with a sickening glide, then thudded onto the bloody floor with a wet plop. Peter sagged against her, thickening, growing heavier and more substantial as he fell. Winnie staggered backward under his weight, aiming at the winking lights again, firing again. She had to silence those mocking blue lights for good, disable them and never let them return. That Peter's head happened to be underneath them was, it felt in the moment, of only distant concern.

She let his body slide to the floor. Gripping the gun in numb hands she fired another shot into the sputtering blue lights, then dropped to her knees and smashed them with the bloody butt of the pistol, again and again, until she was absolutely sure she wouldn't have to do this again next time.

AUTHOR'S STORY NOTE

My dad's a folklore scholar and musician, so I grew up with an appreciation for oral tradition and a certain mode of storytelling, where repetition and musicality are central to the plot, character, or mood of a piece. As a child I was particularly attracted to murder ballads, death ballads, these little personal histories of tragedy, struggle, and loss recounted as sweeping sagas. My dad studied a lot of arcane and lesser known stuff, but in more popular culture—think certain songs sung by Johnny Cash, Joan Baez, Tom Waits, The Decemberists—anything that draws on that ancient tradition of telling a narrative of woe and strife, murder and heartbreak, repeating a refrain to frame a story you don't soon forget. I think this influences a lot of my work in any genre or form, though "Redux" distills it to its simplest state, while twisting a couple of the traditional tropes sideways.

OUT HUNTING FOR TEETH

WILLIAM GRABOWSKI

Published as an ebook short story by Oblivion Press

"That which is done out of love always takes place
beyond good and evil."

—Friedrich Nietzsche

THESE WEREN'T LIKE THE OLD DAYS, Jerfastilhak mused. No. In
this black age nothing like that peace could be found. They had
pain-birds now, killing-birds. Great screaming, swooping demons
that raked the sky and shat fire—rattled the bones brittling across the
cave's floor.

These death-birds were not all they had.

One bright morning, while gathering food for himself and his lover,
Moazirith, Jerfastilhak had idled a few moments sprawled among yellow bursts of primrose. A cool, flowered breeze washed over the hill.
Suddenly the sky caught fire; a second sun rose and blossomed into a
blazing mushroom. The earth shuddered, then rumbled as if about to
open and swallow its children.

The flash blinded Jerfastilhak—wild terror surged through him.

When sight and stability returned he saw a horror . . .

Below the hill on which he stood, far away from the yellow flowers,
the colony of the ugly-ones burned. From this vantage point Jerfastilhak
was spared nothing, could see the colony lay flat, twisted, and unrecognizable, save for one tall structure near the river.

Scattered fires raged. Cries of the maimed, the dying, could be heard,
borne upon the burning wind.

At that moment two wishes choked Jerfastilhak's heart: *I wish these
visions, these sounds, did not exist . . . and I wish to forget them.*

MOAZIRITH, upon hearing the tale of annihilation from her lover, sank
into sorrow.

Nothing Jerfastilhak did could lift from her this dark veil.

The crushing of rodents went unnoticed.

Seven carapace-cracking dives from the tallest cliff barely took her
attention off the lazy arc of a falling leaf.

Levitating Moazirith into the air merely lulled her into fitful slumber.

She hardly paid his antics any attention, not even when Jefastilhak
raised a pincer, punched into his abdomen and drizzled the molten gold

117

that pulsed inside over a scuttling hermit crab.

So profound was Moazirith's anguish she refused even to wear the gilded gift around her neck, despite the considerable difficulty Jerfastil-hak endured trapping the squid—hostile and slippery—whose entrails he braided into a string for the plated crab.

Was there no way to cheer her? Had Jerfastilhak's news of the devastation been solely responsible for his lover's distress? Leaving Moazirith cloaked in sorrow, he went searching for some remedy that might restore her.

Sad and alone, Ushiro Funikoshi climbed the steep trail that cut through the land above his secluded cottage in Kamuri-Yama. Ushiro had fled the bleak horrors of war and spent each morning running toward the sky in green silence, exhaling the stink of his past. In these hills, along this twisting, secret path, he hoped to sweeten the bitterness poisoning his heart; fill the void in his days once occupied by his father. Tadashi Funikoshi, strong as the bamboo and pine around the family home, had given himself to the Rising Sun as a pilot in the suicide-force know as the Divine Wind. He died the "noble" kamikaze death. Ha! What was noble about it? *Kamikaze:* "Divine wind" indeed!

Father was dead. Ushiro's photographs of him possessed, in their abandonment, a weird dignity; at once iconic and mocking. Unbearable.

The Americans and their atomic bombs had drained the spirit from Japan. No divine wind ever imagined could have extinguished *those* infernos.

Ushiro rounded a weedy bend, sensed something deep in the forest pacing him. He stopped, heart hammering his ribs. He listened . . .

From the undergrowth leaped a pair of chirping crickets.

"Oh!" Ushiro cried, and laughed.

They hopped across the path, flitted into dense fern.

He stepped into the dark woods.

Here among fern and flower was a small pool. The waters emanated a fragrance of drowned lilies, and Ushiro counted nine on the bottom, white stars set in green.

A praying mantis clicked across his sandals, but Ushiro stood still as the pool. The exotic insect had as much right to live as he. *Perhaps more; at least you, stick-legs, take life only when you hunger, or in self-defense.*

As if reading his mind, the mantis deftly snatched a cricket from the pool's edge and—with a crack—pinched off its head.

Ushiro shuddered, beheld his pale reflection in the pool. Rain began to fall, spatting ceaseless circles. The young man's image shivered and blurred.

A downpour ensued . . . leaves wept. Behind Ushiro a twig snapped. He pulled his gaze from the pool. *Great bushi* . . .

Whether what towered above him was dragon, hummingbird, or beetle, Ushiro could not decide. The sight of it stopped his breath and sense.

This must be *furyu*, a reminder of the imperfection in perfection. Or, something whispered in Ushiro's heart, was it just the opposite?

Bending at one scarlet joint, the *furyu* bowed its gold-green head and with some effort drank the pool. Delicately it raised itself; steam sighed from lemon mandibles.

And it was not without awe that Ushiro beheld those unblinking eyes of emerald, glittering in the rain like two fantastic jewels.

The *furyu* gazed down in judgment, fixed the man in place with those mesmerizing disks. Ushiro's terror abated . . . tranquility bloomed. With this came a flood of images: father leaving for war . . . mother not weeping until that night, alone in the bedroom . . . lightning at dawn, a violet fork stabbing the sea . . . doves scattering from the eaves of a dead temple . . . the drunken painter in Kyoto splashing snow cherry, cobalt, orange, lime . . . Ushiro seated in the overheated schoolroom, his shoes too tight—

Ushiro's last thought, before this perfection ended him, howled like a winter tempest:

Great bushi, *thousand-year-old samurai, I go with you to join my father!*

JERFASTILHAK wandered the solemn pines for days. Light and dark went unnoticed, beneath his attention. Soon thirst would kill him, but his olfactory lobes detected water. Thirst, though, was a minor concern compared to his pulsing dread.

What if no way could be found to deliver Moazirith from her misery? Should she perish, there would follow nothing but blackness and solitude, for where did others of her kind exist? Jerfastilhak concluded that life without his lover would be unbearable. If she died he would engineer his own demise rather than live in desolation, sentenced for eternity to the prison of loneliness.

There—straight ahead to the water.

Something approached. *Plip* plap *plip* plap *plip* plap *plip* plap—

From the sound, a sizable creature. Fleeing some beast larger still?

Dashing toward water?

Ahead, shards of sunlight cut through trees: a clearing.

Jerfastilhak quickened his step, careful not to cause a stir. Fat rain-drops began falling.

In seconds dark clouds dumped water in torrents, pummeled the ferns. Green saplings nodded, as though confirming Jerfastilhak's plight. But the rain could not mask the ever-rising scent.

Their scent.

This was not strong; probably just one of them. Hardly a threat. Never had Jerfastilhak stood near an ugly-one, so curiosity ruled his behavior as much as thirst. He broke through the undergrowth.

Here was a quiet pool. The ugly-one glanced up, its face pale and moist.

How tiny you are, Jerfastilhak thought. The other appeared impossibly soft and fragile, face revealing every nuance of emotion! Could such a being actually slaughter its own kind?

Jerfastilhak drew closer. Fright quivered the flesh of the ugly-one who, after all, really was not so ugly. *It fears me. I must not cause fear . . . must not trouble this one.*

What if the tiny creature led others to the pool?

Jerfastilhak ended this possibility by bending nearly in two . . . and drinking the pool.

Ahh—life! Relief! Soothing cold!

The ugly-one stood solemn.

Jerfastilhak stretched across the empty pool. *I shall console you.*

He grasped the creature by its neck. **No, no—do not struggle—do not fear!** shrilled Jerfastilhak, unaware that his voice, to the limited hearing of the other, shrieked unintelligibly.

Jerfastilhak's hold weakened, and in his haste to regain it clenched his pincher—severing the head of the ugly-one, when he had meant only comfort.

The head spun through rainy air, spewing blood and smashing against a rock—cracking open and flinging bits of gray, white and red across the ground.

Oh—oh! What have I done?

Warm shards oozed over Jerfastilhak's clawed feet. **I have ended it!**

Then he saw: tiny white bones scattered through the moss.

Fascinated, he dropped the leaking corpse into the weeds, stooped, and plucked several bones from the springy moss. *Beauty. There is beauty and perfection in these.*

One bone—incredible!—bore a gold plug, or seal. How had this creature procured blood from one such as Jerfastilhak? *What secrets might we have shared had I not ended you?*

Into his mouth went the bones; mandibles clacked shut. Powerful digestive acids flooded the orifice, dissolving the ugly-one's teeth, gold mingling with that of Jerfastilhak's circulatory system. After a few moments, there came a strange elation.

Energy, unlike any before, thrummed through his limbs. The white bones must possess curative effects! *Perhaps these should be fed to Moazirith? Hope! Hope!*

Sudden pain spiked his thorax.

With a pincher he punctured his shell, probed . . . and located the irritant.

Wrenching it free revealed a malleable white mass larger far than the original bones ingested. Some strange alchemy must have occurred between them and their taker's digestives, but Jerfastilhak would not be intimidated.

Curious, he played with and molded the warm blob. This conjured a memory: once, while cooling off in a rushing river, he had scooped clay from the weedy bed.

Moazirith had taken this and, with skilled, sensitive pinchers and mindsight, sculpted it into a likeness of her lover.

Could *this* material be likewise formed? Already it grew firm. He must hurry.

Bracing the mass with a pincher, he took the other and squeezed, scraped, stippled and pulled.

Mindsight added further detail. An inspired burst of activity created the figure of a hopping croaker—an albino with eyes golden and bulging. *This must be good . . . must be.*

THE headless body of Ushiro Funikoshi lay undiscovered for months, until one autumn night when crickets creaked and the moon daubed his bones with its luminous brush. A spider crept onto them . . . spun a chaotic web between two ribs and, where once pulsed a young man's heart, assumed its silent sentinel, glittering in moonglow like a jet crystal.

If Ushiro's starving ghost haunted the place of his death, it did not disturb one thread of the spider's net.

JERFASTILHAK saw his lover lay dying and shrilled her name.

Every bird, beast, and insect fled that unearthly howl.

He stood over her, offered the white figure. **Eat of this, my Moazirith.

You *must.***

Weakly she opened her mandibles, eyes brightening but for a moment as she recognized what the object represented. Her lover fed her the albino croaker. With an effort, Moazirith broke down the hard enamel.

She shuddered . . . vibrated her thorax. **What charms does this conceal?**

Jerfastilhak leaned close. **I do not know, but it filled me with the breath of youth.**

Gazing into the twin gems of her eyes, he could see fiery life. Would she live? Thrive as before?

Moazirith, after absorbing the figure, produced no precipitate. Her lover reasoned that his own caustics must have greatly weakened whatever catalyst activated the process. What else could account for this?

Two sunfalls passed, during which Moazirith shone floridly in good health. On the third, as twilight spilled deep blue into the cave, her robust demeanor dwindled, then wholly failed. Alerted by her hollow tone, Jerfastilhak knew something was terribly wrong. **The white croaker,** she managed, **bring me more . . . bring me *many . . .***

Creeping shadow settled over her like a shroud of doom.

Embracing her, Jerfastilhak again tasted the dread of solitude. Moazirith, of course, did not know where the albino croaker originated, nor what her lover had done to obtain its ingredients. Jerfastilhak, as strongly as he loathed to repeat the act, feared more losing his beloved to the black waters of the river of Death.

Lover, she pleaded, **hurry!**

Her golden tongue traced Jerfastilhak's plated throat. Easing her onto the cool cave floor, he determined to hunt day and night, gather so copious a cache of bones he need never leave Moazirith's beauty again. Any pain, any horror, was preferable to a life barren and loveless.

He must hurry; go out into the world and collect what must be collected.

Any living thing that dare stand in his path would know the face of Death.

HERE rose a hill, a view, a special place. The bleak hunter surveyed the province of the dead.

Would not there be a nearly limitless supply of the tiny bones here, free to harvest?

Jerfastilhak ascertained he was not being watched, and climbed down from his perch.

Beneath purple twilight the burial ground stood stark and silent. Trees, twisted and black, clawed at the moon's silver scythe. At the heart of this necropolis, a tall light-post ticked with moths. Honey-sweet whiffs of paraffin and incense lingered in the air, phantoms of some recent ritual.

The hunter moved among ranked stone monuments, some taller than he. Any grave would suffice.

There came a sensation, as nameless as it was novel. (Ushiro Funikoshi, were he alive and not suffocating in the endless night of transmigration, might have called this *awe*.)

The hunter had never seen another of his kind in death. All he knew of his, and Moazirith's, existence was that both were immensely old. Of their origins he knew nothing.

He paused before a bulky gray monument which bore the chiseled likeness of an ugly-one: slanted eyes; long mournful expression, as though the face might slide from the stone like shadow crossing water. Below this, rows of sharp etchings like marching insects. From this grave the hunter absorbed an aura of violence, hatred, and betrayal. Did this originate with its attendants, or the occupant?

At once there bloomed a vision: a solitary figure perched on the edge of a chasm boiling with crimson mist. Above this the sun towed a flaming raft of clouds. The figure cried out, jumped into the abyss . . .

Whoever lay below in black silence was not mourned.

Jerfastilhak bowed to the earth, extended his pincers; spread the lemon blades of his mandibles and scored the soil.

At first its dead solidity resisted, but soon the exhumation was finished.

The hunter's pincers scraped against something harder than the musty dark earth.

He straightened to his full height of thirteen feet, and drew huge breaths from the gloom.

Finally, braced about the grave's periphery by four of his spiky limbs, he reached into the pit and gripped the coffin.

Slowly, he raised it toward dying twilight . . . brasswork gleaming beneath the moon's cold face. Brighter stars jeweled the sky, indifferent suns flaring nothingness.

The hunter rested his prize on the ground and—with a violent stroke—smashed its lid into long splinters.

Offended by the strong odor, Jerfastilhak's olfactory lobes twitched.

The corpse's flesh shone pale green, patched here and there with gray rot and shiny with moisture. The hunter lifted the body from its seclusion, eased it onto dewy grass. Death lent the face a composure both stern and tragic, as though this ugly-one's sleep stirred still with dreams of ruined empires . . . of love lost.

The hunter touched the flesh.

Its taut chill unsettled him, and for the first time he wondered what life as an ugly-one might be like. What terrors? What hopes? What joys?

With a delicacy belying his size, the hunter prized apart the corpse's jaws, took the flat sides of both pinchers and clamped the skull, squeezing until—with a loud report—it split like a rotten log.

Thick, putrid fluid welled up. Unanchored teeth were gathered; others pried from dry sockets. Abruptly the hunter sampled one.

Rage blazed: useless. These bones were *useless!* Dead—all traces of life-force gone.

Waste! My struggles and sorrow futile! Dead! Dead!

In his fury, the hunter walloped the gravestone, smashing it into jagged pieces.

Heedless with despair, he turned from the pit and shambled toward the looming hills . . .

Though unaware, the hunter bled droplets of molten gold from a fissure in his carapace. After a few moments, these cooled in dewy grass. Perhaps on the morrow some mourner, sad and starved, might gather them. Follow their trail to the desecrated grave, and wonder with drumming heart and wide eyes why some terrible goblin had felt compassion enough to scatter such riches along this path of misery.

DAWN.

The sun sailed above the horizon like a blob of molten bronze. The sky blushed a marriage of rose and flame.

From his concealment the hunter regarded this vista with anticipatory calm. Only the jewels of his eyes broke the mirrored surface of the pond in which he lay. Now and then dragonflies with rainbow wings lit upon them, hummed and buzzed and clicked, before taking to the air once more.

Not far from the pond stood a fence of crosshatched steel, the top adorned with razored loops of barbed wire. Beyond this stretched black runways, seemingly endless, blurred by heat-shimmer.

As the hunter watched a silver sky-raker raced toward him gaining speed with each moment, then nosed sharply into crisp morning air. The thing whined over the pond and headed for sunrise.

The hunter rose dripping, locked his emerald gaze and—focusing his mindsight—pulled the aircraft from the sky.

With great velocity it plunged earthward, engines screaming their torment. Sunlight flashed across a row of windows. An instant before impact fifty-two minds wailed their common doom, piercing the hunter's resolve and nearly undoing him.

The ground shuddered with the crash. The aircraft plowed through a thousand feet of tall grass, shrieking, crumbling, scattering a fiery litter of metal, plastic and people.

Heat wavering from hissing fires did not deter the hunter, for the gold of his very blood burned hotter far. He must hurry—harvest what he came for lest the ugly-ones spot him. *Quickly, quickly!*

Hooked by a mangled engine cowling, the armless torso—and the head—of an ugly-one smoldered. The rest of him must be lost among the widely strewn wreckage.

The hunter loomed over his prey, bent at his scarlet abdomen and prized open the broken mouth, deftly extracted those bones intact enough for use. These he deposited into his own mouth for storage.

Farther along the path of burning debris he found his fortune.

Here was a fantastic union of bodies: two females, locked in an embrace; squashed onto them an obese male whose open back revealed layers of yellow fat, shattered bone, and the head of one of the females. Fused by flame into a single entity the threesome became, in death, more intimate than any fevered fantasy in life.

Although he did not care for the stench of this collage, the hunter carried out his duty.

Finally, heading back toward the pond, his path lay hindered by a melting seat. Still strapped in, an ugly-one burned. Little more than blackened bone, smoking hair and gristle, it screamed at the sight of Death's angel.

Shock surged through the hunter, but he soon regained focus and emptied the smoldering skull of its fare.

He continued collections for a few minutes, when the eerie wail of rescue sirens drove him to escape.

Mouth heavy with teeth taken from the newly dead, the hunter made for the hills. Ghosts of annihilation wailed from the field of wreckage.

With each stride of his insect legs the hunter's mouth rattled its catch, as if hail battered the inner surface of his skull. It tasted strange, that music.

MOAZIRITH lay unconscious. Jerfastilhak parted his lover's mandibles, and dropped the tiny bones into her mouth.

She cooed softly, acknowledged his presence. All at once she convulsed. **Swallow them!** Jerfastilhak demanded.

No good; she was choking.

With a pincher, Jerfastilhak probed into her, unseated the mass and consumed it.

Moazirith gave a feeble wheeze.

Caustic juices welled into her lover's mouth to liquefy its morsels. Immediately he felt the pulsing fullness in his thorax. Punching through his carapace he extracted the white glob—spattered the cave with a rain of burning gold, a shower that would end any other creature. Smoke swirled like morning mist.

Left with no alternative, Jerfastilhak force-fed his lover, shrilling all the while, **Please, please, please!**

A clacking, as of submerged seashells, sounded inside Moazirith.

She rose, extending eight green-spiked limbs, carapace flushed with the iridescent gold of health.

My Moazirith. Jerfastilhak embraced her. Their golden tongues twined, untwined, when Moazirith gently released from her lover's heat.

I doubted your return, she shrilled, **but you've shown me the folly of such thoughts.**

Jerfastilhak surged with guilt over his recent musings . . . his abominable self-pity.

His gaze met hers, and he saw there a violent beauty.

The hunter's heart boomed. Around Moazirith's head formed a brilliant nimbus, nearly unbearable to behold.

She levitated until taller than her lover.

At that moment Jerfastilhak would gladly have given himself to Death, so searing, so erotic, was this vision! In the face of beauty, dread is annulled.

It is fortunate, shrilled Moazirith, **that you have triumphed and returned. I would not relish the task of raising our offspring alone.**

Dizziness invaded Jerfastilhak. All at once it did not matter that he and Moazirith were alone in the ugly-ones' cheerless world. Were they not, by virtue of their very existence, *miracles* in such a place? One offspring—glorious!—pulsed within Moazirith's womb; would not others follow, fill the emptiness of their days?

The *ages* we have seen, Jerfastilhak shrilled, **and shared . . .**

Something must be done to honor those whose lives had been ended so that Moazirith could keep hers.

Jerfastilhak took in a large quota of bones. After a few moments he

punched into himself, showered hot gold everywhere.
Already his carapace began resealing. His lover dripped nuggets.
White mass in pincher, he began.

THE ugly-ones had not died in vain.
For the artistry of their Death angel sculpted a replica of the sky-raker in which they had ended.
Prideful, Jerfastilhak shrilled, **A plaything for our young!**

AUTHOR'S STORY NOTE

"Out Hunting for Teeth" is proof that I wrote Bizarro before it was cool—way before. In 1986 I'd been reading a lot of Yukio Mishima, and also a lot of Clive Barker, whose *Books of Blood* I reviewed for the late David B. Silva's World Fantasy Award-winning *The Horror Show* magazine. I also was fortunate enough to be one of the first American writers to interview Clive. All of this highly charged, often lurid and shocking, stuff reached a flash-point in my 27-year-old head. I became fascinated (oh all right—obsessed) with the more horrifying end of Francisco Goya's paintings, and had a nightmare after one long exploration of a fat volume of these. Over the years, and many revisions, "Teeth" had been purchased for two horror anthologies, both of which died on the vine. Its acceptance by Randy Chandler and Cheryl Mullenax for this superb Comet Press anthology proves, I guess, that old saw: "Third time's the charm."

KOZMIC BLUES

ALESSANDRO MANZETTI

From *The Monster, The Bad And The Ugly*
Editor: Jodi Renée Lester
Publisher: Kipple Officina Libraria

GIVE ME SOMETHING STRONG."
The barman of The Croix Inversée prepares the transparent polyplastic cylinder, carefully brushing its rim with his special slush of Amphetamine S, and then pours the synthetic tequila all the way to the brim. As a final touch, he throws in a frozen slice of Nova Scotia lemon, full of parasites, letting it fall into the cylinder where it floats, then sinks like a submerged mine in the waters of old Normandy. This mix of things is called "yellow hail"; the microscopic eggs of the parasites clinging to the lemon pulp contain toxins that, in small doses, can fuck up your brain for a week.

The sweet little animals with their darting tails have transformed the lemons into delicious psychotropic fruits, very fashionable in South Paris 5, the apocalyptic district of the city, inhabited by assholes, psychos, and organ collectors, bitches with their nails varnished with toxic blue paint, small cobras with tits, organized groups of cannibals, rapists with sharp, motorized prostheses, philanthropists with live biomechanical statues on their porches, pushers of Cloud 6 and 7 with first-row tickets to Limbo, Hell, and Nirvana. But the biggest sons of bitches are the mutant rats that rule over the Seine, beasts weighing seventy kilos that hunt at night, always hungry for human prey.

South Paris 5 is one of the ghettos of high apocalyptic impact, the New France, the new world; defeated and forced to its knees, it has been swallowed by Chaos. Ghettos are everywhere, reproducing quickly, fucking like mad, devouring the still-healthy organs of the city like a toothed cancer.

FLEUR drinks her usual drink, exchanging a look of complicity with Fakhr, the Egyptian barman who always knows how to serve, be it synthetic tequila or something else. After all these years, it seems like he can read her mind, as if he kept a special hygrometer under the counter that can measure the humidity of her pussy.

A vintage, primitive music pours out of the blue walls of the Croix Inversée, the broken notes of *Kozmic Blues* by Janis Joplin, who sounds as if she's got a rattlesnake in her throat, a two-hundred-year-old song which stirs the amniotic liquid of the ornamental aquariums in which the embryos of alien-looking calves slowly fry in their state of oblivion. Back in the good old days, aquariums were filled with lobsters, but uncontaminated animal proteins are now rarer than diamonds, rarer than splinters of dilithium.

Fakhr gives Fleur a rag, winking. The hands of the woman are stained with blood; she's just finished working her last customer. Best get clean, despite the low lights and the faint consciences of the customers at the bar, blind pilots of the Parisian night. Fleur quickly scrubs her hands and wrists, like a surgeon in the antechamber of an operating room, and then she licks her fingers and smiles at her favorite Egyptian, reflecting the white of his teeth in the heavy silver medallion hanging on her breast. The medallion is engraved with the Virgin Mary of Zeitun breastfeeding a calf. Syncretism, chaos, superstitions, and broken hopes.

"GIVE me something strong."

The man is hanging by his arms from the ceiling of Fleur's hideout, an apartment on Rue Bodard, wedged in on the sixth floor of a square building with rotten ribs and crumbling balconies, which keeps leaning to the right, a centimeter more each month, slowly sinking in the dark sperm of mud. Christ, South Paris 5 will turn into a fucking swamp in less than ten years. Just like everything else, maybe. Soon, good ole Earth will stop being a planet inhabited by humans, but a vast sewer that will shoot out crocodiles and corpses everywhere like nuclear missiles.

And to think that until that moment, people had imagined the Apocalypse as a giant explosion or implosion, something immediate and spectacular like the Big Bang or a Big Crack, possibly a new Universal Deluge, which, instead of pouring from above, was going to come up from the ground, flooding everything with the shit of trillions of corpses, gushing out, still warm, in gigantic geysers. There were some who believed in the collision of a massive meteorite, the kind that had once wiped out entire species of dinosaurs. They certainly weren't expecting to observe the falling stars of the new millennium: a swarm of forgotten, rotten satellites that crashed to Earth on a daily basis.

In any case, no prophet had imagined this slow, unavoidable and heretical decadence of flesh and conscience, with the intermittent fall of scorching rains of sulphuric acid, which at least cleaned up some of the mess.

"GIVE me something stronger."

The man is fanatically ecstatic for the pain caused by leather belts tightening on his skin, his balls, neck, and arms. Fleur knows how to make her customers enjoy the performance, no matter how depraved the sons of bitches are.

Stronger, you say? The woman lowers herself from the ceiling, sadistically equipped like those of the ancient Grand Guignol theatre, a steel chain with a strong hook from a slaughterhouse trailing her like a shiny tail.

"Hey, what the fuck are you doing?"

The creator of his own dismemberment blinks, he's likely still high, and the ghostly dogs of the Cloud 6 are biting at his calves, and biting hard, accelerating his hallucinations.

"You said stronger, did you not?" Fleur whispers, bending to the floor, freeing the pile of steel, the coils that eagerly await the instant they will tighten on Ambroise's flesh; he's a city council member with Renaissance-like sideburns that reach down to his jaws, an earthworm with obstructed balls who's just spent a thousand credits for two hours of treatment with one of the most creative and hungry mistresses of South Paris 5. The earthworm is sweating like a pig and keeps staring at the hook.

After putting on latex gloves, Fleur begins to circle her customer, whispering a sequence of words, a horrid litany that would make anyone shiver.

Suspension. Gun with a captive bullet. Stunning. Bleeding. Decapitation. Depilation. Skinning. Evisceration. Sectioning.

"Christ, this is not funny! Undo everything; you have your money, bitch."

But Fleur can't hear the prayers of her daily earthworm; the room is flooded by the music of *Kozmic Blues*, by the voice of Janis Joplin's snake. They scream together, the earthworm and Joplin. Each time the music stops the man swears. Bloody blues. Fleur starts dancing around that totem of fresh flesh. Her wide purple skirt, stained with prints of big moths, opens like a fan, showing her long legs and releasing that sweet almond smell that comes from her panties, like Zyklon B for the greedy tongues of the many earthworms and legless souls.

Ambroise opens his jaws until they creak, he can't even scream anymore, unable to emit the slightest fucking sound. The hook sinks in at just the right angle, tearing open his back, splintering his spine, making its way through his flesh for a good, solid grip. Fleur stretches the steel chain using an electric pulley and raises the man's body higher; he's now swinging left and right, waving like a pirate flag, a living Jolly Roger against a blood-red background, a stylized slice of large intestine sticking out in the center.

"Would you like another?" Fakhr mutters. Like the rest of the population, he too is super high and adrift at the Croix Inversée. Nomadic souls
that migrate from one table to another, dragging their feet from one hole
to the next, sinking their ass cheeks or faces into the flesh cushions for
rent in the back rooms, equipped with the latest generation of electric
pumps and a rich collection of coin-operated sex dolls for those who are
too shy or can no longer get a boner. The auto-fucking armchairs are,
of course, also available for the ladies who prefer the autopilot mode
to cylinders of flesh that don't always guarantee good performances.
Rhythm is what is needed, damn it!

"No, I'm okay for now. And you should slow down with that stuff,
too, your hands are shaking and you look like shit. You're drooling, for
Christ's sake!" Fleur replies, bitter. She's the alpha female of this strange
couple, and she never misses an opportunity to remind poor Fakhr. She
would have told her Egyptian partner to go fuck himself a long time ago
had it not been for his long cock and ability to procure excellent flesh
targets for her. The counter of the Croix Inversée is a perfect observation
deck for hunting. Naked bodies, gray and pink, solid or faded, knotted
in the cubes of Plexiglas rooms, forming confused, random orgies, small
paradises of floating cellulite, anchored to the ground by the viscous glue
of bodily fluids, and by the telluric dance of tits and asses of all sizes.
From his privileged position, Fakhr is able to examine, albeit superficially,
the quality of all that fucking flesh, discover their stories, and only then
carefully choose.

"Aside from you getting off, have you thought about us? See any interesting specimens tonight?"

Fleur is like that, beautiful but a real pain in the ass, demanding and
jealous. Satisfying that flesh-eating Amazon was no easy task. With her
cover as a bar whore, she had an easy time amid her colleagues ravished
by super-drugs, hanging from the counter with their skinny bug-like arms
and shadows of Purgatory in their watery eyes. Between their legs they
had the rugged tubes of desperation and the twisted, oxidized conduits of
their waning years. Fleur was the only one among the sluts who worked
at the Croix Inversée with the ability to choose her customers with care.

"Sure, honey, I never miss one, you know that. Have a look at table
seven—do you see that big boy? He's a rude jerk who just arrived yesterday
from Marseilles. He looks really healthy and in good shape, compared
to all this filth. He said that he's been taking Cloud 6 for only a few days,
so there's no time to lose—his flesh will turn bitter in about a week. He's

already been cooked to perfection—I served him three 'special' cocktails. Right now he'd fuck just about anything, even a three-headed sheep, the kind bred in the Mesoamerican Republic. People say that . . ."

"You think you're so funny? Go fuck yourself. Tell those jokes to your bitches, to the druggies that you like to rub against. By the way, keep your hands off that bitch Mirabelle if you don't want to lose your balls . . . All right, now I'm going to see the jerk. Give me half an hour and I'll bring him home and turn him into a good meal. Look at those beautiful buttocks, it almost looks like a girl's ass. I hope he's not a fag. See you later, at home."

"Can't wait, honey. I bought two bottles of Montrachet for dinner. They come from the thermo-ground harvest . . . this is the real deal, eh, they cost me more than your fake tits."

"I already told you to go fuck yourself. You must be deaf rather than stoned."

Kozmic Blues. Again.

Ambroise pissed on himself. Fleur stuck a sponge in his mouth to silence him. She draws near the hanging meat, listens to the cracking of his shoulder blades. With a gentle push she makes him spin, increasing the torque so the steel hook penetrates deeper between the scapulae, as she walks in the opposite direction around the carousel, a blues carousel of stifled groans that fade and come back, the walls spinning fast, flying flesh. The living fountain begins to work as it should, throwing splashes of red in all directions, drawing arcs of blood in the air which break before landing on the floor in squiggles and abstractions.

Through her nostrils, Fleur inhales the smell of fear from the man, holding it for as long as she can in her lungs. It mostly smells like shit, of course, but also of boiling broth and mint, wet dirt and peeled apricots, a smoothie of adrenaline and crushed pine nuts. Fleur is discovering that the smell of those hanging from a hook always differs; it's the aroma of their memories and their fear.

Ambroise is still conscious, but he won't be for long. The stunning awaits him, the same procedure used for horses, cows, and pigs when their ignorant journey on this planet comes to an end. While the oscillations slow to a stop, with the last rattling of the steel chain, Fleur leaves to load the captive-bolt pistol that will kill the man's brain before his body is turned into food. A gradual transformation, Ambroise will travel very soon, shattered, through the digestive tunnels of Fleur and her companion.

Fleur takes the ladder, approaches Ambroise's suspended body, and climbs to the height of his head. She grabs him by the hair, turns him to face her, then kisses him on the forehead.

She puts the gun to his forehead. *Remain still, damn it, be a good boy* . . . the retracted bolt will finish the job quickly and cleanly, bursting through the skull and erasing his brain: the blackout of bipolarized neurons. Total unconsciousness arrives at a speed of 73 meters per second, you don't even see it coming. Nirvana arrives in all its glory, with its golden horizon and its hills looking like tits made of chalk, after a few seconds of muscle contractions. She just needs to take good aim, calculate the right angle to hit the brain cortex. *Remain still, damn it, be a good boy* . . . Fleur pulls the trigger, a deafening, simple noise. Ambroise's shoes fly off with the last vital spasm of his body; it looked like someone stuck a high-voltage cable up his ass. *Remain still, damn it, you're dead* . . .

There is no time to lose, the meat might go bad or toughen up. Fleur pushes a metal table under Ambroise's deflated body, still dangling. She bends his legs a little in order to place the body on the table, then she finally pulls the chain from the ceiling, and the ninety-two kilos of human flesh come raining down. The body remains upright for an instant, somehow managing to keep its balance, a priest electrocuted by his own god, then at last falls face down with a crash.

Fleur hears an ambulance siren screaming louder and louder, a high-pitched noise that manages to slip through the cracks of the windowless walls of her apartment's slaughter room.

The voracious Amazon smiles, knows that there is at least a fifty percent possibility, in this sewer of South Paris 5, that the emergency room of the hospital to which the ambulance is going is no better equipped than her slaughter room. Doctors will already be sharpening their makeshift tools . . . white, blue, and red codes for meat that is inedible or at risk of contamination by prions; code yellow for those who will become food for the sake of the overcrowded communities and the delicate tastes of extravagant rich people who can afford human delicacies and dilithium cutlery. It's always best to remain standing in South Paris 5, at the cost of holding your guts in with your hands to prevent them from spilling out.

Fleur holds the scalpel tight, slicing Ambroise's body from the sternum down to the pubes, opening him, as if she was pulling down an imaginary zipper. This is the moment she likes best. She takes off her latex gloves and sticks her bare hands into that purple and red crevasse, wanting to feel the still-warm organs, first pulsing between her fingers, and then the throbbing stops. She thinks she can touch the soul of her victim, before the body cools. She imagines being able to grab the soul by its slimy tail, if only for a fleeting moment, before letting it evaporate and start its new journey.

If not, the bio-freezer in the basement would contain many extinguished souls, trapped in stews, steaks, and human thighs, lunches and dinners for the next few weeks.

"CAN you buy me a strong drink?"

Fleur, after sashaying through the room, sparking a boner pandemic in the bar, sits at table seven in the Croix Inversée, where the jerk from Marseilles is sitting, dishevelled. The man is drinking the third green ball blocker that Fakhr has prepared for him, all the while enjoying the company of two other whores, the Indian twins Padma and Karuka. Two sluts worth only a few credits, two monkeys who always work in pairs, who make ends meet only thanks to the magical third breast of Padma. A wonder of nature, the cleavage that bitch exposes, bordered with sparkling purple psychedelic stones that reach down to her navel. She has a small gecko with blue spots tattooed on her third, central tit, just above the nipple. The claws of the reptile are anchored to her flesh, like the other thousands of invisible fingerprints of loyal customers who breastfeed from that alien dune.

"You don't look like the kind of guy who's easily pleased." Fleur shakes the cloud of her red hair to free the man from Padma's third tit. She succeeds, like always.

"Wow, and where do you come from?" The man from Marseilles jumps, taking the bait. Fleur is not one who goes unnoticed, even amidst the fever of naked bodies that go up and down like a neurotic tide: an apocalyptic version, vulgar and stoned, of *The Turkish Bath* by Ingres, with tons of extra flesh.

"Well, you know, from a secret trapdoor under your feet . . . this is the hour when the bar pulls out its best stuff."

The two Indian monkeys withdraw immediately, getting up from the table, going off to rub themselves against other drunken customers; all it took was a glare from Fakhr, standing behind his crescent moon-shaped counter a few meters away. *Fuck.*

Fleur comes closer to the Marseillaise, who is wiping his wide forehead with a handkerchief. She charms him with the tissue paper pallor of her face, which allows all the parallels and meridians to concentrate around her big black eyes. A close-up onto an oasis of greenery and springs in a desert of fucking nothing: This is always the impression that Fleur releases in the thoughts and testicles of the customers. The scarabs of pleasure with their sclerotic wings, eager to fly again one day, begin to run with their hot tiny legs along the man's back. He is ready to jump into the void, into any hole, as long as Fleur is there waiting for him.

"Don't call me Marseillaise—name's Serge. And yours, beautiful?"

"My name? A hundred credits to learn it. Just think how much the rest is going to cost you . . . Marseillaise."

The bait is deep in the man's throat now, and he looks at Fleur with his tongue hanging out. He is ready to spend all his wages for that goddess, the four thousand credits that have just been uploaded to his account to buy name, thighs, breasts, pussy, and ass: In short, everything that is hers.

Serge is the sous-chef at Le Miramar, his forte is the bouillabaisse, of course. They say that his secret consists of adding chopped celery and walnuts to the dish, which he uses together with saffron when cooking the fish in the pan, then mixes everything together and creates an unmistakable Provincial soup. Who knows how many scorpion fish, gurnard, mullet, and crabs have passed through his big, strong, and generous hands. The same hands that now begin to reach for Fleur's legs that are accidentally rubbing against his.

"Hey, stallion, keep your hands to yourself and dry your forehead, you're staining my dress . . . we'll do the math later . . ."

Fleur can't finish her sentence. She is looking toward the counter to give Fakhr an *Okay, the prey is trapped,* but then she sees Mirabelle approaching her man, whispering in his ear. He smiles lasciviously, with the sneer of someone who's tasted the first course and can't wait to have the full menu. Mirabelle bends beneath the counter to get a stack of trays; the bitch doesn't miss the opportunity to nibble at Fakhr's cock, which is exploding inside his striped pants.

"You're going to pay for this, asshole, right here and now . . ." Fleur thinks aloud, but Serge hears her, misunderstands, and quickly answers, with a smile as big as one of his ovens: "Anything you want, baby, looks like you're running the show tonight . . ."

Fleur bites her lips. She tries to keep her cool and think about the business at hand. She nervously touches her dilithium ring, twisting it around her middle finger. Okay, first of all she needs to get rid of the Marseillaise stallion, who is about to lie down on the floor to lick her thighs. Then she'll think about Fakhr, that well-hung bastard.

"Well then, let's get out of here, Marseillaise."

Fleur drags Serge across the room, the sound of her high heels wakes an old customer from her apocalyptic torpor, a woman who's fallen asleep with her face in a puddle of tequila, her right calf has been nibbled on by someone who snuck under the table and seized the opportunity for a light blood-snack.

Fleur and Serge pass quickly in front of the counter. Fakhr sees them and smirks. Mission accomplished, he thinks. Fleur responds by staring into his eyes for a few seconds, biting her lips purple, and then she disappears with her new friend. They'll meet at home, as always, once Fakhr ends his shift at the Croix Inversée.

Hunting and a midnight supper are a heretical ritual for the two bastards. Meat for dinner, like the privileged few in the city, the cannibalistic elite who have adapted to the status quo caused by the global pandemic of edible animal protein. Predators, be they rich or poor murderers, reign. And they still eat meat. Who knows what delicacy Fleur will be preparing tonight, Fakhr thinks, licking his lips in anticipation. Meanwhile, he can devote himself to Mirabelle; his hot mistress's workshift is about to end. He has to hurry if he wants to pound her again in the kitchen tonight. He must take advantage of the fact that his tigress is not around. But where the fuck has Mirabelle gone? He doesn't see her in this mess, in this port of forgotten souls and sharks of all races with their oblique fins ready to raid and to strike.

Even among sons of bitches there is competition.

FAKHR has finished his shift, the glass door of the Croix Inversée opens, sliding on its rails, showing him South Paris 5 cloaked by night. The stagnant air slams his face, condensing on his moustache and nose. It's so damn hot, no matter what time of day it is. He walks up the usual stairs of Rue St. Antoine, kicks an abandoned Vagyx extractor, a makeshift pregnancy test used by whores. The small tube bounces toward the knees of a homeless man camped out on his own personal square meter of Hell, busy tearing out his yellow hair, one by one, and cursing everyone. Fakhr turns right; the Seine reveals itself with its invisible crust of solitude and shadows of big rats on its banks, busy dragging their dinners to the shore, down to their dens, food that's still wearing pants, whose hands and fingers desperately cling to irregular protrusions of Roman brickwork in a futile attempt to free themselves, to delay the end, to steal an extra day or two in that rotten repetitive Samsara. They are those who've been fucked by the night, and they are many.

Fakhr caresses the Darden injector hooked to his belt, his little portable flamethrower. If there's one thing those beasts hate, it's fire, apart from the bitter flesh of druggies.

He passes in front of the old Church of the Holy Trinity, transformed into the most celebrated porn show in the neighborhood. A large luminescent rubber phallus covers the skeleton of the ancient slender steeple, which towers over the crumbling rose window of the Renaissance façade. Fakhr stops a moment to admire the continuous variations of color displayed by the horny, twenty-meter long synthetic totem. He waits for the summit to activate its automatic water jet, which sprays fake sperm in a large radial pattern up into the black sky.

He resumes his fast pace and within five minutes reaches the narrow and sloping sidewalks of Rue Bodard and the smashed building where he lives with Fleur. The lights of the apartment on the sixth floor are all on; his predatory partner is waiting for him. Midnight dinner.

"Hey, you did things in style tonight!" the Egyptian calls out soon after he's closed the door.

The oval table in the living room looks like it's been set for a special occasion: The mottled tablecloth sparkles red, orange, and blue under the crystal glasses, the ones from long ago, with their thin, transparent bellies already half full of white wine. Fleur must feel inspired tonight; she's opened the precious bottles of Montrachet that he had bought. In the middle of the table, the highlight of the evening: an elliptical dish in Nortex alloy, full of small bite-sized morsels of meat, covered with a layer of fried eggplant. The reflective edges are trimmed with green beans and rohu eggs.

"Eggplant? Green beans? For fuck's sake, did you buy this stuff in Nova Scotia? These things cost a fortune. What have I done to deserve all this? I know, you want my cock . . . I bet that's the minced Marseillaise under that eggplant, eh? I hope it's as tender as I imagined he would be; he had a good look about him. Have you already tried him, honey?"

Fleur walks into the living room, beaming, wearing the wedding dress she had been hiding in the closet for more than two years. Her boobs flash out of the white silk dress, an altar worthy of worship. The bodice shines of dilithium crystals sewn together in the form of vortices, microscopic satellites at the mercy of chaos, attracted by the gravity of her hips. The tight, glossy skirt frees the fabric on one side, with sharp fringes at its extremes, leaving her left leg bare all the way to the groin. No jewelry, her hands still stained with cold blood up to her wrists, a cobalt glaze. She says nothing, simply looks him in the eyes and bites her lip.

Fakhr just stands there with his mouth open; his cock is waking up between his legs: She really looks like a goddess. "Christ, if this is a proposal, there's no better way to present it!" He immediately gives Fleur his handkerchief to wipe the blood off her hands; that too is a little ritual of theirs. It would be a shame to stain that nice dress.

Fleur passes the cup of wine to her stallion, and then takes hers; an anthropophagous toast while the meat is waiting on the warming tray. Fakhr downs his Montrachet, chews the titbits, swallowing ecstatically, commenting on the dishes, all the flavors of the food prepared by Fleur, as she chews those precious human proteins with more enthusiasm than usual, continuing to remain silent. The Egyptian follows her lead. He's having fun, only thinking about the moment he's going to fuck her, without even taking off that hot wedding dress; not until his stomach is full, though.

The walls of the hall begin to spin, Fakhr thinks he's drunk too much wine: Fleur's face merges with the background, her piercing black eyes multiply, and they are everywhere, staring. His nose bleeds, he feels the warm fluid dripping down his neck, lowers his head to see it flowing onto his pants, which slowly absorb it. When he finally manages to raise his eyes, he realizes that the room has not stopped spinning; now he thinks he is seeing tiny butterflies, the color of cobalt, moving into space, toward him and away. A spiral tunnel opens under his chair, seeming to lead to strange and deep crevasses. He tries to hold on to the tablecloth but is sucked away, down into the unknown chasm. The sound of chains, a horrible creaking, the dark, and then a blinding flash of light. Fakhr covers his eyes and tries to focus on the shadow hanging in front of him, which continues to swing left and right. *What the hell did I drink that fucked my brain up like this? Where's Fleur?*

That damn shadow before his eyes finally stops, assuming sharper edges. Now he can see everything, even if he cannot move a muscle or swallow his saliva. He looks up slowly, following the rings of the chain hanging from the ceiling, seven, ten, fifteen, then he finally sees the eyeless face of Mirabelle, his favorite whore, with her tongue sticking out, her tits gray and livid; farther down, the ugly stump of her right leg, severed cleanly, from which small drops of blood fall to the floor.

Plik, plik, plik.

While Fakhr is slowly pissing his pants, Fleur's tongue licks his ear, the voice of his partner is suddenly back: "You always liked that bitch, right? Tonight, you've finally tasted her . . . inside. Her flesh is so delicious, don't you think?"

The man feels tears slipping down his face, and then something sparkles, almost blinding him. It is the steel hook that Fleur is passing before his eyes, making it spin in the air.

The notes of *Kozmic Blues* resound again in the slaughter room.

AUTHOR'S STORY NOTE

I wrote this story listening to *Kozmic Blues* by Janis Joplin; Her voice sometimes plays a role as an invisible protagonist of my stories, and once again it came in the tale, passing through a small crack in the wall between reality and fiction. I imagined a pair of cannibals who share love and lust, who prey on human flesh to continuously cross the threshold of pleasure. Their hunting ground is the Croix Inversée, a bar on the outskirts of a future, dystopian, cruel Paris. Fleur and Fakhr, the pair of lovers, they will discover new flavors, this time, and the spice of jealousy which will season a new frenzy. There are always new thresholds to be crossed, passionately, and you're in the right place.

SELECTED POEMS FROM BROTHEL

STEPHANIE M. WYTOVICH

From the Bram Stoker Award winner *Brothel*
Publisher: Raw Dog Screaming Press

BLIND OBEDIENCE

You're still and you're blindfolded
arms bound with my satin sheets
and I need you to be quiet,
but I want you to beg;
Now shhhh . . .
and listen to me close,
I'm going to have you now
and I need you to do
exactly what I say, when I say
now kiss me,
kiss me
and tell me you love me,
then get on all fours,
and let me hear you
scream.

BROTHEL

There's a brothel in my hand and it's open for business,
providing me with pleasure while I pay it with my pain; I close my eyes
and see,
see for the first time as immeasurable desires wake
inside me, screaming, panting: legs spread apart,
arms open wide, lips pursed, parted. The women are my
invitations, the men my RSVPs, and I'll accept their summons
to come, to stay, to eat and drink the fruits and juices of the sweet gardens
in front of me—pulsing, dripping, rich with
honey, sweet with wine.

My mouth is open and I'm ready to inhale,
ready to swallow, and they've promised
they'd fill me, that they'd keep me nice and full;
I slip my fingers through the front door and
I'm met with a warm hello,
as I'm taken inside—as I'm taken—and I
think I'll stay here for a while, locked inside
my brothel where the animals like to breed.

VICIOUS GIRLS

Creatures,
creatures are what they are—
violent Eves, rotten apples,
victimized damsels, Salem witches;
they bit the snake that fed them
drank his poison,
pulled out his fangs
and now they bleed,
they bleed once a month for his death,
the death of the devil who cursed their wombs
for they are vicious,
they are venomous
they are women, and they will wait,
patient and persistent,
ever-enduring
and damned
and they will sing,
sing in covens, sing in brothels,
sing for men,
sing for whores
and their words will kill
they will damn
they will puncture
for they sing with lips,
lips not of mouth but of sex
sex that weakens, that confuses,
that traps
and once they have you
have you between their legs,
they will kill you,
they will eat you,
and they will love you
the only way
that they know how

GRATIFICATION, SCARIFICATION

I took off my shirt and slid onto his lap
Get inside me
He kissed me soft, bit my lip and pulled

Make me bleed
He smiled and took out the knife,
grabbed the back of my neck, licked my throat
"beg for it"
I gasped, pleaded with my eyes, my dark fuck-me-eyes
and he cut my black bra down the front,
threw it against the wall—
the blade inched across my chest
spilled my rubies while I came hard
against his thigh.
Back arched, tits out, I laughed
Mark me, brand me, make me yours
He slid two fingers in my mouth
Made me show him how I suck
"you already know you're mine—
but I'll make sure you never forget."

MISCARRIAGE

The child twisted inside me
desperate for escape;
It broke its bones,
shed its skin,
used my blood as lubricant
to slide out between my legs;
It/he/she made its/his/her appearance,
silent, static
a premature suicide
a stillborn angel.

YOUTERUS

You
are inside me,
me/ me and you
and you tear us,
you hurt, you claw,
you rip your way out
I bleed/ bleed strong
bleed red
it hurts, but you come,
you breathe

you tear us/
tear me
in half.

HARDCORE

Beaten black and blue, the girls told me this was occasionally part of
the job,
that some Johns got off on the violence and that I'd better find a way to
deal with it
if I wanted to maintain clientele. I bought extra concealer, darker foundation to cover
the ink blots on my body, but no amount of powder or liquid skin could
disguise
the pain on my chest, my arms, my thighs. I hated this weak, rag doll
costume, despised the way they'd come when I screamed, when I flinched,
when I bled, and so the next time they hit me, I hit them back. And some
of them never got up.

AUTHOR'S STORY NOTE

Brothel is an erotic horror collection that straddles the line between pain
and pleasure, sex and death. I wanted to write an assortment of poems
that stimulated the reader, just as much as it frightened them, not just
for the sake of repulsion, but rather to show readers that the relationship
between arousal and fear is thinner than we might think. These poems
are war cries to those who have been abused, who have been broken
and beaten, or who have ever felt out of place in their own bodies and
minds. *Brothel* takes off the patriarchal blindfold and shows that women
aren't victims; it reveals that sexuality is fluid and not taboo; and most
importantly, it shows what happens when the body and spirit has been
pushed to the brink of exhaustion, and has no choice left but to fight
back to survive.

COMING OF THE DARKULA

ANDREW DARLINGTON

From *Literotica: Sci-Fi & Fantasy*

THERE'S MOVEMENT, from the floors below. So she's pacing on the raw stalks of nerves.

Strange days. Scared of what every sound portends. Been sealed up here for a month, keeping the mad world at bay. Keeping to shadows. But she steps out into the stairwell, in her white leatherette jacket, cinched at the waist, black stretch-pants and high-heel boots. She steals a glance down, sniping glimpses past the dust, the garbage and the giant bug carapace. There are figures moving in and out of shadows. Three men, no four. But yes, they are men. Can't be sure these days.

Out beyond the skyline of city blocks the mauve radiation-glow shimmers across the river. Watch the skies. Between the stars, pinpoints of light flit and dance. Since the coming of the Darkula you hide from the sky. And the empty streets below are ghost-haunted by rad-mutants, and others. Those warp-infected by alien microbes. A distant explosion climbs the sky, roiling a deluge of vivid flame.

Stand still. Let them see you. They're pointing up at you. One of them climbing the stairwell towards you. An impulse to turn and hide. Fight the terror. Wait. As he gets closer, you can see he's tall and bearded. A soft denim hat. And a high-velocity rifle slung over his arm. The others stumble up behind him, they're armed too. The man-tall creature-shell is precariously skewed, furred with mildew, its interior liquefied to green slime. The man halts on the level directly below, squints past its segmented obstruction, and looks up.

'You alone here?'

'Yes, I'm alone. Been here since it began. Hiding out.'

He visibly relaxes, but stays alert. Flattens against the wall as he lopes up the last stairs. Brushes past her. Kicks open the door and levels the rifle at no-one.

It's only then he fully eases. 'I'm John Roxton Lord. You got supplies here?'

She shakes her head. 'I'm Grace. I did have supplies. Stockpiled it ready. But I've been here a month. There's not a lot left. You're welcome to what little I've got.'

When he makes to move into her apartment, she follows him. Heavy drapes curtain across the windows. The TV is dead. He sits on the chair arm. Three more guys file in behind him. An eager younger kid, maybe nineteen, heads for the kitchen and begin ransacking the freezer. Tries the faucets. No water, of course. An older paunchy guy slouches off his cap and mops his sweaty forehead with it. She watches them warily. The fourth guy stands at the door, covering the stairwell, in case this is a trap.

'So where is everybody? Your partner. Your family.'

She pouts. 'Don't want to talk about that . . . There were four of us after it hit, after everyone else fled. That bug attacked and we managed to kill it. But one guy was wounded, got sick. They had to put him down. Eventually, my other friends, Rael and Miko, they ventured out, scavenging for supplies, and never returned. I'm guessing they were killed. Can't be sure. But there's only me. Where exactly are you making for?'

Roxton looks up at her. 'Earthfort. It's a military stronghold upriver from here. Two, three days away.'

'I heard something about that on TV, when there was TV, before it went down.' She laughs bitterly. 'Is it real?'

'We've gotta believe it's real. A bunker. A consolidation centre, to organise and strike back. Rico here . . .' he indicates the youth, 'he's a smart boy, he's wired a solar-nav which picks up signal-guides.'

'Will you take me with you?'

He glances this way and that. 'Sorry, can't do that. It's hazardous out there, we cover each other's backs. You'd slow us down. You stay here, where it's safe, until things normalise.'

'You're a liar. You think things will normalise? This is it. It's not gonna get any better. Not yet. Not for a long time. If ever. These are shit days. And I can't stay here. Like I say, food's about gone. I'd starve.'

'Sorry. You're safer here. We can't take you.'

'You must.'

The young guy—Rico, comes back. 'Truth. Nothing here, nothing.' The porky man turns, makes to leave.

'Wait, you can't go, please. You can't just leave me here like this.' She stands to block their path back out onto the landing level. The sky behind her changes colour. Ripples like some vivid aurora borealis effect. That's the way they arrive, the Darkula, from whatever alien continuum that spawned them. More incoming.

Roxton stands and unhooks his rifle. 'Look . . .'

She tenses. Bites her lip. Reaches up to the neckline of her jacket. Opens it slowly. The breasts spilling out are large, the darkly-pigmented nipples squinting slightly outwards. 'I can be useful to you.'

The porky guys is grinning a big goofy grin now, fresh sweat breaking out across his forehead. 'Whoo-Eeee. All four of us?'

She smiles in what's intended to be a beguiling way, her jacket still open. 'If that's what you want.'

'Whaddya say, Roxton?' he defers to his companion, his attention transfixed on her, eyes never leaving her nipples. A pleading impatience in his whine.

Roxton shrugs. 'It's not for me to oppose, if that's the collective decision, Randall.'

Randall grins. He heads off across the suite, shoves the bedroom door opens, turns and beckons. She hesitates for less than a moment, before submissively following him. Once inside, he looks around the confined space, there are sliding mirrored wardrobe panels, plush mauve-patterned floral duvet, a spill of old glossy style magazines.

'Randall, how do you want me?'

'You sure you're OK with this?'

'If it's what you want.'

'Then on your knees, Babe, on your knees.' He's less confident than he tries to make out. Unfastening his pants, fingers fumbling the zip as she squats down, compliantly. Shuffles closer towards her, angling a fat uncut cock in at her face. She looks up at him just once, a derisive smirk on her face. She opens her mouth, and devours his cock in one slurpy gulp. He flinches, his head shocks back as she sucks hard. Her head burrows deeper into his groin, dark hair fanning out across her shoulders, a tent to conceal what she's doing. He can scarce believe. Her tongue on him, her lips tight around him, her warm moistness pulsing along the length of him. She moves her head a little side to side, up and down only slightly, keeping him inside her mouth so she can work. The hint of teeth on his glans, an excruciating pleasure. He bites his lip and whimpers. He can't hold back. Can't control. His legs are water. His buttocks clench so hard. He groans, and shoots into her. A gurgling slobbery sound . . .

The air is electric. Rico watches from the door, leaning up against the jamb. A big grin splitting the dark features of his slightly skin-pocked face. He swaggers across, unzipping, flipping out a long thin cock. As Randall withdraws and steps back on shaky legs, Rico replaces him. His cock sliding easily between her lips and into her mouth. She sucks at him. He stands with his legs parted, like he's taking a long piss. 'She's lush, ain't she, Randall? Huh—whaddya think?'

Randall slumps back, makes a lazy waving gesture, as though drained. Rico runs his hand through her hair as she tunnels her head into his groin, then pulls her back off him and up. 'Pants off, girl, on the bed.'

She wipes her mouth luridly with the back of her hand. Slips her jacket off and carefully drapes it across the chair. Leans up against the bed to reach down and pull off the left boot, then the right. Hitches her thumbs under the waistband of her black stretch-pants, and skims them down and off in a single fluid motion. Her skin is pale. A neat patch of pubic hair is jet black, the upper opening of her pussy clearly visible as she lounges back across the mauve floral duvet. Rico struggles his own tight jeans off, then launches in between her splayed legs, brandishing his saliva-glistening cock like a weapon. He nuzzles it around the soft wetness, locates her cunt, and eases his cockhead in. She arches her back, and he drives in up to the balls. She gasps audibly, and his buttocks start pumping above her.

The third guy, L'Estrada, has left his post guarding the outer level, props his machine-pistol up against the wall, and now stands watching. He's fiddling with his belt buckle.

'Yeah-yea,' yells Rico as he slams into her. 'You ready, Grace? You ready for it. Yeah-yea, here it comes . . . !' He buries in deep. They can see his bare arse clenching. He gives out one long low exhalation. L'Estrada shuffles in behind him, as Rico pulls out of her, he slides his cock in. Her legs spread as wide as they'll go, she grunts as he enters her. She lies on her back, breathing heavily with every thrust, biting her lip in defiant concentration. L'Estrada lasts a little longer. He slows to a halt, rests inside her, then speeds up again. They can catch the rich fug of her arousal on the air. Hear the squelch of juices, the slap of flesh on flesh. She makes a little mewling noise as he cums inside her.

He withdraws and stuffs his softening cock back into his pants. The three men hang together, catching their breath. As Roxton enters they intercept his stern gaze, and file back out into the lounge, leaving the two together. He's been raiding the bathroom cabinet. He carries a dispenser of perfumed oil. He indicates to her, a switching gesture with his hand. She catches his meaning, and turns over, into a crouch, lifting the rounded curves of her ass towards him. He moves close, loosening his pants with one hand, pouring oil into the valley between her buttocks with the other. His fingers follow its dribbling path down, seeking out the puckered anal aperture, massaging the oil around in wide circles, then smaller circles, smoothing it into the tight opening, his lubricated finger dipping in. He spills more oil, works it in, his finger dipping further in, opening and easing.

His cock is out, in his hand. He applies oil down its length, masturbates up and down until it glistens. Then he applies the oily glans to the primed butt-hole. She braces. He applies slight pressure. There's tight resistance. He forces a little more. She relaxes her muscles as best she can, to receive him, then gasps as the cockhead opens her. Then he's inside, beyond the sphincter ring, sliding deeper. His hands hold her hips, nudging in, slipping up into her. He fucks in and out, dribbling oil. His pace increases. She's tight and deep, convulsing warm around him, the flesh of her buttocks rippling as he slams in at the point of maximum penetration. He doesn't last long, until she feels the kick inside, the sudden warm deluge. He doesn't utter a sound, but stays inside her for a long moment, before slowly pulling out.

Roxton glances down at his solar watch. 'It's late now. We stay here tonight, start out in the morning, OK?' She settles back on her heels, naked, reaching up to tease her hair back into shape. Her smile is aloof, satisfied. She's taken all four of them. They're tired and beat. She's triumphed. She's in control. She lies back on the bed. Roxton returns to the lounge and stretches out on the couch. Randall takes the chair, pulls his peaked cap low over his face. Rico and L'Estrada alternate lookout duties, pacing from window to window, checking the door and the landing beyond. The night is uneventful.

Roxton leads the way down at first light, Rico and L'Estrada a step behind him, covering him. Grace and Randall bring up the rear. Past the bug carapace. The street beyond is empty, a low breeze blowing garbage where grass and weed is already bursting up through asphalt. A flurry of birds rise and swoop. Rico consults his solar-nav, and indicates a direction. They set off up the slight incline. There are two autowrecked vehicles collided at an intersection, the crumpled bodywork already rusting. The group feel exposed as they cross beneath the hostile open sky, until swallowed by sheltering shadows on the far side.

There are grotesque lumbering shapes down a sudden alleyway. Six of them, hideously deformed, they switch dulled diseased attentions around and lurch forward towards Roxton's group. Infected by alien spores that settle and germinate inside their bodies, there's no cure and no immunity. L'Estrada lines his machine-pistol and takes the first one, its head exploding like overripe fruit. Rico guns the second down. They set up a wall of lethal fire. They slither forward with no awareness or fear, crumpling down into twitching heaps of spasming limbs.

Roxton's group move on. A brilliant sphere of light, a captive sun spins down between high city-blocks. They shelter inside a looted store as it hovers just above the highway surface, too bright to look at directly. It moves slowly along the central reservation, as though questing. It's brilliant luminosity casting flickering shadows. Soundlessly it hovers away into the distance, until it's safe to emerge. Darkula . . . ? A new species. A parasite or slave species? Who knows?

Roxton runs his eyes up and down Grace's figure. Her white leatherette jacket zipped low so her cleavage is full. 'Those boots,' he says, 'they're not safe for travel. You can't run in heels like that. You gotta change them.' She pouts.

Randall glances around the smashed glass storefronts lining the street. 'Department store across the way. We could try in there.' She nods, and he leads the way inside. The others wait outside as he forces the door, an accumulation of grit and weed slowing him. Inside, the light is low, but shafts of illumination pick out displays of women's fashion garments and designer gowns. She walks down the aisles, picking clothes at random, holding them against herself, checking for length. The elevator is dead, naturally. On the next floor there are shoes and heavy-duty hiking boots. She sits down on a low stool and begins trying them on for size.

Randall coughs. She looks up. He's unfastened his pants and lowered them, his flabby thighs and stubby cock aimed at her. She smiles and looks up at him, 'Mr Randall, really. You want your cock sucked again?'

'Well, as I recall, it was part of the agreement.'

'No worries, come over here.' He shuffles across to her, she reaches up and takes his cock in her hand, flexing it up and down as it stiffens. She dips her head in and begins mouthing his fat balls, sucking each one into her mouth in turn. Then reaches up to kiss the rubbery cock-tip, and lick it up and down. He groans as her lips close around him and she starts sucking. He holds steady as she works him, his fists clenching and unclenching. His stomach grows and recedes, grows and recedes.

'Jeez, you're good.' His hands come down to seek a way through her deluge of hair, and grip the sides of her head, so he can fuck her mouth. She moves to meet him, timing herself, taking him deep, sucking and tonguing. He moans and curses beneath his breath as the sensations radiate through him from that exquisite point of contact. He flinches, like he's been kicked in the guts, and jets white fluid into her throat. She gurgles a little, and settles into sucking him some more.

He draws back, wiping his cock with a handkerchief. 'I can't believe you swallow like that.'

She looks up at him, tying the laces of hiking-boots. 'What do you expect me to do, gargle with it?'

He laughs nervously. 'No, it's just that I have no redeeming social values . . . and before, y'know, no chick'd ever do that for me.'

She shrugs. 'It's different now. Everything's changed, morality is different. Survival is all that matters. We do what we have to do.' It's not the answer he wanted. 'Tell me, what is it about Roxton, what's his story?'

'He's English. We went to public school.'

'So he fucks me in the ass because he likes to imagine I'm a boy?'

Randall seems agitated. 'You happy with those boots, yes? Time we wuz going.'

Outside Rico has forced his way into a camper van parked on an adjacent lot. Against the odds, the battery is still charged. He's jump-started the engine and it purrs into unsteady life. The fuel indicator is at half. They whoop and dance in a circle, like a crazy barn-dance. Roxton stands apart watching them with an amused smirk. The five of them pile in, and Rico drives it unsteadily across the yard, through a smashed wire-mesh gate, and out onto the roadway, picking up speed. Roxton sits in the passenger seat, scanning the sky and the buildings flashing past outside, as the others relax.

They make good time, following blips on Rico's nav. To emerge on the wharf, looking out across the river. 'We need to get cross-river at some point. But we have to travel inland a way, so we take the first bridge we get to.'

In the sullen tropical warmth, there are gaudy birds re-colonising the waters, nesting in abandoned warehouses since the city depopulated. There are supposed to be wolves too, and deer in the park, spilling out through walkways and precincts into empty shopping malls. Europe is gone. Transfigured into a methane rainforest of tubular purple growths, altering the global climate. The caliphate chain-nuked a thirty-mile-wide corridor to halt its spread, then began plague-dying due to rad-polluted rivers. Until the last com-link went down. Now, no-one knows. The group turn and follow the road-grid parallel to the river, moving inland. They stop at a couple of gas stations, without results. The third one still has a tank of gas from which they top up the camper van, and move on. There are bridge-towers ahead which they zero towards.

Then Rico slams the brakes on, and they shudder to a halt. Across the access-ramp approach to the suspension bridge there's a barricade made up of cars, metal panels and junk stacked across the road. Two armed men atop it, one with a heavy-duty machine pistol, the other shouldering some kind of rocket-launcher.

'What now?' says Rico, throwing his hands up.

'We need to get across. Could take us miles off our course if we have to seek an alternate crossing-point. Even if we reverse now they could blow us off the road if they so choose.' Roxton jerks the door open and steps down onto the road surface. His hands raised. They watch as he strides determinedly towards the barricade. And stops.

Two men survey them from the barricade. Another emerges through a crude concealed gate in the ramshackle structure, two more armed men a pace behind him. They move to within metres of Roxton, and stop. 'This is our turf,' yells the leader. 'I'm Commander Harriman, you come through here, you pay my toll.'

Roxton makes an expansive gesture. 'We got nothing you need. Some tubs of clean water. Cans of food. You're welcome to that. We just want to cross the bridge, that's all.'

'Where are you making for?'

'Earthfort. We want to join the fight-back from there.'

Harriman laughs and scuffs in the dirt. 'Yet, you gotta cross here to get there. But let me put you in the picture. We've created a safe enclave here. We keep it clear of Darkula, spooks, Goon Squad looters and Zees. You cross my bridge, you need our permission.'

'Do we have your permission? I'm asking you politely.'

He knuckles his chin thoughtfully, deliberately savouring his power, stringing the negotiation out. 'We'll take your water and your cans. We'll keep the camper van too. I like the camper van. You go on to Earthfort, you can walk.' His two companions cackle dutifully.

Roxton extends his arms, palms down in a conciliatory gesture. 'You got it. Now let us through.'

'One more thing. You have a woman. As a token of mutual goodwill, we use your woman, you use ours.' Harriman makes one sharp wave over his shoulder. A fourth man emerges through the crude gate, he leads a naked woman by a leather chord around her neck. The woman walks submissively with her hands clasped behind her back, her head slightly bowed, long blonde hair cascading around her face. Across her large rounded breasts the lettering 'S.L.U.T.' has been inked.

'Wait,' says Roxton. He retreats, careful not to make a sudden movement that could be misinterpreted. The camper van door gapes open and he clambers inside to face Grace. 'They're living out some weird Mad Max fantasy. I can't ask you to do this.'

'Seems to me we have no choice.' She meets his eyes unflinchingly. 'Let's do this.' She pulls her jacket off as they watch, pulls her boots off and shimmies out of her slacks. She straightens up nude. 'C'mon, guys, make it look good. Make me look like she does.'

Roxton slips his belt in a loose noose around her neck, she holds her hair aside to facilitate it. With a shaking hand Randall rummages around and produces a felt-tip pen, to write 'SLUT' across her breasts.

He stands back to admire his handiwork.

They file out of the van, leaving the weapons inside, standing together. Roxton a pace ahead, leading Grace by the leash. The sun is low in the sky. There's no sound.

In the space between, they've unrolled a length of carpet across the asphalt. Four of them waiting, with the naked blonde girl. Her head still bowed. Harriman indicates to her, and she slumps down onto her knees, falling forward so that she's crouched passively on all fours.

Roxton glances nervously as Grace. Her jaw is set. Her eyes betray no waver of indecision. When she reaches the carpet edge, her bare toes encountering its softness, without inducement she lowers down onto all fours, side by side with the blonde girl. The two glancing at each other curiously. The men stand around in an awkward silence. Harriman coughs.

It's Randall who makes the first move. Unbuckles his pants, moving forward as they fall away, crouching down towards the blonde's head, she comes up to meet him, her mouth gaping. She takes his cock without hesitation. Then all hell breaks loose. Harriman laughs, moves in behind Grace, and slides a fat cock up between her parted legs, her hips raised to receive him. Another moves in at her face, and she sucks him simultaneously. Their bodies moving together, her free-hanging breasts shivering with each thrust. The other men circle closer, taking their orifices of choice. When Randall pulls out of her mouth and moves around to her rear, Rico takes his place in the girl's mouth. The moist sounds of sex seem amplified, flesh slithering on flesh, gurgles and choking noises, grunts and moans.

The men work in teams, two simultaneously, switching mouth to cunt then cunt to mouth. The anonymous bodies blur, one after the other. Grace hears a choking gasp, glances across at the blonde girl. Their eyes meet. The other grimaces in a weird pained pleasure. Looking back over her shoulder she sees Roxton, and knows exactly what he's doing to her, and why her expression is so conflicted. Then her mouth is required by the next man. Until at last there are no more. Both girls stay crouched, unsure, awaiting instructions.

Harriman approaches Roxton, hand outstretched. 'Great way to bond, eh?' Roxton shakes the proffered hand warily. He indicates irritably at the girls, and they struggle uncertainly to their feet, brushing dirt from their knees.

'We get to cross the bridge now?'

'Sure, we're all friends here, ain't we?' But Harriman strides towards the camper van, climbs up into the driver's seat, and fires the engine.

Roxton reaches out to help Grace, and they pace across to climb into the back. She retrieves her white leatherette jacket and pulls it around her shoulders, using a wet-wipe to clean her face, then down between her legs.

Harriman steers the vehicle carefully forward, through the gate in the barricade. The ragged trail of men file in behind them, the blonde girl too. Grace watches keenly. There are more armed men inside the protective barrier. Too many of them. The ramp of the bridge rises beyond, leading to the river's far shore. She sees it all, frozen in strange clarity. Her mind still buzzing, surging with the multiple-fuck sensations, as though her senses are heightened. The light is unnatural. Casting tall mauve shadows. As though she's hallucinating unreal aftershocks.

No. There are two suns in the sky. The second, mauve sun, descending through cloud layers, in between the tower-blocks. So bright it's dazzling, too painful to look at directly. She shields her eyes. There's panic outside, some are scattering, others assume defensive positions, blasting sporadic bursts of fire at the incoming globe. It's gliding in low. Its light prickling exposed areas of skin with radiation-burn.

Harriman slams on the brakes, judders the van to a halt. As he starts to his feet to dismount, Grace smashes him in the face with a tyre lever. He staggers back, she hits him again so he crumples down into the well. She scrambles over the bucket seat, releases the door catch so it swings open, and kicks him hard. He falls back against the doorframe, loses purchase, and head-over-heels out towards the tarmac. She guns the engine.

The alien sun as spinning like a blazing comet, passing low now. Roxton is at the door as the van accelerates. 'Rico, Randall . . . here!' She steers in a wide arc. L'Estrada leaps aboard. Rico too. Randall pulls the blonde girl by the leash, hauls her into the van.

'You wanna get out of this? You want to come with us?' yells Roxton.

'What would I want to do that for?' spits the naked woman.

'The way they treat you. You're better with us.'

'Lemme go. I don't need this. They look after me, protect me.'

'You're choice,' says Grace over her shoulder, as she decelerates long enough for the girl to jump clear, then hits higher gear and spins the wheel towards the ramp, yawing and canting. There's an explosion ripping the facia off an overhanging building complex, igniting in eruptions of flame sparked by the spinning sun-sphere. She hits the ramp towards the bridge, thrumming across the span, the shadows of support-beams spoking across them. The startle of gunfire fades in their wake. There's no pursuit. The sun already re-climbing the sky.

'Right,' says Rico, consulting his sat, 'take us right.' Off the far-side ramp and onto a new endlessly deserted highway. She throttles back to cruising speed, avoiding the rusting corpses of wrecked autos.

'You did fine, Grace,' concedes Roxton evenly.

'What the hell was that flying fire-cracker anyway?' says Rico.

'Sentient, robotic, programmed AI . . . who knows? When the Darkula open their portals, other stuff gets through too, bugs, microbes, seeds. Could be their equivalent of rodent infestation. Just be glad it arrived when it did.'

'If it was coincidence,' points out Randall. 'It's almost like it meant to be there, helping us.' He shrugs, suddenly flustered when they turn to him. 'Hey, don't bug me, I'm just saying . . .'

Eventually they pull off the main strip into a mall to stay overnight. The sky rippled by tides of strange light. Rico and L'Estrada investigate the upper mall levels, gunning down a group of rad-muties sheltering in a storefront, disturbing the stench of putrefying flesh. There's a supermarket below. Forcing through concertina door-shutters into the rear stockroom, most of it is ransacked, but there are crates of untouched cans and even bottles. In an enclosed central court they ignite a huge roaring fire, sparks dancing into the vault above, and break out the food, heating it up on a makeshift grill overhanging the blaze. The bottles of surprisingly good lager help. The three—Rico, Randall and L'Estrada stand around her now with a new easy familiarity, and she sucks each of them in turn. Then they fuck.

Eventually she stands, naked, brushes herself down, teases her hair back, and seeks out Roxton. He's sitting in an alcove dismantling and reassembling his machine-pistol. He looks up as she approaches. 'This time,' she smiles, 'it's on my terms. This time, you get to know just how good a woman feels.' She crouches down to unfasten his pants.

EARTHFORT, the following day. Concrete bunker above surrounded by gun-tower emplacements. A ramp opens to admit them. Swallowing them underground. Armoured figures circle them, fumigate them, x-ray them, cat-scan them. Doctors take swabs, blood-samples, oral and rectal probes. They're documented, interrogated. Then dropped down further subterranean levels where vast machinery powers strikeback arsenals of mighty doomsday weaponry, to quarantine cells, in naked antiseptic isolation.

Roxton nods as they're separated. 'It's fine. They've got to be certain. Once through this we're in, part of the retaliation. It's only a matter of time. Wait.'

Grace slumps in the cell corner. Crouches down, head in hands. Lightning bursts in vivid storms across her retinas. Flashbacks of the bug clattering up the stairwell. She sees it all, frozen in strange clarity. Rael and Miko loosing off tracer bursts spattering its chitinous shell. Nerve-shredding terror, in the formic acid urine-stench. While Oliver, from below, works around its thorax, lodging grenades, so it erupts in a larval deluge of sloppy flame and streaming gut, threshing jointed legs, mandibles screaming so high-pitched it splits eardrums numb. Oliver drenched in its fire-stream, scarred and melting, dragged to safety into the suite. She sits beside him, as he turns comatose, then shrieking. When his face caves in it's squirming with corpse-white maggot-larvae. Rael and Miko toss him from the balcony, he howls all the way down with what's left of his mouth, to splatter-impact. It's only in the silence that descends afterwards that she feels silver scintillas of ice-pain, and hears the maggot chomping its way through her brain-tissue. Blackness. Forgetfulness. Sleep. Nightmare. Terror.

She slumps. Crouches. Her mind buzzing, surging, as though through heightened senses. The light is unnatural. Casting tall mauve shadows. As though she's hallucinating unreal aftershocks. No. There are now two suns. For she's becoming one of them. Her skin is glowing, beams of intense lights pricking out through flesh-punctures in energy-spikes. Her outline shivering, melting, slurring into a single radiant mass. A spinning sphere of light. No thought. No consciousness. Racing towards her programmed detonation . . .

COMMANDER Harriman curses, spits down from the heights of the barricade. Shields his eyes against the sudden glare. A nuke? A retaliatory strike at the Darkula? No. The massive eruption beyond the skyline is inland, from the direction of the supposed Earthfort. The last human stronghold. No more. He surveys the compound below him. The scattered men and women safe, for the moment, behind his own fortifications. This, he thinks, is now the final human redoubt. He, its last commander. He watches the sky.

AUTHOR'S STORY NOTE

When I first began writing fiction for what was dubiously termed 'Men's magazines' I drew up a set of rules for myself concerning my Feminist sensitivities towards women. I enjoy sex, but not sexism. And so there'd be no gratuitous exploitation or disrespect. I'm not sure if 'The Coming Of The Darkula' strictly adheres to these guidelines or not, but the positive response to its publication has come overwhelmingly from women. A Californian artist friend immediately engaged in a long detailed analysis, insisting I should extend the story into a novel, exploring Grace's motivations further, and that the ending should be tweaked to enable her reprogramming, and salvation. She's even commenced on a screenplay, along these lines. But the post-apocalypse setting—to me, is part of an established SF trope that includes George R. Stewart's *Earth Abides*, Richard Matheson's *I Am Legend* . . . clear up to TVs graphic-novel adaptation of *The Walking Dead*, which is why—while I'm happy to use that precedent as homage or reference, I'm maybe reluctant to develop this story beyond its present form. I enjoyed writing it, and I'm delighted that it will reach new audiences in this book.

LITTLE SISTER, LITTLE BROTHER

SARAH L. JOHNSON

From *Suicide Stitch: Eleven Stories*
Publisher: EMP Publishing

AVAILABLE FOR IMMEDIATE OCCUPANCY.
Furnished 1BR suite in the historical Leighhaven building.
Conveniently located just outside downtown.
Quiet, well maintained, with live-in management.
Email cymbria.william@leighaven.com

* * *

The kid had a staring problem. From behind the first floor window, her dark eyes tracked Tate as he approached the wide stoop. Tiny hands splayed against the glass, tangled hair spilling over her shoulders—Tate figured she was five, maybe six years old. Whole milk in a plastic cup with Oreo sludge at the bottom. Maybe.

Tate didn't know much about kids, though he had two nephews. Countless times he'd stood on his brother's deck, peeling the label off a Heineken, while the boys savaged each other on the lawn. Occasionally they'd return to their respective corners for a slug of cherry Kool-Aid and Brad would offer booming encouragement as he swaggered over the grill.

Doesn't get any better than this. You're missing out, little brother. What about Shelly? Her divorce is final. Think maybe she's ready to test the waters . . .

Do not set me up.

You're thirty-five, Tate. The business is solid. You're looking good. What are you waiting for? What about the Internet? There's that plenty of fish thing.

Sounds like a good way to get crabs.

Man your age shouldn't be alone. Have some potato salad.

No thanks.

Fuck's the matter with you, lately?

It's mayonnaise.

One good dinner won't hurt. C'mon, Val worked all day on the food, made your favorites . . .

Jesus.

How many matchmaking attempts had he endured? How much mayonnaise had he eaten just to be polite? How many times had he covered at the bar because someone's crotch dropping had a ballet recital, or tae kwon do, or anthrax?

But that was then and there. This was here and now. Hundreds of kilometers. A trail he'd followed into the woods, and overnight everything changed. Because it had to.

The little girl in the window slapped her palm over her mouth. Tate swore he heard giggling through the glass. He raised a hand in a hesitant wave. Were you supposed to wave at kids you didn't know? Had he just done a Creepy Thing? With a flap of dingy skirt, the kid turned and vanished into the apartment.

Above the heavy door, a sandstone arch bore the engraving 'Leighaven Est. 1901.' Tate pressed the old fashioned buzzer and watched for movement through the smoked glass panels. He buzzed again. He waited.

As Tate reached for the handle, the door swung inward. A woman stood in the entryway. Tall enough to ride the roller coaster but short enough for him to see scalp through a razor sharp part running down the middle of her head. Dark hair bracketed her pale face. Old enough to rent a car, young enough to wear red flannel without looking frumpy. Huge, dark eyes. She stood with one hand braced against the door and one behind her back, as though expecting him to foist a Book of Mormon on her.

"You must be Tate," she said.

"Are you Cymbria?"

A groove creased her forehead and her mouth stretched diagonally. "You're thin."

"Beg your pardon?" he asked, feeling the tips of his ears sizzle.

"Never mind." She twirled and started down the dim hallway, hair swishing down her back. "Come on in, Tate. Enter, if you dare."

Lager. One of those snotty craft brews in a pint glass.

The heels of her purple Mary Janes thumped on the runner as she led him past a door marked OFFICE and into a windowless stairwell.

"Hope you like exercise," she said, her voice echoing off plaster. "We don't have a . . ." She snapped her fingers. Once. Twice.

"Elevator?"

"Right." She aimed a finger-thumb gun at him. "Can't put one in either, on account of all the rules around preserving heritage sites."

She reminded Tate of an anime character with her snub of a nose, crooked smile and eyes taking up half her face. Not much under that flannel, but from his vantage point three stairs down, she filled out a pair of black leggings just fine.

Tate dropped his eyes to her shoes. He didn't want to be *that* neighbor. Live-in management, the ad said. Probably she ran this place with her lumberjack boyfriend. He'd wear a matching flannel and carry a wrench the size of Tate's leg over his shoulder. *You're thin . . .* Tate sucked in his stomach as he followed her dainty ass up the stairs.

On the third floor, she opened a door connecting to a hallway where sconces cast nominal light over the papered walls and stamped tin ceiling. She pointed to another door with a tarnished '9' over the peephole.

"I am," she said.

"Huh?"

"I'm Cymbria. Not used to introducing myself is all. Been ages since we've had a new tenant."

Tate scanned the deserted hallway. "You could hear a hair drop in here."

"Pipes make most of the noise in this place." She pointed down the corridor. "Halls are L shaped. Around that corner there's two more suites."

"Are there many kids in the building?"

"Is that a problem?"

"No," Tate said, too quickly. "I saw a little girl, in the window out front."

"That's the office."

"Oh."

Tate waited. Cymbria stared. Maybe she was a private person. The kid had the same hair and eyes. Could be her daughter.

Without breaking eye contact, Cymbria stuck her hand down the front of her shirt and pulled out a key. "You want to do it?"

The body-warm brass melted into his hand. He slid the key into the lock and opened the door to number nine.

Crown molding joined yellow walls to the ceiling and a parquet floor gleamed in the afternoon light. Pink sofa, coffee table, and corner kitchen with a few cabinets and checkered curtains drawn across the plumbing beneath the sink. Tate poked his head into the bathroom, noting the old spotless fixtures. The bedroom had a southeast-facing window. Tate imagined the sunrise pouring onto the white duvet, spread without a wrinkle over the queen size bed.

Cymbria's shoes tapped along behind him. "Mattress is new and the sheets are fresh."

Tate waded through the mellow scent of floor wax. "This is . . ." Scotch. Single malt. Twelve years. "It's perfect."

Cymbria clicked her heels together. "No place like home."

Tate chuckled. "Got a pen, Dorothy?"

"Oh!" She clapped her hands. "You know that book?"

"Saw the movie as a kid," Tate said, digging in his satchel. "I'll give you first, last, and a deposit right now."

"But you just got into town." Her hands curled into fists over her stomach before she forced them down and smiled, her crooked mouth almost pretty. "Need help moving in?"

"I've got a change of clothes and my laptop in the car. Once I bring those up, I am moved in." A sheepish note crept into his voice. Tate herded it away. Wasn't like he'd abandoned a flock of small children. If he wanted to drop everything and go on a vision quest that was his own goddamn business.

Cymbria's smile didn't falter, but her throat rolled as though she'd dry-swallowed an aspirin. "There's no rush, Tate. Make like a butterfly and settle. Drop the cheques by the office tomorrow. I'll be around." She retrieved another key from her shirt and before Tate could ask how many she had in there, she'd dropped the hot brass into his hand.

"That's for the front door."

"Okay?" He trailed her as she all but fled the apartment.

"Welcome to the building!" She tossed another bent smile over her shoulder and the spring-hinged stairwell door shut behind her.

"No place like home," Tate muttered.

He sprawled on the sofa, enjoying the silence, getting to know the smell and the light. When the sun began to sink he decided to grab his bag from the car. Just as he opened the apartment door a child's laugh rang out, clear and silver.

Tate stepped into the hall. "Hello?"

Pattering footsteps. Tate wandered down and peered around the corner. Another hall with a window at the end, creating the illusion of being in a tunnel, or a mineshaft.

Two doors, one on either side. Tate glanced back at the sunlight slashing through the open door of his own apartment. Three units to a floor then. That made for nine suites total. Number nine. The highest room in the tallest tower. The cherry in the Shirley Temple ordered by the vocally sober or tacitly pregnant.

The floor creaked as Tate approached the window. Not a bad view. Streets lined with poplars, and the downtown skyline beyond. Tate liked the idea of living in an old building in a strange city. So long as that kid wasn't running the halls at all hours. He turned from the window and when he rounded the corner, he found himself in the dark. The wall sconces had gone out, and the door to number nine was closed.

*   *   *

Eighty-one squares on the ceiling, each stamped with concentric circles, like ripples in a puddle. Nine rows of nine. Tate lay on his back in the white bed and counted the moonlit squares again. He waited for sleep.

"What the hell am I doing?"

A reply came in the form of muffled groans and pops. The shuddering language of an old building tucking itself in for the night. Yesterday, Tate had responsibilities. He had roots. Now, he was alone in a strange bed in a strange place. No one demanding. No one needing. It didn't feel good yet, but he expected that to change soon.

Yesterday, he'd been at the bar, pouring and bussing on his own because surprise, surprise, Brad and Shelly both had family hurricanes blow in on the same night, which happened to be Thursday. The worst night in the industry.

The shift started out okay. Tate traded syllables with the math teacher who shambled in every day at four to down a variable number of rum and cokes. Bacardi dark, no lime. He'd paid his tab, left his customary five-dollar tip and shambled out. Tate had an hour of quiet before Thursday People descended. Customers looking to start the weekend early, but with the responsible adult stick still wedged far enough up their rears to ask about gluten-free menu options.

After that it was loosened ties, and high-heeled shoes dangling from painted toes. Embryonic infidelities. Cab sav and chard for the ladies, beer on tap for the gents, and a steady flow of gin and tonic filling gaps in the gender binary. Open tabs paid on plastic. Lime juice under his fingernails.

Just after ten, some hipster sashayed through the door with his scarf-twirling entourage. Eyes glued to his phone, he typed one-thumbed while snapping his fingers in the general direction of the bar. He ordered a round of sidecars.

Fucking *sidecars.*

Tate threw his rag down and walked out.

On everything.

He'd meant to go outside for a few minutes, get some air. But then he'd dipped a hand into his pocket and felt his car keys.

A few hours later, he stopped for gas. He threw his phone in the squeegee bucket. Sploosh. Gone. He didn't know why, didn't have an answer. Why? Why what? He didn't even know the question.

He just knew.

That life was done. It didn't exist anymore. He'd followed that broken line on the highway to a creaking pile smelling of damp wood and dust. Leighaven was creepy as hell, and the second he crossed the threshold, Tate knew he'd come home.

*   *   *

Tate knocked on the office door. When no one answered, he twisted the knob and poked his head in. "Hello?"

The suite was laid out like his but instead of a couch and TV, there was a desk with a printer, monitor, penholder, and a stack of unopened mail. Bookshelves stuffed with hundreds of paperbacks lined the far wall. The bedroom door was closed.

"Lost?"

Tate spun around, nearly bumping noses with the man standing behind him. Hair the color of black coffee fell over large eyes set in a pale, angular face. Taller, broader, but the resemblance was unmistakable.

"Sorry, you startled me," said Tate.

"Yeah, well." The man shoved past Tate, setting his toolbox on he desk. He dropped into the chair and reached into a basket on the floor. A pair of knitting needles emerged, trailing a mass of yellow yarn. He began casting stitches on the empty needle, hands working at a tempo you could set a metronome by. After a dozen beats, he glanced up at Tate. "What do you want?"

"Just dropping something off. For Cymbria?"

The needles clicked. "You're not sure?"

"Pardon?"

"You said it like a question." The man glowered through the hair hanging in his eyes.

"Rent, and deposit." Tate pinched the cheques between his thumb and forefinger. "I'm the new tenant in number nine."

"Right. Number nine. Here to breathe some life into the place." The man pushed his sleeves up his slender forearms and extended a hand, but not to shake. "Give 'em to me. I'll take care of it."

Tate laid the cheques across the man's palm. "Wasn't sure who to make them out to. Figured you might have a stamp or something."

"Tate Sutton," the man read off the cheque. "What the hell kind of name is that? Tate?"

Tate gritted his teeth. "And, you are?"

A smirking version of Cymbria's smile stretched across the man's face as he flipped his hair out of his eyes. "I'm Will. And I'm the fixit around here, so if you got needs, lemme know."

Jäger. That would be Tate's first guess, except tall dark and sullen here didn't have the requisite neck tattoo. So, not Jäger, but something that made a statement. People like Will took up knitting for a reason. Otherwise, they'd be serial stranglers.

"I'll tell Little Sister you stopped by."

Tate headed for the door. "Good to meet you, Will."

"Welcome to Leighaven, Tater Tot. Enjoy our stairs."

The clicking of needles started up again as Tate closed the door behind him with more force than necessary. Blood pulsed hot in his ears. *Tater Tot.* Dick. There was no way Cymbria's brother could possibly . . .

Screwdriver. That was it.

Perfect for Leighaven's crafty maintenance man. Nothing said, *I'm an alcoholic and I don't even care that you know,* like bottom shelf vodka with a splash of O.J. for breakfast. The get-it-done cocktail. That was Will.

In the stairwell, water stuttered through the pipes running up the walls like painted snakes. Lights blazed, but Tate froze as a sense of darkness engulfed him. Surly brothers and grouchy plumbing aside, there was a sickness about Leighaven. Something chronic and crippling. He ought to run upstairs, pack his shit, and get the hell out. Or not. He had his wallet and keys in his pocket. He didn't need anything else.

He ought to leave. Right now.

He tipped his head back, squinted at the ceiling three floors above, and knew he wasn't going anywhere.

* * *

Vanishing without a trace held a certain romantic appeal, but the last thing Tate wanted was to be reported as a missing person. The proof of life email he'd sent his second day at Leighaven wouldn't hold them forever. Tate stared at the pre-paid cell phone in his hand and dialed.

Brad picked up on the second ring. "Hullo?"

"Hey."

"Jesus Christ," Brad shouted into the phone.

"Thought I'd check in. It's been a few weeks."

"It's been a month and a half! What the hell? What happened? Where are you?"

"Doesn't matter. Just wanted you to know I'm okay."

"Well that's real nice, Tate. Except Val's worried sick, the boys ask about you every day, I've been tearing my hair out trying to run the bar by myself."

Tate envisioned his brother's scrunched up forehead. "I know you're pissed. I don't blame you."

"What the fuck is going on?" Brad breathed heavily into the phone. "Are you in trouble? Is it drugs? Did you get a girl pregnant?"

Tate chuckled. "No, Brad. Nothing like that."

"You're really okay?"

"I really am."

"Need money?"

"I've got money."

Between his savings and a part-time gig shelving books at the downtown library, he had enough to live on and plenty of time for reading, jogging, exploring, and lately, writing. Thirty-five years of keeping his mouth shut had left him with a surprising lot to say. But not to Brad.

"How are the boys? I miss them," Tate said, aware that it wasn't entirely true, but it seemed like the thing to say. Two minutes of conversation with his brother, and already, Tate was falling back on old habits.

"If you miss those boys, man up and tell 'em yourself," Brad gruffed and then sighed again. "This isn't like you, Tate."

"People change, Brad. Sometimes they have to."

"Look, I'm not even pissed, not really. But I trusted you to have my back, brother. You've let me down, you've let us all down . . ."

Commencement of the 'I'm not angry just disappointed' speech had Tate appreciating Will's brand of open hostility. He wished Brad would just give him hell. Then Tate could shovel it right back. Point out that it was easy to feel let down when you weren't used to hauling your own goddamn weight. Remind Brad that until six weeks ago Tate always had his back. Always. But in the three decades prior, when exactly did Brad ever have his? Fat Tate never had anyone behind him. Because Fat Tate was the omega. Always.

"A man works hard and takes care of his family . . ."

Christ almighty . . . Tate pinched the bridge of his nose.

"Now, that means something to me, and it used to mean something to you . . ."

He had clothes in the dryer downstairs. They'd be done about now. Brad went on scolding. Tate shoved the phone between the pink sofa cushions and walked out, shutting the door to number nine behind him.

A blur whipped around the corner of the hallway. Shadows had a way of coming to life at Leighaven. Things moved. Loud cracks and what sounded uncannily like wordless shouting erupted at all hours, keeping him on his toes. Tate felt awake here. Present and engaged in a way he'd never before experienced.

Fluorescent tubes buzzed on the basement ceiling, illuminating windowless cinder brick walls, painted an institutional green. Just a laundry room. Not like it had to be airy and tastefully appointed. Still, something a little less cryptacular would be nice. He'd only ever had reason to enter the laundry room but if he did take a stroll around the bend in the corridor, he'd be disappointed not to find a pair of skeletons tossing bourbon down their fleshless gullets and telling each other knock-knock jokes.

A rivet on a pair of jeans branded Tate's arm as he pulled his clothes out of the dryer. He wondered if Brad was still hectoring the recesses of the old sofa. With a smile in his heart, he picked up his full laundry basket.

The lights stopped buzzing. Tate gripped the basket handles, his palms slick on the plastic. Fluorescent tubes flickered, and died. Darkness dropped like a black bag over his head.

Tate's breath rolled in his ears. Then he became aware of another sound creeping toward him. Around him.

Pat, pat, pat.

The lights crackled on. She stood in the doorway, the ragamuffin from the window, the girl with the silver laugh. Her little chest heaved as she breathed hard but noiseless. She smiled. If smile was the right word. It might have been, if not for the drool oozing through the gaps between her teeth, running over her chin and dripping onto the concrete floor. *Pat, pat, pat.*

Tate followed the trail of viscous blobs over the floor where they led back to him. Circled him. Her ghoulish grin widened, then she turned and ran.

"Hey." Tate chased after her and stepped into the stairwell, just in time to catch a glimpse of her scuffed, yellow rain boots. Her footsteps stamped up and around, up and around, all the way to the third floor, his floor, where he heard the door open and shut.

Another face appeared over the rail at the top floor. Small face. Small boy. *So,* Tate thought, *there are two of them.*

"Stay away from her," the boy said in a pitchy snarl. He and the girl shared the same wild dark hair, and that attitude was all Will. There had to be some relation.

"Lights went out," Tate said. "I didn't mean to scare her."

"Scared? Of you?" The little boy scoffed and turned away from the rail. Tate heard the door open and snap shut again.

"Brats," Tate muttered.

When he reached the third floor, he heard no laughter, or disembodied footsteps. No sign of the kids. They had to live in one of the other two units on his floor. Tate unlocked number nine, stepped onto the sunny parquet floor, and left all consternation behind. He was glad he'd blocked the number to the burner phone and deactivated his email account. It was nice to come home and not dread sorting through messages. It was nice to come home.

* * *

The office door was ajar, nevertheless he knocked.

"Hi Tate, come on in."

He walked in to find Cymbria sitting cross-legged on the desk, dipping a graham cracker into a can of frosting, eyes glued to the tablet balanced on her knee.

"How'd you know it was me?"

"Lucky guess," she said without looking up. She took a bite of the loaded cracker and sprayed crumbs as she whooped with laughter. She held up the tablet, showing him a video of a kitten wrestling with a balled up piece of paper. "Isn't it the funniest?"

Tate had opinions about the sort of people who watched cat videos. But it was hard not to smile at a kitten being a kitten. Just like it was hard not to laugh at Cymbria's latest wackadoodle get up. Denim cut-offs over orange tights and pink Converse sneakers. She also wore a slouchy yellow sweater. A sweater Tate had last seen several weeks ago on her brother's knitting needles.

Little Big Bird's eyes slid over him as she stretched out her endless orange legs.

"Want some?"

"Pardon?"

She held out a graham cracker and the can of frosting. "It's the best snack I ever invented."

Tate shook his head. "Sounds great, but it's not for me."

"Y'know, people with nothing to lose usually come to a bad end. Think about that before you give up everything good in life."

She looked so utterly serious, and Tate couldn't help himself. He swiped a dot of icing from the corner of her mouth with his thumb, and licked it clean. "I haven't given up *everything* good."

"We'll see about that." She grinned and brushed crumbs off her orange tights. "So? How may I serve you today?"

Tate splashed through the brackish convergence of thoughts at the inlet of his mind, trying to locate the reason he'd popped into the office.

"There's a couple kids living here. Boy and a girl?"

Clueless eyes stared up at him.

"Do you know who they belong to?" he prompted.

Her nose wrinkled. "That's a terrible question."

"It is?"

"Who do you belong to? Who does anyone belong to?" She stuck out her confetti-hued tongue. "That's super personal. You can't just . . .

It's a weird question. You're weird for asking it."

He was weird? Maybe she wasn't craft beer. Maybe she was something else. Like a syrupy white zin. Any self-respecting grownup would be embarrassed, but somehow, she turned it around so he was the loser, in business casual, with his glass of pinot noir.

Tate jammed his hands in his back pockets. "They run wild. Follow me around the building. I hear them outside my door. Couple days ago they were in the basement, skulking about. Someone just needs to tell them it's not cool to sneak up on strangers, and I'm not sure it should be me."

Cymbria tilted her head. "Are you strange?"

"I'd like to speak to their parents," he said. "I should probably meet my neighbors, anyway."

"Do you want to meet them?"

Tate considered it. He heard water running, footsteps, and latching doors. He received either a cheery wave from Cymbria, or a grudging nod from Will almost every day when he passed the office on his way out of the building. Otherwise, it was easy to pretend he had Leighaven all to himself.

"Guess I've been enjoying the bubble," he admitted.

A curious smile slanted across Cymbria's face. "Did you get yourself a present?"

Tate followed her pointing finger to a cardboard slab resting against the wall. "Must be the desk I ordered."

Her face fell. "That's not a present. People use desks for work."

"Or watching cat videos." Tate crouched in front of the box, inspecting the bill of lading taped to the side. "But work is the idea, yes."

Cymbria knelt beside him, her elbow not quite touching his. She gathered her hair, exposing her pale nape before tossing the dark mass over her shoulder. She smelled like kindergarten—graham crackers and hot, sticky hands. "What do you do for work, Tate?"

"Shelve books at the library."

Cymbria ran the tip of her tongue along her upper lip. "I mean before you came to Leighaven."

Not the name of the city, or even a vague 'here.' Leighaven. Like it had been his plan, all along.

"Speaking of personal questions." Tate stood up. Cymbria remained on her knees, staring up at him, her mouth soft, damp, and open just a little. He gripped the edge of the box. "Uh, I ought to get this put away, but if you want to come by later, I could pour you a cup of coffee and tell you all about it."

She blinked, a slow sweep of eyelashes. "I should get Will."

Granted it wasn't Tate's smoothest move. The kind of invitation usually met with some version of, 'Jeez, I would but I have jury duty.' It was Cymbria though, and because she had to be weird about everything, she shut him down with one unexpected syllable.

"Will?" he asked.

Cymbria bounced up and drummed her fingers on the cardboard. "To help you. Little Brother moves heavy stuff all the time. He's really strong."

Rejection, followed by three flights of hate-face?

"It's not that heavy."

It was very heavy.

"Once I get it on the first step, it'll slide up, no problem."

He said a prayer for his back.

Sweat prickled along his hairline and his shoulder ached. He focused on the door to the third floor. One more flight. He gripped the sides of the box and shoved. His toe slipped off the edge of the stair, the box slid back, hitting him in the chest. Tate's hand flew out, but his fingertips only grazed the rail as he fell backward.

His tumble stopped suddenly as it started, when a hot manacle locked around his wrist.

Will stood above him, one hand holding the box, the other holding Tate. Dark eyes blazed behind his shaggy hair. Heat from Will's hand travelled up Tate's arm and gathered in his chest. It was the first time in weeks that someone had touched him. Despite the severe expression on Will's face, despite being suspended mid-crash over the stairs, Tate felt oddly cared for.

"Thanks," he said.

Will's forearm corded as he pulled Tate upright. "Looking a little doughy there, Tater Tot."

"What?" Tate yanked his wrist free and his stomach sucked itself in, retreating from the pointy words. "Doughy?"

"Pale, like bread dough?" Will explained, as though it were the most obvious thing in the world.

"Good timing," Tate said, gripping the bannister. "Could've broken my neck."

Will grunted. "What a waste that would be."

"Where'd you come from, anyway?"

Will glanced over his shoulder. "Most people call it a door."

"Right."

Will leaned his hip against the rail, one hand steadying the box like it weighed precisely nothing. "What are you doing, trying to move this by yourself?"

"Didn't seem that heavy at first."

"They never do."

Will hauled the box up the rest of the stairs with grace. Bastard. Cymbria was right. Will was strong. And naturally thin. And good looking. Not quite handsome though, like his sister wasn't quite pretty. Both attractive, but in an androgynous way. It was Will's attitude that lent him a caustic masculinity.

Outside number nine, Tate dug in his pocket for his key.

"Need help setting it up?" Will asked.

"Think I can manage." Tate slid the key in the lock. "Thanks again. I owe you one. Really, if there's anything I can do for you, just ask. I'm happy to help."

Will's annoyance swarmed around them like a cloud of wasps. "If you wanna blow me that bad I won't stop you. But I'd just as soon leave it here, yeah?"

"Consider it left."

"Try not to stab yourself with a hammer." He clapped Tate on the back. "Later, Tater."

The door squealed shut behind Will, muting his footfalls down the stairs. Tate stood in the hall, the skin between his shoulder blades stinging. He listened for silver giggles or footsteps. Silence. Cymbria never did answer his question.

Inside the apartment, he opened the box and found all the parts and hardware he needed. Cymbria was right. He planned to use the desk to work. The work had already begun, in fact. He had plans.

Tate's eye wandered to his computer, currently sitting on the coffee table. Maybe he should contact Brad? That last conversation hadn't ended well. Tate did miss his brother and his nephews, but in a detached way. It didn't sit right. He wanted to miss them more. They were the only family he had.

The desk went together easy enough. As Tate tightened the final screw, he noticed the discoloration circling his wrist. Pink and tender, like a sunburn. In the shape of a handprint.

* * *

A knock at the door wrenched Tate out of his computer screen trance.

"Shit," he muttered, noting the late hour. He pushed away from the desk and shuffled over to the peephole. He yawned and opened the door.

Cymbria held up a plate of cinnamon rolls. "I made you a special treat."

The smell smashed into him, neither good nor bad, just overwhelming. He stared at the floor, searching for his words. "Cymbria, what the hell are you doing here?"

"You asked me to come by later."

"It's past midnight."

One eye narrowed as she pressed a finger to the bow of her upper lip. "Too late?"

"Well, yeah." He rubbed a hand over his face. "Or too early, depending on how you look at it. Jesus."

"Shoot, I've never been good with these . . ." the finger snap again. "Conventions."

Tate couldn't help noticing her chalky face, the purple shadows under her eyes, and the way her collarbones punched up too hard under her skin. "Cymbria, are you okay?" he asked.

"I screwed up." She shoved a flour-streaked tendril of hair behind her ear. "When you visit, you're supposed to bring something. It's polite. But it took longer than I thought and time is like, something I don't really notice, and I do things without thinking them through, at least that's what Little Brother says, but he's wrong, because I think a lot, about all kinds of things, but they're always the wrong thing, you know?" She thrust the cinnamon rolls at him. "Anyway, here."

He took the plate and caught her arm as she pivoted to leave. "Wait."

Her face swiveled back to his, eyes bigger than ever. "I'm sorry, Tate."

Sorry. The sound of that word coming out of her mouth, the shape of it on her lips. It felt wrong. He never wanted her to say it again.

"Don't go," he said. "I was up anyway. Please, come in."

"I should leave you alone."

He pressed his thumb firmly into the hot crease of her elbow. "Come in."

She shivered as he pulled her across the threshold. Once inside, she slipped through his grasp, inch-by-inch, until her fingers glided over his. She clomped across the parquet floor in knee-high shitkickers, paired nicely with her white wife beater, like Johnny Walker and cigarettes. In between, a pink skirt flounced down her legs, and a matching ribbon secured her sloppy ponytail.

Goodbye Big Bird.

Hello Kitty.

"Wow." She stomped around his living room. "You've done a whole lotta nothing with the place."

"It's a good scotch," Tate said. "Doesn't need much. Just a few drops of water."

"You drink a lot of scotch?"

"Not as much as I've served. Before I came to Leighaven, I was a bartender."

Cymbria mimed a free pour. "That's always a sexy job in the movies."

"Yeah, a sexy consequence of an English degree."

Her mouth turned down. "You like to ruin the fantasy, don't you?"

"Constant source of disappointment, right here."

"Didn't mean it like that." She gave his arm a squeeze, a simple, tender touch that demanded nothing in return and stirred him more deeply than it should have. "Can I ask you something?"

"Go for it."

"It's personal," she warned.

He gave her a look. "I let you into my apartment in the middle of the night. Just ask."

"People quit their jobs all the time, Tate. You quit your whole life. Why?"

Tate paced back and forth for a long moment. "It's complicated. My brother thinks I've cracked up. That I'm selfish."

"Brothers are a chore sometimes."

"But it is selfish, isn't it? To suddenly blow town without telling anyone?"

Cymbria perched on the edge of his new desk, smoothing her cotton candy skirt over her knees. "A lot of things look sudden, Tate. Maybe some things are. But not people."

Tate continued pacing. "You know that content look people get on their faces when a person falls exactly in line? When all expectations are met and you've neatly slotted yourself into the space where they think you belong?"

Cymbria nodded, her eyes following him back and forth.

"My whole life," he said. "I've tried to be the guy my family and friends needed. I never stepped outside of the parameters they'd set. I'm a responsible business partner, a tireless worker, a last minute babysitter, a good brother, and by necessity the second best son, a place to crash, a bank to borrow from, a comic foil . . . whatever they wanted, I made it happen. I existed to put that look on their faces. I never questioned it."

Cymbria swung her crossed ankles. "They were happy. You thought you were happy too."

"That night, I realized my life wasn't even mine. I was a drone, performing as programmed. I saw a way out. So, I followed the trail."

"Into the woods," Cymbria said, catching his hand as he passed, arresting his pattern. They shared a moment of silence until the smell of cinnamon drove him to distraction.

He lifted the edge of the plastic on the plate. "It's a little late for me, but do you want one?"

"I already ate four." She clutched her stomach. "Can't help myself. Treats always make me happy. For a while, anyway."

Tate gazed at the pastries. "Sometimes that's enough."

"Are you writing something?" Cymbria touched the word-filled screen of his laptop.

Heat blasted into his ears as he snapped the screen down. "I was. Before you inappropriately neighbor'd me."

"A story?"

"Sort of, I'm not sure yet." He rubbed the back of his neck. Why was he telling her this? Why was she here? It was all so personal.

Cymbria hopped off his desk. "I love stories, so does Little Brother. For the longest time, we read the same old books over and over. But now, with the Internet, you can get anything you want, anything in the whole wide world!" She threw her arms out and twirled around his living room. Her skirt flew up, displacing cinnamon scented air and exposing her creamy thighs. Also, no bra.

He rubbed his eyes. "Can I ask you something now?"

"Want to play twenty questions? I love that game, even though Will hates it."

"Is there anything he doesn't hate?"

Cymbria's gaze dropped to the floor. "You don't like him."

Tate bobbled around all the words that wanted to go first. "I don't think he likes me. Or that I'm here, at Leighaven."

"He's a barky dog, but he'd never bite anyone who didn't deserve it." A softness crept into her expression as she defended her brother. "What was your question?"

"At the library, I found a book on the city's historical buildings. Leighaven was in there."

Cymbria's hands fluttered to her stomach. "So?"

"Wasn't much information. Stuff about the architecture and that it was built by Reinhold and Glory Leighaven in 1901."

"Guess there's not much to tell."

"Maybe, but I was interested, so I went down the street to land titles. Sweetie-pied a clerk half to death, hoping she could dig deeper into the building's history. Turns out Reinhold and Glory died just a few months after the building was finished, and ownership passed not to any family, but to The Leighaven Group, Reinhold's investment firm. In 1970, the Leighaven Group successfully lobbied the province to have the building declared a heritage sight, and they're still paying the taxes on it today out of a trust. Administered by Cymbria and William Leighaven."

"And we would have gotten away with it too, if it weren't for you pesky kids," she crowed. "Nice work, Scooby."

"I've been living here almost two months. We see each other almost every day. Why didn't you tell me your last name is Leighaven, or that you own this building?"

A dark look clouded her face. "Most times I feel like it owns us."

His heart squeezed out a run of irregular beats. "I get that."

She clutched his hands, her fingers threading through his wherever they found a gap. "Since we're confessing stuff, I may as well admit that when you emailed your application, I searched you up on the Google. I found an article on food and beverage spots. There was a picture, of you and your brother, in front of your bar. So, when you showed up last week . . ."

Tate pulled his hands free. "You expected a fat guy?"

"You've been preparing, Tate. Even if you didn't know it. You came here empty, just waiting to be filled up again. I knew you were the one to let in."

Cymbria didn't know Fat Tate. She didn't know that Fat Tate was a lot nicer than not Fat Tate. But Fat Tate was a doormat. Fat Tate couldn't say no. Fat Tate laughed it off but still cringed inside when his brother or his friends employed varied sobriquets like 'Tubs' or 'Tits' or the crowd favorite, 'Tater Tot', unwittingly resurrected by a certain lanky bastard in residence.

Cymbria dragged her finger down the middle of his chest. "I never expected Ken to turn up on my stoop."

"Ken?"

"Barbie's boyfriend. You know, blond and handsome." She scraped his hair back from his forehead. "I always wanted to be glamorous like Barbie."

On impulse, Tate tugged the pink ribbon on the back of her head. The bow slipped open and her hair tumbled down like a warm pelt. "You look better than any Barbie." His thumb brushed over her suddenly flushed cheek. But people were never sudden, were they?

Her hand closed around his wrist. "Tate, don't write about Leighaven."

"Why?"

"Because history is never over. It's never dead. You get real close and real quiet and you'll see it breathing."

Her queer-eyed stare held a plea, a warning, and something else. An affliction. Tate couldn't get a fix on her. Charming. Puzzling. Shifting to the left whenever he thought he had her pinned. A child with her goofy outfits. A woman, braless and knocking on his door in the small hours. Or a creature, with hidden fangs and dark eyes full of old secrets.

Cymbria Leighaven.

Her arm hooked around his neck and she pulled his mouth down to hers. They kissed with uncoordinated tongues, held breath, and clashing teeth. Everything terrible about first kisses, except it wasn't terrible at all. His hands slid under her shirt over the bare skin of her waist.

"Oh my god, you're hot," he said.

She giggled, not realizing he hadn't meant it colloquially. He boosted her back onto the desk and she pulled him between her legs, drawing him flush against her body. He fought the urge to recoil, like he would if he'd laid his hand on a hot stove.

"Cymbria, are you feeling okay?" he said. "You're really—"

"Shh."

Tate closed his eyes, falling into the taste of cinnamon, sugar, and butter. Everything good and satisfying in the world and all of it plated up so nicely on his new desk.

"Tell me what you want," she whispered.

Trick question? To hell with it. He ran his hands up her long legs, under her skirt. He hooked his thumbs into the sides of her panties. "I'd like to get you out of these."

He didn't know how long they kissed like that, his hands on her hips under her skirt. She wasn't craft beer, nor was she a cloying white zin. She was Tequila, straight up. Anejo. The good stuff you insist on but always regret.

Cymbria whimpered and wriggled against him. He tugged her panties down and wrestled them over her boots, lace snagging on steel hooks and chunky rubber tread.

"I'm sorry, Tate. I'm so sorry."

"Stop . . . saying that," he said between kisses, scalding his mouth on her neck and along her shoulder. His hand inched up her inner thigh, until he scorched his fingertips on slippery flesh that turned his brain to soup and his cock to stone.

"It's too soon," she whispered. "I shouldn't . . . it's too soon."

His hand stilled between her legs. "Want me to stop?"

"Mmm, and would you?" She rocked against his hand. "If I asked you to, right now?"

This was not the time for an interrogation. He was in a far too honest place. *You have questions? Ask away. Don't be shy. Let's get personal.*

Yes. Within three minutes of making her acquaintance, he'd wanted to fuck this bug-eyed weirdo blind. Yes. Her warning about Leighaven chilled him on a basement level of himself he didn't understand. And yes. If she asked him to stop now he would but . . .

"Barely," he whispered and caught her mouth under his again.

She'd started this. She had. Hadn't she? And now he needed it, needed her, like all the light in the universe would gutter out and he'd freeze to death in the dark if she were to push him away.

Her laughter rippled down his throat as she reached between them. He was in her hand. Then he was in her. Tate flinched as intense heat gloved him. Was she full of lava or something? This wasn't normal. She had a fever. She sure as hell looked sick. Whatever it was, he hoped it wasn't contagious.

Speaking of contagious. No condom. This was beyond idiotic.

Sweat slicked down his back under his shirt. Cymbria clawed at his shoulders and those awful boots scraped his hips. The desk creaked. His socks slipped on the floor. Her hair caught between their mouths, tying their tongues together.

The bartender always gets laid. An embarrassingly true stereotype. However, losing almost one hundred pounds had a curious effect on his game. He got more looks for sure, more flirty smiles, arm petting, and phone numbers scratched on napkins slid across the bar at him from the insanely hot Stella-from-the-bottle Thursday Girls that never would have looked at him twice before. But when it came to the women he genuinely wanted to get to know better, they were less receptive than they'd been when he was pudgy. Ergo, the last sex he'd had was over a year and fifty pounds ago. A long time. And now it was too soon. Too late.

"Cymbria."

"Wait." She pushed her forehead hard against his. "Almost there."

Distraction. Delay. Provincial capitals, the Greek alphabet, open gut surgery. But for whatever reason, an image of Will formed in his mind. Prince Charmless, with a morbidly obese chip on his stupid, perfect shoulders. Will, with the same pale skin, long limbs, and black velvet eyes full of I-know-something-you-don't.

Tate buried his face in Cymbria's hot neck as he came. Not a second later, she tensed around him. And the noise that came out of her. No exaggeration. The woman roared.

Murmuring nonsense, they bumbled their way to the bedroom.

"I tried not to . . . thought maybe just touching you a little . . . but you feel so good." Words dropped like wilted flower petals. "Couldn't help it . . . did you mind?"

"Stop talking," Tate said. "And I'll show you how much I mind."

He stripped her like the Barbie doll she'd always wanted to be and they fell onto the white duvet. A slower pace, yet not a moment to spare for sober second thought. In the dark she clutched him, pleading, repeating, a chant, a mantra.

"Please, Tate. Please let me . . . just let me . . . please . . ."

"Yes," he whispered into her soft, wet mouth, holding her hips against his. The question didn't matter when there existed only one conceivable answer.

*   *   *

Concentric circles. Nine rows of nine. Tate blinked at the ceiling tiles, pink ripples in the early light. Blinking felt like an accomplishment. Now, if he could only turn his head. The sound of his hair dragging over the pillow was like wire bristles on wooden planks. His neck muscles felt inflamed and tight as they rolled his leaden skull to the left. Toward an empty pillow. Another blink.

"Cymbria?" he croaked, not really expecting an answer, not really expecting the gummy meat of his throat to produce sound.

He shambled out of the bedroom. The only evidence that it hadn't been an acid-etched hallucination was the plate of cinnamon rolls on the desk. That, and the big bastard of a sex hangover that couldn't have been worse if he'd downed a fifth of Patrón. The parquet floor went swirly. His stomach lurched.

"Ugh."

Cymbria. She'd been an animal, a lion. She'd run him down and ripped him open. Even as she ate him alive, his body reported only pleasure. Metaphor or not, it freaked him out.

Tate rubbed the glue out of his eyes. Shower. The most glorious idea of all time. Hot water. Soap. Yes.

He pulled the shower curtain around the inner circumference of the freestanding tub. Water hissed. Tate stood under the spray, listening to the downpour hit the bottom of the tub in a steady rumble.

The warm water turned to freezing rain when an outline of a face slowly pushed in on the opaque shower curtain. Two shadowy hands pressed in on either side of the face. Tate yanked the curtain aside. White tiles, toilet, pedestal sink, painted pipes. His towel on the rack.

Slick plastic slapped against his back.

Tate whipped around, slipping on the enamel and taking the curtain down with him. He hit his head on the edge of the tub. Black fog obscured his vision and the pattering of water on the curtain exploded into gunfire. In the midst of it, he heard giggling. Silver bullets.

Hastily dressed in sweat pants and a t-shirt, Tate fought off waves of nausea from the throbbing gull's egg on his head as he stalked down the dim hallway and around the corner. Two doors, one on either side of the corridor. The kids lived in one of these units. Every time they disappeared on the third floor.

His knock echoed in the empty hall. He listened for movement, watched for a shift in the light creeping through the gap between the door and the floor. He knocked again. Waited. Crossed the hall. More knocking, listening and watching. Someone had to be home. Tate raised his fist, prepared to bang on the door. He paused. Maybe there was a better way to do this than terrorizing potentially innocent neighbors.

On the ground floor, Tate didn't knock. He shoved the office door open. Two near-identical faces fixed on him from opposite ends of the room. Will behind the desk, hands frozen mid-stitch on his needles, and Cymbria in the corner kitchen, yawning as she twirled a spoon in a mug.

"Oh my god, Tate!" Cymbria dropped her spoon and snatched up a white tea towel.

"The kids," Tate snapped. "Where do they live? I want to speak to their parents."

Will resumed his knitting. "You know you're bleeding from the head, right? Like a medium amount?"

Tate touched his temple and his fingers came away scarlet.

"What happened?" Cymbria skittered over, pressing the warm towel to the cut.

"They broke into my apartment, at least the girl did. I heard her."

Will glanced at Cymbria. "You sure, Tater? This building makes a lot of weird noises. Old pipes and what not."

"It wasn't the fucking pipes, Will. I was in the shower. I saw a face through the curtain. I heard them. That damn creepy giggling."

"Come sit, okay?" Cymbria guided him to an armchair and knelt at his feet, keeping the towel on his head. "They didn't break in, Tate. I left the door unlocked behind me. I shouldn't have, but I didn't want to wake you."

Tate felt Will's gaze incinerating them both.

"I'm sure she didn't mean any harm," Cymbria said, gripping Tate's hand. "She just likes to play. If she'd known you were hurt . . ."

Will strolled over, giving Tate's shoulder an ungentle nudge. "You don't waste any fucking time, do you?"

Tate stood, looking Will in the eye. "That's none of your business."

Cymbria wedged herself between them. "Will, don't."

"Don't what?" Will glared her down. "Don't spread 'em for number nine?"

"Hey, that's enough," Tate said.

"You really wanna get into it with me, Tater Tot?" Will snarled so ferociously that Tate actually stepped back. So Cymbria wasn't the only poorly domesticated animal at Leighaven.

"Shh, there's no need for that." Cymbria cupped Will's face in her hands, stroking his cheeks with her thumbs. "No need, no need . . ." Will jerked his chin out of her grasp. Vertigo clapped Tate right back into the chair. Cymbria turned to him. "Let's get you upstairs. You need to rest, and you should eat something."

Will snorted. "Like that's going to help? Damage is done, Little Sister."

Cymbria quailed under her brother's scorn. Tate didn't understand. Where did this crabby, son-of-a-bitch get off, shaming a grown woman like he would a misbehaving child?

Didn't help that Cymbria was dressed like a damn toddler in overalls and a purple t-shirt. Tate found it hard to reconcile that just a few hours ago he'd been inside her. Hard to believe her cinnamon-sweet mouth had dripped onto him filth that would've made a roughneck blush.

She also looked a hell of a lot healthier than she had last night. Her cheeks pink and plump, eyes sparkling, hair shiny. Now that he was paying attention, it looked like whatever had been draining her had latched on to Will. Bruised circles bagged under his eyes and where his sister's skin was heavy cream, his had the bluish tint of skim milk.

It was the first time he'd seen both Leighavens in the same room. Maybe it was the concussion, but together, they were even more bizarre. Like aliens zipped up in humanish skin. Passing, but barely.

"Please, don't be cross," she said softly to Will, her thin arms flexing as she gathered handfuls of his shirt. "I'm not as strong as you are."

"We'll talk about this later," Will said, and then he turned to Tate. "I'll sort out your trespasser problem. Now go home, get some sleep, and lock your goddamn door."

"Tell the parents to get a leash on their kids. Next time I'm calling the police." Tate took several lurching steps down the hall. When he looked back, Will leaned out of the office door, like a frost glazed bottle of vodka rolling out of an open freezer.

"I told you to stay away from her," he said.

Tate bobbed his head. Acknowledgment, rather than agreement. The truth was, Will had never told him any such thing.

The stairs took forever. His pulse boomed in his temples and he kept losing his balance. In his apartment, he searched every corner, cupboard and closet. Satisfied he was alone, he noodled into his desk chair. The blood on the side of his head itched. The plate of cinnamon rolls was within arm's reach. When he peeled off the wrap, the spicy smell hit him and his dick semi-hardened in his sweats. After last night, he was surprised the thing wasn't dead.

He picked up a pastry and took a bite, chewing slowly. Saliva flooded into his mouth and his stomach shivered. What was she? A freak in the sack. A god in the kitchen. He stared at the handful of heaven in his palm, one bite missing. If he ate any more, what was to stop him from eating them all?

With a flump they slid into the trashcan. Fat Tate would be appalled over the waste, but mostly, over the rudeness of it. How much of his weight problem was gluttony, and how much was his crippling desire to please?

Staring at those cinnamon rolls in the trashcan, Tate couldn't pretend he wasn't conflicted, but he'd made the decision. He'd had his taste and now they were gone.

* * *

It had to happen sooner or later. He'd been lucky to avoid it as long as he had, but after nearly a week, Tate's uppance had come. Outside the laundry room, around the bend in the hall, he heard a series of scrapes and thumps. He poured detergent into the drum, shut the lid, and started the machine. A diffuse glow bled around the corner of the hallway.

Tate hadn't explored this part of the basement. Instead of another hallway, he found a large open space with three massive boilers, a modern electrical panel, shelves loaded with cardboard boxes, and Will, dragging a rolled up carpet over the concrete floor.

"I expected skeletons," said Tate.

Black eyes glittered in the low light. "Say what?"

"Decent creep factor down here. Just seems like there should be skeletons."

Will grunted. "Make yourself useful, yeah? Grab the other end."

Fibers from the cut edge dug into Tate's hands. "What is this?"

"Old stuff I ripped out before you moved in. Last tenant ruined it. Never got around to feeding it to the bin."

Tate's arms strained. "You were going to move this yourself?"

"See anyone else lining up to help? Little Sister's more about the play than the work, as you might've noticed," Will said with a pointed look. "C'mon."

Tate puffed as they lugged the carpet down the hall and through the stairwell door. "Thanks for dealing with the kids for me. No sign of them since that day."

"They were just having fun, Tater." Will took the first few stairs, pulling the roll with him. "Don't you remember what it was like to be a kid?"

"I never broke into people's homes."

"They've been at Leighaven their whole lives. They think of the entire building as their home."

"Are they related to you?"

Will stopped halfway up the stairs, abruptly dropping his end and letting the full weight of the roll rest against Tate. "Could say that."

"Uh . . . Will, could you maybe . . ." Tate groaned under the strain.

"Jesus, Tater Tot." Will picked up the carpet, tucking it under one long arm. "We gotta work on your upper body strength. There, just give'r another shove. That's it."

They manhandled the carpet out of the stairwell, down the main floor hall and out the back door. Together, they tipped the roll into the dumpster. A thick plume of dust shimmered in the sunset.

"Thanks," Will panted.

"Anytime," Tate said, and surprisingly, meant it. It felt good to be useful. He had scratches all over his arms, but the sting was satisfying. In his old life, he'd resented being the only one hauling a sledge loaded with several people's burdens. But with Will in harness right next to him, pulling just as hard, it was different.

Will braced an arm against Leighaven's exterior sandstone, hanging his head. A faint wheeze accompanied the outline of his ribs heaving through his t-shirt.

"You okay?" Tate asked.

"Fine . . . just . . . dandy." Will flipped his head back. Sweat gleamed in the hollow of his throat and the sinking sun deepened the shadows around his eyes. "What're you looking at?"

"Not a thing. D'you want to come up for a beer?"

The combination of his greyish pallor and lopsided smirk made Will look downright sinister. "Don't think it's a good idea, Tater."

"Okay." Tate tried not to look disappointed.

"I'm not saying no," Will added. "I'm just . . . saying."

"Right." Tate paused. "But, I'm just saying, the last ghoul-faced Leighaven to walk through my door walked out looking like a million bucks."

Will's eyes narrowed to the size of regular eyes. "Man, you got a hell of a cheek on you."

"Are you coming or what?" Tate opened the door and stepped into the gloomy hallway.

* * *

"It's not that I hate kids." Tate reached into the fridge, fingers closing around two cold glass necks. "I have two nephews."

"Angels, I suppose?" Will produced a pocketknife and pried the caps off the bottles.

They sat down on opposite ends of the pink sofa. Tate took a pull from his beer, letting it drain deliciously thick down his throat. Usually, he couldn't justify the calories, but Russian stout was created for Monday nights with awkward company.

"My nephews are a lot like my brother," Tate said. "So they're kind of awful, but great, too. They laugh until they fall down, they're noisy, messy, and when they hug you, it's like getting tackled by a rhino. They go at life so hard, you know?"

"Sometimes."

"But the kids here, they aren't like that. They're sly. Almost feral."

Will said nothing. They stared straight ahead at an empty yellow wall, filling the silence with quiet gulps of stout while dusk barged through the window and fouled the apartment with shadows. Within minutes, Tate couldn't make out much more than a silhouette of his guest. The silhouette tilted its head and Tate felt dilated pupils fix on him like spotlights. Or the exact opposite. Focused beams of zero illumination. Notlights.

"Saw a thing on TV once, about feral kids." Will's smoky voice curled through the darkness. "Babies ditched in abandoned tenements in Ukraine."

"Scary."

The shadow man shrugged. "These kids develop differently. They can see in the dark, smell a storm two days away, and hear a spider walking on its web. They learn how to forage and stay warm. Some of them even figure out how to trap live meat."

"No kidding?"

"By the time they get 'rescued', they're more animal than human.

They've got a totally different nature. Can't be civilized. So, they get locked away."

Tate downed the last mouthful of stout, no longer cold. "You think they're better off living like animals? That Remus and Romulus stuff is a myth, Will. Kids left on their own, even if they can find food, they'll eventually get sick or hurt. It's not like the fairy tales."

"Where d'you think fairy tales start? Someone lost in the woods. Maybe they curl up under a tree and die, or maybe they keep going. The will to survive is powerful. Especially in kids. Powerful enough to bend the fucking universe."

Tate wondered. Was there a situation here? Abuse or neglect? Was Will telling him to leave well enough alone? Leighaven creaked and popped around them. Pipes juddered as water was called forth. A police siren careened by on the street below. Tate peered blindly across the couch at a shadow he suspected could see just fine. Something about being watched when he couldn't see unnerved him beyond his tolerance. He reached over to switch on the desk lamp.

Will hissed, his hand flying up to shield his eyes.

Tate held up his bottle. "Want another?"

"Why not." Will drained the last of his beer and scratched his finger over the pink upholstery of the couch. "This thing."

"What's wrong with it?"

"Ugly as hell. I could make you an afghan. How d'you feel about grey?"

"Swell." Tate took the empties to the kitchen. "What's with the knitting, anyway? Not many guys are into it."

Will didn't fire a smartass round from his retort cannon, but rather, stared at his hands, resting palms up on his legs. "Like how it feels is all. Life is hard. Yarn is always soft. What am I doing here, man? Seriously."

"Seriously?" Tate pulled a loaf of bread out of the fridge. "I'm going to make sandwiches. You hungry?"

Will's eyes gleamed in their deep hollows. "Starved."

"Good. I'll fix you up."

"You would offer it just like that."

"A sandwich?"

"Jesus, Tater, develop some trust issues like a normal person, yeah?"

Tate shrugged. "I've got turkey."

"Cheese?"

"Nope."

"Course not."

Tate made the sandwiches. Lettuce, tomato, and mustard. No

mayonnaise. Whole grain bread. Between that, the stout, and the turkey, it was Carb Christmas.

"Call it an olive branch." Tate offered Will a fresh bottle and a sandwich. "I'd like to get right with you. I'm sorry about Cymbria."

Will rolled his eyes. "Did you rape her?"

Tate nearly coughed out his first bite. "Is that what you think?"

"If I did, you'd be in the dumpster, rolled up in that rug." Will set his bottle on the coffee table and chomped into his sandwich. "You got nothing to be sorry for. It's called seduction, Tater. Believe me, you didn't stand a chance."

"She told you?"

"Didn't have to. I know her."

Tate slouched back on the couch. "I've stopped by the office every day, sometimes twice a day, but she hasn't been around. I think she's avoiding me."

Will chuckled. "Someone's got a crush on Little Sister."

"Laugh it up," Tate muttered into his bottle before taking a drink. "Why d'you call each other that? Little Sister. Little Brother."

"Family joke. She's smaller, I'm younger—by about ten minutes."

"Twins?"

"Hatched from the same meatsack, or so says the paperwork. Not that there's much of it. I suspect the adoption arrangements were shady as fuck, but fat cats have a way of writing their own rules, don't they? They wanted kids so they went out and bought a pair. Like shoes."

"You're not close with your folks?"

"Gave us their name, this mausoleum, and not much else." A scowl swept over Will's face. "They're gone, now. Dusted."

"Mine too."

"You miss 'em?"

"All the time."

"You're tight with your brother though."

"I thought so. But could you walk out on Cymbria like I walked out on Brad?"

Will shook his head. "She'd hunt me down and drag me back. Little Sister's stronger than she looks."

"No shit." Tate said, catching his tongue too late. "That came out wrong."

Will's hot hand clamped around the back of Tate's neck. "Relax, man. Probably seemed weird, me going berserk over you and her. Thing is, Cym's got impulse control issues. Does things without thinking them through. She's all I have, Tater. And I protect what's mine."

Protect her from what? From unsafe sex with strangers? Was it a pattern? Will did seem more pissed than surprised at the whole thing. Tate made a mental note to get himself tested for everything from the clap to SARS.

"To family." Tate raised his bottle and Will clanked his against it. A shrill twittering bounced off the walls, floor and ceiling. A moment of silence and the twittering repeated.

"Speaking of our resident succubus." Will dug in his pocket and pulled out a phone.

Tate hadn't heard a phone ring in almost two months. And now, to have one shrieking in close proximity? He could confidently say it was the most god-awful sound in the universe.

"Uh huh . . . upstairs with number nine . . . yeah, really . . . you should come up . . . just get your ass up here . . . see you in a few."

Tate shoved Will's shoulder hard with the heel of his hand. "What're you doing?"

"Getting you out of your own goddamn way." Will jammed the phone back in his pocket. The movement dragged the waistband of his jeans down exposing a taut slice of abdomen sweeping like a snowdrift to the crest of his hipbone. "Cym's a tricky bird, Tater. Never gonna fly into your cage just because you leave the door open. Has to be something in there she can't say no to."

"Like what?"

"Like me."

Tate sucked back the bottom third of his beer and banged the bottle down on the coffee table. "William Leighaven, you are the devil."

Will flashed an honest-to-god smile that promised only sin. Lots of it.

Cymbria waltzed in without knocking. Tate stared at her outfit. Flip-flops, basketball shorts, and a Hawaiian shirt knotted beneath her breasts, exposing a long arc of midriff. She'd changed the game on him again. This wasn't tequila. This was Malibu rum, pineapple juice, and coke. Trailer park colada.

Tate wrenched his eyes upward. "Hi."

She ignored him, homing in on her brother. "This is the last place I expected to find you."

Will shrugged. "Guess I know when I'm beaten."

She glanced at Tate and then back to Will. "But you said—"

"Forget what I said." Will braced one hand on the back of the couch and pressed his eyes shut for a moment. "We both know it's too late."

Cymbria's features melted into something like sadness. Something like grief. She walked up to her brother, held his head in her hands and burrowed her fingers in his hair. "You look awful. You need this."

Will opened his eyes and stared into hers. "I had some."

"A scrap here? A crumb there? That's not enough."

Tate stepped forward. "Hey, if you want another sandwich, there's plenty of—"

Will thwacked him with a glare so hateful it seemed to form a dark halo around his head, sharpening the angles of his gaunt face. Minutes ago, they'd been having their first real conversation over Russian stout. Will almost seemed to be enjoying himself. But with Cymbria's arrival, Little Brother was back to grouch city.

She pressed her cheek to Will's. "You're running hot."

"Why do you think I called you up here? It's time."

"Okay then." Cymbria looked over her shoulder at Tate. Her lips parted slightly and her tongue flicked between her teeth like a snake tasting the air. "Miss me?"

Tate took a reflexive step back. "Just wanted to see how you are."

"Dandy as a dandelion." She slithered over and dragged her nail over the scab on his forehead, sending threads of fire down his spine. "Does it hurt?"

"This helps." Tate's arms reached out of their own accord, finding the hot skin of her waist. Maybe it was the stout, or perhaps it was what he'd come to think of as the Leighaven Effect. Prolonged exposure to the building and its management had a way of heightening the senses while rounding off the edges of reality. Tate didn't care anymore that something massively odd was afoot. Or that Will was still glaring from the other side of the room as his sister steered Tate onto the couch and straddled his lap.

"Don't you want some?" Cymbria asked, looking over her shoulder. Will shook his head. "You first."

With a smile she turned back to Tate. "Little Brother likes to watch."

Sweat beaded along his hairline. He was on the wrong side of their language barrier. The smoldering woman-creature in his arms squirmed closer. He forced himself to let go of the need to understand, and when she kissed him, Tate knew he was lost.

Her lips left his, only to yank his shirt off, and then they were back, on his mouth, ears, face, and neck. He unknotted her Hawaiian shirt, pulled it off and threw it away. Her naked skin threw off a blast of nearly unbearable heat, and Tate wanted nothing more than to burn his mouth on her nearly flat chest and stomach. All the way down.

Then another pair of hands glided over Cymbria's bare shoulders. Tate could only watch as Will grabbed Cymbria's jaw, wrenched her head around and kissed her hard. Cymbria leaned back into her brother, returning his kiss, even as she rocked her hips against Tate's hard-on.

"Fuck, you guys are so weird," Tate groaned, but they didn't seem to hear him over the ravening noises in their throats.

Will slung his arm across Cymbria's collarbones, locking her in place as he kissed her deep and deeper. Until it could no longer be called a kiss, and Tate no longer felt aroused but drugged. His limbs grew numb and heavy. His breath came in labored gusts. The conduit of Will and Cymbria's joined mouths glowed white, even as the dark chasm of their hunger yawned open.

Cymbria flattened her palms against Tate's chest. It burned like a branding iron. He gasped, raising his weak arms to push her away. She grabbed him around the neck and crushed him to her, toasting his face on her breasts. Under her skin, he felt the rhythmic contraction of muscle. Her whole body acted as a pump, drawing not blood but something even more vital from the living pulp of him, and shotgunning it into Will.

Tate found himself thrown back as Will hauled Cymbria off his lap and pushed her down on the sofa beneath him. Tate rolled to the floor, banging his shoulder on the coffee table. Through bleary eyes, he watched their passionate embrace turn brutal.

Will kept his mouth clamped hard over Cymbria's as she whimpered and struggled. Her wrists bruised and her skin blanched as she fought, but Will held her down, appearing to grow stronger as she weakened. Finally, her body went limp and her big eyes rolled back before closing. Will broke the kiss. Then he stroked Cymbria's hair until the last drops of tension drained from her mottled face and she fell solidly unconscious.

Tate couldn't believe the difference when Will slid off the couch to sit on the floor. The heroin addict pallor was gone, replaced by the pearly glow of health, and his eyes glittered like chipped onyx.

Will turned to him with that devil's smile. "You're not looking so hot, Tater tot."

"Wha . . ." Tate couldn't even form the one-word question.

"She wasn't lying." Will took a deep contented breath. "What little you got tastes damn fine. I haven't felt this good in decades."

Tate tried to lift his head. Might as well have been a mountain. He glanced over at Cymbria's blue-tinged skin and purple lips. "Is she . . ."

Will responded with one of his withering looks. "Like I'd shove my only family in the proverbial oven for you?"

"Then why?"

Will grazed his knuckles over the bruise forming on Tate's shoulder. "Little Sister likes you an awful lot. Would've hated herself for killing you, and I can't have her hurt like that." Tate's heart struggled to pound the adrenaline through his body as Will's face moved in closer. "I like you too, Tater. At least I like the person I think you could be. But I could still drain you dead without losing a speck of sleep over it. So the question becomes—what am I gonna do with you?"

The question sank into the murky grog of Tate's mind. He tried to move his fingers and found he couldn't. He attempted to speak, but his voice wouldn't come. His pulse slowed. His eyes refused to focus. Death wasn't as unappealing as it ought to have been, and he'd already left so much behind, it would be easy to drift away. In spite of all that, Tate wasn't ready.

"Good choice," Will said, sliding on top of him. "Try to relax. This might feel strange. For both of us."

Strange was one way of putting it. Strangely repellent. Strangely compelling. Will's mouth tasted like butter and cinnamon, like Cymbria, and his wiry body crushed Tate into the floor. Whatever the mechanism, skin contact seemed to get the job done, but slowly. Kissing—or fucking, for that matter—created a direct pipeline. Typically, the flow went from the prey to predator. Now, Will forced it in the opposite direction, creating violent turbulence. Tate gagged as it gushed into him and tried to pull away but Will bit into his tongue, forcing his mouth wide open.

Luminous energy filled the chambers of Tate's heart and lit up his blood. Strength flooded back into his limbs and he moaned when his revived erection pushed against Will's. It made sense now. This was more than their fuel source. It was a narcotic, an aphrodisiac, an elevator, a regenerator. In its clutches, pain, regret, morality, and identity were rendered meaningless. The cries of extinct animals.

Tate ran his hands under Will's shirt feeling his skin heat to a blaze. Like a shot of ice cold Chopin pouring fire down his throat. The kind of vodka you sip alone, not because you have a problem, but because it's just that special.

Will broke the seal of their mouths and panted against Tate's neck, the harsh rasp of worn out machinery. Tate didn't know what else to do for Will, so he held him.

Until a little girl's laugh rang out in the hallway.

Pushing Will off, Tate scrambled to his feet, wincing as his teeth scraped his bitten tongue. Will propped himself up and licked away the blood trickling out of his mouth. He looked even worse than he had earlier in the evening. Skull clearly defined under his bleached skin. Cheeks flushed with sickness rather than health. Death boiled over.

The girl's laugh echoed through the stairwell.

"Those kids, what are they?" Tate asked.

"Dreams," Will muttered.

"You mean ghosts?"

Will's glazed eyes sharpened. "No ghosts here. Little Sister and I, we clean our plates."

Rage simmered in Tate's rejuvenated veins. "There are no other tenants in this building."

"Think of it as serial monogamy."

"Or serial murder."

Will uttered a weak laugh. "Does a wolf murder a rabbit?"

"Is that what you are? Wolves?"

"Wish I knew. Unfortunately, this ain't a fairy story. There's no woodsman coming to the rescue, or an evil witch with a candy house, or a moldy old book with all the answers. Sometimes the breadcrumbs don't lead anywhere."

"They led me here."

"And it's a good job more people don't know the way. Otherwise, we'd have a queue out the door. Don't act like you don't know."

Tate knew. Sex was only a word, a crude act that couldn't begin to describe the pleasure of that metaphysical energy dialysis. But that's not all it was. He felt something that night with Cymbria. He felt it tonight in the midst of their fucked up three-way, and again, just now, on the floor. He felt cared for. Of course, that was part of their game, wasn't it? Seduction.

"That's all I am to you? A meal?"

"Christ, don't push it." Will managed to sound dangerous despite his exhaustion.

"You wanna hear something that makes you feel like a special snowflake? Listen to your heart, yeah? The fact that it's beating right now makes you special. The fact that I've never, in over a hundred years, done what I just did for you makes you fucking special."

Tate stared at his shoes. "She said I was the right one to let in."

"But not the right time. You're too thin."

Tate's hands covered his stomach. "What?"

"Your soul, dumbass. It's emaciated. Saw it the second I laid eyes on you. Christ knows how long you've been starving yourself of everything good in life." Will's bruised eyes softened. "Cym promised me it would work out, that she could fatten you up. I may be a grouchy son-of-a-bitch, but there's not much I wouldn't do to make her happy."

Tate swallowed hard. "Then let me stay."

Will shook his head. "Go back to your brother and your bar. Watch your disgusting nephews grow up. Do it right this time. Live the life you want. Write that novel. Drink with your friends. Fall in love. Break some hearts. Make a big fat feast of your existence. And when you're stuffed so full you're tearing at the seams, then you'll come home to us. To Leighaven."

Tate shook his head. "But I can't leave the two of you, not like this."

"You can." Will tensed like a feverish panther. "Or I'll take back everything I just gave you with interest. I'll have you in ways you can't even imagine, and I know a part of you wants it, but timing is everything, Tater."

Tate shoved his hands in his pockets and his fingers clutched his car keys. All he needed to escape. If only he wanted to.

Will didn't wait for a final answer. He dragged himself onto the couch where he curled his body around Cymbria's, kissed her ear, closed his eyes, and joined her in a death-like slumber. Twin corpses. Babes in the woods. But instead of a cadaverous chill, they radiated heat so intense it turned the entire apartment into an oven. If Tate stayed much longer, the Leighavens might literally cook him for dinner.

In the hall, Tate heard the tramp of little feet. Dreaming familiars. Echoes of what they'd once been. Human children. Feral and starved, their will to survive bent the universe. Transformed them into something you couldn't bottle. A strange brew.

Tate pulled on his shirt and left number nine. He dawdled down the stairs, past the office, through the heavy front door, and jogged up the block to his car without so much as a glance over his shoulder. When the time came, he wouldn't need a trail of crumbs to find his way back to Leighaven. He had history here, and history never died. No matter how dark, or how still, if you got real close and real quiet, you'd hear it breathing.

AUTHOR'S STORY NOTE

Fairytale retelling is a popular sport amongst writers. We can't resist mining the veins of subtext running through those grim yarns, and Hansel & Gretel in particular always struck me as a story with more to say. About hunger. About losing your way.

What happens when babes in the woods refuse to curl up and die? What happens to the next lost soul to stumble across the gingerbread house? What happens when the fairytale doesn't end at happily ever after?

MISS_VERTEBRAE

ERIC LAROCCA

From *Rejected for Content 4: Highway to Hell*
Editor: Jim Goforth
Publisher: J. Ellington Ashton Press, Wetworks

GREETINGS FROM ELVAGOG

Date: 01/24/2015 7:32 a.m. Elvagog Standard Time

From: miss_vertebrae@elvagog.net

To: louismarsh64@gmail.com

They'll have found my body by the time you read this, lover.

If you think the first thing that expires when you die is pain, you're wrong.

I'm dead.

And the small cyst of pain I've been hosting since birth still tickles me in all the usual places.

————————

DISSECTIONS IN THE KEY OF ME

Date: 01/24/2015 7:59 a.m. Elvagog Standard Time
From: miss_vertebrae@elvagog.net
To: louismarsh64@gmail.com

I wish I could perform my own autopsy.

I wish I could see myself outside of myself.

When I was only seven months old and in my mama's tummy, my father found a baby German Shepard he called Maggie.

She stayed even when my father didn't. Mama said he never loved us.

I always wish I could see myself the way Maggie saw me.

————————

HOLES WHERE FACES SHOULD BE

Date: 01/24/2015 9:17 a.m. Elvagog Standard Time
From: miss_vertebrae@elvagog.net
To: louismarsh64@gmail.com

Did I ever tell you about the man who could regrow separated limbs? This one's better than the one about the man who could defecate with his asshole closed or the woman who taught her vagina how to talk and tell jokes.

He's a factory hand who assembles bits of machinery at one of the bigger warehouses outside of Worcester, Massachusetts. Teaching himself to delight in the invariability of the everyday sameness, he scarcely gripes to fellow laborers and even seems to enjoy the predictability of his post at times. It isn't until his acceptance of tedium turns to utter carelessness that he allows his right hand to be caught in one of the larger machines and the hope of monotony is literally pulverized.

One out of five fingers remains; four glistening red stumps grimace at their misfortune. Strands of fat tendons violently wrenched from the pinkness of rubbery sinew flower from the channels ribboning without any sort of precision or accuracy from the palm of his hand to his forearm. His body stirs, the agony so intense it renders him voiceless as threads of arteries joining his wrist with his hand snap and his hand loosens permanently. Ignoring the pain, he cannot help but feel sadness for his right arm's only relative as it slumps on its side, rejected from the body corporate.

His sadness is suddenly dashed, however, as he senses the tickle of cartilage lengthening where his hand had once been and veins unraveling and furiously curling themselves about the cylinder of the new bones that seem to spider in five neatly calculated geometric directions. He watches, unblinkingly, as new supple and spongy pink tissue proliferate instantly and flesh follows suit. When he no longer senses the enthusiastic disagreement between cartilage and rubbery bands of ligaments as they shift, he tightens and contracts his newly formed digits and watches them flex.

Although the new hand appears to possess the same health and fortitude of the previous one, it seems considerably divorced from the rest of his being and occasionally ticks with the identical cramps of agony as before when it was severed, his fingertips drooling with what appear to be black tar. He's met with equal astonishment as he watches the disjointed hand on the ground stir and shift, making viciously frenetic movements. Its gaping aperture bubbles and foams as rounded pipes explode outward and dark red cables of arteries uncoil neatly around the expanding shafts of white. From the small severed hand on the ground mushrooms the beginnings of a man; one that was just as tall as him and just as lean. A duplicate.

The inauguration of the new being is just as violent and painful as the unbearable process of a proper birth. The thing twitches violently on the ground, making spastic seizure-like movements, as muscle fattens and more veins sprout from the frothing tissue. It isn't long before the entirety of the thing's legs, groin, torso, and shoulders adjust and became fully formed.

He recognizes himself in every inch of the new being—from the dark brown mole ornamenting the instep of the thing's left foot to the small scar on his left pectoral from a childhood injury. Although the thing's development of living matter seems to halt, leaving the being headless, its inability to see or sense leaves it with hardly any handicap at all as it swings immediately at him, tearing at his lips and eyes and making them its own.

It's not long before the beginnings of a head flourish from the severed lips that look like two fat pink slugs. Eyes join them and ears and nose as well. Gaping holes are left in his face where robbed organs and muscles had once been. The gaping duct where his mouth had once been, so miserable over the loss of lips, begin to implode, suddenly collapsing itself inward into a crater making a permanent home in his face. His eyes, nose, and ears eventually do the very same thing until the entire man's front has been compressed.

Although he no longer has ears, he can somehow hear what the thing said to him.

"I'm a better YOU than YOU'LL ever be," it says, tongue flexing and seemingly relishing in the delivery of every syllable. "I can talk better, eat better, work better, and fuck better."

The man does not die as you might think. Instead, enduring the permanent stress of his compression day after day, he follows the thing around until he loses all sense of self and the thing becomes a truer him than he had ever been.

He still sometimes talks, though—a hole where his face should be.

––––––––

SHE LAUGHS AT MỸ LAI

Date: 01/24/2015 11:56 a.m. Elvagog Standard Time
From: miss_vertebrae@elvagog.net
To: louismarsh64@gmail.com

Every nerve in my body shrieked as they tore the flesh from my fat.

I don't miss my skin much.

I feel much more honest without it.

In fact, I'm watching it being hung right now by the two surgeons that took it. They come back to me every now and then and kiss my nakedness, as if praising their craftsmanship. My skin hangs on a hook and looks like a large rubbery body suit; pleats of the excess dangle obscenely and small bees whisper out in droves from the sulking labia. For the first time, I see myself outside of myself and I laugh. They laugh with me and call me, Miss Vertebrae.

There is a group of little naked boys playing beneath it, their skin wound with barbed wire and cemented with ash from mornings in the charnel house where they're usually forced to elect an unfortunate member of their brethren, decapitate him, and take turns shitting down the be-headed spine. I see perhaps twenty-three or twenty-four of them. Some of them lag behind the other ones as if pained, handicapped. Perhaps their discomfort comes from the scalding needles that are typically forced into their scrotums every morning. Sometimes they come around with loud percussive and horn instruments and they serenade the pageant of gro-tesquery while the more unlucky ones are humped by headless wild dogs. Not today, though. When they're not blowing their horns or banging their drums, they shove little scraps of food in their gaping black mouths and make little gobbling noises.

There was a young boy brought to the charnel pit today. They called him "Girlroot." They laid him out and made him suck on the hot-iron prick of the two-headed-ram. Then, they buried him in excrement up to his shoul-ders and lit his hair with fire.

I thought perhaps I had known him. His body, that is. It's strange how you can know the confidence of one's body without actually knowing them. It was then that I saw two empty outlets on both sides of his nose and real-ized how I'd known him in life. You and I had taken his eyes and sold them.

The small band of children will come back tomorrow, short one more member, and play another song.

————————

GIRLROOT

Date: 01/24/2015 1:07 p.m. Elvagog Standard Time

From: miss_vertebrae@elvagog.net
To: louismarsh64@gmail.com

When Isaiah is eleven, he invents a game he calls "Alien Autopsy."

The game's invention is purely an accident at first.

One morning, after a bath, he lays himself out on his bed and, with his mind very much elsewhere, his pubescent hands begin to outline the entirety of his unexplored body. His nipples toughen at the excitement of the self-discovery and possibility of his senses as his index fingers and thumbs pinch both identical rounded pink knobs on his chest. Isaiah pretends his hands are no longer his own, but instead belong to some sort of strange creature with many tentacles that had abducted him in order to study lifeforms on Earth. It never scares him. The thought that he, out of billions of earthly candidates, has been picked for analysis delights him, in fact. He feels special and the painful reminders of his inadequacy in gym class seem so trivial in their sudden insignificance as his alien digits continue their inquiry.

His hands wander further down, gently toying and examining the round divot in the center of his belly. It's when his hands reach his flaccid boy-hood that his mind reels from its comatose state and flowers with minute throbs of untouched bliss. Pulling his foreskin back, he examines it, admiring the configurations of veins running from the base to the tip. He rubs it with the palm of his hand, back and forth, sometimes gripping the hardening shaft and moving his hand up and down the length. To his surprise, the instrument seems to tremble as though its bloating purple head seems to be eagerly anticipating the arrival or dismissal of something.

His hands continue moving up and down for several minutes until a feeling of exhilaration overwhelms his entire body, muscles contracting and shoulders tightening. He rests his hand, body still reeling from the sudden invigoration. Excited and yet bewildered at the same time by the weakening spasms of elation quivering throughout his entire form, he wonders if this is what "getting high" means. The two boys who live next door are always going on and on about "getting high." Isaiah had always thought you need a cigarette and some of those funny looking herbs to feel good and get off. He's relieved to find out this wasn't the case. Smoking always made his lungs ache anyhow. He's content to know all he needs is the strength of his right hand and some saliva.

He wants to ask his father if he knows this method of self-pleasure and, if so, he wonders especially why his father has never told him. The window of opportunity for asking is significantly limited, however, as his father isn't home most nights. Dad's the night watchman at the hospital just two towns over. The nights that he is home, he always brings a lady friend that makes far too much noise with repeated supplications to a deity. *Maybe he's teaching her what I learned,* Isaiah thinks to himself.

Regardless, he learned how to brush his teeth and wipe himself after using the toilet without his father's help; he figures he shouldn't be so surprised to think his father wouldn't share all the prospects of his growing body. He's startled, however, when one afternoon his father sits him down and tells him about the "girlroot."

"What's that?" Isaiah asks.

"It's, unfortunately, what you've got inside you," his father says. "Your mother knew. We talked about it before she passed."

Isaiah can't help but wonder why his father's kept this from him for three years.

"Most boys don't have it, you see? But then, there are some ones that do," he explains. "It's got to be cut out, though. Permanently."

Isaiah knows his father has known for quite some time now what the other boys call him while waiting for the school bus in the morning. "Limp-wrist." "Mary." "Fruitcake." Some of them might be amusing if he weren't taking the brunt of it. Ones like "Oklahomo," "Marmite Miner," and "Chutney Ferret" confused his tears with involuntary giggles. His embarrassment is overshadowed by the pure elation that his father has sat him down and has acknowledged him.

"Where is this 'girlroot'?" Isaiah asks. "What does it look like?"

"It's somewhere deep inside you. Different places for the boys that do have it. But, it's there," his father says. "Remember those spinning wheels we had talked about?"

Isaiah feels pressure in his hairless testicles.

"Yes."

"Maybe it's there?"

"What does it look like?" Isaiah asks.

He watches as his father shifts in his chair, visibly uncomfortable.

"I don't know," he says. "I've never seen one. But you'll know it when you get rid of it. And you have to make certain you do. You'll feel better."

Isaiah wonders if anything on earth aside from his right hand has the potential to make his eleven year old self feel any better or more euphoric than the ending result of playing "Alien Autopsy." Although he figures that perhaps his father's acknowledgement and pride in him might outbalance the excitement of his game of self-pleasure.

He twitches, sensing another spasm of pain in his testicles. The discomfort is inconsiderable at first, but soon begins increasing in duration and frequency. Despite the intermittent throbs of pain, he feels overwhelmed with a sudden happiness, convinced he has located his body's girlroot.

After making certain his father's car has left the garage for another midday run to the package store, Isaiah sneaks out to the backyard and recovers a flat-head screwdriver from the toolshed. Its tip glistens in the light, immaculate and prepared for usage.

Isaiah wonders what his girlroot will look like as he lays the screwdriver on his bed and begins to undress himself. *Maybe it will look like some sort of alien slug or salamander*, he thinks to himself. He can scarcely contain his excitement at the prospect of his father's happiness. He plays the scenario over and over in his head of how it might transpire. Maybe he will simply leave the girlroot on his father's bed, like the head of a slaughtered beast. Or perhaps he'll greet his father at the front door with the dreaded thing being held with a pair of pliers. They could then flush it down the toilet together.

He's trembling with unbridled exhilaration now as he sits at the edge of his bed and works up an erection. *I can't "get high" yet. Not yet*, he thinks to himself; although the temptation is already there and reaching perhaps five inches in his hand. He has decided that the pleasure would be a treat for his victory. Once the shaft has hardened to its fullest extent and the glans of the head inflate purple, with one finger, Isaiah gently opens the small slit. The lips frown at first, dripping tiny pellets of urine from a recent trip to the bathroom; more manipulation, however, and they comply, parting further.

Isaiah grabs hold of the screwdriver and rests its tip at the mouth of his penis, the cold frankness of the metal opposing the warmth of his flaring urethra. With a grunt of determination and an unthinking thrust, the screwdriver goes inside Isaiah. He winces, eyes watering as he works the tip deeper and deeper down the tube of his shaft. Stirring the tip of the screwdriver in its place, he hopes he will recognize what his girlroot might feel like. Instead he feels nothing but a rush of warm fluids. He suddenly feels as though he has to pee. With a quick tug, he nervously jerks the rod of the screwdriver out of his groin's pipe and senses a molten liquid violently spout from its mouth. His father will beat him into a pulp if he finds he has peed the bed and carpet.

Isaiah grabs his crotch and it's then that he recognizes the fluid streaming out from the duct is not urine, but is in fact red. His erection is fountaining out torrents of blood. He cries out, sobbing at the realization. With both panicky hands, he grabs hold of his groin's weakening cylinder and tries to discourage its aim; however, even under the slightest duress of touch, the slit at the head of his boyhood widens with another profound jet of redness, pumping the spray all over the carpet and the wooden train set he had set in the corner and hasn't played with in three years.

Isaiah collapses, his naked body convulsing in a pool of his own blood still draining from his disfigured flute. Although the pain quiets most other senses in his eleven-year-old self, he cannot help but feel an excruciating defeat for not cutting out his girlroot.

His brain lives on for a few seconds.

Dad's going to be disappointed, he thinks; then, he dies.

———————

THE KINDNESS OF STRANGERS

Date: 01/24/2015 3:59 p.m. Elvagog Standard Time
From: miss_vertebrae@elvagog.net
To: louismarsh64@gmail.com

When I was nine, my mother said that the two round duffels of wind in my chest were as unreasonable as I was. They hardly ever inflated and I was always coughing because of their lack of cooperation. The sailors and bankers in suits that my mother would recruit would gripe, complaining that my coughing would depress the little tails poking from their front that would wag with anticipation and press against me.

One evening, an older gentleman in a burgundy colored velvet blazer and black crocodile loafers afforded the purchase of my loins for an uninterrupted twenty-five minutes and only lasted seven of them. Physically uninspired to repeat the activity, he seemed far more interested in the condition of my respiratory system. My body sweating, I answered him with words that probably sounded like coughs to him. He rested his arm on my shoulder and made me hold out my hand. I did and a collection of little white pills slid from his palm and into mine.

I heard him use the word "steroid" and he said these pills would help. He watched me take one and smiled. He never returned to the closet above the laundry room where Mama would make me wait for men, but his memory repeated to me often. The reminder of him grew in little calcified beads all over my body where my hair was supposed to grow. Instead of my girlhood maturing as my Mama had told me with a pelvic girdle wreathed with a tress of sprigs that most men savor, my fingers found the disappointing fossilized dots that would enflame under touch. The pain increased as more grew and I could hardly move without the soreness of the small grains chafing against one another.

Clients dwindled, understandably, and eventually never called again.

That was the winter that Mama died.

_____

TALK NICE TO ME

Date: 01/24/2015 5:58 p.m. Elvagog Standard Time
From: miss_vertebrae@elvagog.net
To: louismarsh64@gmail.com

The soles of his custom-made patent leather Oxfords click anxiously on the tiled floor of the doctor's exam room. Jonathan McCoy can scarcely contain his delight. His hand rests on his wife's thigh as he sits beside her, rubbing her leg, his fingers occasionally harassing the hem of her flower-print skirt. She doesn't seem to mind. Her concentration is focused on the male practitioner, maybe 5'9 and gowned in a knee-length white coat. He stands beside the screen and points to the MRI scan of her brain glorified on the wall. Jonathan notices Colleen's eyes water as the practitioner speaks and animatedly gestures to the monitor.

The highlighted photograph looks like a fileted jellyfish; a small round nugget of silvery whiteness, perhaps the size of a moth, noticeably lines the periphery of the organ. Jonathan's ears do not seem to register the doctor's words as his mouth moves, instead silence blaring between the openings of his lips; infrequently his auditory system records the word "malignant." He catches the words: "atypical," "surgery," "chemotherapy," and "futile" as well. His entire body loosens with joy; one instrument of his anatomy in particular seems to harden with enthusiasm, imagining her body's throbbing kernel of discomfort. He thinks of deleting his online handle, cyst_licker_69, from the frequently visited chatrooms.

He reaches for Colleen's hand and her grip is weak. Biting his lip, anxious for her attention, Jonathan unfortunately goes wanting. He admires her head—her perfect head—and studies the arrangement of hair, neatly pulled back in a bun. The stiffness in his pants toughens as he imagines a small and orderly arranged aperture ventilating her left temple and advertising her cerebrum. The very idea of the integrity of her head's organ spoiled by a minute knob of tissue only excites his growing erection more. Her cranium seems to bloat with the prospect of unlimited variations of sexuality.

She does not say much during the car ride back to the apartment on the Upper West Side. Only a few grunts and one-word answers regarding her headache. She has always been one to talk to herself. But, not today. The silence is unbearable for Jonathan. He notices how the corners of her eyes collect water and her mascara clots in thick lumps.

"Talk nice to me," he hears in an unfamiliarly feminine voice.

He turns and the door to the bathroom closes, Colleen on the other side.

"Did you say something?" he asks.

Jonathan hears nothing other than the vehement arguing of taxicab horns outside down on 73rd Street. The toilet flushes and Colleen opens the door.

"Don't you have to be back down at the office?" she says, passing by him.

He loosens his tie, flexing his esophagus. "They can wait."

Jonathan observes Colleen as she sits at the edge of the bed and kicks off her heels. He notices her flagrant preoccupation with reviewing his leather wallet resting on the nightstand, more importantly the small circular indentation pressing outward along the fold that's about the size of his wedding band. She turns and he's too late to hide his naked finger, undressed from several nightly meetings with bald women who hide small round secrets in their breasts and brains. Sometimes men as well, who keep similar unrevealed truths in their rectums.

"Don't let me keep you," she says.

He gently approaches her. "You don't mind if I stay, do you?"

Colleen says nothing.

Jonathan sits beside her, mouth parting with the intent of words but eventually merely eliminating an exhalation. His hands are awkward and tremble, unsure where to begin. He rests one on her shoulder and she turns from him. He leans closer, pressing his lips against the nape of her neck, and drawing in her scent through his nostrils.

"Talk nice to me," he hears again.

"I will," he moans, running his mouth along the extent her collar.

Colleen turns, seemingly bewildered. "What—?"

Jonathan's mouth is far too preoccupied with her ear to offer an answer. His hands are already beneath her skirt and playfully teasing the knots of pubic hair. He presses his mouth to her face and frenziedly pecks her cheek, forehead, and lips. Dragging down her panties, he tours his finger around her frowning womanhood, brings his thumb to his nose, and violently inhales the dampness of her musk. She rakes her head back on the cushions, making soft cooing noises, visibly enthralled with the pleasure and yet thoughtful to discourage herself to indulge completely in the activity.

He unzips his pants and holds his erection with both hands, envisioning the small lump in her brain quivering the way her clitoris does under correct stimulation. Although he expects she might, she does very little to oppose him as he mounts her. He massages her nose and forehead with the length of his shaft, his appliance finally reaching her temple. His entire body shudders on the brink of orgasm.

"Talk nice to me," he hears again; this time the disembodied voice as fine and as trill as a whistle.

It's then that he notices the left side of her cranium bloat exaggeratedly as though a balloon were expanding from the inside of her skull. Although nothing can discourage Jonathan from concluding the extent of his pleasure, his senses otherwise impaired by the ecstasy of satisfaction are perceptive enough to appreciate Colleen's anguish as a portion of her head continues to swell.

"Wait—!" she sobs, her voice trembling with panic as she squirms beneath the heaviness of his body.

Colleen heaves Jonathan off of her and sprints from the bed to the washroom, occasionally scowling in unadulterated agony, the intense pressure of cranial inflation observably unbearable and remarkable in its profoundness. Jonathan rushes after her, grabbing and pulling at her dress. She screams, sobbing, as she catches the embellished nature of her distended skull in the bathroom mirror. Jonathan throws his naked body at her and she swings both arms at him, shouting until hoarse. She turns again to admire the deformity and her footing is unbalanced. Colleen cries out and her thrashing arms go limp as her head slams against the rim of the toilet.

Her body is still, head draining redness all over the tiled floor. Jonathan turns her over and admires the vent perverted along the side of her head. Cartilage and puffy tumefaction bulge furiously from the yawning maw. Most notably ornamenting the rubbery looking matter is a bulbous wad of otherwise unnatural distension. Jonathan's penis has not weakened in its stiffness; in fact, it's harder than ever as he lovingly admires the tumor in its glistening brilliance. Shutting his eyes, he guides his cock into the outlet and begins to massage the plump tissue already generously lubricated with blood.

His entire body palpitates in euphoria as his pelvis rocks back and forth against the side of her head, the wetness of blood dripping from her hair occasionally tickling the sensitivity of his testicles. As he strokes his erection against the tumor one final time, the duct of his urethra opens and violently launches fat buttery globs of cream all over the exposed colorless tissue and splintered bone. He moans as he strokes the last of the discharge from his tube, smearing it in the grooves of her unprotected brain matter.

Suddenly, he hears it again.

"Talk nice to me."

His eyes return to the tumor, three times larger in size than when previously observed, drenched in blood and wet ribbons of ejaculate.

"What—?"

He feels foolish speaking as he holds his sagging erection in one hand.

The tumor stirs in its place with a jellied gurgle. Its voice is infant-like. "Will you talk nice to me?"

Jonathan lowers his head, bringing his hands closer to the shiny fat wad of material. The growth seems to twitch excitedly at the anticipation of his touch.

"She talked nice to me," it says, wiggling in the oily pulp of Colleen's mashed brain. "She was sweet to me. She can't take care of me now, though. But you can. Right?"

Its impish articulation curls as though genuinely hopeful Jonathan might.

He holds out his hand and the clump slides from the channel of brain matter right into his open palm. It squirms gleefully as he holds it and carries it toward the bed where he rests it on a small pillow. The tumor wriggles, giggling merrily as it rolls onto the cushion.

"You have to talk to me," it demands. "If you don't, my cells will weaken and I'll die. If you talk, I'll give you whatever you want."

"What—what should I say?" Jonathan stammers.

"Tell me a story," it says. "Anything you like."

Jonathan opens his mouth and says whatever comes to his mind. He speaks for hours and hours on end; the tumor merely sits, listens, and occasionally chuckles, bouncing with laughter.

In the morning, Jonathan wakes to a putrid smell drifting from the bathroom. All that is left on the cushion is a small ringlet of blood and semen detailing where the tiny growth had once been. It's nowhere to be found. Jonathan's nostrils flare again at the reminder of his dead wife. He cannot be bothered with that now.

He swallows an Aspirin.

Nothing seems to soothe the intense pressure within his head. It feels as though his brain might explode.

He brings his hand to his ear and his fingers are wet with small beads of blood. His canal feels loosened, enflamed with redness, as though something had just crawled inside.

_____

AFTERBIRTH

Date: 01/24/2015 7:32 p.m. Elvagog Standard Time
From: miss_vertebrae@elvagog.net
To: louismarsh64@gmail.com

They'll have found my body by the time you read this, lover.

My head will be situated in the entrails of Maggie as half of her reclines on the carpet and the other half dozes beside the kitchen table. I found the hammer wet with her blood you must've used lying in the bathroom sink. I cleaned the dissecting scissors and scalpels as well. When I was finished, I took tubes of her intestines as thick as garden hoses and kissed them, looping them around my neck like a pashmina as I lay beside her and listened to her stillness. A small rope of excrement bowed from her anus, probably squeezed out from fear, I imagine. The clotting flecks of dog food never to be finished digesting bulged like tiny calcified nuggets from the cylindrical tissue glazed with red mucous. It tickled my neck. I laughed at her reminder and then thought of you as I looked into the gaping cavity of her divided lower body, most organs gone.

I had hoped you'd return and find us together. But I expected the selfish-ness of your sham deal would outweigh your concern for me once you were handed the money. I'm sure it's all gone by now. You're lucky that pinhead you made the deal with could barely tell the difference between a dog kidney and a human one. I couldn't help but think of his daughter and all the misery that was to make company with their family once they found out. I haven't known true misery in a while. I wondered whether I'd recognize it or not when it came again. I, of course, knew it would; but, didn't know whether you'd bring it or the thing I'd been carrying in my tummy for almost nine months would.

You're worried now.

Or am I giving you too much credit for caring?

After I'd found what you had done to Maggie, I sensed something warm running down my thigh, my body unlocking a new and damp torrent of soreness. I thought I had wet myself. My hands were red and I knew it was the beginnings of her.

A month early.

She didn't take too long to deliver.

Twelve hours.

First thing I did was cut the tether that guaranteed part of her to me with my teeth. I expected I'd feel relief, but none came. Instead I felt sadness, an unshakeable melancholia for her and all the aching she was to inherit.

I knew it wasn't reasonable—how she was helpless from the start. Then, I wrapped her in cloth and laid her out on your pillow. God forbid she went wanting for her father's kisses as I did when I was little. I hope you kiss her often and think of me when you do, knowing she's your daughter and granddaughter as well.

I was so happy to know I'd found you and that you loved me and would talk nice to me. Even if you never really knew me the way a daughter should know her father.

I hope I see you again in death so I can worship the exquisiteness of your agony.

Because if you think the first thing that expires when you die is pain, you're wrong.

I'm dead.

And the small cyst of pain I've been hosting since birth still tickles me in all the usual places.

New ones too.

[miss_vertebrae has deactivated her account]

AUTHOR'S STORY NOTE

I once read that most computer users regularly access only 10% of the internet. That means that 90% of the web, like the depths of our planet's oceans, is hidden and still very much unknown.

While most may thankfully never wander into the secreted space known as "the deep web," almost all know it as a place of things better left unseen—a den of depravity where drugs, weapons, child pornography, and other unmentionables are exhibited and traded. Although nothing quite fills me more with a sense of dread than the unknown, the idea of seeing something I'm not supposed to see is equally troubling.

My fellow millennials' desensitization to violence and pornography may be very well-founded considering what we are able to access online, even so minimally. After all, we are the generation of "2Girls1Cup" and "2Kids1Sandbox"—viral shock videos meant to test the endurance of viewers. Regardless, as somebody who has witnessed the aforementioned videos (and, regrettably, many others of the like), there is still an assumption that nothing can quite compare to what waits for viewers in the darkest corners of the internet.

While the mysteriousness of the "deep web" might cause some un-ease, most can take comfort in the fact that it's inaccessible without the proper equipment and, of course, the stamina to search for the intended sites. Still, the concept of something unprompted coming forth from the "deep web" troubled me greatly enough to eventually become the foundation for "Miss_Vertebrae."

Told through a series of emails, "Miss_Vertebrae" operates as a story-within-a-story. The crux of the tale is founded upon the circumstances surrounding the life and death of the writer of the emails—a dead woman known only as, "Miss_Vertebrae"—as she tries to communicate a gruesome truth with her former lover, writing from a server located in the depths of the internet called "Elvagog." Secondary to her plight are several vignettes written by her—"Holes Where Faces Should Be," "Girlroot," and "Talk Nice to Me."

While the vignettes detail unrelated horrific situations and read as though they are bizarre urban legends lifted directly from the pits of online forums such as, Reddit or 4chan, each of the short pieces is intended to echo the themes prevalent in Miss_Vertebrae's overarching narrative. "Holes Where Faces Should Be" repeats the theme of identity found in deterioration, while "Girlroot" echoes the concept of sexual awakening and disgrace from a parent's neglect. Finally, and most im-portantly, "Talk Nice to Me" exemplifies the exploitation of decay as exhibited in Miss_Vertebrae's criminal profession as a human organ trafficker before her demise.

Perhaps one of the most fundamental themes of "Miss_Vertebrae" is the symbiotic relationship between birth and death. Readers would be well advised to pay close attention to the time stamps on each of the emails, as well as the number of emails written. You'll notice a methodi-cal sequence ebbing beneath the weight of the story that is intended to resemble birth and, consequently, decomposition.

There is an inherent voyeuristic tone set throughout the entirety of "Miss_Vertebrae," and for good reason. You're reading something you're not supposed to be reading. Right now, too.

[Account deactivated]

BED OF CRIMSON JOY

JASPER BARK

Published as a standalone novella by KnightWatch Press

I

ARE YOU SURE THIS IS A GOOD IDEA?" said Stanley, scratching at his grey hair and inspecting the bits of scalp under his fingernails.

His spectacles were perched on the end of his nose, giving him an expression halfway between a squint and a sneer. He was wearing his baggy fawn cardigan and tartan slippers.

For a second, Rose wondered if it was a good idea. Stanley wasn't cutting a dashing figure. "Stop being such a fusspot and come on," she said, turning the key in the back door.

"You're only watering the plants and feeding the cat," said Stanley. "I really don't see why you need me here."

"Just get inside will you." She gave him a push and he stumbled through the door into the utility room. Their neighbours had moved in seven months ago, and had already made extensive renovations.

"That's solid Corian," Stanley said, running his fingers along a work-top. "Nice work too." Rose walked through to the kitchen shaking her head. She'd forgotten that Stanley hadn't been inside since Samantha and Darren moved out.

Naturally he'd want to do all those male things, like inspecting the carpentry and admiring the quality of the materials. She'd have to fin-ish her chores quickly or she'd lose him altogether to his inspection of the new kitchen suite.

That wasn't the reason she'd brought him next door. Even if he hadn't realised yet. Rose sighed; she'd always been the one to take the lead in these matters. A momentary pang of regret welled up inside her. Regret for all the things she'd never had from her relationship.

She wanted to be needed, physically. She wanted a man who would chase her, wherever she led him. A man who would just take her, with-out Rose having to orchestrate the whole thing and lead him through it step by step.

But she was old now. Available men were thin on the ground and she did still have Stanley. He wasn't a passionate husband, but she didn't have much to complain about. Mainly the minor quirks and irritations any long-term marriage has to accommodate. Heaven knows, he put up with enough of hers.

"Are you finished yet?" said Stanley, hovering in the kitchen door. The cat eyed the food she'd put out with suspicion. Rose could never work out if the cat hated the food or just the fact that Rose put it out for her.

"I just have to do the orchids," Rose said. Stanley glanced around the kitchen at the new range cooker and the expensive oak cabinets. "Nice what they've done in here," he said. "They obviously have a bit of money."

"Hmm," said Rose, spritzing the orchids with water. She didn't want to encourage too much interest in the new kitchen.

"Right, well I'll be getting back while you finish that off," said Stanley.

"But you've only just got here."

"I've seen all I need to."

"What on earth do you want to go back home for?"

"The snooker's on in a minute, I don't want to miss it."

"But you haven't followed the snooker in ages."

"I caught a few matches on the iPlayer and got back into it."

"Well you can watch the next one on the iPlayer then."

"It's not the same as watching it live."

Rose let out a short, exasperated breath. She started to question the whole thing. It was just like Stanley to spoil everything before he even realised what was on offer. "There's something I want to show you upstairs," she said.

"We can't go up there."

"Why ever not?"

"Because it's not our house. They gave you the keys. I don't even know if they want me in the kitchen, let alone upstairs. It's not right."

"It can't do any harm. They'll never know."

Rose put her head to one side, tilted her hips and shot Stanley a knowing look. It was a look she'd first given him on Boscastle Beach, back in 1970. A look he recognised straight away.

"Oh," he said, and swallowed audibly, making his adam's apple bob. The look was enough to silence him. Rose took him by the hand and led him up the stairs. He wore the same shocked, yet acquiescent, expression he'd worn forty years ago.

Up until that moment, on Boscastle Beach, Rose had thought Stanley was being a gentleman, out of some antiquated notion of chivalry and respect. She learned, when she seduced him, that fear and inexperience had held him back.

She wished later that she hadn't chosen such a perfect spot for their first tryst. The act itself had been clumsy and embarrassing, and altered Rose's feelings about the secluded cove. She could never recall the location without a sense of awkwardness and regret.

At nineteen she'd been in awe of Stanley's intellect and his talent as a poet. He was only twenty-three when Rose met him and already his poems had been published in several small journals. One of the journals was even stocked by her university's library. She hadn't entirely liked the poems, but she'd admired his achievement. He was the first person in her social circle to be published.

Sadly, as a poet, Stanley had not made good on his early promise. He had improved as a lover, but he'd never quite gotten over the shift in power that sex brought to their relationship. He was threatened by Rose's sexual experience.

Stanley tried to compensate for his inferiority by subtly belittling Rose with his intellect. He wouldn't stoop to an outright insult. He did it all through inference and allusion. Because she recognised the source of his hostility, and because she loved him, Rose had learned to ignore the barbed comments and the subtle taunts.

Rose led Stanley across the landing to the spare room. Stanley was still taking in the reclaimed floorboards and the Farrow and Ball paint that had replaced the flock wallpaper, as Rose opened the door.

"So," she said, making a grand gesture. "What do you think?"

"What do I think of what?"

"Oh come on," she patted the mattress of the king-sized, four-poster bed that dominated the room. "What do you think I'm talking about?"

The four-poster bed took up most of the available space in the room. Rose had no idea how Peter and Bethany had gotten it in there. It was too big to go up the stairs or through the door, or even for them to have winched it through the window.

It was a Tudor style canopy bed, with intricately carved oak posts. A nymph and a satyr chased each other round the dark antique wood of the posts. The carved panels of the headboard depicted an obscene bacchanal, in which few of the sexual positions seemed physically possible. The bedspread and curtains were made of a deep red material with gold brocade stitching, decorated with an intricate crest made up entirely from genitalia.

"Oh it's the bed," said Stanley. "That's what you wanted to show me." He looked relieved, like a schoolboy who's been let off a scolding. "I thought . . . well, I mean, when you . . . anyway, I've seen it now. Come on, we'd better be going."

"Hold on, I'm not finished yet." Rose pulled herself up onto the bed and patted the mattress next to her. "Come join me."

Stanley looked more than a little hesitant. "Look Rose, this isn't right. We don't even know Peter and Bethany. We should be getting along now."

Rose sighed with exasperation. The bed was already starting to affect her. All she needed to do was to get Stanley to touch it.

She remembered the first time she saw the bed, when she popped over yesterday. She'd fed the cat and watered the plants and decided to have a nosey about. She got a delicious, clandestine thrill being in someone's house when they were away. It was like sharing an intimate slice of their everyday life, without them knowing.

After checking the cupboards, the bookshelves and the broom cupboard, and finding nothing of any note, Rose decided to head upstairs. The idea of checking the bedrooms gave her a little frisson, especially when she considered the things that might occur there, but they were disappointingly tasteful and bland.

Then Rose walked into the spare room and saw the bed. This was just the sort of secret she'd been hoping to unearth. The bed looked as though it had been waiting for her. She was appalled and fascinated by the carvings and the motif on the spread. Peter and Bethany seemed so prim and self-contained. She knew there had to be something lurking beneath their respectable facade, but she hadn't expected anything so exciting as this.

In the back of her mind she told herself it was time to go back downstairs and leave, she'd pried enough, and she still had to make Stanley's supper. She didn't listen though. Instead she went over to the bed and ran a hand over the spread. A static charge seemed to crackle up her arm. She didn't feel it in her body so much as her emotions, which gave it more force. Her breathing became quick and shallow and her heart beat faster.

The mattress was high and Rose had to pull herself up on to it. She felt a twinge from her bad hip as she swung her leg up. Rose cursed, and shifted her buttocks to ease the pain. She lay on her back and stared up at the tapestry on the underside of the canopy. It showed a naked woman, with large breasts, easing herself onto a large, erect phallus. The anatomical detail of the woman's labia, as they parted to accommodate the huge shaft of the phallus, was very graphic.

Rose was filled with a sudden yearning to be penetrated by such a huge phallus. To feel it, hard and swollen, pumping furiously inside her.

She slipped her hand down the front of her trousers and lifted the frayed elastic of her knickers. Her fingers searched out her clitoris. Rose could not remember the last time she'd done this. She felt out of practice, lacking both the dexterity and the rhythm she needed to please herself.

Then she looked up at the tapestry again and projected herself into the woman's position, imagined lowering herself onto such a magnificent cock and her fingers began to work their old magic.

The orgasm seemed to come from somewhere deep inside the bed. It seeped into her, moving down her thighs and up her spine, lighting up each of her nerve endings. She arched her back, knowing she'd pay for that in the morning but caring not a bit, and let out a moan that became a sob as her whole physique surrendered to the pleasure of coming.

When she was done, Rose lay panting on the bed. She brought her fingers up to her lips and tasted herself. Something she hadn't done since she was a teen, experimenting with personal pleasures. She was pleasantly surprised to find that, despite being long past her menopause, she still loved the taste of her own juices.

She wanted to feel those juices now. She'd gotten Stanley this far, he just needed one last little push.

"Do you think these posts were carved by hand?" she said. "Or one of those carving machines?"

"A router you mean?"

"Yes one of those, what do you think?"

"How on earth should I know?"

"Well, you're the expert. You have such a good eye for these matters. You know so much more than me."

Stanley went to examine one of the posts. Stroking his ego always worked. "I doubt you could get this detail with a router. Plus it's most likely an antique, they wouldn't have had the technology back then."

"Are you sure?"

"Just look at this finish, and the grain of the wood. This has to be done by hand. See how smooth it is."

Stanley ran his hand along the post and Rose smiled. He looked down at the front of his trousers with surprise. A huge bulge had appeared. He looked over at Rose, and she nodded, reaching out a hand to him as she threw back the covers.

For the first time in their marriage, Stanley didn't need to be led to the bed, didn't need to be guided and gently encouraged. He leaped on Rose.

She tore off his checked flannel shirt and tugged at his thermal vest while he fumbled with his belt.

"Just let me get my glasses off," Stanley said, as Rose tried to wrestle the vest over his head. Rose slipped off her blouse and skirt then pulled off her knickers. She was so excited she didn't even mind that Stanley hadn't noticed they were new.

Her bra was relatively new too. She was about to unclip it when she thought better of it. Better to keep an air of mystery, or at least let Stanley remember her breasts as they used to be. Not as the saggy things they were now.

Stanley was down to his Y-fronts and his socks. One was tartan and one was navy blue. Rose chose to ignore them. She pushed him onto his back, knelt next to him and removed the slightly stained brown and beige Y-fronts.

Stanley sprang free, his erect penis jutting expectantly from a little nest of grey pubic hair. Rose bent and took him in her mouth. He hadn't washed that morning, and he had an old man's musty scent, but he throbbed with appreciation beneath her lips and tongue. A drop of pre-cum trickled over her tongue and Rose felt herself moisten in anticipation.

Stanley groaned and Rose took him out of her mouth. She sat astride him and guided him into her. Rose closed her eyes and pictured the tapestry above her head. As Stanley filled her, she imagined herself as the woman, being taken by the giant phallus.

Rose began to grind her hips. She opened her eyes and caught Stanley's gaze. They smiled furtively at each other, reveling in the forbidden pleasure of fucking in a neighbour's bed.

Peter and Bethany would never expect such a thing. To them, Rose and Stanley were quaint and sexless. An older couple who lived next door. Someone with whom they exchanged Xmas cards and polite greetings in the driveway. People whom they pitied and patronised for their lower income and aging bones.

They certainly weren't the sort of people Peter and Bethany would imagine rutting like animals on their freshly laundered linen the minute they went off on holiday.

When they were done, Rose lay next to Stanley toying with the hairs on his chest. They were so perfectly white Rose imagined them the ghosts of hairs that once lived on Stanley's chest.

"What are you thinking about?" Rose asked him. Stanley chuckled, his mouth set in a supercilious smile.

"I was thinking of Betjeman, and his poem— 'Late-Flowering Lust.'"

"Do I want to hear this?"

Stanley ignored her and began to intone:

"I cling to you inflamed with fear
As now you cling to me,
I feel how frail you are my dear
And wonder what will be—

"A week? or twenty years remain?
And then—what kind of death?
A losing fight with frightful pain
Or a gasping fight for breath?

"Too long we let our bodies cling,
We cannot hide disgust
At all the thoughts that in us spring
From this late-flowering lust."

Rose rolled over on her side, with her back to Stanley. She blinked away the tears she didn't want him to see. For all his learning, Stanley suddenly seemed very old, yet very childish in his spite.

II

Three days later, Peter and Bethany came home and Rose returned their keys, posting them through the letterbox in an old brown envelope. She'd put the incident with Stanley from her mind, trying her best to forget it.

Rose was frying pork sausages for dinner when there was a loud rap at the front door. It was Peter; despite his tan, and his expensive pink polo shirt, he seemed deeply rattled. His long, thin face was ashen and he looked genuinely appalled about something.

"Peter," Rose said, tucking some loose hairs behind her ear. "How was your holiday?"

"What . . . ? Oh, my holiday, yes my holiday . . . it was fine thank you."

Peter breathed out heavily through his nose and looked at the floor. He put his hand on the back of his neck and shook his head.

"Look, there's no . . . erm, easy way to say this. But . . . well . . . just what do you think you were you doing in our spare room?" A cold wave of panic washed over Rose. How could he possibly know. There was no conceivable way. She had laundered all the sheets, put everything back as it was. There was no trace of their passion left in the room.

"I'm not sure I know what you're talking about," she said, trying to hide how dry her throat suddenly felt.

"Oh come on, it's not something you'd miss, is it?"

"I'm afraid you've got me at a loss Peter . . . I don't, I mean . . . I simply watered the plants and fed the cat like you asked. I didn't go anywhere near the spare room."

"What I want to know is how you got it up in the first place."

Rose almost gasped. Her shoulders went back and her brow furrowed with indignation. "I don't think I care for your tone Peter. Now, if you'll excuse me I have something on the stove."

Rose started to close the door but Peter blocked it with his hand. "Look, I'm just trying to make sense of it all. I'm not even really that cross, just perplexed. I don't understand how you got it through the door or even up the stairs. Did you get some men in? Was it delivered while we were away? Did you have to sign for it or something?"

"Peter, I'm sorry, you really aren't making any sense. Did we have to sign for what?"

"The bed of course, the ruddy great bed in the spare room."

"Wasn't that already there?"

"So you've seen it. You do know what I'm talking about."

"I might have glimpsed it."

"But I thought you said you didn't go anywhere near the spare room?"

"I had to get the cat down from upstairs at one point."

"The cat's not allowed upstairs."

"Exactly, so I . . . must have . . . chased her up there and caught a glimpse of it through the doorway. It's quite noticeable."

"I'll say it's bloody noticeable." Peter stared at her intently. Rose could tell he suspected she wasn't being entirely frank, but that wasn't the biggest of his worries. "So you really have nothing to do with it being there? Because it wasn't there when we left and you're the only person who's been in the house."

"Peter, I hardly know you and Bethany. Why would I put a bed in your spare room while you were away? I'm an old woman and Stanley's plagued by his back. How could we get a four-poster bed up those stairs?"

"You didn't pay someone else to do it then?"

"Why would we? We live on a pension. We've got better things to do with our savings than waste them on senseless practical jokes and expensive furniture."

"You didn't see anything suspicious while we were away. No one else calling round with deliveries or something."

"No, not a thing."

"You would tell me if you had seen something, wouldn't you?"

"Of course."

Peter shook his head and stared at the floor, trying to puzzle it all out. "It just doesn't make any sense." He looked up and stared Rose straight in the eye. "No one's threatening you are they? To keep quiet about all this I mean. You can tell me if they are."

"Peter, listen to yourself."

Peter stared up at the window of the spare room next door. Then he turned to go without saying a word of thanks or goodbye. Rose had the distinct feeling she'd been dismissed.

The sausages were burned black when she got back to the kitchen and she had to open a tin of beans instead. Her hands were shaking so much it took two attempts to get the lid off.

She thought at first it was from the confrontation with Peter. When she considered it however, she realised it was the bed that had shaken her. The mysterious bed that had seduced her and Stanley. The four-poster bed that hadn't been in the spare room when Peter and Bethany left for their holiday, but had somehow been waiting, just for her.

III

Late next afternoon, Rose saw workmen carrying chunks of carved wood and a mattress out to a skip in next door's drive. She recognised some of the carvings and the designs on the fabric that the men slung in the skip.

At the end of the day a truck came and took the skip away. Peter and Bethany probably paid a premium to get such prompt service.

Rose was surprised by how upset she felt about the disposal of the bed. It was an antique after all and probably one of a kind. It was wanton vandalism to hack it to pieces and dump it in a skip. It made her wonder what sort of people Peter and Bethany were to treat a rare object like the bed with such violent disregard.

Rose had let go of any foolish thoughts she had about the strange power of the bed. She and Stanley had just indulged in a foolish and uncharacteristic moment of madness that was all. A brief attempt to recapture their youth and deny the stifling hand of age. She was rather embarrassed by the whole incident now, as enjoyable as it had been.

Stanley hadn't looked her in the eye since. He'd retreated into his private world of snooker and DIY catalogues. Rose knew that he felt just as foolish and blamed her for it. It was childish of him, she knew, but he'd get over it if she gave him a bit of time and space.

She didn't suppose that Peter or Bethany would ask her to look after the property next time they went away. She didn't mind too much about this. There were too many memories in the house for her. The extensive renovations hadn't dulled the impact of those memories.

When Darren and Samantha lived there, Rose had been round at least twice a day. Their young children, Paul and Emily, had loved Rose and she was always babysitting and baking them treats. Rose would often have the kids after school once Samantha started work again, to allow her and Darren could keep up with the mortgage.

She and Stanley hadn't been able to have children, though Rose would dearly loved to have been a mother. They tried for a long time but it never happened. Rose had wanted to see a doctor but Stanley wouldn't agree. He felt it was a personal thing that should be kept between the two of them. He didn't want to go sharing these sorts of problems with a stranger, even if that stranger was a trained professional.

In truth, Rose knew that Stanley suspected the problem was with him, and he didn't want that medically confirmed. He already had enough hang-ups about his sexuality and Rose didn't want to make him feel any more insufficient.

Stanley turned to poetry to cope with the erosion of his confidence. For a while he was more prolific than he was when Rose first met him. He even placed a couple of the poems with prestigious publications. One of the poems he showed Rose ended with the line:

"Her womb was an instrument of revenge."

She wasn't entirely sure what that meant, but she knew he was subtly taunting her. Turning his inadequacy into hostility towards her. Making it all her problem. It was typical of Stanley to use his intelligence and learning to goad her in such a way that he remained above reproach, while Rose was made to feel insufficient because of her lesser intellect.

As the years drew on, Rose felt increasingly hollowed out by her broodiness. A deep yearning would chip away at her insides every time she saw a pregnant woman. Whenever she heard a small child call out 'Mummy' in a supermarket, Rose's own need to be called 'Mummy' would echo round her hollow interior like a cry of anguish in a canyon.

On her fifty-first birthday, Rose stopped bleeding altogether. The ticking of her biological clock had been silenced, once and for all, by menopause. She crawled into the bath with a bottle of red wine and tried to drown the emptiness with which she was swollen. The mocking emptiness that had eaten the life Rose longed to feel inside her.

Samantha had instinctively known this of course and, while they were good friends, she didn't mind exploiting it, not when it meant endless free childcare. When Darren left her, quite unexpectedly, for a younger woman he'd met at work, Samantha relied on Rose even more to help with the children.

That's when the problems started. As Samantha fell apart and was unable to cope, Paul and Emily came to depend more and more on Rose for their everyday parenting. When Samantha started to recover, she began to resent this. Rose was only trying to help, but the closer Paul and Emily got to her, the more Samantha hated her.

"You're not their mother," Samantha had screamed in her face, the last time Rose had seen her. "They're not your children, you can't take my place!"

Rose had simply come round with the schedule for the school's parent-teacher meetings. She had offered to drive Samantha there because her car was being repaired, and to wait for them if need be. Samantha had slammed the door in her face.

A month later they moved out and put the house on the market. Samantha didn't leave a forwarding address, nor did she bother to say goodbye.

Paul got in touch with her on Facebook for a while. Rose was over-joyed to hear from him and to find out how he and Emily were getting along. As soon as Samantha found out however, she blocked Rose and threatened her with a restraining order if she ever got in contact with the children again.

A long period of grieving followed for Rose. She was mourning not only the end of her relationship with Paul and Emily, but all her hopes of motherhood. She would never get to comfort or nurture them, or any child, again. She would never see them fall in love for the first time, go off to university, get married or bring home their own first-born child for her to see.

The emptiness that filled Rose made it so easy for people to get inside her. And when they did, something deep within her always died.

IV

The next morning Rose was violently sick. She woke feeling nauseous and only just made it to the bathroom before emptying her stomach.

By lunchtime she felt fine and put the vomiting down to a fleeting tummy bug. Her stomach was quite painfully bloated though, and the front of her pants felt tight and restricted. She sighed at the thought that her waist was growing once again and she'd probably have to let out all her clothes.

Rose opened the fridge to decide what to have for lunch. As she scanned the contents for inspiration, she was gripped with a sudden desire for pilchards and pickled gherkins. She hadn't had either for over a decade. She had no idea where the desire came from, but Rose could already taste them. Her mouth watered and her stomach rumbled its appreciation. They weren't foods she liked, but the need to eat them was overwhelming, as though the oily fish and sour vegetables would instantly fix everything that ailed her.

The next morning she woke just as nauseous and brought up everything she'd eaten the night before. There were no more problems for the rest of the day, other than a severely bloated stomach and a few odd cravings.

This pattern continued for the next few days. The doctor told her it was nothing to worry about, probably just a bug. "Come and see me in a few days time if the symptoms continue," she said, without looking up from her computer. "I'll give you some pills for the nausea." Rose had waited for over an hour and the appointment lasted less than three minutes.

The symptoms did continue, though Rose didn't bother to return to her doctor. The bloating got so severe all Rose could wear was a pair of old leggings and her sweatpants.

She stood in front of the mirror in their bedroom, about a fortnight after the nausea started, and stared at her gut. It was noticeably protruding now. She looked like a famine victim with a distended belly, except she wasn't malnourished, despite the early morning vomiting.

Stanley, who was already in bed, looked up from his book and saw her stroking her belly.

"How Blakean," he said.

"What?"

"Oh Rose thou art sick,
The Invisible Worm
That flies in the night
In the howling storm:

"Has found out thy bed
Of crimson joy:
And his dark secret love
Does thy life destroy."

Rose turned and glared at Stanley with such venomous fury that the smug grin dropped from his face. He looked shocked and a little scared. Like a guilty schoolboy who's just been overheard using bad language. He blinked, swallowed and went back to his book.

V

A week later they were just settling down to watch MasterChef when there was a loud rapping on their door. Rose got out of her armchair and winced at the pain in her lower back. Stanley stood and placed a gentle hand on her shoulder.

"You sit yourself down love," he said gently. "I'll get it."

Rose patted his hand and sank back into her chair with a painful sigh. Stanley was worried about her health. The early morning vomiting had stopped, but her stomach had really swollen. It was heavy and painful. Stanley wanted to call the doctor, but after the last debacle Rose wasn't keen to go back.

"Peter?" Rose heard Stanley say in the hallway, followed by the sound of Peter barging in. "Why don't you come in?" Stanley continued as Peter marched into the living room.

Rose got to her feet to greet Peter, holding her stomach. There were dark bags under Peter's eyes. His clothes were rumpled, his hair hadn't been combed, he needed a shave and there was alcohol on his breath.

"Have you seen her?" he said. "Has she been in touch?"

"Have we seen who, Peter?" Rose said. Peter looked irritated by the question, as though Rose was stupid for asking.

"Bethany of course," he said. "She's disappeared. Has she called round or been in touch with you?"

"No, I haven't seen her in days. When was the last time you saw her?"

Peter stared at Rose with disbelief, as though he couldn't believe she could ask such a question. Then he shook his head and stared at the carpet, massaging his temples with his left hand.

"We went to bed last night, same as normal. I woke up this morning and she was gone. I've called everyone I can think of, no-one knows where she is."

"Maybe she just needed to get away from everything," said Stanley. "Sometimes people do. She might even be back later tonight."

Peter turned to look at Stanley for the first time. Regarding him with such withering disdain that both Stanley and Rose frowned.

"You don't understand," Peter said. "We were in the bed."

"Isn't that where people usually are first thing in the morning?" said Rose.

"Not in bed. *In the bed*. The one we got rid of."

"I'm not following you Peter."

"We went to bed last night in our usual bed. The one that cost a fortune from John Lewis. When I woke up this morning I was in the four-poster. Our old bed was gone and the four-poster was in its place, right there, in our bedroom."

"I don't quite see how that's possible."

"Don't you think I know that! Do you know how much I paid to get rid of it the first time? But there it was in our bedroom."

"Was Bethany in the bed with you?"

"Yes . . . well no. I mean, she was to begin with, I swear she was. I could feel her next to me as I woke. Her back was pressing against mine. I rolled over to spoon, with my eyes still closed, and there was this faint noise, like a hiss or someone wheezing and trying to catch their breath. Then suddenly she wasn't there. The sheets were still warm. I could smell her on them but she was gone, as though she'd just, I don't know . . . fizzled out."

"Fizzled out?"

"Yes," said Peter, getting annoyed with her. "That's the best way I can describe it, okay? That's what it felt like."

"How are you and Bethany getting on at the moment?" said Stanley.

"What business of yours is that?" Peter retorted.

"Well none really, only, looking at this objectively, the most obvious explanation is that she's probably behind all this."

"What on earth are you talking about?" Peter's voice was frigid with disapproval.

"Well, think about it for a moment. Who is best placed to deliver a four-poster bed to your house if not one of the occupants? Someone who knows when you're going to be away. Maybe the second time, she slipped you an incredibly strong sleeping pill, then had the old bed taken away and put you back in the new one before you woke. Perhaps she slipped away just as you were waking, but you didn't see her go because you were still a bit drugged."

"That is the single most ridiculous thing I have ever heard! Why on earth would she want to do that? Why would anyone want to do that?"

"Maybe she's trying to drive you mad. Maybe she wants you out of the way. I don't know, that's why I asked how you were getting on. But how would anyone else manage to deliver two identical beds to your house without at least one of you noticing?"

"But it wasn't two identical beds. It was the same one. The exact same one. That's what I'm trying to tell you."

"It couldn't possibly be the exact same bed," said Rose, in measured tones, trying to calm Peter. "You destroyed the first bed, hacked it to pieces."

"I know, but it keeps coming back. The same bed keeps returning.

You couldn't replicate something this unique. The carvings, the curtains, the throws, they're all identical."

"Even the tapestry on the underside of the canopy?" said Stanley. Peter stopped what he was about to say and glared at Stanley with suspicion.

"How do you know there was a tapestry?"

"Well I . . . I mean I . . . erm . . ." Stanley went dead-white and Rose could have throttled him.

"He saw it in the skip, when you threw it out," she said. "I would have thought that was obvious. Such a waste too, it was unique, it must have been worth quite a bit."

"But we didn't throw the tapestry in the skip. We burnt it separately. There's no way you could have known about that tapestry unless you'd been on the bed. You wouldn't have seen it if you'd just looked through the door of the spare room."

Now it was Rose's turn to go white. "That's not the point," she said, trying to gather herself. "Bethany is missing and someone is delivering beds to your house without you knowing. Let's focus on the important issues here."

Peter wasn't listening. He was staring with horror at Rose's belly. He backed away from her shaking his head ever so slightly. "Oh my God," he said. "You didn't, you didn't, you have no idea what you've done, have you?" The back of his legs touched the sofa and he collapsed on to it, like a rag doll someone had tossed onto the furniture. All the life drained from his muscles. He put his head in his hands and began to cry.

Rose and Stanley exchanged a puzzled look. This was not the response they expected. "Go and get some brandy," Rose told Stanley. She sat beside Peter, settling carefully into position to accommodate the weight of her distended belly.

"You don't understand what you've done, do you?" Peter muttered, staring at his lap. "I'm fucked, I'm absolutely fucked."

"Peter, you're not making any sense," Rose said. Stanley returned with a large glass of brandy and Peter sipped it gratefully.

"Peter," Rose said, putting a hand on his arm. "What is it that you think we've done? What don't we understand? Does it have something to do with Bethany's disappearance?"

"It has everything to do with Bethany's disappearance." Peter drained the last of the brandy from the glass. He seemed to be weighing up how much to tell them.

"You have to tell us," said Rose. "It's important."

Peter sighed and handed Stanley his glass for a refill. "The bed, I've seen it before, that is, before I moved here. Bethany and I are lawyers, used to be lawyers. We worked for a firm that specialised in probate and estate management. That's where we met actually. It was against company rules to get involved with other staff, plus Bethany was already married, which made it even more complicated, but we were the best at what we did, so they let it slide.

"Our clients were old and rich, and mainly came to us through personal recommendation. We had one client, though, who was a little eccentric. He was a recluse called Archibald Trelawney. He had a huge personal fortune and a vast property portfolio. When word got out that he was looking to expand his legal team, Bethany and I did everything we could to get an introduction.

"He never left his home, some crumbling, gothic pile in the middle of his country estate, so that's where we went to meet him. We were carefully vetted before we got an introduction, so I have to admit, we were curious and a little excited to finally meet the elusive Mr. Trelawney.

"A shame then that he made our flesh crawl. We were shown into this little backroom on the ground floor, where he seemed to spend all his time. A poky little space filled with books, lining the walls and sitting in huge piles everywhere. He had a mansion with four wings and acres of land around it, yet he hardly ever left this one room. You could tell by the smell.

"He had these horrid little eyes, sunken into a wizened head. They made you feel dirty just by looking at you. He was well spoken and obviously educated, but he had a way of speaking that made everything he said sound lewd and inappropriate. He smiled the minute he saw us, it was a predator's smile, made you feel someone had rammed an ice pick in your guts.

"We had a pretty slick PowerPoint presentation all prepared, but he wasn't the least bit interested. It turned out he had a proposal all of his own. He didn't beat about the bush or anything, he just came straight out with it. He asked how we'd like to inherit his whole estate, money and all. We thought he was joking, obviously. So we laughed it off and tried to steer him back to employing our company.

"Turns out he was being deadly serious. He wasn't looking for lawyers, he was looking for a couple—the right couple, and he liked what he saw in us. He offered to make us sole benefactors. With one single stipulation, we had to do something in return. Something quite unorthodox . . ."

Peter stopped, shook his head in revulsion and got to his feet. "I'm sorry," he said. "I've said too much already." Stanley also stood, to block

Peter from leaving.

"Wait," Stanley said. "You can't stop there. You haven't told us anything. This is important."

"Look, I've taken up too much of your time. I shouldn't have come here in the first place, you don't know where Bethany is. I need to get as far away as possible."

Stanley moved in front of the door. "Don't leave please, we need to know what the stipulation was."

"No you don't, you really don't. But I do need to leave. I have some posts of yours by the way, the post man delivered it to us by accident. I'll drop it off before I go."

Rose pulled herself off the sofa and put her hand on Peter's shoulder. "Peter, look at me, please. You know something about that bed, about Bethany's disappearance and . . ." Rose rubbed her stomach. "And about what's happened to me. Stanley's right, this is important to all of us. We won't judge you, we might even be able to help you, but we can't do anything unless we know the whole truth. Please, come and sit down, Stanley will get more brandy."

Peter seemed to waver. Rose motioned for Stanley to refill his glass and took advantage of his indecision, to steer him back to the sofa. Peter accepted the fresh glass of brandy and stared straight ahead of him. "You were going to tell us about the unorthodox stipulation . . ." Rose prompted.

Peter sighed. "Where do I start? I mean, I'm a man of the world and everything. Some of my richer clients have had some . . . interesting tastes, but this turned out to be . . . well . . . I mean we thought at first it was just a harmless peccadillo.

"He was going to let us inherit everything, so long as we agreed to . . . to . . . I can't believe I'm telling you this. So long as we agreed to have sex, in a special bed, in his house, while he was in the room with us. We weren't even sure he was serious when he first put it to us. I mean we'd come there to win his business. We didn't expect to be offered the whole estate if we put on some private sex show for the old pervert.

"We asked for a bit of time to think it over, but the old bastard put the hard sell on us, saying we'd have to give him an answer straight away. Well, what would you have done? I mean he was offering us more money than we could spend in several lifetimes. Naturally we agreed.

"But it didn't stop there, the paperwork we had to sign was incredible. I mean, this was our area of specialty but even we were overwhelmed by it and, because of the nature of the transaction, we couldn't employ anyone to negotiate on our behalf, or help us with the more esoteric parts. A huge part of it was in Latin, which I'm not great on. The problem was, a lot of it dealt with laws that we weren't familiar with, some weren't even laws of the earthly realm, that is to say they . . . no, I'm not making much sense.

"Anyway, back to the . . . erm, act we had to commit. We had to do all these strange exercises for about a month leading up to it. We'd be picked up and driven to the estate and some strange people would instruct us to do some very odd things. They'd give us these hideous herbal concoctions to drink as well, it was all very bizarre.

"Then one night we were taken to this bed chamber on the second floor of the mansion. It had magical symbols, drawn on the floorboards in ash and daubed on the walls in blood. The room was filled with erotic art, statues and paintings, most of it was unspeakably obscene. We nearly bolted when we saw it, in spite of all the cash at stake.

"In the centre of the room was the bed. That's where we were supposed to . . . perform. It wasn't . . . it's actually not as easy as . . . I mean I don't normally have any trouble. I've never fancied anyone like I fancy Bethany, but it was different with him in the room.

"When the old goat saw that I was . . . I was having trouble, he . . . No, no I can't tell you . . ."

Rose put her hand on Peter's shoulder. "This is important, I told you we won't judge, but every little detail might be pertinent."

Peter drained his glass. "He put something up . . . look you have to understand that I'm not into any of the funny stuff. I'm not gay, or kinky, okay? But he . . . put something up my behind. A little muslin bag filled with exotic spices. Felt like my arse was on fire, excuse my French, but I don't think I've ever been harder. I didn't have any problem after that and, well, you both know what the bed can do to you.

"When we finished, we heard this weird hissing noise, like someone wheezing or gasping for breath. It was just at the point that I climaxed actually. We looked over at Trelawney and he was slumped over in his chair, dead. A thin trickle of dark green fluid ran from the corner of his mouth. He'd poisoned himself.

"Can't say we were sorry to see the back of the old goat. I mean everything was ours now, or so we thought. The first thing we did was get rid of all the old books and the obscene art, not to mention the furniture and furnishings. We could have sold some of it I suppose, it was all antique, some of the books and the statues were worth quite a bit I'm told, but we were already fabulously wealthy so we didn't need the extra money. Besides, I never really went in for antiques. Most importantly though, we got rid of that monstrous bed, or at least we thought we had.

"Then all these notaries started crawling out of the woodwork, especially when Bethany discovered she was pregnant, which kind of surprised us. Bethany had been told she couldn't have children. It was one of the reasons her first marriage broke down, her husband was desperate for kids.

"There were all these clauses in the paperwork we signed, that we either hadn't seen, or hadn't understood. Most of them were to do with the care and provision for any children we might have in the first year of our inheritance. So naturally the first thing we did was lawyer up ourselves, inasmuch as we could, given the paperwork we'd signed, which forbade challenging the terms and conditions of the will under pain of forfeit.

"We also got some Latin scholars to translate the passages we couldn't follow. There was a lot of references to an *aeternae ultionis* clause, meaning eternal, or unending, vengeance which, if invoked, would result in us being punished over and over and over again. Though it didn't specify how this would be done from a legal perspective, so we weren't too bothered about that.

"What did worry us were our legal imperatives under the *rerum tanta novitas* clause. This specified our roles in a magical ceremony that we had no idea we were taking part in. A ceremony to incarnate a grown man inside the womb of a barren woman, so he'd grow to manhood with all the knowledge and memories of his former life.

"Bethany was pretty freaked out, I can tell you. She didn't like the idea of being pregnant in the first place, she was only three months gone but she looked more like six or seven. It wasn't helping our marriage any either. Then, when she found out about this, it sent her over the edge.

"I mean neither of us believed it was real, not at first. But she knew that something wasn't right with her condition. She said she could feel him growing within her like a tumour, sucking the life out of her. She thought it was like a form of unending rape, having that creepy old goat deep inside her. She even became convinced she could hear his thoughts, goading her and laughing at her from inside her own womb.

"It was driving her mad so we had to do something about it. If that was Trelawney growing inside her, we certainly didn't want to raise him after he was born. Can you imagine that? A little toddler running around with the mind and memories of an evil old man, calling you 'Mummy' and 'Daddy.' Looking into a tiny infant's eyes and seeing that malevolent old fossil staring out of them. I can't think of anything worse.

"We made discreet enquiries about terminating the pregnancy. No one wanted to help us at first, they thought Bethany was too late in her term, because of how big she was. Eventually we found a clinic with questionable ethics and a liking for six figure fees. When it was over we told the solicitors that Bethany had miscarried.

"Unfortunately they followed the money trail to the clinic and exposed our little lie. We lost the whole estate. We'd gone back on our deal and as such we'd forfeited our right to the inheritance. We had to do it though, after the way that bastard had played us. At least we foiled his little plan."

Rose was suddenly reminded of the line from Stanley's poem: 'Her womb was an instrument of revenge.'

"What did you do then?" Stanley asked.

Peter coughed. "Sorry my throat's dry from talking so much. Don't suppose I could ask for a glass of water?" Rose fetched it this time. Peter smiled his thanks and drank it down. "Well we had to move out. There was a fight about what we owned, the possessions we'd brought to the mansion, the things we bought while we were there. That took a while to resolve. We'd salted a little of the money away where it couldn't be found, so we were okay financially. We moved here to stay under the radar. Then we tried to put everything behind us. We thought we'd succeeded until that wretched bed suddenly turned up."

"What are we going to do?" said Rose. She wasn't quite certain what to make of Peter's incredible confession. Part of her wondered how much of it was fantasy and self-delusion? A fantastical tale invented by someone close to breaking point, in order to cover up a more prosaic case of fraud and embezzlement. Another part of her was reluctantly accepting the truth of it, and how it accounted for all the strange little events that had befallen her.

"I'm going to get as far away as possible from that bed. Then I'm going to find Bethany." He got up from the sofa and made his way out of the room. Stanley didn't attempt to stop him this time. Peter stopped in the doorway, turned to Rose and pointed at her stomach. "You'd be wise to get rid of that as soon as possible."

Stanley followed Peter to the front door and saw him out. Rose stood in the living room with her hands round her swollen belly. It wasn't until Peter's parting comment that she'd even begun to consider there was a life growing inside her.

VI

Rose didn't sleep at all that night. She didn't sleep much these days as it was. Sleep was like an old friend with whom she'd once been close, but had now drifted apart. She only spent a few hours in its company most nights.

Stanley, on the other hand, had become much better acquainted with sleep. He went to bed much earlier, got up later and was always dozing off in the afternoon. He'd also developed a dreadful snore which disturbed Rose's light sleep.

Tonight, she was trying to process everything Peter had said. The implications were too much to take in all at once. She had to let them slowly creep up on her, one at a time, so she could mull each one over and process how she felt.

Rose stared at her huge belly in the dim light of the bedside lamp. She couldn't help stroking it in a proprietary fashion. If Peter was telling the truth, and she suspected he was, then there was something wholly unnatural inside her. The simple fact that she was pregnant, more than a decade after going through the menopause, pointed to how unnatural it was. It had never crossed her mind, or her doctor's, that all the symptoms might add up to this.

Bethany had described it as a tumour, a permanent rape. Peter had advised her to get rid of it as soon as possible. Rose didn't feel like doing that just yet. She knew she ought to be appalled. If Peter was to be believed, she'd been used in the most awful way and had dragged Stanley into it too.

But she didn't feel violated at all. She had what she'd wanted her whole life, another life growing inside her. Rose couldn't believe how quickly she'd come to accept this. It seemed a ridiculous thing to contemplate. Then again, she'd known something wasn't right for a while, somewhere at the back of her mind she'd been preparing herself for this. Given every other strange occurrence of late, it made a sort of twisted sense.

Rose knew that it wasn't right. She knew that soon she would have to rectify the situation. But right now she wanted to enjoy the feeling of being pregnant. Of nurturing another life inside her, of filling the aching hollowness that had screamed at the centre of her being for more than half her life. She liked feeling pregnant. Finally, after all these years, she got to know what it was like.

Rose wondered how someone her age would even go about getting a termination. She supposed she would have to go to some seedy backstreet establishment, which wouldn't be cheap.

Rose weighed the alternatives to abortion. Would it be possible to get an exorcist to chase Trelawney out of her foetus, if he was actually in there? How about after he was born, would it work better then? She'd read somewhere that a frontal lobotomy could erase unpleasant and troubling memories. Would that work? Could you erase the entire memory of a past life? Would it be possible to perform a lobotomy on a newborn child?

The more Rose considered it, the more desperate and brutal each of the alternatives seemed. There was no way she could commit any of them on a child she brought into the world. What were the risks attached to bringing a child to full term at her age? Surely there'd be complications. Given how quickly she was growing, she wondered if she'd even have to carry it for nine months.

As the sky outside her bedroom window began to lighten, Rose began to cry silently. Tears spilling from her cheeks in condemnation of the sheer unfairness of her situation. Here she was with a child—or something like it—inside her, and she would have to kill it. There, she'd said it. *Kill it.* That's what she was contemplating after all.

She'd brought this on herself. Her longing had drawn this old man into her and now she was expected to kill him. She laughed with a bitter irony. The emptiness that filled Rose made it so easy for people to get inside her. And when they did, something deep within her always died. Literally, this time.

Rose ran her hand over her stomach and something moved inside it. Despite everything she'd been thinking, Rose felt a huge burst of excitement. She rubbed the spot where she'd felt the movement, hoping to get more.

That's when she became aware of another consciousness, waiting on the outskirts of her own. One that was rooted to the strange life inside her. It was there at the very edges of her mind, she could sense it more than hear it, like trying to see something hovering in your peripheral vision.

The strongest thing she sensed in this consciousness was need. A need for her, like none she'd ever felt before. Need that came in the form of a plea: please look after me, and love me and raise me. Was this what it meant to be a mother? To be needed this badly and this much.

Beneath the need, other emotions festered, tainting the purity of the need for her. There was cunning, and an ability to manipulate, but there was also a definite sense of threat—you better had look after me.

There was another kick inside her and Rose felt herself flush with pride for the clever little thing in her womb. The consciousness on the perimeter of her own almost seemed to form a thought, a little proto-thought: *Look what I can do Mummy.*

Yes my little darling, she thought, in reply. Show me.

There was more movement, but this time it came with a sharp stab of pain. A pain that kept building until it was beyond agony. It knocked the breath of her, and Rose could only open her mouth in a silent wail of pain.

The skin on her swollen belly began to stretch as something pushed against her from inside. The skin stretched further and she could clearly make out the fingers of a hand. Not a soft fleshy hand. The fingers were gnarled and seemed to be made of twisted bone and there on the end of them, through the taut skin of her stomach, she could clearly see tiny claws.

VII

Rose was in the garden when the phone went. She was trying to get rid of a particularly stubborn outbreak of bindweed before she got too big to do any more gardening.

She was growing at an alarming rate and had given up any hope of seeing her feet in the near future. This made clambering up off her knees, and shuffling into the house, very uncomfortable.

The answer machine took the call before Rose could get to the phone. She picked up the receiver but the blessed thing kept recording. Like a lot of modern technology, the intricacies of operating it completely defied Rose. She'd bought the thing under protest because her old machine, that she'd had for nearly fifteen years, kept cutting off callers and mangling the tapes she put in it.

"Hello, hello," said Rose, randomly pushing buttons on the machine.

"Oh . . . hello, is that Mrs. Shotton?" said the young man who'd been leaving the message.

"Yes, that's me."

"Hello there, my name's Keith, I'm calling from the Bridge Hotel. Do you know a Mr. Peter Hince?"

"Yes, he's my neighbour, why?"

"He's been staying with us recently, but we haven't been able to locate him for the past couple of days. There was some post in his possession that's addressed to you. You haven't seen or heard from him recently have you?"

"No, not for the last couple of weeks. Is anything wrong?'

"Well it's rather hard to explain, Mrs. Shotton. Would you be prepared to come and collect some of his things? We're not too far from you."

"Erm, I'm not too sure, when would you need me?"

"Whenever you're available, Mrs. Shotton, but we'd appreciate it if you could come in sometime today or tomorrow."

"And what would you like me to pick up?"

"Again, that's rather hard to explain over the phone, you'd really have to see it for yourself. Shall I expect you later today?"

"Well, okay, I think, but I'll have to check."

"Splendid. Would you like me to e-mail you directions?"

"No, that's alright, I'll find you on the map."

"Okay, Mrs. Shotton, I'll hopefully see you later today, just ask for Keith at reception."

"Okay, bye," Rose said and hung up. She felt more than a little coerced into visiting the hotel, but she was curious about Peter. He must have accidentally taken the letters he was going to drop round with him

Two days after Rose last saw him, an estate agent's sign had appeared in Peter's front garden. Rose hadn't seen anyone come to view the house, but a team of cleaners had called round to spruce the place up. Rose hadn't expected to hear from Peter after that, so she was more than a little intrigued by the call from the hotel.

The Bridge Hotel was a shabby, modern building, just off a busy A road. It was a bland, featureless building with a large gravel forecourt. It looked like a Travelodge or Holiday Inn that had seen better days.

The reception area smelled strongly of air freshener and needed a lick of paint. Rose asked to see Keith and was introduced to a tall, thin man with spiky blond hair and bad skin.

"Mrs. Shotton," Keith said. "Thank you so much for coming in." Keith was having great difficulty taking his eyes off Rose's stomach. She supposed it didn't quite gel with her grey hair and crow's feet. It was actually the first time in about three decades that a man hadn't been able to make eye contact with her. Sadly it wasn't her chest that was drawing his gaze, but she thought he could be forgiven, under the circumstances.

"I wonder if you could just sign a few forms for us and then you can pick up Mr. Hince's things. Oh, here's your post by the way." Keith held up a few official looking letters in brown envelopes as Rose waddled over to the reception desk.

"What sort of forms?" she said with a little suspicion.

"Oh nothing too important, just some silly legal stuff."

"What kind of legal stuff? I thought I was just doing you a favour by popping by to pick up Peter's things."

"It's nothing major, don't worry. It's just something our legal department said you had to sign."

"Why?"

Rose shifted uncomfortably from foot to foot. Her arches hurt from standing.

"Just so that the hotel is covered legally, when it comes to damages and transportation."

"Well, I brought my car, that's all the transportation we'll need isn't it?"

"Not for everything I'm afraid."

"But surely he just brought a few suitcases."

"Yes, but there is one item that's . . . shall we say—rather cumbersome . . ."

"What on earth do you mean?"

"Look, it's a bit hard for me to describe. I think I better show you Mr. Hince's room."

Keith took Rose down a series of ground floor corridors towards the rear of the building. The walls were hung with bad watercolours of old cathedrals. The paper was coming away in places and the carpet was well worn.

Keith stopped beside a wood paneled door with chipped white paint. "The thing is," he said, slipping the electric key in the lock, "We have no idea how Mr. Hince got this in the room. It wasn't there when he booked in. We only discovered it after he disappeared. As far as we can tell, he left everything he had in the room, car keys, phone, you name it. We tried everything we could to get hold of him, but he's nowhere to be found. You were our best lead."

Keith opened the door and stepped inside. "You see what I mean. He couldn't have gotten this through the window or down the corridor. No one saw him carry it in the entrance. It's not on the CCTV footage. Where did it come from?"

Keith was standing in the doorway with his back to Rose, so she couldn't see into the room. Nevertheless she knew exactly what he was going to show her before he ushered her inside. The poky little room, scattered with Peter's clothes, was utterly dominated by a four-poster bed. Rose felt her stomach lurch as she recognised the carved posts, the bedspread and the obscene tapestry on the underside of the canopy.

"Why would anyone do something like this?" said Keith. "Is it some kind of sick joke? I just don't understand it."

Rose couldn't bring herself to answer Keith. She knew that their efforts to trace Peter's whereabouts would come to nothing. Just as Peter's attempts to find Bethany had been futile.

She felt the unborn creature inside her start to kick at the proximity of the bed. Rose winced and put a hand to her stomach.

"Are you alright?" said Keith.

"Yes, I just felt a kick, I'll be alright in a moment."

"So you are actually . . . I mean, at your age . . . is that possible?"

"It came as a great surprise to me."

Rose staggered. At the back of her mind she felt the foetus's brain come to life. Its thoughts seeping into hers like bile leaking from a ruptured spleen. They were half-formed and struggling for comprehension, a still growing consciousness trying to recall something from a former life.

Rose recognised what the unborn life was trying to grasp at though. It was a clause in a contract. *Aeternae ultionis*, meaning eternal, or unending, vengeance which, if invoked, would result in being punished over and over and over again.

Rose felt her legs go from under her and she sat down hard on the floor. "Is everything okay?" said Keith.

"No," Rose replied. "I've got to go."

"But what about your post, and Mr. Hince's things?"

"You can keep them."

"And the bed?"

"Hack it to pieces and burn every single last bit of it."

VIII

"Rose, love, you need medical attention." Stanley was really worried now. He'd been trying to wheedle Rose into seeing a doctor for the past five days. Ever since she retired to her bed.

Her stomach had become so huge that she couldn't carry the weight of it. She was at least twice the size of any normal pregnant woman at the end of her third trimester. Her calf muscles and joints were inflamed, her ankles were swollen and her lower back was pure agony.

Stanley was being ever so sweet to her, for a change. He rearranged her pillows whenever she asked him, brought her soup, and any other food she demanded, and even gave her frequent sponge baths.

As a consequence Rose was being frightful to him. She bullied and berated him at every turn, until he was cowed into submission. And Stanley was so concerned that he took whatever abuse she hurled at him.

"It's not natural, love," he said for the fortieth time that day.

"And just what am I going to tell the doctor, if you do call for him? That my husband and I had sex on a magical bed and now I'm pregnant, even though I'm in my sixties?"

"You're not pregnant, love, you can't be."

"And why not?"

"Because you're too old and you're too big. No one gets that big when they're pregnant."

"Then what have I got growing inside me?"

"I don't know, a parasite or something, like a tapeworm perhaps. Maybe it's just a bloody big tumour, but it's not a baby. It can't be, it's not possible."

"I can feel him moving inside me. I can hear his thoughts, I know he's there."

"No you can't, love, you only think you can. You're not well and you're imagining things."

"I am not imagining things!"

"You are, and it's bloody well got to stop, right now!"

Stanley pulled his mobile out of his pocket, much to Rose's amazement. It was an ancient, cheap thing she'd bought him from Argos. He drove her mad most of the time because he refused to carry it anywhere and even when he did, he left it turned off so she could never reach him. He must have thought the situation was grave to have actually charged it.

As Stanley began to dial the number, Rose felt a kick. Urgency and alarm emanated from her womb. A voiceless plea burst into her mind. *He's going to hurt me mummy. They're going to take me away from you. Please don't let them take me away from you!*

Like a lioness whose cub is in danger, Rose felt a wave of murderous anger engulf her. She remembered there was a kitchen knife under her pillow. She'd put it there when she became bedridden, at the insistence of her unborn. She hadn't given it much thought at the time, but now she realised why she'd been prompted to hide it there. Many things she did these days were done unconsciously for the good of her unborn child.

Stanley was still dialing when she rolled off the bed, reared up on her feet and lumbered towards him. The pain in her spine and the back of her legs was almost crippling. If she hadn't been filled with adrenaline and spurred on by homicidal intent, Rose would have collapsed on the floor in agony.

She raised the knife over her head and lunged at Stanley with her other hand. She grabbed his shoulder and they toppled to the ground. Stanley gasped with pain as the air was knocked out of him and Rose's immense weight pinned him to the ground.

The phone fell from his hand. Rose brought the knife down. Stanley yelped with fear. She smashed the point into the phone's screen and shattered it.

Rose brought her face right up close to Stanley's. "You are not doing anything to endanger the life of my baby," she growled.

Stanley whimpered with pain as Rose shifted her weight, crushing his arm beneath her. She rolled off him onto her back and started to push herself back towards the bed with her legs.

Stanley got to his feet, wincing with pain. "Here, let me help you," he said. Rose waved the knife at him.

"Don't you come near me," she shouted, in a deep, ragged voice that sounded nothing like her own and surprised her with its viciousness.

She caught Stanley's eyes. He looked deeply wounded. Unable to believe that she could treat him this way after forty years of marriage.

Part of Rose wanted to reach out to him. To apologise for her manic behaviour, take him in her arms and soothe his hurt. But that part of her was not in charge.

She was not in charge. In that moment Rose realised that her mind was now the consciousness on the periphery, and the iron will of the being inside her womb was in full control of this situation.

"Get out," she screamed. "Get away from me, damn you, go!"

Stanley slunk from the room. His face showed shock and disbelief. His hands were shaking and his shoulders were slumped with dejection.

Rose pulled herself up onto the bed and cried out with the torment from her back. She rolled onto her side to relieve the immense pressure from her swollen front. Her unborn was still agitated and she stroked her stomach to soothe the both of them.

She lay like this for several hours. Sometime in the early evening she heard Stanley let himself out of the front door. She didn't know where he was going, but she was suddenly seized with the knowledge that it was the last time she would ever see or hear from him again.

Rose began to cry, her body wracked with deep heaving sobs. Her chest swam with regret for all the things she'd had to sacrifice, including her marriage, in order to finally be a mother. She'd had to rid her life of everything that filled it, in order to stop feeling so empty inside.

It's time, mummy, her unborn thought, and she knew he was right. She circled his mind like a satellite sentience, sensing his intent from afar, without fully comprehending it.

There was a faint hissing noise coming from far away, rising imperceptibly in volume. The louder it got the more it sounded like someone wheezing and struggling for breath. Rose knew what it was. It was the sound of her former existence, breathing its last.

The sheets beneath her began to change in consistency, coarsening from crumpled cotton to finely pressed linen. She was aware of four objects approaching the bed, as if from a great distance, each with a trajectory that ended on a different corner. As they got closer, Rose saw they were carved wooden posts. A canopy with a tapestry on its underside descended upon the bed as if from a steep height.

Rose was filled a sense of déjà vu, as if she had dreamed all this many times before. Only it wasn't quite something she'd already seen, so much as something she'd already lost. As though her former life, and everything she'd been experiencing until now, was a distant memory that had returned briefly to taunt her with everything she'd forsaken.

Rose looked around her at the four-poster bed and the oak paneled room filled with obscene art. She'd never seen its lewd furnishings, or the magical symbols daubed in blood on the walls and formed in ash on the floor. However, she knew exactly where she was.

It begins, thought the life within her womb. And though he had yet to leave her body, Rose had never felt more distant from him, nor more afraid.

IX

Rose had studied every stitch of the tapestry on the canopy. Sometimes, as she lay on her back and looked up at it, she liked to imagine how it was woven, reconstructing its composition. She would picture the weaver working the threads of the weft back and forth through the warp. Working their way up and along the tapestry until it was done. It was a good way to keep her mind off what was happening to her.

The obscenity and eroticism of the image were long since lost on her. She'd been staring up at it for such a length of time it had lost its power to shock. Even so, Rose had no idea how long she'd been on the bed, trapped by the horror in her womb. All she knew was the endless carnage she had to endure. She may have been there months, but if felt more like years.

She thought often of Stanley and how they'd parted. She wondered about the lengths to which he'd gone to find her. Had he been as out of his mind as Peter? Rose wondered if Peter would have been so desperate to find Bethany if he'd known where it would lead him?

She scratched at her leg. The blood coating her thighs was dried and flaking, making her raw skin itch. Pints and pints of it had poured out of her this time. The sheets and mattress had absorbed it all. Drank it down until there was hardly a faded stain left. The bed always devoured it. Rose had come to believe that was how it fed.

There was often cartilage or shreds of torn flesh in the blood. One time Rose saw an eyeball, with the optic nerve still attached. She had screamed then, and beaten her fists against the distended skin of her huge stomach. But it did no good. It didn't stop him. Nothing could stop him.

Once the blood had been fully absorbed by the bed, the whole process generally started again. Knowing what was going to happen next didn't make it any easier on Rose. She gripped the bed sheets and ground her teeth. The muscles in her calves knotted as her toes curled into her feet. She'd come to hate the waiting worse than all the other indignities she had to suffer.

The child within her wanted to be fed and a true mother will do anything, go to any lengths, to take care of her child. Rose's child did not draw sustenance from an umbilical cord, nor from her dry and sagging breasts. Her unborn wanted vengeance, to suckle at the teat of the *aeternae ultionis*.

Rose neither ate nor drank any more. Whatever was in her womb was doing that for both of them. Though her term was long overdue he refused to leave her. Her body was his to do with as he pleased now. His hideous appetites kept her alive, even though she did not share them.

The flesh along Rose's stomach began to ripple, a violent tremor made its way across the whole of her midriff. This was how it usually started. Rose felt, once again, the immense internal pressure that came with the process.

The skin around her midsection began to stretch and grow out of all proportion, as something pushed its way up from inside her. Rose groaned and screamed. An outline of shoulders, and the back of an adult head, could be clearly seen beneath the skin. Where it came from, how it appeared and grew so quickly, Rose had no idea. All she knew was the sudden, unbearable pain as her womb expanded well past its breaking point.

Her intestines and other internal organs shifted to accommodate the immense new bulk with an agony that was beyond Rose's power to express. She simply had to bear it. To endure the intrusion of this fully-grown human form where it had no natural right to be.

Sometimes she could tell whether it was Peter or Bethany. She could catch a stray thought and identify it, in the same way she perceived her unborn child's brooding mind. Usually she was only aware of their terror.

Terror, and the dawning realisation that they were trapped inside an impossibly small space, a space that should be the beginning of life, but was now the site of endless, endless death.

Trapped with a tiny, vicious creature they had wronged, to whom they had promised life but brought only death and double-cross.

A tiny, vicious creature with impossibly sharp teeth and claws and an insatiable need to be redressed.

Their screams and pleas did them no good. The contract was watertight, they were lawyers, they should have known. There was no escape, they were to be punished over and over and over again.

Stanley had been right. Rose's womb was an instrument of revenge. The emptiness that filled Rose made it so easy for people to get inside her. And when they did, something deep within her always died.

AUTHOR'S STORY NOTE

I'm not a genre purist, especially not when it comes to horror, I don't worry whether zombies run or shamble or talk. Nor do I worry about being labelled a horror writer. I don't try and pretend I write 'weird' or 'dark' fiction so my mother won't be ashamed to mention my work at her weekly sewing circle. When I see the word 'horror' on a book or a film I think: 'yes, I'll probably like this', so I'm happy to have the label on my own work.

This said, a lot of my work is a mash-up of genres. I don't do this consciously, it's just that other genres seem to creep into my stories more or less organically. The following novella is a mash-up of sub-genres, namely Quiet Horror, Erotic Horror and (given that this is a hardcore anthology) Extreme Horror. Each sub genre tries to do something a little different with horror. I'm generalizing here, but Quiet Horror tends to make you uneasy, Erotic Horror aims to turn you on while it scares you and Extreme Horror wants you to lose your lunch. By mashing them up I was curious to see if I could subvert the genres a little. Rather than relying on the atmosphere of Quiet Horror to unnerve you, for instance, I wanted to see if I could use the Erotic element to do that, or even to outright repulse you? I'll leave you to decide how successful I was.

"Bed of Crimson Joy" comes from a 'what if' moment. We live next door to wonderful older couple who often look after our house when we're away. As we were leaving for one vacation, my mind started to wander in a strange direction (as you might imagine, this happens to me a lot), a direction that deeply disturbed me and one that I couldn't get out of my head. In fact, it proved to be so disturbing that I thought: 'hmm, there's probably a story here.' Six drafts, and some 15,000 words later, it seems I was right.

PLEASE SUBSCRIBE

ADAM CESARE

From *Splatterpunk's Not Dead*
Editor: Jack Bantry,
Publisher: Splatterpunk Zine

UPLOADED 1 MONTH AGO
"Hey guys. Melody here and this is my first of what I hope to be many videos."

We're in a typical webcam medium shot.

The girl on screen is attractive but not the most attractive we've seen. And that's okay, because she's got stiff competition. We do watch *a lot* of videos. And once she watches a few more, herself—some tutorials on proper lighting (the difference between key and fill), a couple of make-up how-tos—then maybe she will rank among the most beautiful.

"I'm new to this whole thing, but I see that the surefire way to get likes and subscribers is to live-stream myself playing video games. But, and I hate to break this to you, Internet, but: I'm not a gamer. Unless phone games count.

"No. My content is going to be . . ."

She scrunches up her nose in a way that can only be described as self-aware. It's a calculated movement. Calculated, but we are all in agreement that the nose-scrunch is undeniably *adorable*.

Yes, her first video isn't of the highest quality, but this is a girl who knows what she's doing. This channel will get more interesting. It's definitely worth sticking around for the remaining two minutes and thirty-four seconds of her first video.

"Well, I actually don't know what the content on my channel is going to be. And I'm hoping that maybe you guys could help me decide. Leave me a comment and slap a like on this video to help me get some views. But, before you leave, let me tell you a little bit about myself."

She begins a list, counting off her attributes on her fingers like she's only got the ten.

The list goes:

She's eighteen.

She doesn't say where she's living now, but she'll be attending Rutgers in the Fall. That gives us a general location, if she's going away for college but not too far away.

Melody Bliss, her channel name, isn't her real name. No duh!

Her interests include music (classical music, actually, she was first chair violin in high school and hopes to continue the instrument in college), volleyball, and watching bad TV with her friends. And that's not an editorializing on our part, she actually calls it "bad TV", which is a

249

level of self-reflection that many young women do not possess. Especially young women who post cell phone videos of themselves online.

She has two dogs. Which is boring.

But she also has a hermit crab that she got at the boardwalk two years ago. She seems proud she's been able to keep him alive this long. "He's molted three times!" she tells us. We're not sure what that means, but her enthusiasm is quirky and adorable (that word again) and already on-brand.

But there's a big clue in that hermit crab discussion, because she called going to the beach going "down the shore." That means we've successfully triangulated her to the tri-state area. Probably Philly or South Jersey.

Melody signs off—as most of them do—with a plea to subscribe to her channel.

So we subscribe.

UPLOADED 3 WEEKS AGO

"Hey guys. Did you miss me?"

She's back. Very few young vloggers stick to a schedule. Some never even make a second video, forgetting about that silly dream of internet stardom after their first video fails to break fifty views.

But *this girl*. She's got moxie. We're all in agreement there.

Moxie and a black eye. She's tried to hide the injury with concealer, but she must not have watched a tutorial on that, either: the bruise is glaringly apparent.

Whatever happened to her eye must have happened not soon after she recorded her last video, because the mark has already begun to heal. There's a thin crescent of discoloration against the bridge of her nose that's brownish instead of a dark, attractive purple.

Her makeup technique is no better, but she's learned some video production tricks.

This video has a custom thumbnail. Also the lighting and framing is worlds better.

This is *quality content*.

"So I got a few responses to the last video, some comments, and I thought I'd go through and address some of them."

We all lean a little bit closer to our screens at hearing this. It doesn't matter the size of the screen, even if we're watching on a phone and could more easily lift the screen closer to us, we *still* lean forward.

Because maybe she's going to address our questions directly.

Maybe she's going to say our name.

"The request I received the most was if I could play you all something on my violin. And maaaaaybe I will if we can get my page to 100 subscribers by next week, but I don't think I'm feeling up to it today."

She touches the side of her face with the bruise, but doesn't address it directly.

Melody: you're holding out on us.

How did you hurt your eye?

We all want to know.

"And then there were some comments that were . . ." she pauses, searching for the words in, by this point, her trademark, cutie-pie way. "Let's call them rude."

She looks deeper into the camera.

"I had to delete many of them. Sorry, pervs! This is a family show."

She smiles, changing the subject, switching gears with an almost audible click as her smile brightens.

"There was one other common viewer request that I think I can give you all the hook up with."

She reaches both hands under the frame and our collective hearts leap because not only can we see a little further down her shirt, but she comes back up holding . . .

A fish tank?

An empty fish tank, with a fog of condensation on the sides and cling wrap over the lid.

"You all wanted to meet Pablo the hermit crab. And he wants to meet you!"

She removes the lid, lifts out a pathetic little creature in an oversized shell. She places Pablo flat on one hand. A few seconds elapse as she waits silently for him to poke his antennae under his shell. He tastes the air, then pops his eyestalks and legs out and makes a beeline for the edge of her hand.

"Nope. Yer not allowed to play outside of your cage, buddy," she says, not to us but to the small land crab.

"Well, that's Pablo. I feed him pellet food I order online, mostly. But occasionally I'll chop him up some fresh vegetables or give him some peanut butter. But that's just on special occasions. Right, Pablo?"

"Si," she says, in Pablo's voice. The choice of language and accent, coming from this white girl, is . . . problematic. Then she drops the little critter back into his cage.

"If you all want to get your own crabs, I've linked some good care instructions down in the description. Be sure to check those out, because there's a lot more to taking care of hermies than just the wire cage they give you at the beach."

Deep breath. Here comes the plea.

"If you want to see more of me or Pablo, please like this video, then hit the subscribe button. I'll see you here next week and maybe even play you a song, if we hit our goal. Remember: I'm still not sure what this whole thing is, so any suggestions are appreciated."

We hit like.

Then we prepare our comments.

UPLOADED TWO WEEKS AGO

Melody doesn't say anything to kick off her latest video. There's ten seconds of silence, her staring at the camera with her mouth closed around something.

The pose is like she's holding her breath under water, puffing her cheeks out.

The bruise is still there. Barely. But still there, some slight discoloration that only serves to make Melody look tired, not battered.

Then she opens her mouth and Pablo crawls out over her tongue and plops into her waiting hands.

In Melody's much-improved lighting, his shell glistens. But other than the sheen of spit, Pablo seems none the worse for wear. He cleans off one antenna with his smaller front claw.

Then Melody begins laughing, an embarrassed but unrestrained outpouring of "can you believe I just did that?"

Coming from many other YouTubers, the laughter would read as self-conscious and cloying. But on Melody it's endearing.

"I watched a video that explains you have fifteen to twenty seconds to capture your audience's attention."

She holds Pablo up to the camera so we can see that, yes, he is indeed okay. Maybe a little bewildered. But it's hard to read any emotion in his tiny black eyes.

"Do I have your attention?"

Yes she does.

The video then cuts to a bumper. It's a simple fading in and out of Melody's name, but when we cut back to her, there's also an annotation that pops up on the side of the screen imploring us to subscribe. She has come so far, so fast. Learned so much.

Without her cheeks puffed out to hold her pet inside her mouth, it's becoming apparent that Melody has lost some weight since posting her first video, two weeks ago. She doesn't mention it, but we can see that the line where her neck meets her chin is a little sharper.

Her cheeks are less full, but it looks good on her, accentuates the dimple on her left side. You could lose a penny in that thing.

We all sigh when she smiles wide enough to flash the dimple. We like her better this way. We'll tell her so in the comments.

"I'm sure many of you know by now, but we did reach our subscriber goal, so I'm going to play you a song at the end of this video, but first I wanted to put a question out there: what are your essential dorm room items? I, like, just this morning found out that I'm going to be in freshman housing, in a double, which means that I'm going to have a roommate. I hope she's cool. So, on my list I've already got Christmas lights, collapsible hamper, and flip flops—for the showers."

She exhales, inhales. She's getting better at talking to the camera, but still needs to work on pacing. "But I'm sure that there's a ton of stuff I'm not thinking of. Leave me a list! Give me some life-hacks!"

We can all think of a few suggestions.

We take our eyes off Melody for a moment and look around the frame at what else we can see in her bedroom. There's a pile of laundry that she maybe doesn't realize the camera's picked up, because on top of that pile is a little pink bra.

"Moving on," she says, leaving a slightly awkward pause in instead of editing it out, as she seems to have done in her previous two uploads, which are so tight.

She's not getting lazy. She's just allowing herself to appear more human, less processed. We approve.

"A few of you had noticed that I have a black eye and wanted to know what happened. I guess I'm not as good with makeup as I thought. Or you're all very perceptive [dimple smile]. But no, nothing scandalous. That's just what happens sometimes on the court. The volleyball court. I'm not like, being abused or anything. My videos aren't a cry for help or something. Just want to reach out."

Then there is an edit, no pause, and in the next set-up, more zoomed out, Melody has her violin resting under her chin.

"I read somewhere that videos over six minutes don't do well. So this is going to have to be a quick song," she says and begins to play, beginning with a down stroke, a deep sound. There's a little bit of echo in her bedroom, but she has the camera far enough from the instrument that there's no feedback.

We alternate between watching her hands as she plays and watching that pink bra.

She's quite talented. The song isn't mopey, but it's not joyous either. It's neutral, fast without being particularly invigorating.

"That's all for this week," she says, ending mid-song, it would seem. She tells us to like and subscribe and share.

We are left wanting more.

UPLOADED A WEEK AGO

"A knife, garbage bags (the heavy-duty kind), condoms (all sizes), a shovel," she says, reading off a list.

"You guys are hilarious, but those aren't the kind of dorm room supplies I was talking about."

God, between this week and last week she must've lost fifteen pounds.

The bumper cuts back in after she's done talking. She's got this "starting with a hook" thing down to a science. Who wouldn't want to keep watching?

Not us.

She's rearranged her bedroom. We can no longer see the pile of clothes. Or the bra. She's moved a bookshelf to the edge of her desk and put Pablo's cage on top of the shelf, so we can see him in there, clinging to a knotted length of driftwood.

"Got a lot of comments on last week's video. Also got a lot of hate for my trick with Pablo. Some people called it animal cruelty. Some called it just plain gross. But you know what I say?"

No, what do you say?

"Eff the haters! Efff them right in the ear!"

It's like she can hear our applause from the other side of time and the internet, because she pauses to let her bold stand against "teh haterz" sit for a moment.

Yeah. Eff them. Eff those fucking fucks.

"But those people are in the minority. So thanks to all my *viewers* who left me comments of support. And for those of you looking for me to do something bigger and crazier . . . all I have to say is stay tuned."

She almost, almost, said 'fans' instead of viewers. The hesitation was microscopic. But we all felt it.

We detected that wriggling diva larvae. The diva that we've planted deep inside the base of Melody's skull. The diva seed.

She longs to call us her *fans*, wants us to tear at the hem of her garment, wants us to tear each other apart but she won't get it. Not yet. As of this video, we are a united front.

There's been no indication as to what the content of this video will be and there's less than a minute left to it. Hardly time for another song or stupid pet trick. What are you going to show us Melody? Is this even a full episode? A measly two minutes is supposed to be our weekly fix?

We are unimpressed.

"Today I . . ."

"Today I . . ."

It's like she's stuck, but then we notice the drip that streaks down below her left nostril. There's a watery red line drawn above her lip. She's gotten a nosebleed but she doesn't cut the camera. Instead she covers it with one bent finger, trying to stopper the nostril with a knuckle, and keeps talking.

"That's all the time I've got for today, check back soon for something really spectacular, keep those comments coming in and make sure that you like and subscribe, if you haven't already."

Before the video ends she gives us viewers a quick wave, not with her free hand but with the one she's been using to staunch the blood.

The flow has trickled down, from the knuckle of her pointer finger down so that it drips off the end of her pinky. It's like she's made of marble and in the middle of a Roman Fountain, the water pumping from her a dark red.

Her wave is such a quick motion that the blood forms a fan. The video cuts off right when the spatter peppers the side of her desk, the bookshelf and Pablo's tank.

Getting only a two-minute video seemed like a rip-off at first. But we've watched it, collectively, 5,000 times by this point, a mere three hours after it was uploaded.

We pay special attention to that last twenty seconds, trying to map out where all the droplets of Melody Bliss will fall.

UPLOADED JUST NOW

We're beginning to suspect Melody may have an eating disorder.

Or suspect that she takes comments on the internet way too seriously.

We feel that she's done what she swore she would never do. She's let the haterz get the better of her.

Ironically, she's grown an immense audience in a short amount of time. We hope that she knows that this type of success is atypical. We've never seen anything quite like it. It's not like she has millions of views. She hasn't gone viral. But it's fair to say that she's got a cult audience.

No, that's not a pun.

At the start of this video—freshly uploaded but we all get to it at the same time because we've all set up to be sent email alerts whenever Melody Bliss posts a new video—we're all praying that she gets help. Maybe once she gets to Rutgers, visits their dining hall, she'll put on the freshman fifteen and all will be right with the world.

If she pulls out of this tailspin then we'll have her to internet adore and internet whisper to for many years to come.

We'll be with her when she gets a lucrative sponsorship deal or writes a coffee table book or marries a Hollywood star who's *actually famous*.

But then she speaks for the first time in this video and it seems pretty clear that none of those things will come to pass.

"Hey guys, Melody here. Just a quick video I made about something I've been getting asked about and have wanted to talk about." Her speech is halting, labored even. She's not annoyed, just tired and unable to concentrate on the words that she's so clearly reading off her computer monitor. They aren't good words.

We'd be able to tell she was reading from the slight, tennis-match back and forth of her eyes, but then she makes it more obvious by squinting at a few words.

"First, I want to say that I appreciate those of you who've reached out to ask if I'm sick," she coughs, in bold defiance of what she's about to say: "No. I am not ill, and I am not sick in the head, either. I *do not* have an eating disorder, but I *have* been on a diet."

She swallows hard, gets wistful. "Summer used to be such a fun time, but I guess this is what growing up's about because I'm so . . ." she searches for the word, she's either going off-book or she's lost her place.

"Stressed. I've become stressed. I mean, I used to worry about tests, but when I asked for dorm room tips and got to talking to some of you about your college experiences, it got me caught in a kind of cycle."

We don't notice it until now, but the lid is off Pablo's cage and he doesn't appear to be inside.

"I spend all day worrying about every little detail. The future is terrifying y'all."

That last bit isn't a southern-ism, it's more of a youthful borrowing of urban slang. And it feels like it's meant as a joke, but we aren't laughing.

Oh, Melody. We really *did* believe in you.

Maybe it's not too late, we all think, nearly at the same time, all across the country, the English-speaking globe, really, because Melody even has a small but fierce following in Germany. Who knew? Not Melody, because she doesn't seem to know how to check her analytics, at least she hasn't given any indication that she does.

It's not too late if we all go into the comments, right now, even before this video is finished, and we all write *one nice thing*.

One thing about Melody that makes us happy. Makes us proud to be a part of her community, her subscribers and, yes, her fans.

You're the best Melody.

OMG. Hair's so cute today!

There's some kind of *sound*. We're missing action as we type but we must press submit on our new comments.

More Pablo! Love him!

The *sound* again.

You need closet organizers! They're lifesavers in a dorm.

The *sound* is a smack.

Can you shoot a vid showing how you do your make-up?

Fuck you. Kill yourself, slut.

Oh, we all recoil at the dingus among us who felt the need to write that last comment. We bristle as a collective organism.

But a few bad apples . . .

By the time we all scroll back up after typing out our positivity, Pablo's on screen.

Cute little Pablo! If Melody keeps making videos, one of us is going to have to make Pablo his own Twitter account where "he" can share cute memes and aphorisms. We wouldn't want any money in exchange for doing something like that. We'd just want Melody to acknowledge what a nice gesture it is.

Pablo looks troubled, he's crawling across the desk, searching out a place to hide.

And he finds it in Melody's hair. Her chestnut curls are so wide and well-kept that Pablo is able to use one of them as an impromptu cave.

Melody's hair has fallen across her desk, pushed her keyboard away, apparently bumping the camera to a lower vantage.

She's performed a literal headdesk.

But it's only once the blood begins to spread, the salty blackness of it chasing Pablo out of his hiding spot so he slips off the desk—we hope to land unharmed on the carpet—that we realize that those smacks we heard were repeated headdesks.

Putting her face down onto the desk and into a kitchen knife that Melody has held horizontally (not vertically, like would make more sense). The flat of the blade is flush with the particleboard of her Ikea desk. The sharp part is embedded in Melody's forehead.

It's sad. And she's unresponsive, but the thing we all marvel at is: How did she manage to get this video uploaded? There must be a program or function for it that we've never heard of. Maybe a Google Chrome extension?

Amazing. Melody went from a nobody to a seasoned expert in less than one month.

Oh well. There's nothing more for us to see here, the video is over, the pool of blood from the gashes in her skull spread as far as it's going to go.

The video ends.

We unsubscribe.

AUTHOR'S STORY NOTE

"Please Subscribe" was solicited by Jack Bantry, editor of *Splatterpunk Magazine*. It's the third story of mine he's purchased and I thank him for continually publishing my work (and Randy and Cheryl for reprinting it). My books have moments of extreme violence, but mostly I think that my long work is too goofy and/or tame to be considered "hardcore" in any real capacity. I'm happy to have a respected editor telling me to cut loose in short fiction . . . even if the results are sometimes more sadpunk than splatterpunk.

I wrote "Please Subscribe" while trying to get my own YouTube channel off the ground (as of writing this, it's still going, if you want to see my dumb face talk about movies and books). Clearly, the story is not autobiographical, but while researching the scene and what it takes to gain subscribers/view traction I found myself asking: "Why would anyone want to put themselves out there like this?" And more importantly: "Who the hell is supposed to be the audience for vloggers?" The answers I arrived at are probably depressing and slightly confused.

BACKNE

TIM MILLER

From *A Gathering of Gore*
Publisher: GutWrench Productions

JERRY HATED WORKING IN A FACTORY. He'd been a material handler for almost three years and it sucked. Some guys loved it. He would admit any day of the week he liked driving the forklift. Well, most of the time. Sometimes unloading trucks and having to place loads into super high places was the worst. You couldn't see where the fuck shit was. One time a skid got caught on something, as he pulled the forks out, the skid came with it and two fifty-five gallon drums of cleaning solution came crashing to the floor.

Fortunately, no one was standing nearby or they'd have been killed. Since that incident he was much more careful. Half the time he didn't even know what was in most of the barrels. They all had hazmat labels on them. That was all he needed to know. Not to mention they always smelled something awful. Even when they were sealed his eyes watered just from the odor.

When possible he wore a respirator when hauling the things around, but that wasn't always an option. They took too long to put on, and usually didn't help. Sometimes they made it all worse, trapping the odor inside. Totally nasty. It always felt like fire was going up his nose. At least what he figured fire going up his nose would feel like, as actual fire had never physically gone up his nose.

One day they received a shipment of some especially strange looking barrels. These were green drums stacked onto a skid, but didn't have any hazmat labels. Not that it mattered to Jerry. These would go onto another loft on the far side of the warehouse. Unfortunately, they would have to go on the very top. Jerry's least favorite, as he wouldn't be able to see what he was doing. Had to play it by feel.

He lifted the skid and elevated the forks as he backed away from the truck. He drove to the loft and raised the forks as high as they would go. Once it was raised up, he tilted the forks backward slightly to get a good angle, when something dripped onto him. First it got onto his helmet, then it came down faster until it was pouring down in a steady pour.

"Motherfucker!" Jerry yelled as he undid his seatbelt and jumped out of the seat. He made it out, but not before a bunch of the ooze hit the back of his collar and ran down his back. It was warm and gooey whatever it was.

"Jerry! What the hell are you doing?" Carl called out as he ran over. Carl was the plant supervisor.

"Those fucking barrels are leaking. That shit got all over me. Look!" Jerry turned around. He hadn't seen what the actual substance was but could hear Carl gasping.

"Jesus fuck. What is that shit?" Carl asked.

"I don't know. The driver had the MSDS for it. There were no hazmat stickers on it."

"Shit. Does it hurt?"

"No. What's wrong?"

"Nothing man. If it doesn't hurt. Just go home. Maybe get it checked out if it bothers you. That shit is all green and sticky looking."

"What about the forklift?"

"Just leave it. I'll have someone take care of it. Get out of here."

Jerry nodded and headed home. He could feel the sticky substance along his back but still hadn't seen it. When he got home, he stripped out of his work clothes and held up his shirt where he saw the green sludge for the first time. The entire back side of his shirt was covered in it.

"What the fuck?"

He climbed into the shower and began to rinse off. Whatever the substance on his back was hadn't bothered him at all until the water hit it. The second the water touched his back, his whole body burned. He screamed and jumped away as white-hot pain shot through his entire backside.

"Holy shit! Fuck! Shit! Fuck! Shit!" He jumped up and down, almost slipping and falling, but keeping his balance after grabbing the rail. He stepped out of the shower and toweled off. The burning in his back continued, but subsided slowly. Looking at himself in the mirror, he cranked his head around to see what his back looked like.

The green goo was gone, but his back was bright red as if it were badly sunburned. The pain was gone by the time he'd toweled off and dressed. However, he did suddenly feel exhausted. Jerry climbed into bed and pulled up the covers. Before he knew it, he was sound asleep.

When he awoke, his back was throbbing. Climbing out of bed, he headed into the bathroom to look at his back again. This time, he almost threw up at the sight. His back was covered in bright red pimples. Hundreds of them clustered together. Some of them had whiteheads already. Others were just red and puffy.

"What the fuck?" he said to his reflection. He needed to go have it checked out, but also needed to get to work. He was already running late. He couldn't let something as simple as a breakout cost him his job. His plant only allowed three sick days a year and all were unpaid. Carefully he pulled on his shirt before he finished dressing. Once his boots were laced up he headed out to work.

Most of the day had been uneventful. Typical loading and unloading of various trucks. No one mentioned the strange barrels and leak the day before. He'd wanted to ask his boss just what was in there, but Carl had been tied up in meetings all morning. Jerry was relieved when the lunch bell sounded. He climbed out of the forklift and headed to the break area when someone from behind startled him.

"Holy shit!" the guy yelled.

Jerry turned around to find his co-worker, Mike, standing behind him looking horrified.

"What's wrong?"

"Dude, your back is all wet. What the fuck." Mike took a step closer. "God and it stinks."

Jerry reached over his shoulder, feeling along the back of his shirt, and sure enough, it was completely saturated. But with what?

"Jesus Christ," Jerry said. Out of panic, he began to remove his shirt right there. His co-workers in the break area looked on horrified and confused as he pulled his shirt all the way off.

"What the fuck?" Another co-worker yelled. A female worker screamed as people started backing away from him. Jerry felt something running down his back. He ran into the bathroom to look in the mirror. When he saw it, he screamed himself. His entire back was covered in huge, yellow zits. Many of which had burst. Greenish/yellow pus oozed all down his back. Some falling off in large clumps.

Sirens sounded as Jerry stepped out of the bathroom. There was an ambulance pulling up outside. Two paramedics came in, a guy and a girl, both carrying medical bags and wearing rubber gloves.

"Are you the one with the fluid discharge?" the male medic asked.

"I guess so. I'm not sure what's going on." Jerry turned around.

"Oh my God!" the female medic said. "Any idea what caused this?"

"Some shit spilled on me yesterday from a barrel I was unloading. I have no idea what it was, and no one will tell me. I woke up today all broke out. Now it's like this."

The male medic stuck his finger into one of the holes in his back. More greenish syrup oozed from the opening. The medic held the finger up to his nose and took a sniff.

"Smells like acid," he said. "Does it hurt?"

"Not really. Did you just stick your finger in there?"

"No. Let's get you on the ambulance," the woman said before grabbing a blanket and throwing it over his shoulders. He hoped once they got to the hospital they could figure out what it was. Except as they were walking out, Jerry noticed several of his co-worker's faces were covered in red and yellow zits. Some didn't notice, but others were looking at each other and freaking out.

The medics looked at each other as the girl finally spoke up.

"I think we need to quarantine the whole plant," she said. "Including us."

"Are you serious?" the guy asked.

"Yes I'm serious. Look at this. Everyone is getting whatever this guy has."

Jerry's face and arms began to itch. He reached up and felt thick bumps all over his cheeks and forehead. Looking at the medics, their faces were breaking out as well. None of the current breakouts were as bad as his back. Except he was about to be in worse condition than everyone else. The other employees began screaming at him as the paramedics looked on.

"What did you do to us?"

"What the fuck is wrong with you? You infected all of us!"

"Are we turning into zombies?"

Jerry tried to back away as they closed in on him.

"I didn't do anything to you. One of the barrels spilled shit on me! Seriously! I woke up all broken out. I just thought it was a rash. Then at lunch my back looks like this. I had no idea! I didn't know!"

Some of them were holding various tools in their hands. One man he didn't know approached. His face had gone from red and puffy to yellow and greasy looking. It was covered with whiteheads that were throbbing and ready to burst. He stood inches from Jerry.

"You did this to me," he said. "Now I'm gonna kill you!" The man lifted a hammer and reared back. Before he could swing, Jerry punched him in the face. As his fist connected, dozens of zits on the man's face popped at once. Yellow pus and fluid splattered onto Jerry's face and into his mouth. It tasted salty as he gagged, trying to keep from throwing up. The man fell to the ground and looked up. He looked as if his face was melting off.

The entire right side of his face was covered in yellow clumps of pus and sludge. The others' faces began turning yellow as well. When the man's face began oozing yellow slime, they all attacked Jerry at once. He swung in every direction as many jumped onto his back. One person grabbed him in a chokehold, but he was able to slip free as greasy pus lubricated his face and neck.

The entire mob fought like mad as their zits continued popping and squirting. They rolled and tussled around in a huge pool of greenish yellow sludge. One man shoved another man's face into a puddle of pus, holding him down until the man drowned. Jerry felt someone thrust an entire hand in an opening in his back. The person's hand fished around as if it were looking for something as more slime oozed from the opening. Jerry broke away to see it was the female medic. He couldn't even make out her face under all the pus that caked her hair to the side of her head as huge clumps fell from her face. Her eyes were wild-eyed as she screamed and jumped at Jerry, digging her nails into his face, ripping his flesh and zits free. Bloody pus dripped down his face and nose as he tumbled backward, hitting his head on the floor, and knocking him unconscious.

When he awoke, he was lying in a hospital bed. Looking around, he saw the room was dark and there was plastic lining the walls. Someone stood over him wearing a fully encapsulated hazmat suit.

"Jerry. Glad you finally woke up," the robotic voice from the suit said.

"What's going on? Where am I?"

"I'm Dr. Cole. You're at the CDC in our special quarantine unit. You had quite an ordeal."

"I guess. I thought it was just a nightmare. I had this really bad acne on my back and everyone at work got it too and attacked me. It was so gross and freaky."

"I'm afraid that was no dream. It all happened. You were exposed to some rare bacteria that caused the breakout. It also causes temporary dementia and paranoia."

"Yeah, I noticed. What was in that barrel? That stuff that fell on me?"

"That barrel contained the actual pus from another set of victims. I'm not sure why it wasn't marked. The fluid itself contains some valuable properties."

"What does that mean? Do you have a cure for it?"

"Cure? No. I think you're mistaken. We are harvesting it. This stuff can be easily weaponized. It is very potent and you of all the victims seem to have an endless supply."

"What?"

"Yes. That's what all the tubes hooked to you are."

Jerry looked at himself and for the first time he noticed dozens of tubes connected to his back, arms and legs.

"What is all this?" Jerry asked.

"Think of it like this. You are one giant Slurpy. So we have several people with straws hooked up to you to make sure we don't miss or lose a single drop. Just a few ounces of that stuff is worth a fortune."

"You can't do this!"

"I'm not. The Pentagon is. I just work here. Sorry kid. Don't worry though. I left you some DVDs to keep you company during your stay." The doctor held up a box containing a bunch of movies that looked like they just came from the Wal-Mart bargain bin. "I think they have Piranha Shark vs. Bugnado in there. That's a good one. Anyway. Here you go. I'll be back in a few hours to check on you."

As the doctor turned and walked way, he knocked on a steel door that made a hissing sound as it was unsealed. The doc stepped through and the steel door slammed shut. Jerry looked around and flung the box of DVDs across the room. He tried to climb out of bed, but the tubes kept him in place. They had been surgically embedded into his skin. Panic began to set in as the reality of his situation hit. He'd spend the rest of his life in this place as a one-man pus factory for the government.

"You can't do this!" he screamed. "Let me go! You can't do this!" Tears ran down his face as he looked at the ground. He caught sight of one of the DVDs. It was called Attack of the Pus Monster. He threw his head back and laughed. Once the laughter started, he couldn't stop it. He laughed hysterically at the irony of the whole thing. Attack of the Pus Monster? He was the Pus Monster. But that gave him an idea. He reached back and began tugging at the tubes, despite the pain he'd ripped one free. Chunks of skin and pus dripped from it as he pulled on the next one. When the doctor came back, he was in for a big surprise. A surprise from the real life pus monster.

THE GIRL WHO LOVED BRUCE CAMPBELL

CHRISTA CARMEN

From *Corner Bar Magazine Vol. 1 #4*

No Bottom Pond might have had a bottom, but as far as the three clammy and restless individuals that sat in the idling car by its banks knew, it very well might not. The cold sweats and body aches would not assail them for much longer; the lankier of the two males divvied up the wax baggies of brown powder, and each in turn began their own sacred ritual of preparation. It took only seconds for the first of the three to realize a key element was missing from their assorted paraphernalia.

"Dammit," the stocky male said. "Does anyone have a water bottle?"

There was no reply as each of the three checked the space around their feet, and the nearest cup holder.

"Now what?" the lone female asked. "We can't hit a gas station. We need to stay off the roads for a while, someone may have seen us leave that house."

There was murmured agreement from the two men, followed by a morose silence. The lanky man broke the quiet with a snort of derision. "This shit's fried our brains," he said. "We're sitting next to a lake, complaining about not having any water to shoot up with."

"It's not a lake, it's a pond," the woman said.

"Technically, it's not even a pond. It's an estuary. And we can't use that water because it's brackish." The stouter man sounded matter-of-fact.

"What's brackish mean? That it's dirty? Please, I've seen you use the water from the tank of a gas station toilet, dirty should be the least of your worries." This, from the woman.

"No, not dirty, *brackish*. It means it's half freshwater, half salt. We can't shoot that, it might mess with our bodies' electrolyte levels or something." Now the stocky man sounded less sure of himself.

The lanky man opened the car door. He reached for an empty Dunkin Donuts cup discarded on the floor of the passenger seat, removed the lid, and looked suspiciously into its depths. Shrugging, he started for the pond's weedy shore.

"I didn't just get away with a B&E and buy dope from the shadiest dealer in town to let a little saltwater stop me. It's only *half* salt anyways," he called over his shoulder.

The woman and the stout man watched him creep toward the water's edge. He folded his tall frame in half and scooped a cupful of water into the Styrofoam. He did this in the light of a moon so close it seemed to

269

be perched atop the hill that loomed over No Bottom Pond, a luminous cherry on top of a black forest cake.

The first full moon to rise on Christmas in forty years had occurred the night before. "A Christmas miracle," the woman had said sarcastically as they listened to a radio talk show host lament the previous night's fog cover on their way to Shore Road, and the house they'd been casing most of the past week. The upscale home had yielded extensive reserves of jewelry, cash, and three guns. There'd been a safe, but they had no use for a safe. They only took what they could trade quickly and easily to their dealer, and Pablo had no interest in safes.

The lunar display of December twenty-sixth happened to be free from a smothering blanket of fog. As the woman watched the tall man return, she noticed that in the bright moonlight, the water's surface had a strange sparkle to it, was almost phosphorescent in the gleam. Parts of the pond were the shiny, black, oil slick of water-in-moonlight she'd expect. Having spent her whole life in the seaside town, she'd seen water undulating under the moon enough times for the sight to be commonplace, but No Bottom Pond seemed greenish in its radiance, and seemed not to steam as much as gurgle, like the stew in a witch's cauldron.

She forgot her inquisitiveness over the appearance of the water when the passenger door slammed shut. Three syringe tips plunged greedily into the captured pond water, transporting water from cup to three waiting spoons. Mysticism, Rhode Island was a small town (the population was reduced by half in the winter), and the heroin dealers had been tapped into the same pipelines in and out of the closest major cities for decades; the three longtime users expected the same cut and purity of dope they'd had both the previous day, and on the occasion of their first use. Subsequently, no lighter flicked on to form dancing shadows on the car walls, no Butane-fueled flame burned prospective toxins out of the contents of their spoons, spoons that had shed the innocence of their kitchen days for something more sinister. They each shot up, one, two, three, and each fell into that first nod of euphoria, a scarecrow short of Dorothy and her friends in the poppy field.

At the same time that legions of fish were rising to the vaporous surface of No Bottom Pond, dead and already beginning to putrefy, small boils began to pop up under the skin of the three beings in the car. The tall man thought he'd injected a "hot shot," while the woman jerked out of her nod in wild agitation to inspect the tip of her needle, convinced she'd given herself "cotton fever" by neglecting to free the point from Q-tip remnants. Both of them were wrong.

The mutations occurred quickly and the changes were profound. When the transformation was complete, the three beings were no longer satisfied with the heroin that flowed through their veins. They were hungry for more. Hungry in a way that made every torturous withdrawal symptom or harrowing mental craving of the past seem like a petty annoyance, a mere itch that could go without being scratched.

Two hours earlier, a local scientist named Craig Silas stood on a dip of Watch Hill Road, a dark silhouette overlooking the river that rushed into No Bottom Pond. Craig worked at a nearby pharmaceutical company, and the previous year had snuck a project home to his basement laboratory to continue his work free from the oversight and ethical regulations of his employer.

In the wake of a country-wide opiate epidemic, Big Pharma had sufficient incentive to develop an opioid-free painkiller, eliminating the potential for abuse and addiction. Craig had stumbled on an unanticipated side-effect of the chemical compound he'd been studying, and upon bringing his research home, further unlocked the potential of the drug. Characteristics included superhuman strength, laser-point focus, and a complete inability to feel pain. Craig spent weeks hypothesizing on the drug's seemingly limitless prospects, until he'd descended the basement stairs one morning to find one of the pink-eyed lab rats feasting on his cage-mates' brains. It seemed that with every possibility of experiencing pain eliminated, the rats' behavior had morphed into something much more ominous . . . and much more deadly.

After driving up and down the streets of Mysticism with the concoction swishing around a large vat in his trunk, Craig noticed that the adjacent river ran under the road and into a wide inlet. Theorizing that the body of water before him was the equivalent of a dead end street, he pulled onto the narrow shoulder and muscled the vat onto the guardrail before another car could appear. Craig Silas had left No Bottom Pond ten miles behind him by the time his miracle drug had seeped into the pond's ecosystem, and was home in his favorite armchair with his feet up by the time the first transformations began to occur.

SOPHISTICATED cognition already reduced to animalistic compulsion, the three addicts, who had become fiends of a different nature, were barely able to recall the chain of events that had led them to their last high, brought to the utmost intensity by the unorthodox mixture of heroin and pond-dispersed, opiate-free analgesic. But they were able to recall enough to know what they needed to do to feed the hunger that gnawed at their insides like so many of Silas' lab rats. And so they began to move.

KARTYA watched the spray of blood waterfall through the front door of the cabin, and grabbed Kit's arm.

"That . . . was . . . awesome!" she cheered, the arm-grabbing escalating to arm-slapping. She turned to face her boyfriend. "How much time is left?" she asked him.

"Kar, just watch it, I'm not messing with it again. It's thirty minutes long, like all the other episodes."

This appeased Kartya enough to watch the last ten minutes in silence. She twirled a ringlet of cherry-coke-colored hair around blood-red fingernails. When the show was over, she turned to Kit again, eager to hear his opinion on the latest installment.

"Well," Kit said. "They definitely set us up for an epic showdown at the cabin."

"Agreed!" Kartya paused. "I wish there was more than ten episodes. That was a good one though. Buckets of blood!" A mischievous smile turned up the corners of her lips.

"Twisted, gory, and hilarious," Kit said. "The dead cop put her fists through those campers' skulls, and turned them into corpse puppets!"

"Let's be serious, the other characters only exist to compliment Ash. To give the directors a springboard for Ash's amazing one-liners. And so we can see some different weapons brandished against the Deadites. 'Cause, you know, it can't be all about Ash's chainsaw arm and 'boomstick.'" She mimed obliterating Kit with a shotgun blast to the face and snickered.

"Also, did I tell you that Ash, err, sorry, Bruce Campbell wrote an autobiography a few years back . . . called *If Chins Could Kill?*"

Kit gave her a look that conveyed both incredulity and reverence, and broke into a hearty chuckle, no doubt visualizing the B-list movie actor's signature square chin.

"Are you kidding me? That's amazing. You need to get that book." He gestured to two bookshelves flanking the television, which still rolled the blood-splattered credits for the show.

Kartya nodded with enthusiasm but did not turn to regard the bookshelves, pointing instead to the two Vinyl Pop characters facing off from their respective posts atop surround sound speakers. The superbly detailed plastic Ash and an *Army of Darkness* Deadite had been Christmas gifts from her mother the previous morning. Though she didn't share her daughter's love for horror, Kartya's mother knew Kartya and Kit harbored a cultish enthusiasm for Ash, and all things *Evil Dead*, from the campy originals to the 2013 remake, and now, the new original series. She had wrapped the figurines, knowing it would bring appreciative smiles to their faces.

"Instead of that wobbly speaker, a hardcover copy of *If Chins Could Kill* could be mini-Ash's battleground in the fight against evil," Kartya said.

Kit surveyed the current setup displaying their action figures, smiled, and got to his feet.

"You're cute, babe. I love that you love blood and guts as much as I do." Kit stretched his six-foot-three frame toward the ceiling and let out a groan. "But the party's over. I have to get to work."

"I can't believe you agreed to work the night after Christmas," Kartya said. She tried to pout, but a yawn claimed her features instead. "Although to be honest, you won't miss much. I'm beat and will be asleep fifteen minutes after you leave."

As Kit dragged himself up the stairs to change, Kartya heard a muffled chime, and realized she was sitting on her phone. A preview of the text message scrolled across the screen. Kartya's friend Laura had written: "Better lock your door . . ."

Laura did well as an emergency room nurse, working as an independent contractor in different hospitals from Hartford to Boston. She vacationed often, and had just returned that morning from her fourth trip to St. John since the year began. Kartya thumbed at the screen until she could see the rest of the message. In its entirety, it read: "Better lock your door . . . because my house just got broken into."

A fat worm of fear speared itself between the layers of Kartya's intestines. There had been numerous reports of break-ins in Mysticism over the last month, and Laura lived less than a mile from the riverfront home Kartya and Kit rented. Her fingers jerking in furious spasms, Kartya texted Laura back: "Were you home? Are you ok? What did they take?"

As she waited for Laura's reply, Kit trudged back down the stairs. He was able to read the worry on her face with a single glance.

"What is it?" he asked.

"Laura and Seth's house got broken into. I asked her what they took and if they were home. She hasn't answered me yet."

The concern on Kit's face mixed with anger. With a grim headshake, he reached out to pull her off the couch.

"No way. This isn't happening. No way I get switched to the night shift a month before the worst string of burglaries this town's ever seen. Follow me."

"But why? Where are we going?" Kartya asked him, her attention split between his grip on her forearm and her phone announcing a newly arrived message.

Kit gestured up the stairs, but let go of her so she could navigate to her text message app. She read silently, her brow creased, then raised her eyes to meet Kit's.

"She said they were out getting drinks and they came home to a broken window in the living room. They'd been on vacation for the past week so someone obviously anticipated an empty house. They took jewelry, cash, some other valuables . . ." Kartya tried to trail off effectively, as if this was the extent of stolen goods.

"And? What else?" When she didn't answer, he said, "What else did they take, Kartya?"

"Three guns were missing," she said, knowing this information would fan Kit's anger and apprehension into a full-blown blaze.

Motivated anew, Kit took her hand and resumed their ascent. In the guest bedroom, he retrieved a lockbox from an opaque-fronted entertainment stand.

"I would never forgive myself if something happened to you. I know you're going to protest, but agree to it for my sake." He pulled a handgun from the box and spun the cylinder, counting bullets.

"Kit," Kartya objected.

"Please, just come here so I can give you a quick refresher on how to . . ."

"Kit—" She was about to insist on an end to this surreal conversation. Instead, Kartya sighed and took the gun from Kit's hands, showing him that she remembered how to wield the weapon properly, cocking the hammer and adopting a shooter's stance.

"You've dragged me to the range a hundred times. I know what I'm doing well enough to defend myself if it came to it."

Kit nodded, but he seemed distracted. She uncocked the gun and returned it to the lockbox. Spinning on her heel for the hall, she stopped short when she heard the scrape of something much larger being unearthed from the closet.

Without turning, she said, "Kit, I do *not* need the shotgun to be within arm's reach when I go to bed tonight. End of discussion."

Torn between Kartya's obvious intention to refuse the shotgun and his need to be assured of her safety, Kit placed the shotgun on top of the stand.

"Fine," he said. "But I'm leaving it here, just in case. The revolver is going on your nightstand. And that's also not open for discussion."

"Whatever," Kartya said, believing that the house was impregnable. "Drive safe please, and try to have a good night at work."

Kartya let Kit lead her into their bedroom, saying nothing as he placed the revolver on a paperback, two feet from where she was to lay her head down on the pillow. He kissed her goodnight and turned off the bedside lamp, and Kartya listened to his footsteps on the stairs as she nestled beneath the covers. Fewer than fifteen minutes after he departed, she was sound asleep.

A NOISE woke her, what sounded like the skeletal finger of a winter-dead tree tapping on a window. She sat up, disoriented. Had Kit forgotten something, perhaps his badge, or the food she'd packed for him to eat on his break? She groped for her cell, found the button to illuminate the screen. Ten forty-five. Kit would be forty-five minutes into an hour-long commute, so it wouldn't be him tapping. She strained to catch the sound again, but it had stopped. Kartya sunk down onto the pillow, drawing the comforter up to her neck, then groaned. She flung the comforter back, forcing herself to bear the cold trek to the bathroom before returning to sleep. Halfway there, the tapping began again.

Kartya froze. There in the hallway, equally removed from both the revolver and the shotgun Kit had set out for her protection, vulnerable in her bare feet, with full bladder and panic fluttering in her brain like a moth trapped in a lantern, the details of the nearby break-in came roaring back, having been temporarily stolen by the fugue of sleep.

As she stood rooted in paralysis, her rational mind attempted to quell her fears, reading from the familiar script all terrified souls call upon in times of need: 'It's nothing, it's just the wind. There's a perfectly good explanation for this.' Repeating those words with the same tenacity as a drowning swimmer flailing for a rescue buoy, she started down the stairs in the dark.

Kartya's bare feet sunk into the shag carpet as she crossed the living room to the big picture window on the right, struggling to see in the all-encompassing blackness. Wondering why the moon refused to aid her in her endeavor, cursing the peaks and gables of the house's roofline, she moved from the window to the front door, whacking her hip on the corner of the heavy, oak desk in her blindness, and switched on the outdoor floodlights.

Slowly, giving the desk a wider berth, she crept to the right, so focused on the grate-free expanse of the window that she didn't notice the shadow stretched across the ground in front of her.

A hapless civilian had become possessed by the Kandarian Demon and turned into a Deadite . . . or at least this was the only explanation that occurred to Kartya when she came face-to-face with the diseased-looking monstrosity separated from her by only a half-inch of glass. For one breathless moment, Kartya thought she was dreaming, or perhaps had slipped on the stairs and knocked herself out, and was now subject to some trauma-induced hallucination. Then the demon-thing cocked its head to one side and emitted a guttural chuffing noise, and Kartya knew that somehow, what she was seeing was real.

She may have stood staring into the black pits of the creature's eyes, a creature who had once been a tall, lanky, human, until Kit returned home from work the next morning, but the spell was broken when the now-inhuman thing's arm shot out as if from a cannon, smashing through the six-foot tall window pane with no more effort than a man punching his hand through a piece of paper.

Kartya did not think, not in any conscious, deliberate manner. She ran to the stairs on reflex, sprinting up them two at a time, her body knowing where it was taking her, seeing her destination in her mind as clearly as an earlier scene from *Evil Dead*. Though it defied logic, though an hour ago it had seemed impossible, she had to get to the revolver if she wanted to survive. As she flew down the hall for the bedroom, she had the wherewithal to dart her arm into the bathroom and flip the switch, the overhead fixture just bright enough to allow a half-moon of light to spill into the hallway.

It took all of Kartya's willpower not to shut and lock the bedroom door behind her, but knowing how easily the thing had infiltrated the ground floor, she knew it would behoove her to leave the door open and see it coming, rather than be ignorant to its diabolical design. She grabbed the gun from the nightstand and slid along the front wall of the bedroom. She molded her hands to fit around the butt in what she hoped was a relaxed position ("Never choke your gun," the range attendant had told her, "that's a surefire way to hit everything but your target.") and crouched by the closet, the thinnest rectangle of hallway visible from her spot on the floor.

The sound of footsteps shuffle-dragging up the stairs after her was interrupted by a second downstairs window imploding, and then, horribly, a third. Kartya wanted to curse. She wanted to scream, or cry, or curl up in the fetal position on the floor. Instead, she pulled the hammer back, prayed for consistency, squinted one eye, and kept perfectly quiet.

The thing made it to the top of the stairs and turned the corner. The hallway was short and Kartya had a clear shot, but forced herself to hold fire. The thing took a long, lumbering step, then another. It was wearing jeans and a plaid flannel shirt with the sleeves rolled up, and as it stepped into the crescent of light filtering out of the bathroom, Kartya saw strange marks on its forearms. The thing moved forward again.

The first shot shocked Kartya with its loudness, and she realized she'd never experienced gunfire firsthand without protective earmuffs. She recovered quickly, as she had to, concentrating on readying a second shot despite the knowledge that the thing hadn't been halted or even slowed in its pursuit. She'd hit it three inches below the chest, a mark devoid of any major organs. Kartya figured this could be why the creature was still on its feet, but she had a sneaking suspicion that it was not the only thing spurring the demon forward.

Kartya hit the creature again, in the shoulder, and again, clipping its neck, spurts of blood exploding from the torn flesh, and again, another shot to the stomach. Still it stalked toward her, so Kartya took a deep breath and held it, steadying her hands and her gaze, and aimed for its right kneecap. She hit it dead center, and the thing's leg seemed to fold backward, threatening to topple the creature ass over teakettle, but it would not go down. Before it could fully right itself, she aimed for the left kneecap. Another direct hit, and when the thing's jeans tore and knee shattered, Kartya thought she saw a substantial fragment of bone go catapulting through the air like a haphazardly thrown Frisbee. Again, the creature stayed on its feet.

Kit had considered the possibility of a break-in serious enough to warrant planting the revolver by her bedside, but not serious enough to provide her with extra bullets. The thing had swayed like a drunken sorority girl in too-high heels, but when it took another step, hesitant, but advancing all the same, Kartya knew she had to enact plan B.

Before she could change her mind, she rushed at the thing with calculated strides, coming to a stop before she reached the end of the damask-patterned runner. She bent before the creature, loath to take her eyes off it for even a moment, and took the corner of the rug up in her fingers. She knew she couldn't yank the runner hard enough to accomplish her end goal of toppling the creature over the bannister and initiating a free-fall to the ground floor below, but she hoped to knock it off its feet enough to start that process. Luck was on her side, however, and the creature had already begun to fall off balance, so that when she yanked the runner with a throaty grunt, its back was already pressed against the bannister, and the upward movement of the rug functioned to throw the creature's legs up and over its head in a graceless backflip over the railing.

It fell the distance of fourteen hardwood steps and crashed to the floor below. Flipping on the hall light, Kartya leaned over and peered into the abyss. The thing had already gotten up and was placing one splintered but still-operational leg onto the bottom step.

"You have got be kidding me," Kartya said out loud, scuttling back from the edge and heading for the guest bedroom.

Kartya had only fired the shotgun on one prior occasion, and even then she'd almost passed on the opportunity, preferring to refine her technique with the handgun. Before she exited the bedroom, she slipped her feet into a pair of red Victoria's Secret slippers, the left foot embroidered with the word *naughty* in white stitching, and the right with the word *nice*. It occurred to her that it would be immeasurably easier to fight Deadites without a full bladder, so she walked to the bathroom to relieve herself, pointing the shotgun at an opening in the bannister rails as she did, counting herself lucky when she heard what sounded like a scuffle amongst the creatures at the bottom of the stairs, delaying their climb. She declined to flush, not sure if the noise would send their zombie-like brains into a frenzy, and stood at the threshold of the passage to the stairs. *What would Ash do*, she thought? She looked down at her feet.

"Time to put the *naughty* foot forward," she said, forcing a half-grin, and stepped her left foot out into the hallway.

Kartya marched down the stairs, beholding the scene below her, and cocked the shotgun. There were three creatures, as she'd guessed from the equal number of shattered windows, and they appeared more akin to Deadites than she'd have thought possible apart from being on the set of *Ash vs Evil Dead*. They appeared to be undeterred by pain but incapable of reason, and they were unable to begin their onslaught of the second floor because they couldn't decide amongst the three of them who was going to go up first. Kartya helped them out by blowing the arm off the shorter, stocky man on the left, who looked down to regard the blood and sinew hanging from his shoulder with serene detachment.

The thing to the right of the tall creature had been female in its human form, and Kartya made the mistake of pulling the trigger as she moved down another step, throwing off her aim and catching the she-thing in the upper portion of the skull, blowing off the top half of its scalp and rocking the thing's head back on its neck. The head snapped back to its original position. Kartya recalled the catchphrase of the popular children's toy that refused to be bowled over: "Weebles wobble, but they don't fall down." With dark amusement, she wondered if anyone had tried to knock a Weeble down with a double-barrel shotgun.

Kartya told herself to focus on this next shot. She aimed for the center of the tall one's head and in her nervousness whispered to herself, "Boom."

The shot was absolute in its devastation, the shell forging a hole in the thing's skull like the point of a pastry-bag digging through a jelly-filled donut. Kartya was ecstatic to see that with its brain dislodged and projected somewhere into her living room, the Deadite-thing was finally incapable of pursuit.

So that's it, she thought. *Although they don't appear human, they can be killed as such.* The *Necronomicon* proposed three specific ways to release a possessed soul: a live burial, bodily dismemberment, or purification by fire. Thinking that she liked her house, and would rather not burn it to the ground, and that time did not permit the digging of two graves in frozen soil, Kartya re-cocked the shotgun. Wistfully, she pictured Ash's chainsaw hand. Bodily dismemberment would be a hell of a lot easier with her hero's weapon of choice than by the excruciatingly slow process of fortuitous shotgun hits, but beggars can't be choosers.

Oblivious to the flecks of blood and brain matter peppering her body, Kartya closed the distance between her and the two evil things still standing. Needing to make it to the front door, she had to descend the stairs low enough to shoot the creatures sideways, preferably one to the right and one to the left. Getting within arm's reach of the things was not her idea of a good time, but neither was wasting two barrels of the shotgun into anywhere but their heads.

Kartya had properly determined the direction the things would be propelled in, but she wasn't lucky enough to replicate the angle of her shot to the taller creature's head. Though the things were knocked to the floor and out of her path, they were reanimating quicker than she would have liked. Grabbing her car keys from their hook, wishing she had time to find a coat, Kartya fled into the cold night in only her slippers, t-shirt, and sweatpants, the ash-grey shirt darkened in several places with the demon-things' blood.

Ten steps down the front walkway and the moon made a glorious reappearance, lighting Kartya's path to the garage and keeping her from tripping on a bizarre pile of items laid out at the base of her driveway. Allowing one second for curious inspection, Kartya stooped and beheld the needles, spoons, and a random Dunkin Donuts cup of what appeared to be coffee-tainted water. Then the water hissed, geysering from the cup in an angry spout, and she reevaluated her first interpretation.

"Crazed junkies or the infected victims of a science experiment gone wrong," she said as she jogged for the garage. "Either way, no thanks."

The garage door groaned in protest as Kartya flung it open. She unlocked the Jeep's doors with a terse beep, praying the noise was not enough to attract the evil things. She surveyed the driveway and as much of the yard as was visible: nothing came for her. Hopping into the car, thinking she could be at the police station in less than five minutes, hoping this was quick enough to bring back reinforcements before the creatures could abandon her place for somewhere else, she threw the car into reverse and prepared to backup. The stout male thing and the lone female one took up the entirety of her rearview mirror.

"I don't think so," Kartya said, and flooded the gas. The things disappeared under the Jeep and Kartya flinched as she registered the sounds of splitting flesh and crunching bone. It sounded like someone had thrown a cantaloupe onto pavement from six stories up. Then, there was quiet.

Kartya sat in the driver's seat, feeling her skin slide over the leather under its coating of gore. She had time for one profound exhalation before a figure blotted out the moonlight streaming through the passenger's side window. As she regarded the reanimated corpse-woman with horror, the driver's door opened and Kartya was pulled out of the Jeep by a pair of rough hands inserted under her armpits.

At the last second, before her legs had fully passed the frame of the vehicle, she found purchase and launched herself backward. The thing hit the pavement again with a wet thump, and Kartya managed to disentangle herself from its clutches.

The house was too far so she ran for the garage, hoping to find a pair of gardening shears. Instead, her headlights illuminated a beautiful sight, the most beautiful sight she'd ever seen. She said a silent apology for ever nagging Kit about cleaning out the garage, packed full with junk from previous tenants, and sprinted for the chainsaw.

She flipped the start switch and placed the saw on the dusty floor, gripping the handlebar with her left hand.

"Here goes everything," she said, and pulled the starter rope like she'd seen her father, Kit, and Ash all do on numerous occasions. The saw popped, but did not start.

"Dammit!" she yelled, as she watched the first of the possessed-things, which after its run-in with her Jeep had lost even a passing resemblance to a living human, approach the mouth of the garage. She jimmied a black lever on one side and tried the starter rope again. The saw came to life with a deafening rumble.

Kartya had been a vegetarian for eight years, so the extent of her experience with chopping flesh was limited. By the time she'd finished a violent vertical dismemberment of the stout man, she was so thoroughly covered in blood that she did not imagine the second creature's vivisection could be any worse. It was coming for her, the female, and though Kartya almost slipped in the lake of blood that covered the two-car garage from wall-to-wall, she was ready for it.

"I must say, you're taller than Chuckles over there, so this could take a while," Kartya told the demon-thing.

Kartya missed the creature's hellish reply under the unforgiving tremors of the chainsaw.

HEADLIGHTS announced the approach of a vehicle. Drenched from head to foot with an unfathomable amount of blood, Kartya was not curious as to the identity of the driver until the car passed the entrance to No Bottom Pond Road and started down the driveway. Wiping a film of blood from around her eyes, she was surprised to see Kit's Volkswagen nearing the carnage.

When the car turned slightly and illuminated the blood-covered specter that was Kartya, Kit threw the car in park and was at her side in seconds.

"What the hell! What the—" his hands grasped her shoulders and he surveyed her wildly, looking for a wound.

"It's ok, it's not my blood," Kartya told him. She gestured behind her where four halves equaled two bodies.

Kit's jaw dropped. He was incapable of speech.

"I'll explain everything, but we should probably call the police at some point. I think they either took some sort of recreational drug that turned out to be far from recreational, or were infected with something that turned them into zombies. Or . . . Deadites." She said these last words hesitantly, as if despite the very concrete evidence of chaos behind her, Kit would think she'd lost her mind at the mention of the purportedly fictional walking dead.

"Jesus, I can't believe this. I'm so glad you're alright. I pulled into the lot at work and said 'What the hell am I doing?' The night after the holiday, the night our friends get robbed, I shouldn't have left you. I should have been here for you. So I called in sick from the parking lot and came home. You should have called me, Kartya. No, you should have called the police right away!"

Moved past the point of revulsion to Kartya's blood-saturated state, Kit pulled her into a savage embrace. She let him hug her, still a bit shell-shocked, then stepped back and took it all in.

The gore packed into her Jeep's tire treads winked in the moonlight. The dismembered bodies glistened in wide pools of blood near the still-purring chainsaw. The pile of syringes and infected water sat in the foreground of the house's smashed windows. The house itself, a looming skull with its two front teeth knocked out. Her eyes came back to settle on Kit, and she smiled.

"There was no time to call anyone. I didn't have much in the way of options, didn't really have time to come up with a plan. I had to rely on myself, I guess, and on my own tenacity. With a little inspiration from a certain groovy guy." She paused, wiped a smear of blood from under her cheek, and continued:

"But the important thing is that I'm ok. And that you came back for me . . . now come here and gimme some sugar, baby."

AUTHOR'S STORY NOTE

What's not to love about the King of Groovy? A long-time fan of the Evil Dead franchise, a fun evening of binge-watching Starz's *Ash vs Evil Dead* last December was interrupted by the chilling news that my good friend's house had been broken into, and several firearms stolen. On the heels of this unfortunate text message exchange, my now-husband cheerily announced, 'Alright, time for work,' and promptly left me to embark on his normal shift . . . the night shift.

Alone, over-active imagination whirring, I lay in bed and contemplated how I would go about stopping a band of burglars should they choose to break into my place next. The opioid epidemic had long been gaining traction in the New England region I call home, and I theorized that the individuals breaking into homes to steal pawnable items like jewelry and guns were doing so to fund drug habits. Christmas 2015 concluded with a blazing full moon; I have commenced with many a story from a single strange or striking image, and the image of a trio of heroin addicts setting up their next round of shots on the banks of the brackish water inlet across the street from my apartment, illuminated by the hazy moonlight, seemed as good a starting point as any.

Like an action sequence right out of *The Evil Dead*, my bloody descriptions of dismembering, eviscerating, and decapitating Deadites were so campy and so cathartic, they seemed to take on a life of their own. I was thrilled when the editor of *Corner Bar Magazine* felt similarly, and published 'TGWLBC' in the Ostarablot issue of March 2016, and even more thrilled when Bruce Campbell himself retweeted my announcement of publication! Now the story is having new life breathed into it by *Year's Best Hardcore Horror, Volume 2*, and there's just one thing left to say: Hail to the King, baby!

THE IMPLANT
BRYAN SMITH

From *Seven Deadly Tales of Terror*
Publisher: Bitter Ale Press

AWARENESS OF SOMETHING WRONG dawned slowly for John Stark that morning. He awoke with what felt like an ordinary stiff neck, the kind that occasionally resulted from sleeping with his head turned at a bad angle. That he awoke lying flat on his back as his eyes fluttered open didn't matter. He'd been having some restless nights lately and might have shifted sleeping positions any number of times between bedtime and sunrise.

He was groggy at first and felt little motivation to do anything about the discomfort he was feeling as his consciousness continued its slow, lethargic return from dreamland. When his head was a little clearer, he would raise himself up a bit, maybe double-fold the top pillow for added cushioning, and wedge it carefully against the sore area. Then a bit later he'd get up and take some Tylenol. That should take care of things.

In those first moments, though, he was content to simply lie there as he attempted to hold on to fragments of the sex dream he'd been having prior to waking. In the dream, he'd been kidnapped by a gang of beautiful and glamorous female criminals. The babes lived a double life, working as fashion models during the day and committing elaborate heists at night. They took him to their mansion and forced him to be their sex slave. He felt like it'd been probably the most amazing dream of all time, but it was already breaking apart, the few remembered fragments growing fuzzier with each passing moment. Soon, he suspected, he wouldn't remember it at all.

Bummer.

In a few more moments, his eyes opened wider as the grogginess continued to clear. He remembered the basic premise of the amazing dream, but little beyond that, just one or two fleeting images. With the return to full consciousness almost complete, he rose up some, double-folded the pillow beneath his head, and tried to get comfortable.

It was then he began to realize he was dealing with something more than an ordinary stiff neck. Shifting position did nothing to alleviate the ache. Instead, it heightened awareness of the hard center of discomfort. He tried twisting his neck to see if this was some kind of kink that could be worked out, but all this resulted in was a sharp jab of pain he felt all the way down to his toes.

Frowning, he lifted up his head and slipped a hand beneath his neck to probe gingerly at the knot of discomfort. His breath caught in his throat and his heart did a little stutter as his fingertips skidded over the hard, round lump protruding from the flesh just beneath the base of his skull.

John sat bolt upright and probed at the object with a little less delicacy. This resulted in additional jabs of pain, but he couldn't help himself. There was something sticking out of his neck that didn't belong there, an alarming development to say the least. Any pain he was feeling from the stings that resulted from each poke of the object was overridden by other concerns, primary among them being a single basic question—*what the fuck is this fucking thing sticking out of my fucking neck?*

It did not feel like a natural object.

This impression was a good thing in the sense that, if accurate, it ruled out the sudden protrusion of a long-developing malignant tumor. The measure of relief this insight afforded him was not insignificant, but it was swept aside by the lingering mystery of what the clearly foreign object embedded in his neck actually was.

He was able to discern the basic shape of the thing with a bit more gentle probing. It was an almost perfectly round knob and felt like it was about half the size of his thumb. He tried pulling at it slightly, but this resulted in a jolt of pain sharper than any of the previous jabs.

He was breathing heavily and his heart was beating faster as he tossed aside the blanket covering his body, got out of bed, and hurried out to the bathroom down the hall. The bathroom door had a tendency to stick in the frame. After shouldering it open, he traipsed across the small space on legs turning more rubbery by the moment. He stopped at the sink and peered at his reflection in the mirror above it.

John knew what he had to do.

But he was reluctant.

There was something in his neck that shouldn't be there. It hadn't been there when he'd gone to bed. That he knew for a fact. He'd gone to bed stone sober, just as he had every night for the last five years, following his fifth (and final) DUI arrest. He'd been in full possession of his senses until lights out, no question about it.

So, again . . . *what the fuck?*

He lingered there in frozen terror a moment longer, knowing he needed to visually appraise whatever it was. Until he did that, he couldn't even begin to figure out what the thing in his neck really was or how to remove it. And yet a very frightened part of him didn't want to see it, was, in fact, *terrified* at the very idea. Whatever this thing was, someone else had put it there.

Or some*thing* else.

Aliens, maybe.

The idea was ridiculous on the surface. He'd always scoffed at tales of alien abductions and experiments, treating the stories with the same disdain he felt for kooky conspiracy theories. Only now, with this goddamn thing stuck in his neck, it was hard to discount any of the wild possibilities he'd once treated with such contempt.

"I've got to do this," he muttered, his voice too loud in the otherwise empty room. "I've got no choice."

He turned to his side, craned his neck around, and lifted up the little scraggle of dark hair at the nape of his neck. The object protruding from his neck was pretty much as he'd envisioned it from his initial tactile examination, except that the hard knob was a shade of light blue rather than the dark brown or black he'd expected.

Leaning over the sink, he put his head as close as he could to the mirror, his eyes swiveling and straining in their sockets as he tried hard to get the best possible view of the thing. He still couldn't tell whether it was made of metal or some other hard material. With the fingers of his other hand, he pressed down as hard as he could on a patch of flesh adjacent to the protrusion, hoping for a glimpse of the part of the object that was actually inside his flesh. This resulted in a series of minor stings that were bearable and nothing compared to the sharper jabs that came when he applied direct pressure to the object.

By doing this, he was able to catch a brief glimpse of something silver attached to the bottom of the blue knob. He was only able to observe it for a few seconds before the stinging sensations became more than he could tolerate. Though minor at first, they became steadily more intense the longer he pressed down on the flesh adjacent to the object.

He took his hand away from his neck and let out a breath.

A rod or bolt of some sort, apparently made of metal, had been inserted in his neck while he slept. How this had been accomplished without waking him or causing excruciating pain, he did not know. He stared at his reflection and wondered what to do.

Get it out. Now.

Well, that was easier said than done, wasn't it?

The object was deeply and firmly embedded in his flesh. Removing it would require a significant amount of force. Judging by the jabs of pain triggered by simple prods of the exterior knob, any attempt at removal would likely result in waves of mind-bending agony. There was also the issue of the placement of the object to consider. It was lodged dangerously close to critical areas such as his brain stem and spine. By trying to forcibly extract it, he might inadvertently cause some kind of debilitating and irreversible damage.

John nodded, still staring at his reflection.

What he needed was the help of medical professionals.

On the other hand, what if his wildest imaginings were true and the object in his neck was some weird piece of alien technology? Once this was determined to be the case, he might be taken into custody by the military and shipped off to fucking Area 51 or some other secret place from which he might never return. Where once he might have dismissed such a notion as paranoid and absurd, it now seemed all too plausible.

John Stark *really* didn't want to spend the rest of his life locked away in a secret underground laboratory. He also didn't much relish the prospect of doing nothing and leaving himself at the mercy of whoever had implanted the object, regardless of whether those responsible were actual creatures from somewhere beyond earth or some sinister and equally mysterious earthbound organization.

Several more minutes of thinking it over resulted in no revelatory insights, but he did come to a conclusion about what he needed to do next. He shuffled back to his bedroom, grabbed his phone from the nightstand, and called Mike Carter.

Mike was his oldest and most trusted friend. They'd known each other since elementary school. They'd been through thick and thin together. John had been best man at both of Mike's weddings. Mike had bailed him out of jail a couple times back when he was still drinking and getting into trouble. His old friend might not have a solution for him, but he might be able to steer him in the right direction as far as what course of action to take.

That initial conversation was brief. John didn't want to tell the full story over the phone because it would make him sound crazy. Mike would think he'd suddenly started drinking again, which would be a logical enough deduction to make minus the visual evidence. Instead, John kept it simple, effectively imparting a sense of urgency and direness in just a few terse sentences.

Mike said he'd be right over.

He got to John's house inside of fifteen minutes.

At first he expressed the expected skepticism when John told him what had happened and his suspicions about it. The skepticism faded, however, when John showed his friend the object embedded in his neck and invited him to press down on the flesh adjacent to it in order to glimpse the silver bolt.

They were in John's living room at that point. The morning light spilling in from the sliding glass doors overlooking the patio and large, leaf-scattered back yard was muted, the day overcast and drizzly. Only a single lamp was on in the living room. The semi-gloom imbued the moment with a disquieting sense of the funereal.

Mike drew a hand across his mouth and scratched at his jaw. "Maybe you're not paranoid, after all."

John let out a shuddery breath and nodded in an emphatic way. "Damn right, I'm not. That thing is there. It's weird, but it's real. And I want it the fuck out of me. What the hell do I do?"

Mike took his hand away from his mouth. "There's only thing you *can* do."

John's brow furrowed in confusion. "And what would that be?"

Mike smiled.

For the first time, John experienced a mild tingle of trepidation where Mike was concerned. There was something in that tight little smile that was not at all friendly. But surely that was just more paranoia, right?

Mike reached inside his jacket and took out an automatic pistol. "What you need to do, John, is put this gun in your mouth and wedge the sight up against your soft palate. Once it is firmly in place, squeeze the trigger."

John laughed, albeit nervously.

This *had* to be a joke.

Only it didn't seem like a joke. And that gun was very real. "This isn't funny."

Mike nodded. "Unfortunately for you, John, I'm not attempting to elicit a humorous reaction."

John flinched but did not retreat as Mike approached him and pressed the gun into his right hand, forcing him to curl his fingers around the grip of the pistol. Once the gun was securely within John's grip, Mike moved back several steps, glanced briefly at the smart watch strapped around his hairy wrist, and shifted his gaze back to John.

His tone was stern and devoid of even the slightest trace of mirth as he said, "Put the gun in your mouth, John."

John glanced at the gun. He tried willing his fingers to uncurl and allow the ugly weapon to fall to the floor. Instead the gun came to his mouth. Then it went inside his mouth and in another moment the sight was wedged painfully against his soft palate. He trembled and whimpered and longed to yank the gun away, but he just stood there, powerless, no longer in control of his own actions.

Mike's expression remained mostly emotionless, but there was a small hint of smug satisfaction at the corners of his mouth. "You're probably wondering how this is happening. And you're probably wondering why your best friend since childhood is compelling you to do this."

John could not nod. He just whimpered some more. His bladder loosened and a flood of piss stained the crotch of his briefs.

Mike's nose crinkled slightly in distaste. "The answer is simple. I'm *not* your best friend. In fact, before I walked through your front door a few minutes ago, you'd never met me before. Everything you know about our history together is a fiction. It is an elaborate tale woven into the code of the implant in your neck, which was not put there by little green men. Since you're about to die and take the secret to your grave, there's no harm in telling you that it's an experimental mind control device developed by rogue elements of your own government, for whom I work, albeit in a necessarily secret capacity." Now he smiled again, more broadly than before. "Your tax dollars at work."

John couldn't believe any of this. It was crazy. He'd shared so much of his life with this guy, countless things that were an integral part of the fabric of his existence. No way could those things all be products of computer code.

Mike sighed. "You don't believe me."

John managed to mutter the word "no", though it was muffled by the barrel of the gun.

"Device," Mike said, his tone turning more precise as he pitched his voice louder. "Cycle red, directive one, wipe."

The moment the word "wipe" was spoken, John knew he was staring at a stranger. Everything the man had said was true. The truth about his life came back in an instant. He was a lonely, broken-down alcoholic. He had no friends. None that were still alive, anyway.

Tears spilled down his face.

His heart thudded painfully in his chest.

Mike cleared his throat, straightened his tie, and said, "I'll take the device with me when I leave. The angle of the shot about to split your head wide open should erase any evidence of its insertion. The gun is registered in your name. Yes, I know you've never owned a gun before. We've arranged everything, all the paperwork and the suicide note you were compelled to write before device insertion last night."

"Please," John managed, the tears spilling faster and hotter down his face. "Don't."

Mike ignored this plea and said, "Your country thanks you for your service and your contribution to our ongoing mind control studies."

John screamed. He glared at his hand, tried again to regain control over his body and pull out the gun.

To no avail.

"Device," Mike said, again speaking in that loud, clear tone. "End program."

John's forefinger began to squeeze the trigger.

He managed one last muffled scream.

The last thing he saw before the bullet blew out the back of his head were the unforgiving, soulless eyes of the stranger, which were faultlessly observant and appraising to the end.

FATHER OF DREAD

MATTHEW CHABIN

From *Cthulhu Lies Dreaming*
Editor: Salome Jones
Publisher: Ghostwoods Books

N O ONE KNEW WHAT POSSESSED them to do it. An unusually powerful spirit of iconoclasm, perhaps. Maybe they'd hoped to purge the land of idols yet still mitigate the world's outrage—unlike when the Taliban dynamited the Buddhas at Hajarazat. Still, it is hard to imagine how sane men, capable of all the necessary calculations, could have arrived at such a "solution."

The great Sphinx of Giza was a 200-ton monolith. It was extracted, intact, by the most exacting and expensive stratagems, and placed upon a massive iron float. This was then ferried for more than a hundred miles down the Nile, requiring constant dredging, and causing frequent, deadly mishaps. Finally, it was towed out beyond the breakers at Raz El-bar, only to be cut loose and left to drift away. To do all this in a time of war, with limited resources and the world falling down around them . . . It was one of the maddest undertakings in the history of the human species. And yet they did it. Then, when the pride of the pharaohs was a vanishing speck on the waves, when the engineers had been dismissed, when the baffled soldiers had been debriefed and sent back to the front, the planners of the feat, those inscrutable midwives, took cyanide and put pistols under their chins—both measures in tandem—and spoke no more. No one knew why they did that, either.

The Sphinx, once liberated, moved steadily west. It was seen from the island of Crete, from the shores of Tripoli and Tunis. Past Malta and Malorca it drifted apace, and like a key guided by an unseen hand, found its way to the Strait of Gibraltar. On a night when the waves tilted blackly against the coastline, and crimson lightning lanced the cadaverous skies, this progeny of the ancient world slipped through into the cold, heaving wilds of the Atlantic.

The Australians attempted a recovery, but were thwarted by a sudden squall. The Russians tried for it, and lost two of their ships and fifty-nine men in a terrible, freak collision. Bad weather and bad luck attended it like grim handmaidens, and in the turmoil of those years the errant beast of Giza ceased to be a *cause célèbre* and became instead a baleful sign of the times. Mariners told stories—how it lingered over the graves of the *Titanic* and the *Athenian Venture,* as if hunting the souls of the dead. How it dwelt among strange currents and mysterious swells and eerie, subaqueous glows. How it was notoriously *hard to sneak up on.* How, even at a distance, its dead gaze tended to settle upon the lookout, and how that man who first spied it was changed by his misfortune, troubled in his sleep, anxious in his work. A good bet to meet with a bad end.

At length the Sphinx became what it must have been to its conscripted builders and wretched supplicants of old. A monster. A dire and unaccountable *thing*, rampant upon the earth.

THE more he tried not to look, the more Walter became convinced that the man loitering in the hall beneath the yellowed tympanum of the Resurrection was looking at him.

True, the light was bad, at least for a reading room. The green lamps in their vine-shaped Art Nouveau sconces hummed and flickered on a pinched current, and the high cupola windows admitted only a wan, leaden daylight. It was also true that Walter was prone to misread visual cues. Just the other day he'd been parking his car in the dim catacombs under the Woolworth Building and had mistaken—if only for an instant—a standard poodle in the neighboring Cadillac for an old woman grinning fox-fangs at him. It had given him a serious jolt (not just that such a thing could *be*, that that it could be out *driving around*). Other people in the same situation might have laughed, but Walter didn't. His history, in conjunction with certain recent developments, made laughter quite out of the question.

In any case, he *was* being watched. The gaunt, elderly gentleman wore a herringbone vest, and had an overcoat draped about his shoulders like a cape, and was definitely watching him. He held a tabloid newspaper in his lap, but his eyes kept creeping up from the page, and with a sly angling of the head their gaze consistently tacked to Walter. There was something intense, something unhealthy about that gaze. Walter wasn't sure, but he thought the faint, brittle clicks he heard from all the way across the room were the man's teeth grinding.

Walter looked the other way and saw with some relief that Maureen had returned. He got up and walked over to the help-desk. She was a comely young woman, with a glass eye, a stylish bob, and a wry manner. She looked up and smiled. "Mr. Church?"

"Maureen. How'd we do with that list?"

She placed a stack of books in paper sleeves on the counter in front of him, an index card with a list of titles taped to the top. "All but one," she intoned gravely. "That one's checked out, and—" her library voice dropped even lower— "and between you and me, Mr. Church, I hear the Department of Homeland Security is after it. Section 215 of the Patriot Act. Don't worry, I kept your name off the query list."

He adjusted his glasses and scanned the card, tapping pensively with his index finger.

"Of course they don't tell us *why* they want it. There's a rumor—" her voice cut to a whisper— "that *OBL* had a copy on him when they, you know . . ." She made a subtle shooting gesture, and rolled her good eye. The glass one stared straight ahead. "They're worried about codes. Mad Arabs bombing the subways—"

"I say, Maureen . . ."

"Hmn?"

"Do you see the man sitting in the hall back there, your eleven-thirty, on the bench?"

She craned her neck. "Yes?"

"Do you suppose he's . . . all right?"

She looked again. "Has he been there for long?"

"Well, he seems to be—"

"Oh, there he goes."

Walter looked. The man was walking down the hall, tapping about him with a long cane and drawing glances from a group of uniformed grade-schoolers coming the other way.

"My God," said Maureen. "Have you seen this?"

"Hmn?" He looked down at the newspaper she'd turned around for his inspection. The headline read "Five Arrested in Plot to Dynamite Ancient Treasure," and surmounted an image, familiar by now, of a dark silhouette against the Manhattan skyline.

At Battery Park, three months and seventeen days ago, Walter had been standing with a crowd of several thousand, pressed against the rail with a front-row view of the harbor. He'd seen it emerge from the dense fog that lay on the water, immense and impassive, blackened by the sea, gliding along on its iron bed beneath screaming throngs of birds. A gasp went through the crowd and a few starkly isolated shouts rang out as the great beast of Giza came fully into view. Six thousand miles it had traveled, dreaming upon the illimitable deep. Walter had the unnerving impression that it was looking right at him.

The harbor masters were ready and had sent tugs to guide its passage, but their exertions did little to persuade two hundred tons of limestone-freighted inertia. Of its own volition, it headed toward the mouth of the Hudson and finally came to rest about a thousand yards off Governor's island. From Walter's vantage, it skulked about the fog-dimmed skirts of Lady Liberty like some bastard offspring, come to ransom its legacy.

A helicopter circled above it. Water began to feel dizzy. He turned and shouldered his way through the crowd.

As days went by he found himself increasingly taken with the strange, brute charisma of the thing. In this he was not alone. Almost immediately, "tourists" started coming by the boatload, boarding the iron platform with ladders, ropes, ramps, whatever they could use. Some of these immediately stripped naked and crawled fawningly over its outstretched paws, or kissed the stone, or feigned to suckle at its flanks, encouraging others to take pictures. Others tagged it with spray-paint, or chiseled souvenir fragments to keep or to sell. Still others tried to scale the limestone shelves, carious and slick with sea-grime as they were. Many fell and shattered their bones, or banged off the lip of a barge and were drowned. This toll continued until one morning at dawn, when a squadron of harbor police took the platform and beat the pilgrims back into their boats. From then on a regular guard of men in riot gear stood ready to discourage further encroachment. A semblance of normalcy returned. Walter's approach was rather the opposite of the enthusiasts'. It was distance, not closeness, that he sought. The distance to comprehend the breadth circumstances, the space to discover the truth. That, he believed, had always been humanity's best response to plague, to calamity, to war and genocide. It still was. The best way to shake the irrational feeling that he, Walter Church, at fifty-two, was living in somebody's nightmare.

JOEY Church dangled his legs over the stage in the Rockaway High auditorium. Long, curly hair veiled his face. He was 16 and good-looking, with a leading role in the school play—a play ostensibly written by Joey Church. He had his grades locked up for the semester, and visions of being the next Edward Norton or Robert Downey. He didn't give a fishtailed fuck about some 5,000 year-old piece of crap rotting in the harbor. Joey Church was the real deal, the Sphinx of Rockaway High!

"Okay, people bring it in." Ms. Ortega rapped her clipboard and settled in a swirl of skirts and perfume on the stage next to Joey, a little close for his liking. He'd considered her hot at one point—like, *really* hot—but recently her bohemian style and gypsy camp manners had struck him more like sloppy affectation. A lot of things were disappointing him lately, though he mostly kept these sour impressions to himself. Apart from his sister and maybe Fox Creasy, there was no one he felt like confiding in.

"We open exactly one week from tonight," said Ms. Ortega, "and some of you still don't have your lines down. That makes my brain bleed and hallucinate little green gnomes eating you alive, but I know it's no use calling you out here. You know who you are, you know what to do." A few guilty groans and murmurs answered her. "Get it done!"

"*Mea culpa*, Ms. O, *mea culpa*!" wailed Clay Widerski, swooning dramatically. Fox jiggled his wrist over Clay, and Joey screwed up his lips to keep from grinning.

"Now, a few of you have asked to have your lines cut down. Normally I'd just give you a straight answer, like *no*, or *hell no*, but since the playwright is sitting right here on his gifted little tuchus . . ." She jabbed a painted nail at Joey. There were some appreciative chuckles and a knowing smirk from his sister. "I guess he's your daddy. Mr. Church, you have those chops under review?"

"Yes, ma'am."

"I need your ruling by tomorrow. Please be kind to your fellow thespians, some of those lines are pretty ornate. But keep the *Book of the Dead* stuff. I'll murder you if you chuck that. 'Kay. Questions? No? Get out. Go home and practice."

Joey was popular with the drama kids, but not in general. The only time he liked attention was when he was on stage. If he'd known his father's batshit script would actually win the contest and become the school's fall production, he might have turned in his own work instead, the one about the Garden of Eden reality show. Now here he was, playing the Sphinx in some kind of baroque, schizoid cross between Oedipus and the Wizard of Oz. Which was cool. Sort of. Better than clomping around in cowboy boots singing about corn, or watching Clay Widerski's Puck OD on fairy dust. On the other hand, some of the dreams he'd been having made him feel like a stranger to himself. They weren't just the usual 'fuck, what's my line?' dreams, but not exactly screaming nightmares either. More like *really* dark, immoral fantasies. His backpack was in the first or second row of seats, he was sure—but now he didn't see it. He walked along, scanning the rows, and jumped when Fox Creasy slapped him on the back.

"Hey! Whoa, you okay?"

"Fine, why?"

"You look a little . . . I don't know . . . Still in character."

"Na." He smiled. "I'm all right. What's up, we rollin'?"

"Yeah, well . . . Me and Allie was gonna catch a cab over to Forest Park, check out those sculptures she's been on about."

"Naw yo, I can't. Promised moms I'd pick up the dry cleaning. They close in two hours."

"Oh right. Then . . ."

There was a pregnant pause, and Joey realized he'd declined a non-invitation.

"Ay, Joey, son, you know me an' Allie been spendin' time an' shit. I hope that's okay wit' you, cuz, you know I'd never disrespect her or nothin' right?"

"Naw, naw it's cool yo, just be good, y'know, don't get lost out there."

"Naw, f'sure, we'll be careful. I'll have her home by ten."

"*Ten?*"

Fox frowned. "What . . . like eight?"

Joey held the glare for a good three seconds before Fox saw a crack and they both broke into laughs. "Shit, son."

"Fuck outa here, man."

They slapped hands and Fox retreated quickly down the aisle. Allison was waiting at the door, and blew Joey a kiss. Then they were gone, and Joey stood in the empty auditorium. He looked to his left. As if by magic his backpack was there, second seat in, practically under his nose. He shook his head as he shouldered it. *Fox and Allie, huh.* He figured he ought to be happy—who did he trust more than Fox? Just felt kind of weird.

He was almost to the door when something made him look back. The auditorium was empty—looked empty, *felt* empty. But something had just rippled the curtains. He felt like he had dreamed this moment, like he *was* dreaming it.

He shrugged off the shiver that ran down his neck, re-slung his bag and banged through the door. *Fuck it!*

WALTER's fellowship had dried up almost six weeks ago. The university had lost interest when his work took a turn into what they politely referred to as "more speculative territory." Now from his tiny garret in Upper Manhattan, he worked on borrowed time and borrowed money, with all the English tenacity his father had bequeathed him. He wanted to see the thing through and make his mark. At fifty-two it felt like a losing prospect. *Still, if you can fill the unforgiving minute . . .*

It was Friday, his day of rest, his day to stop off at The Cloisters to tarry amongst the herb gardens and translated monasteries of his beloved Europe, his intellectual Eden. Usually he meditated on the Unicorn Tapestries, those marvelous minglings of pagan and Christian heritage. Today he found himself in a different gallery contemplating an illumination, *The Procession of the Flagellants* from the Duke of Berry's *Belles Heures*. The men in this delicate rendering wore wide-brimmed, black hats and white gowns that clung precariously to their hips. They walked in stately ranks, two abreast. Two in the foreground were on hands and knees, receiving lashes from two others in masks of white cloth.

Walter marveled, first at the hand that could do this, second at the rather blatant homo-eroticism—one of the men was whipping himself with one hand and caressing himself the other—and finally that an act of self-debasement should be rendered with such superlative grace. He felt a kinship with these men, who in their time, in their peculiar folly, had also believed their efforts were holding up the heavens, holding back the darkness.

Of course the real scene must have been somewhat less picturesque: naked fanatics beating themselves bloody in the street. More like Goya had painted it. His eyes drifted up to the anguilliform dragon, either swimming in the barred abstract of sky or else impaled on one of the cross standards. The latter would imply a horrible blasphemy, would it not? The fiend crucified in place of Christ?

Walter felt ill. The room turned about him, and the venerable air of the place grew musty and close, like a tomb. The next thing he knew he was out in the corridor, vomiting against the wall. People murmured, and a guard's radio crackled. Shamefaced and retching, Walter went for the first exit he saw, and staggered out onto a stone landing overlooking a river. The river, once called the Hudson, was now called something else—some terrible name he couldn't remember, couldn't pronounce. "Oh *God!*" he groaned, mopping his sweaty face. He wished that he could vomit it *all*, get it out of him, this muck of accumulated knowledge, this tired, unclean store.

He looked again. There was no sanctuary. The sky was a leprous purple and red. Every saturated cloud was an evil, floating brain. The river was a lamentable afterbirth. It drained away in the shadow of the Jersey Palisades, which Walter understood to now be serving as execution grounds.

"Yo, your pops is a fuckin' genius, yo."

It was a cold, blustery afternoon and Canarsie Pier was almost deserted, just the way they liked it. The three of them had taken over a bench, looking out over the water and passing a bottle of citrus Mad Dog. The sauce was just a tune-up for the real road show, due to start any minute now. In an hour they wouldn't even remember they'd drunk it.

"Fuckin' genius," Fox repeated, leafing through the pages of the script. "Kinda fucked up, though. Like that part where the Sphinx marries Ed to his mother, and his father comes back from the dead. That's pretty fuckin' seven-thirty, yo, but I like it. Like Shakespeare on shrooms, yo!"

"Yeah, whatever," muttered Joey. "You didn't have to live with him."

"What's he like?" asked Allie. "You never talk about him."

Allison was Joey's stepsister. Her own father was a jolly Puerto Rican stevedore who lived in the Bayview Projects, just ten minutes walk away. Dark skin and crystal-blue eyes made her a fetching study in contrasts, no less so than her Catholic faith and penchant for boys and drugs. Joey was not especially tough, but he'd decided at a young age that he was willing to go to prison for her sake. Most guys understood this and acted accordingly.

"Jo-ey," she said. "Jo-jo. You at home, bro? Those caps kickin' in?"

He looked at her. "Huh?"

"I asked you what your old man is like."

"Oh . . . Professicus? Maximum Over-choad? I don't know, imagine growing up in the London Natural History Museum." He tipped bottle, took a swig. "With weekends at the circus."

"Fuckin' shrooms taste like garbage," muttered Fox, picking at his teeth. "Give me some skeezies, yo."

Joey took the bag of Skittles, placed one in his open hand. "One." He placed another. "Two." He reached into the bag and placed a third— "Three" —then hit Fox's hand from below and sent the candy flying. "Fuck outa here."

"Oh you fuckin' gloryhole cunt-mugger . . ." Fox's punches hooked into Joey's back and shoulder as he laughed.

"Here, bitch, take 'em." He shoved the candy into Fox's hands and winged a hook of his own.

"Okay-okay," said Allie, "the English history part I get, I mean I know that part. Tell us about the circus."

Joey sighed, looking up the shoreline. The wind rifled the cordgrass and made the salt flats shimmer with fanning textures of light. The marshes were dying here, little more every year. No one knew why. For some reason he thought of that thing floating in the adjacent harbor, like a big rotting tooth. That thing he didn't give a fuck about. *That* one. Was that what his father's loopy play was about? Some kind of whack-job fuckin' allegory? He hoped it was something like that, and not . . .

"The circus," he said after a long silence, "was him going through my mint-condition *Alien vs. Predator* comics with a red fuckin' sharpie, saying he's finally figured it out, the reason for the Holocaust." He looked over and met their blank stares. "That's right. The Holocaust. The one in Europe. You probably thought it was Hitler's fault, huh?" He shook his head. "Batman and fuckin' Predator."

Fox burst out laughing. Allie looked sad.

"He's nuts," continued Joey. "He spent a whole year in a loony bin. That's why Moms got custody. Oh, and he cheated on her with his research assistant. Brian."

"Fuck!" shouted Fox, belting it over the water like a war cry, and Allie gave in to a sad mirth as she stroked her stepbrother's back.

"Goddamn, I'm *feelin'* it," said Fox. "Yous feelin' it?"

"Mmn."

"Lil' bit."

"Come on, let's run through it." He leapt up, brandishing the script. "You're the Sphinx. Daddy's takin' a dirt nap. Momma, wassup wit' *dat ass?*" He pulled Allie off the bench and she laughed, slapping his hands away. "Sphinx, your line."

"Naw, you two go ahead," said Joey. "I'm gonna sit for a minute."

Fox shrugged and followed Allie over to the rail. The sun was going down in a red bath to the west, and the bay made a rippling, blood-purple backdrop to their rehearsal. The mushrooms were *indeed* kicking in. His body felt like a thing apart, a suit of crawling, alien armor, a busy android housing his brain. The edges of his vision unraveled and re-knit with seamless fluidity, and Fox had Allie in his arms and Joey knew it was just the scene playing out, but . . .

It was as if he had two minds, the one frightened of the other, frightened at the anger, the resentment, the *jealousy* that flowed up from secret, poisoned wells and flooded his entire body. The wind in the trees became a throaty roar and the hassocks bristled like great hogs in rut. He watched his best friend kiss his sister, not a stage kiss, a real kiss. She was *letting* him.

And somehow these two minds, one of rage, one of terror, abided within him like sun and moon behind an impassive face of stone. A face that gave nothing away. A face that could look for five thousand years upon the wretched fate of the world and never. Once. Blink.

"I USED to be afraid I was losing my mind."

Dr. Edison—a tidy, owlish man with a goatee, silvering hair, and a habit of chewing his nails in session—did not reply. He smoothed his notepaper and waited, as if for something more noteworthy.

"Take these pills, for instance." Walter reached into his jacket and produced a bottle with his name on it. He set it on the table between them. "You hear that?"

"Hear . . . That?"

"Exactly. Quiet as a choir of church mice."

Edison's forehead wrinkled.

"At night I can hear them crawling around in there. Oh yes. If I hold it by my ear, I can almost count them by the . . ." He skittered his fingers on the tabletop. "Or if I hold it up to the light, I can see their shadows, crawling up the sides. *Open* it . . . they're just lying there. Little blue pills, looking so very innocent. And I take one, I do. I tell myself that the one I take will make the others settle down and behave."

"I see."

"Do you?" Walter was quiet for a moment, stroking his chin. Then he reached into his pocket. Edison tensed, ever so slightly. "Doctor, have a look at this, will you?" He took out a newspaper and spread it on the table. Pointing to an article in the lower left-hand corner, he read aloud, "'City Breaks Ground on Audacious New Building, Purpose Unknown.' Did you hear about this? They killed three people at the opening ceremony. Volunteers, they said. Clubbed them like fish, right in front of the cameras, cut their throats and mixed their blood with the mortar. Now does that not seem a tad . . . atavistic to you?"

"It upsets you?"

Walter sighed. "For once, Doctor, please consider that my reaction may be immaterial. It only occurs to me that we didn't use to do these things. Or rather we *did*, a very, very long time ago, and now our sensibilities are in regress." He leaned back and rubbed his eyes as Edison jotted a note. "I used to be afraid I was losing my mind, Doctor, but now I fear it's much worse than that."

Edison glanced at his watch.

"Yes, I know." Walter rose and gathered his things, the pills, the newspaper.

"We might try you on a different medication, perhaps—"

"Doctor, pardon me, but how did you come by that painting?"

Edison turned to look at the enormous oil behind his chair. "Oh? You know, I don't remember. Do you like it?"

It showed a medieval hall, an ape-like creature seated at a table lit with candles, wearing a crown, devouring the naked corpse of a man.

A RAIN of cherry blossoms (pink confetti) fell over the courtyard, covering scattered weapons and fallen soldiers. This was the final scene, the aftermath of a great battle. In the background, an imposing replica of the Lincoln Memorial glowered blindly. Its gouged eyes wept blood, and King Laius slumped at Lincoln's knees, awaiting his resurrection. There was shout, a puff of smoke, and Joey entered stage left in headdress, beard, wings, and pendulant, jeweled breasts. (The arts department had outdone themselves). The groan of metal horns and the beat of drums sounded from the speakers. The house lights went dark and black-lights flooded the stage, making the set glow and drip neon color. Gods and surviving mortals alike reeled in awe.

(He wanted to be away. Everything about this was fake and ridiculous and he wished he really could strangle his *fellow thespians*. Especially this motherfucker. Right. Here.)

"Daughter of Orthus, Father of Destiny, take us into your house. You have made us victorious. Now make us one flesh. Marry us!"

"Oedipus, behold thy mother." *My fuckin'* sister, *you*— "Would you tread upon the laws of heaven and earth? Look how these divinities and powers hide their eyes for shame at thy brazen words."

"These gods and powers are hypocrites unrivaled, born of incest, every one!" The gods staggered and groaned. "This woman is my mother, aye, and mother to us all. Shall the star of Heaven lack her consort? I say again, marry us!"

(*Marry you, I'll fuckin' rip your*—) "Answer my riddle, and be you wed. Answer false, and be you *dead*."

A seeping tide of green light crept over the stage, and hidden fans stirred the banners. "Agreed. Ask."

"I," intoned Joey, his voice reverberant through the speakers, "am your first enemy and your last friend. Know me, I make you. Forget me, I unmake you. I am in your hand, but look, I surround you. What is my name?"

The king looked down at his sword, at the field, at his slain father. "Your name . . ." —the living and the immortal host leaned in to hear— ". . . is Death."

(*No. Death is only . . .*)

"Step forth and be married."

King Oedipus (Fox Creasy) took Queen Jacosta (Allison Santiago) in his arms and kissed her fiercely. "Mazel tov!" shouted a dead soldier (Clay Widerski), and everyone laughed, Fox, Allison, the gods, even Ms. Ortega in the front row.

All but one.

WALTER sat on the pier at Liberty State Park, sipping black tea with cane sugar and watching a fiery, orange dawn break over the Manhattan skyline. For the moment he was content. If he could separate the world and its troubles from his troubled perception of the world, then he could take his problems with him when he went. He just had to take things in stride, and focus.

He took the last drink of tea. A cold, damp wind was blowing off the water and he turned his collar up as he walked to the edge of the pier. The Sphinx had drifted considerably in the last few days, further into the mouth of the old Hudson. This, the easternmost pier by the old CRR train shed in Liberty State Park, was the closest point of landward approach. At less than a hundred yards, it was also the closest Walter had been to it, close enough to hear the racket of the birds and read some of the graffiti that covered its lower flanks (if he could bring himself to read that junk, that is). Two harbor police were manning the barge, one pissing over the side while the other pointed his finger at Walter and mimed shooting him. Walter paid them no mind.

He stepped behind a brace of coin-operated binoculars, fed his quarters through the slot, and stooped to look. The shutter clattered open and he saw before him a frozen waste, with snaking ribbons of ice blown by the constant wind. The Sphinx was exactly the same size, but now icebound, minus the guards, and bearded with hoary icicles. Behind it the metropolis that had once been Lower Manhattan was going down under a mountainous glacier. The skyscrapers gathered in its embrace like broken toys, tipping into one another, their steel girders distended like burst ribs through the failing concrete. Behind the incessant scrolling blast all was still, all except one moving shadow, a black thing with long, jointed legs climbing the white ruin of the Chrysler Building. Walter thought of the pill bottle on his table at home, and the strange seeds that an ocean of time would bring to hideous flower.

He straightened and blinked into the sun. The position of the Sphinx was the same, exactly, so perhaps what the binos showed was not the future, but a radically different *now*. Was it possible that two such parallel realities could mingle? Could the madness of a single man be the conduit for their association? But that would mean he wasn't mad, would it not? Oh, he was feeling confused again.

He walked back to the bench and sat down, lightheaded, missing his tea. He took out his map and marked the position of the binoculars. He took out his morning paper and scanned the headlines. The border-closing ceremony at the Lincoln Tunnel had turned violent (three dead, twenty injured), several landmarks had been rechristened with names he didn't dare read, even in his head, and there was an editorial calling for a number of prominent people to be arrested and chemically mummified.

The weatherman predicted snow by the end of the week.

"Mr. Church?"

"Mm. Yes?"

"Can I have a word please?"

Walter glanced up at the elderly woman in the droopy cotton hat and aviator glasses sitting next to him. "I'm sorry, do I know you?"

"Not exactly. You may have seen me around. You can call me Terri."

He looked again more carefully. There was something familiar about her, the gaunt frame and bushy eyebrows. Her jaw moved, and her teeth clashed loudly in her mouth. "From the library!"

"That's right. I was hoping this little chat wouldn't be necessary, but you're very persistent."

"I'm sorry," said Walter, "but you were . . . dressed differently last time."

"I change," she said. "Frequently, and in any way I can. It keeps me on the outskirts, out of his dreams, more or less."

"I'm sorry, I'm not sure I underst—"

"Mr. Church, time may be extremely short. What would it take to convince you to forget this whole thing and go back to your old studies?"

"My . . . Well, you see—"

"What if I told you it could save your life, your sanity? What if I told you that forgetting certain things you may have noticed is absolutely your only hope?"

Walter could think of no reply.

The woman, Terri, removed her glasses, and the tiny pinpoint pupils of her eyes bored into his. "Take it from someone who knows, Mr. Church, someone who's been around. That thing on the water isn't just a statue—it's the ark of his dreams. How many people meet those eyes every day? A thousand? More? The sensible ones feel a shiver and look away. But you don't have the shiver gene. You look back, you take notice. You become *involved*. He's dreaming of you, Mr. Church, dreaming *through* you. He can reach right through your heart and touch the ones you love. Perhaps he already has."

"What are you talking about?" snapped Walter. "Whose dream? Who the fucking bloody hell sent you? What do you know?"

"I *know*!" she said, with such sudden ferocity that Walter drew back a little. "I know well enough not to speak that name! I know how dangerous this conversation is, for both of—" Her whole body jerked and went rigid, her eyes rolled up into her head, and her jaw worked frantically. The clash of teeth was so loud it sounded like she was chewing rocks.

This spell lasted for several seconds and then she slumped out of it, took a breath, and put on her glasses as if nothing had happened.

"Our obsessions take us far afield," she said, gaining her feet and letting her folding cane deploy. "When, Mr. Church, was the last time you checked in on your son? Joey, is it?" She walked quickly away, tapping around her and muttering something that might have been a prayer.

"HAVE you seen him?"

"Hell yes! I was in the bathroom and I came out of the stall and—swear to God—there was this face in the mirror!"

"Nu-uh!"

"I don't know how to describe it. It was—"

"Hey," said Joey. The girls, one dressed as the Delphic Oracle, the other as the cat goddess Bastet, stopped talking and looked at him. "What's that about?"

"Oh," said the Oracle, "we're talking about the Sphinx! It's totally going around. Bethany saw it, and Clay saw it, and now this loopy bitch here she says she saw it too."

"I did see it! It was *so* tripped out!"

"They say you only see it for a second, and it changes your whole perspective."

"Have *you* seen the Sphinx, Joey?" Bastet's tone was suggestive. The girls tittered.

"No," said Joey in a cold, flat voice, and their smiles dropped away. He got up and walked out of the greenroom. There was a bathroom right next door, but it was full of geeks, and he wanted solitude. He walked the length of the hall and turned into the deserted east wing of the school. *Ol' Fox Creasy, he's a foxy one. (Shut up) Think he's foxed his way into her crease yet? (Who is that?) Have his foxy red rocket in her by the end of the month, whad'ya wanna bet?* He grabbed his hair in fists and squeezed. *(Shut the fuck* up, *you're not me!)*

The boys' room was empty, dark. He flipped the switch and the lights flickered on. On the mirror above the sink some wit had scrawled *FAG* in black marker, with an arrow pointing up, and above that, a pharaoh's headdress with beard, lopsided tits, and outlined eyes framing his reflection. They even knew how tall he was. His stage makeup—a pale base, blue lipstick, and imitation kohl darkening his eyes—made him look like a painted corpse, a zombie clown fleshing out the crude cartoon. He skinned back his blue lips and grinned at himself, then hit the water and started splashing his face.

Remember three years ago? 'Member vodka summer, home-alone summer? How you two played? Do you remember what it felt like to put your hand down her pants, how she shivered, how she looked at you? You're just gonna let her forget?

"Ooagoddamyou!" He left the water running as he banged into the stall and fumbled with his zipper. His cock sprang up, hard as a steel rivet, and found his wet hand. He swallowed and breathed, remembering that day, drawing his whole self from that memory, *there, no sister by blood*, the words a mantra, *no sister just . . . just . . . Allie!* He whispered her name as he came, splattering the toilet wall. He opened his eyes and a rich, narcotic blast of endorphins and guilt rolled through him. He snatched some toilet paper and cleaned himself up.

He stepped out of the stall and grimaced at his slinking, ghoulish reflection, the half-washed makeup smeared down his face. How could he have let this happen? More than anything he hated and feared the stigma of his father's madness, the trace of it *in him*, the knowledge that he was likely genetically marked. And yet here he was, courting it, taking it to the ball, acting out his father's artfully scripted insanity. *Wanting* his sister. *Hating* his best friend. But what, then? He would drop out, quit, go away. Everyone would think he was batshit, that he'd caught the family bug, but fuck it, let them. He'd be saving the best part of himself.

"Joey."

He spun around. He was alone. The voice had come from the hall. *Not* in his head, he was sure.

"Joooe-ey."

He opened the door and peered out. The hallway was empty, but what was that? He started walking. *Something,* way, way down at the southeast end, was going around the corner. He quickened his pace, almost running to the end of the hall. He turned the corner and saw the door to the gym was open. It was dark inside. He stepped through the door. *(Get out of there!)* "Hello?" *(Don't speak to it!)* "Someone in here?" *(Run!)*

The face, the pale, oval face with the placid smile and sparkling black eyes, floated out of the darkness at midcourt. At first it was just a face, but as he walked to it—his heart knocking in his chest, his breath coming in shallow little sips—the rest began to take shape. That smile of perfect serenity, that doting, generous mien . . . "Joey," it said, with a voice like dribbled honey. "Let's have a word, shall we?"

WALTER's TV dinner tasted bad tonight. Worse than usual, as if it had been thawed, left to turn, and then re-frozen to seal in that little gift of decay. He stopped eating halfway through, pressed the 'mute' button on nightly news, and picked up the telephone. It had been so long. He couldn't remember the number until his thumb was on the keypad and then he knew it by touch. The little code of sequential beeps unlocked something in him, a dark room painted in sad shadows where he had spent far too much time already.

As he waited for her to answer, his tired gaze took in the room. Cold radiator, bookshelf, liquor cabinet with French and Latin volumes crammed between the bottles, old Singer sewing table he used as a writing desk. These things were the same. That was something. The TV was showing a handheld shot of a home interior, cluttered and rundown, zooming in on a blood-soaked sofa, with the caption "Horror at Red Hook." It seemed the news was positively chock-full of horrors these days.

"Hello?"

"Amanda. It's, um . . . it's Walt."

"Walter. Hi. Is everything okay?"

The words stuck in his throat. He shook his head.

"Walter?"

"Fine," he blurted. "I just, um . . . Well I know this is a bit how-do-you-do and out-of-the-blue, but . . . I was wondering how Joseph is doing?"

"Oh. He's fine. He wanted me to thank you for the play."

"The play?"

"The one you sent him to use. *Father of Destiny*, or something like that? He told me the school is actually putting it on."

"I'm afraid I don't . . . Are you sure that was the message."

"You don't remember? He told me you said it was the best thing you've ever written."

"Wh—ah—when . . . Amanda, when did I give him this . . . *play?*"

"July? August? I'm sorry, Walter, I don't remember. But they're opening tonight. I can't make it, I have to work. But you should go if you have the time."

"I will," said Walter. "I certainly will."

"I'm sorry, Walter, I have to go."

"Not at all, I—" But the click told him she was gone.

Walter glanced over at his pill bottle. Silent, for now. He un-muted the news. Apparently there'd been a string of disappearances along the East River. Mysterious drownings. No bodies.

He watched a cockroach preen its antenna under the radiator.

Like an intruder through an unlocked window, a terrible, icy premonition crept in through the back of his mind. He knew in that moment that something dreadful had happened—was happening—was *about to happen.*

"He can reach right through your heart and touch the ones you love."

He got up and walked out the door, leaving the TV on, heading for the stairs. His car was parked three blocks away, and by the time he reached the street he was running.

Opening night at Rockaway High, and the audience had been promised "something unique." So far, *The Father of Destiny* had delivered. There'd been laughs, shrieks, cheers, a few indignant walkouts (the better to weed out the lames), but Ms. Ortega, watching from the balcony, hadn't counted a single yawn. The scene where Oedipus rescued his mother from the house of the dead—by weighing his heart against a feather and matching wits with a baboon—had been a great sell, really drawing them in. They had that blissfully mesmerized look that audiences get when a show really starts to score. Their eyes were drinking in the story, primed for the big showdown with Laius on the steps of the Lincoln Memorial. It was like bringing a dream to life, cast in living flesh, and for once she had no regrets about her career. At least a small part of her wanted to track down Joey Church at the after-party and jump his precocious bones.

If Joey, brooding in the darkness backstage in full Sphinx regalia, looked like death, it might be assumed he was getting into character.

It was just Joey and Allison now. The rest of the spare cast had been drafted into one of the armies. She wore a shimmering gown of blue gossamer and pearls, selected to make her eyes pop in the black light. It gave her a fierce, numinous beauty. She was pacing the wing, pricking her thumbs with her fingernails and mouthing her lines. Joey's eyes followed her, the only part of him that moved.

"Where is my mother? Summon her!"

Fox's command from the stage meant her big scene with him and Laius was coming up. Suddenly she ran to where Joey was standing and hooked him round the neck. She nuzzled his shoulder, mindful of his makeup, and whispered, "I love you, Joe. Thanks for being so cool, brother." She started to go for her entrance, but his hand shot out and caught her wrist. "Eh? Joey, wha—"

"Don't go out there," he hissed, his eyed brimming with sudden intensity.

"What, what are you—"

"*Please,* Allie! The play, it—it—it's bad! Th-there are secret lines my father wrote . . . Allie, it doesn't end how you think it does!"

"Hey. HEY! Joey, let . . . GO!"

"Please, don't go. I can't stop it if you do! I love you Allie, please, we can go, we can leave right now and be together, we can—"

"Hey . . . Crazy *fucker*, let go!"

His grip faltered and she snatched her hand back. For a moment she saw the deep pain in his eyes, but only for a moment, before it hardened into a flat, nothing gaze. A dead gaze. She shrank from it and practically ran for the light of the stage and Fox's outstretched hand.

The scene unfolded with crackling aplomb. Allie was rattled at first, but managed to find her stride within a few lines. Once or twice she glanced back at the wing and thought she saw her brother back there—his eyes at least, glimmering in the shadows. The battle raged around her and she was Jacosta again, her passions torn between her husband and her son, and anxious moreover for that part of her that defied them both, the secret, smuggled heart of a woman. And then it was over. Laius lay dead. Oedipus Fox, victorious, drew her close and kissed her in front of gods and men and left her breathless and dazed. The drums and the metal horns sounded and the theater went dark. All eyes looked to the wing. Allie Jocasta looked.

And her mind broke in two.

For what now took the stage, with heavy thump and shuffling drag, aglow and ghastly in the cold blue light? What taxidermist's nightmare, what unnatural abuse of form, what desecration of life, what dread ancient now cast its shadow on the audience and fixed them in their screaming shock? What now addressed the bloodless face of the king with a voice that blew the speakers out and sent a wave of despairing groans through the onlookers?

"Speak!"

"D-Daughter of Orthus," sputtered the king, helpless to stop the words from forming, "Father . . . t-take us . . . m-make us . . . marry us!"

"Answer my riddle."

The eyes of the king refused, pleaded, begged to be reprieved, but he had no power to refuse what was written, and trembling he replied, "Ask."

"What is my name?"

"Your name . . ." whispered the un-made king, tears streaming down his face, "is Death."

"No. I am one who dreams a million leagues below death. Death is only the beginning. You will see. I will show you. You are mine!" It reached for them, took hold of them, and they screamed louder than all the rest, if not as long.

WALTER got out in front of Rockaway High auditorium, leaving his car to idle in the street. People in disheveled eveningwear were trickling out of the entrance like poisoned bees from a rock. They tripped over their own feet, searched the ground with blasted vacuity, or tilted strange grins to the starless sky. One dusky woman in voluminous skirts looked up at Walter as he hurried past, her scooped-out eye-sockets weeping blood. He fought his way through the door, down the dark hallway full of gibbering, reeling, reaching forms, and threw open the auditorium doors. The air was thick, syrupy with death, full of mutters and groans and half-articulate lamentations. What remained of the audience rolled and swayed in the murk of the reflected stage lights. A man traced invisible signs in the air, a woman clawed at her naked breasts while a mass of tentacles wriggled from her mouth, a teenage girl held up a toddler with a broken neck like an offering . . . All of these were but shadows, poor stewards to the towering horror of the stage.

"*Joseph!*" he screamed over the woeful din. "*Son!*"

It heard. It looked up from its abominable labors and turned its gore-slathered face to him. It pawed the ruined bodies. "Father!" it said in a voice dredged from the gutters of Hell. "Behold your work!"

"No, no, no—" chanted Walter, the last and only word he would ever know or speak again. "No, no, no—"

"Father, I am born!"

"No . . ."

"Sehk noth l'tak'gn!"

"No . . ."

"Behold your son!"

AUTHOR'S STORY NOTE

The title of this story comes from the Arabic name for the Sphinx of Giza, *bu al-Hawl,* which is commonly translated as *The Dreadful One,* but literally means *Father of Dread.* Like the Sphinx, it is a found artifact (as good titles so often are).

This was originally written as a Lovecraftian Mythos story for the *Cthulhu Lies Dreaming* anthology by Ghostwoods Books. Obviously the ancient world is fertile soil for this sort of thing, and the figure of the Sphinx allowed me to draw on a convergence of Greek and Egyptian mythology.

The Greek world was never a totally closed cosmological horizon like those of the monotheistic religions. Before the Olympian Gods there were the Titans, and before them there were more shadowy figures like Chaos and Gaia rising out of primeval darkness. The Greeks' awe and trembling before the Fates and the Furies, their spiraling obsessions with space and time, their majestically dark theatre with its origins in primitive rites, all fit very well with the Mythos tradition. And the Egyptians, well, read the *Book of the Dead*—baboons feeding human hearts to crocodiles!

Monotheistic religion came along and suppressed what dark, irrational currents in paganism it could not incorporate. The psychological law says that when darkness is repressed it loses its virtue of balancing against light and becomes absolute evil, absolute other, an alien consciousness waiting for its chance to revenge itself up on the waking world. That, I think, is the psychological core of Lovecraft's best work, and what I was aiming for here.

ON THIS SIDE OF BLOODLETTING

STEPHANIE M. WYTOVICH

From *555 Vol. 2: This Head, These Limbs*
Editor: Joseph Bouthiette Jr.
Publisher: Carrion Blue

THE HANDS OF A SEVERED POET

I often think about what it would be like to cut off my hands, to have two stumps that plop and bang rather than fingers that glide over keys, make words and tell stories. I wonder if people would listen to me if I went silent, if they would make poetry with my mute remains.

INSIDE OF ME, SHE BLEEDS

There's a monster in my veins. Her name is my own and she bubbles and bleeds, tries to convince me to let her out, to let her play. Sometimes I make an incision. Just enough to give her a taste. But still she cries, still she screams, screams pleas of amputation, cries operas of pain.

BRUSHING WITH BLOOD

The walls in my room were white, but everything in my mind was red, red like the cherries I ate, red like the pomegranate juice that dripped down my chin. I liked red, liked the way it stained my teeth, the way it complimented my gums when I brushed my teeth with the morning's blood.

OEDIPAL SOLUTIONS

I wasn't happy. The world was ugly and I didn't like what I saw, what I was forced to look at every day. Outside it was bright. It hurt to be alive, hurt to watch. But I felt better when I took out my eyes, because then the world went dark. Then, I could see.

POSTMARK TO PAIN

My body has 555 cuts on its skin, each made with love, each made with careful consideration, for I, myself, am a mailbox of suffering. Learn my address. Postmark your hate mail, send it straight to my heart. This is who I am. I'm made for it. 555 slots for sorrow. I can take it.

DATING MY DEATH WEAPON

Knives are what I know, what I trust. They don't fail me. They don't walk away. In fact, their slim, metal bodies are the best lovers I've known. Dependable. Efficient. Consistent. Their foreplay is torture. Their penetration is climax. When I fuck them, I bleed. When we make love, they write notes on my back.

MAKE ME BLEED, MAKE ME HISS

I wanted to pierce my ears, so I took a needle and shoved it through my lobes. They barely bled, except for a drop or two, so I pierced my nose. When that didn't bleed, I took scissors and cut out a section of my tongue. I swallowed the cube of flesh muscle. Hissed breaths.

HUMAN PINCUSHION

The spikes hugged me in my body drawer, in my metal casket, and I was the Iron Maiden, the girl who slept with the thorns and dressed herself in holes. My skin, polka-dotted and infected, beat shades of red and pink. I dressed my wounds with the tears I laughed. I cried my blood away.

ARSONIST LULLABY

Father Fire sings me my lullaby, his voice burning the world as he lulls me to dream with ashes, tucks me in with flames. When I drift off to sleep, there's a match in my hand, when I wake up in the morning, there's destruction on my breath. I am his death phoenix, his redemption.

DARK ROAST

She cried hard into her coffee when she wanted to mix the cream and sugar, and silently wept into her mug when she took her caffeine black. The trick to a strong cup was the amount of suffering she put into it. If her heart wasn't black enough, the dark roast never came out right.

ELECTROCUTION JUNKIE

The hurricane screamed itself raw with its booming voice and electric words, and the girl took each strike, each hit, as her ragdoll body was flung side to side, beaten and bloody near the front door of her mind. She'd come around. Always did. Most women were made for madness. She was made for storms.

COMMIT THEM TO MEMORY

There's a code to this trade, a set of rules that I follow, rules that keep me on schedule, that prevent me from making mistakes. I never take trophies, have no need for reminders. I commit each detail—every name, every taste, every article of clothing—to memory. I know I'll never forget my girls.

HE'S BETWEEN MY LEGS

I cut his name into my thighs with a piece of broken glass from the bottle

I knocked off the desk when he walked away. He was the only man I saw when I spread my legs, so I marked him in flesh, in memory for how he still fucks me even though he's gone.

MY VAGINA IS A ZOMBIE

I don't bleed like a normal woman, because I'm not a normal woman. Every 28 days I hemorrhage until I die, a lifetime of deaths served by the slit between my legs. I have the axe wound that never heals, the river that always runs red. My vagina is a zombie, a reanimated gore machine.

MY MEN DON'T BRING ROSES

If I had to choose between lovers, I would choose the one who scares me, the one who makes my heart beat fast out of fear. I need a partner who's going to bring an axe to the bedroom every once in a while. I like a man who knows how to make me scream.

BLOOD MAPS

I puked razor blades and knives, threw up needles and a pair of shearers, and still my body takes the abuse, still it begs for more, more cuts and incisions, more holes and puncture wounds. When will the blood maps that I've drawn in scars be enough? When will those pictures lead me to recovery?

RED IS MY FAVORITE COLOR

There's something about the color red that gives me peace, that lets me open my lungs and breathe a breath of fresh air. I've painted the walls in my house crimson, soaked all my clothes in wine, and I suck on veins for breakfast, lunch, and dinner, happily starving in scarlet, cynically crying in carmine.

JACKSON POLLACK, REVISITED

I smiled when I read the headlines. They saw me for who I was: a visionary, a connoisseur of culture, of philosophy, of art. I wanted to capture the idea of rebirth, silence the notion of death. It was sacrifice, expressionism in blood. I laid down my paint, my bodies, a canvas of organized chaos.

SHOOT TO KILL

I'm a visual learner, a Pinterest picturesque plotter. I don't see people for who they really are until I see them through my camera lens, and once I snap their picture—once I commit to a subject—they're imprinted in my brain; a face forever hanging in my gallery, a mental collage of pre-inflicted pain.

THE MAP OF OUR RELATIONSHIP

I am many things in this life, but I'll forever be the cartographer of your scars. You're my canvas, my journal of pain, and every time I look at you, I look at the map of our relationship, trace it back to where it started, to the first mark, to where our love story began.

FAMILY TRADITION

This machete has been in the family for ages—passed down generation after generation—but it's been shadow sleeping, retired too long. The blooms of rust call to me, the decade-old blood stains weep, and it makes me nostalgic for the good ol' days when pleading filled the night and grandpa laughed himself to sleep.

DIRTY LAUNDRY

I wet the bed until I was thirteen. Mother made me sleep in my mess, refusing me clean sheets, denying me comfort until I learned to stop; but I didn't stop and mother hated me. Now my sheets look different. They're practically soaking in all the red. I think Mother would maybe love me now.

SLEEPING WITH THE ENEMY

There's an abandoned house that I go to sometimes to sleep with the man who broke my heart. One time, I took an axe with me. I wondered: would I have stopped swinging if he apologized, if he repeatedly begged me to stay? I'm not sure, but the body next to me is baffled, too.

GUILLOTINE GIGGLES

Most of the time their last words are prayers, prayers or maybe confessions, every once in a while an apology or two, but this one, this one just giggled, giggled until the blade dropped, until his head hit the ground, and even then I swear he was laughing, smiling as he rolled and rolled around.

BENEATH THE FLOORBOARDS

It's cliché and it's Poe, but it makes me happy that I get to walk over your grave every day, that I get to trap you like you trapped me, but unlike the story, your murder doesn't drive me mad, for it's the phantom beating of your heart that allows me to sleep, to dream.

MY WEEK-OLD SEX DOLL
It's been a few weeks, and he's losing the color in his cheeks; I added some blush to help him come back, some foundation to take out the bloated hue, and if I squint, he looks just like his old self again, only this time more sophisticated, more debonair. The sex has never been better.

STALK, STALK, PREY
It's waking up in the morning and knowing what your soon-to-be victim is having for breakfast. It's knowing his favorite pub to visit on Wednesday nights, just like it's studying his approach to picking up girls. It's dying your hair black because you know he prefers brunettes to blondes. It's obsession, practice. A widow's skill.

BECOMING THE BUTCHER
At first, I refused to believe that I did it. That I was capable. *How could I be so stupid?* I needed to go back, to try again. I waited all my life for their bodies, and now their dismemberment disgusted me. I was a hack. A butcher. They deserved better. I needed more practice.

THE EXECUTIONER'S DIARY
Murder is a game, but when I take the players to my basement, my secret chamber of penance, of retribution, there's no God waiting for them. It's just me, me and my notebook, an executioner with a plan. I scribble their sins in poetic eulogies, tell them to close their eyes. To count to ten.

CARRY-OUT CONFESSIONAL
The man at the counter looked at me strange. He asked if I was planning on killing someone, and I smiled as I looked down at the rope and the gasoline, at the shovel and the nails. I told him not today, and he laughed as he handed me my receipt. Tomorrow is another day.

PSYCHODRAMA
There's an unspoken competition between psychos, a silent battle that's similar to the fights of most teenage boys. Everyone wants their knife to be bigger than their friend's, and in the end, most of them just lie to impress the others, to live out a fantasy. In fact, most of them have barely even killed.

THE TAILOR

I've been watching you, and I can see that you're the type of person I could wear. Your skin, it's soft, subtle, more enticing every time you walk past me. I find myself mentally sizing your chest, counting the inches between your shoulders, the centimeters between your thighs. You're going to be a perfect fit.

UNDERWATER WARDROBE

My wardrobe is a pair of cement shoes and a pocket full of change. *I should have listened.* A fish sucks on my nose but you can't see my tears, not in this garbage heap of an ocean where bodies decompose and all my prayers are wet. *I would have preferred the severed horse head.*

SELF-CANNIBALISM

Last night I dreamt that I didn't have any legs, that I pulled my half-severed corpse around the apartment like a zombie when my stomach started to growl. When I made it to the refrigerator, there were two legs of meat on the shelf. Thighs were always my favorite, even when they were my own.

ORAL FIXATION

Sometimes I think about eating my teeth, but I'm not a dentist, so I'm not sure how to extract them so they won't lose their gritty taste. I called around, but no professional would willingly remove 32 healthy fangs, so I ripped them out myself. My blood acted as a nice Merlot with my meal.

DIAMONDS ARE A GIRL'S BEST FRIEND

The rain sounded like diamonds falling against my window. I opened the door and walked outside, eager to bathe in the crystal waters, but the droplets cut my skin like sharpened teardrops. The gems dug their way inside me and I stood there, shining like a fallen star as I bled rubies over the yard.

FEEDING THE GARDEN

I noticed a new flower in my garden yesterday. It was purple and yellow and it smelled like lilac and honeysuckle. When I bent down to touch it, it bit me, each petal full of a hundred mouths and a thousand teeth. I smiled and fed my garden, my blood turning its yellows to oranges.

MY GIRLFRIEND WANTED TO SCISSOR

My girlfriend wanted to scissor, so I took off her pants and pushed the blades up her slit. She screamed, and she always screamed when she liked it, so I kept pumping her full of metal until she came in waves of cherry and tears. Afterwards, she slept like a baby. I wore her out.

BLOOD BATH

The sky rained cherry-sized droplets that stabbed my eyes when I woke up this morning. I slept outside because I liked the coldness of the ground. It chilled the heat running through my body, and the red clouds that hung above me made me thankful that I wasn't the only one painted crimson that day.

WOMEN ARE TAUGHT TO BE SILENT

He told me we couldn't talk for two months, and I nodded my head. Bit my lip. I went in my bedroom and opened the wooden box I kept on my dresser. I took out the needle and I sewed my lips together so I could practice being silent, because effort is attractive in relationships.

THE ANGELS ARE GONE

Night-time is the worst. My demons speak loudest then, convincing my heart that I'm alone while my mind battles to tell me I'm in good company, but the truth is, my angels left long ago. They dragged me into the sea, like Annabel Lee, and every night I jump off of cliffs when I sleep.

PHANTOM PAIN

Sometimes I like to imagine that I'm dead, that no one can see me here, that the pain I feel is akin to an amputee's agony over a phantom limb. I try to imagine myself without a heart, try to become a sociopath in the off-hours when the world is asleep and I'm still living.

THE NEW FLESH

It's cold in my apartment tonight, but that's what happens when you take off your skin suit. You freeze. You shake, tremble. It's therapeutic. Hydrotherapy without the water. I tore it all off a week ago. Threw it in the trash. Since then, I haven't touched anyone. And most importantly, no one has touched me.

MY SOUL BELONGS IN HELL

There's a distance there that goes beyond miles, and my mind wanders lost highways and off-road sites while I look for you even though I already know where you are. It's a devil's game, a crossroads, and I sell my soul for a chance at love even though I've damned myself to hell twice before.

THE PUNISHMENT OF ABSTINENCE

My body is a festival of sin. That's why he won't touch me. He knows, knows that I am walking filth, a culmination of lust and regret. My flesh, tortured with invisible scars, weeps under the blankets at night. I wrap my arms around my chest. Every time he doesn't touch me, the Devil laughs.

WHATEVER HELPS YOU SLEEP AT NIGHT

Every night at 2:37 a.m., I walk outside my apartment complex, naked, and I stand in the middle of the road and scream. I scream loud enough to wake up my neighbors, long enough that my voice goes hoarse. One time, I almost got hit by a car. I slept better than usual that night.

GIRLS WATCH THEMSELVES CRY

When I cry, I like to watch myself in the mirror to see if I look pretty. Sometimes I look tragic and beautiful while the mascara runs down my face and my cheeks turn red. Other times, I look ugly. Defeated. So I practice—so I cry—every day until I get it for you.

HOMEMADE BOTTLE FULL OF VOODOO

There's a bottle of red wine that sits on my shelf buried behind books I haven't read. It's filled with pins and needles, with rosemary and sage. I sealed it with the wax that I dripped from a lit red candle as I whispered wishes and prayers, curses and hate. I like knowing it's there.

I DO NOT

When I wake up in the morning, I hear your voice telling me all the words I've been waiting to hear. You tell me you're sorry, that you should have tried harder, loved more. But my tongue is sandpaper and I choke on the marriage proposal that I've been practicing in my bedroom every night.

NAME-CALLING IS BODY TRAUMA

I scratch words on my arms to remind me of who I am: monster, child, victim. I look at them every day while I stand naked in front of the mirror wondering how to dress my pain. My identity is my body, but my body is a canvas of your words. Speak kindly to me.

THE OTHER ME

I disassociate when it gets dark. My Hyde takes over my Jekyll, and I, myself, become a different person. This other girl, she's better. Her eyes are dead, her lips blue, but she is confident, unafraid. I like her more than the version of myself that walks during the day. I wish it was night.

THAT NIGHT ON REPEAT

I try to sleep but the nightmares come faster than usual. I drink valerian root in my tea, rub lavender on my temples. Nothing helps. I can still see the house, still feel your breath. Sometimes, when God is feeling exceptionally cruel, I can hear your voice as if you're sitting right next to me.

INSIDE MY DESK DRAWER

I keep a notebook of all my bad memories. It helps me write poetry, and it keeps the pain fresh, makes the hurt still feel real—*as if I could ever fake it*—and I've noticed, lately, that it's dangerously full, so I made a notebook of blessings instead. God laughed. I threw it away.

I-71 NORTH

I drive until my head starts to shake, until my eyes twitch, until I see the dead girl on the side of the road. It's 1:00 a.m. I've been going for two and a half hours, but she's been here much longer than me. Usually, she watches me drive by. Tonight, she extends her hand.

A EULOGY FOR MYSELF, NOT YET DEAD

This is me telling you goodbye. This is me leaving. This is me walking away, saying farewell, wishing you the best as you move on with life. Except this isn't me disappearing. I'm imprinting myself in your memory, committing myself to this page. I live forever in ink, in the black letters of this eulogy.

AUTHOR'S STORY NOTE

Blood. Body Dysmorphia. Amputation. I'm fascinated by the beautiful grotesque, by the welcoming of pain, by the imperfections of self and what that means in regards to the human body and mind, and as such, my work tends to writhe along the sidelines of cuts and bruises, hack-jobs and botched surgeries. I'm fascinated by anatomy, a fictional female-Frankenstein if you will, and despite centuries of doctors searching for ways to heal our meat sacks, both physically and mentally, it is my job to peal back the flesh and show you what lies beneath the body suit when we can't, or prefer not to, stitch ourselves back together again. I ask readers, what is really living inside the rotted, damaged parts of our brain? What happens when compulsion and phantom pain become too much to bear, or when a broken heart starts to peek through the skin? Madness is an illusive awareness, a heightened state of fear and worry, and it is my pleasure to guide you through it on this side of bloodletting.

AUTHOR BIOS

MICHAEL ARNZEN is an award-winning author of horror and dark suspense fiction, a poet, and an English professor. His trophy case includes four Bram Stoker Awards and an International Horror Guild Award for his often funny, always disturbing stories. The best of these appear in the Bram Stoker Award-winning career-length retrospective, *Proverbs for Monsters*, which Dread Central called "a guided tour of insanity and the macabre, with a few moments of touching grace combined with repulsive terror . . . [which] serves to document the evolution of a great writer."

Arnzen holds a PhD in English from the University of Oregon (where he researched his non-fiction book, *The Popular Uncanny*) and he is presently a Professor at Seton Hill University, where he teaches horror and suspense fiction in the country's only graduate program in Writing Popular Fiction (http://fiction.setonhill.edu).

Arnzen resides near Pittsburgh, PA, with his wife of many years, Renate, and a brood of deranged cats. His website is http://gorelets.com

JASPER BARK is infectious—and there's no known cure. If you're reading this then you're already at risk of contamination. The symptoms will begin to manifest any moment now. There's nothing you can do about it. There's no itching or unfortunate rashes, but you'll become obsessed with his books, from the award winning collections *Dead Air* and *Stuck on You and Other Prime Cuts*, to cult novels like *The Final Cut* and acclaimed graphic novels such as *Bloodfellas* and *Beyond Lovecraft*.

Soon you'll want to tweet, post and blog about his work until thousands of others fall under its viral spell. We're afraid there's no way to avoid this, these words contain a power you are hopeless to resist. You're already in their thrall and have from the moment you clicked onto this page. Even now you find yourself itching to read the rest of his work. Don't fight it, embrace the urge and wear your obsession with pride!

MARVIN BROWN is the author of suspense novels *Jigsaw Man* and *Covet*, as well as the nonfiction work *The House the Lord Built*. He is a regular contributor to *Insomnia & Obsession* magazine. Marvin lives in Akron, Ohio, with his wife and two daughters. Visit his website, www. marvincbrown.com, for book excerpts, blog essays and book reviews. Marvin's movie reviews are available on the Internet Movie Database (www.imdb.com). Follow him on Twitter: marvbrown9 and Instagram: marvincbrown

CHRISTA CARMEN's short fiction has appeared in WolfSinger Publications' *Just Desserts*, the DreamFusion Press anthology, *The Book of the Macabre*, *Devolution Z Horror Magazine*, *The J.J. Outré Review*, *Jitter Press*, *Literally Stories*, *Fiction on the Web*, *Corner Bar Magazine*, *pennyshorts*, and *Dark Fire Fiction*. "Four Souls of Eve" was published by Frith Books as a standalone eBook, and is soon to appear in their *All Hallows'* anthology, and "The One Who Answers the Door" took Best in Genre for Thriller/Horror in *wordhaus'* Trick or Treat Fall Story Contest. Additional work is forthcoming in the *Mad Scientist Journal* and the speculative fiction ezine, *Anotherealm*. Christa works at Pfizer in Clinical Trial Packaging, and at a local hospital as a mental health clinician. She lives in Rhode Island with her husband and a beagle who rivals her in stubbornness.

ADAM CESARE is a New Yorker who lives in Philadelphia. His books include *Mercy House*, *Video Night*, *The Summer Job*, and *Tribesmen*. His work has been praised by Fangoria, Rue Morgue, Publishers Weekly, Bloody Disgusting, and more. His titles have appeared on "Year's Best" lists from outlets like Complex and FearNet. He writes a monthly column for Cemetery Dance Online.

MATTHEW CHABIN is a writer from Portland Oregon. He worked as a journalist in the US Navy and studied literature and philosophy at Southern Oregon University. His work has appeared in *Gravel: A Literary Journal*, *Southern Pacific Review*, and *O-Dark Thirty: A Veteran's Writing Project*. He currently lives in Nagano Prefecture of Japan with his wife and two cats.

His story, *Father of Dread*, originally appeared in *Cthulhu Lies Dreaming*, an anthology from Ghostwoods Books.

JOSE CRUZ is an author and freelance writer whose work has appeared in print and online venues such as Nightscript, Turn to Ash, bare•bones e-zine, The Terror Trap, Classic-Horror, and Paracinema Magazine. He lives in southwest Florida with his wife and a very furry child.

The first thing ANDREW DARLINGTON had published was the poem "Anthem For A Lost Cause" in Barnsley-based "underground"-arts magazine *Sad Traffic* (no.5, May 1971). It was also the first poem he'd ever written. It name-checks Homer's *Odysseus*, and the Edgar Rice Burroughs *Martian Tales* establishing the recurring technique of using the trash Junk Culture of cheap pulp SF (and loud Rock 'n' Roll) to reference personal issues—the "lost cause", of course, being himself! Over 3,000 published items follow, extending across a widthband from Music Journalism to Erotica, from closely-researched historico-features on Science Fiction to interviews with culture icons William Burroughs, the Kinks, Kurt Vonnegut, Stone Roses, Byrds, Craig Charles, Peter Green (Fleetwood Mac), Robert Plant (Led Zeppelin), Cabaret Voltaire, Carolyn Cassady (Kerouac's lover), EC Tubb, Jack Dee, and many more (a selection collected into *I Was Elvis Presley's Bastard Lovechild*, Headpress, 2001).

He was born 18th September 1947—to coincide with the Roswell UFO Incident in New Mexico, and pubesced through the fantastic graphic-strip exploits of "Jet-Ace Logan" (a SFictional hero he later scripted for). Fiction was the first form—in New English Libraries *Stopwatch* anthology (editor: George Hay, January 1975) through multiple magazine and hard/softback appearances around the world (including German and Flemish translations) to the 2015 *The Mammoth Book Of Sherlock Holmes Abroad* (editor: Simon Clark, 2015). In fact, space restrictions mean that elaboration of the Alternative Cabaret "Stand-Up Poet" work, the vinyl records as part of UV Pop, editing *Ludds Mill* alternative-arts magazine, the *Don't Call Me Nigger: Sly Stone & Black Power* biography (Leaky Boot Press, 2014), new fiction collection *A Saucerful Of Secrets* now available from Parallel Universe Publ. and poetry collection *The Poet's Deliberation On The State Of The Nation* (Penniless Press http://www.pennilesspress.co.uk/books/poetdeliberation.htm). His website is: www.andrewdarlington.blogspot.com

PAOLO DI ORAZIO, born in Rome, Italy, in 1966, is a writer, painter, drummer, and an HWA active member. He has published short novels, long fiction and comic books since 1987 in Italy. The very first splatterpunk author of his country, his first book raised a Parliamentarian scandal in 1990—for instigation of murder (*My Early Crimes*, Raven's

Head Press, 2015).

In English, he published stories for *Heavy Metal* (2000-01), and *Kipple* (*Dark Gates*, with Bram Stoker Award Alessandro Manzetti, in 2014. *The Monster, The Bad And The Ugly*, anthology). His short novel *Hell* was recommended by Ellen Datlow in The Best Horror Of The Year Vol.7 (2014).

STEFANIE ELRICK is a writer, artist and performer from Manchester. She's toured fantasy stage shows with Hawkwind, The Levellers, The Age of Glass, Peaches Christ and others as well as devising the immersive *LABOLIS* theatre series. As a performance artist she's blood-lined poetry into her skin, been strapped to a 12-foot spinning timepiece and escaped Houdini like out of mod-roc cocoons. Her written work has been published in *Cthulhusattva: Tales of the Black Gnosis* and she has lectured at Manchester University and Wimbledon Art College. She's particularly fascinated by hybrids, shape-shifting and magic. www.stefanieelrick.com

WILLIAM GRABOWSKI is the author of 9 books (ghostwriter of more), most recently the techno-thriller *Infinity Point*, media tie-in *Castro's Cadillac* (from the screenplay by Michael Sayles, optioned for filming on September 12, 2016 by CuffLink Productions), Amazon bestseller *Black Light: Perspectives on Mysterious Phenomena*, and *Traces of Oblivion*—a collection of best short stories including his 2004 novel *The Untold*—a conspiracy thriller. Five years with World Fantasy Award-winner *The Horror Show* earned Grabowski a Best Writer nomination from SPWAO. Over 350 of his articles, essays, interviews and reviews have appeared on Forbes dot com, *Philadelphia Business Journal* digital edition, Hellnotes and elsewhere; in magazines *Cemetery Dance, Beware the Dark*, NPR-associated *Wireless* and others. He's a popular guest on radio and podcasts, and a contributing editor with *Library Journal*, Metaphysical Circus Press's *See the Elephant*, and JournalStone Publishing.

SARAH L. JOHNSON lives in Canada with her family and two bewildered felines. Her work has appeared in *Shock Totem, Crossed Genres*, and the Bram Stoker nominated *Dark Visions 1*. Her short story collection *Suicide Stitch* was released by EMP Publishing in 2016.

ERIC LAROCCA's horror fiction has appeared in various literary journals and anthologies such as, *Of Devils & Deviants: An Anthology of Erotic*

Horror and *Stiff Things: The Splatterporn Anthology.* He is also the author of several plays, which have been developed and produced by various theater companies including, Gadfly Theater Productions, Hartford Stage, La Petite Morgue, and Love Creek Productions. He currently resides in New Hampshire.

ALESSANDRO MANZETTI is a Bram Stoker Award winning author of horror fiction and dark poetry, editor and translator. His work has been published extensively in Italian, including novels, short and long fiction, poetry, essays, and collections. English publications include his collections *The Monster, the Bad and the Ugly* (co-written by Paolo Di Orazio),*The Massacre of the Mermaids, The Shaman and Other Shadows, Dark Gates* (co-written by Paolo Di Orazio), *Stockholm Syndrome* (co-written by Stefano Fantelli), and the poetry collections *Eden Underground, Venus Intervention* and *Sacrificial Nights* (co-written with Bruce Boston). His stories and poems have appeared in Italian, USA and UK magazines and anthologies, such as *Dark Moon Digest, The Horror Zine, Disturbed Digest, Illumen Magazine, Devolution Z Magazine, Recompose Magazine, Polu Texni Magazine, Bones III Anthology, Rhysling Anthology* (2015 and 2016), *HWA Poetry Showcase Vol. III, The Beauty of Death, Mar Dulce, I Sogni del Diavolo, Danze Eretiche Vol. 2, Il Buio Dentro* and many others.

His dark poetry collection *Eden Underground* won the Bram Stoker Award 2015 and was nominated for the Elgin Award 2016. His dark poetry collection *Venus Intervention* (co-written by Corrine de Winter) was nominated for the Bram Stoker Award 2014 and the Elgin Award 2015. Some of his poems were nominated for the Rhysling Award 2015 and 2016. Six of his stories were recommended by Ellen Datlow for the *Best Horror of the Year* Vol. 7, and two of his poems made the long list of the Honorable Mentions for *The Best Horror of the Year* Vol. 8.

He has translated works by Ramsey Campbell, Richard Laymon, Poppy Z. Brite, Edward Lee, Graham Masterton, Gary Braunbeck, Gene O'Neill, Lisa Morton and Lucy Snyder. He is the owner and editor-in-chief of Independent Legions Publishing, HWA Active Member, Italy Representative and member of the Board of Trustees.

More about Alessandro at his website: http://www.battiago.com/biography.html

TIM MILLER has dedicated his life to writing stories that will both scare readers and make them cringe.

Over the years, Tim's writings have evolved into darker realms. He released his first horror novel, *The Hand of God* in 2011. Since then his books have become progressively more violent and gory. With the release of *Family Night* in 2013, Tim had moved into the world of extreme horror where he continues to push the boundaries of human suffering.

Tim is now an international best seller as well. His books, *Hell, Texas* and *Family Night* have recently ranked high on Amazon sales charts since their release in Germany under German publisher, Festa-Verlag.

Tim is very active on social media and loves interacting with his readers. You can find him at his website at http://timmiller.org.

ALEXANDRA RENWICK is the US/Canadian author of the award-nominated collection *Push of the Sky*, which was a Powell's Books SF Book Club reading selection and received a starred review in *Publishers Weekly*. Her fiction has been translated into nine languages and performed in audio and on stage. She currently lives in a crumbling urban castle tending to a pondful of voracious koi she's been warned not to name. More at http://alexcrenwick.com.

JEREMY THOMPSON is the fictionist responsible for the novels *The Phantom Cabinet* (Necro Publications) and *Let's Destroy Investutech* (Bedlam Press). His stories have appeared in a number of magazines and anthologies, including *Into the Darkness*, *Under the Bed*, *DarkFuse*, *Sanitarium*, and *Walk Hand in Hand into Extinction*. A San Diego State University graduate, Jeremy resides in Oceanside, California.

TIM WAGGONER's first novel came out in 2001, and he's published over thirty novels and three collections of short stories since. He writes original fantasy and horror, as well as media tie-ins. His novels include *Like Death*, considered a modern classic in the genre, and the popular *Nekropolis* series of urban fantasy novels. He's written tie-in fiction for *Supernatural, Grimm, The X-Files, Doctor Who, A Nightmare on Elm Street,* and *Transformers*, among others. His articles on writing have appeared in Writer's Digest, Writer's Journal, and Writer's Workshop of Horror. He's been a finalist for the Shirley Jackson Award and the Scribe Award, and his fiction has received numerous Honorable Mentions in volumes of *Best Horror of the Year*. In 2016, the Horror Writers Association honored him with the Mentor of the Year Award. In addition to writing, Tim is also a full-time tenured professor who teaches creative writing and composition at Sinclair College.

WRATH JAMES WHITE is a former World Class Heavyweight Kickboxer, a professional Kickboxing and Mixed Martial Arts trainer, distance runner, performance artist, and former street brawler, who is now known for creating some of the most disturbing works of fiction in print.

Wrath is the author of such extreme horror classics as *The Resurrectionist* (now a major motion picture titled *Come Back To Me*) *Succulent Prey*, and it's sequel *Prey Drive*, *Yaccub's Curse*, *400 Days Of Oppression*, *Sacrifice*, *Voracious*, *To The Death*, *The Reaper*, *Skinzz*, *Everyone Dies Famous In A Small Town*, *The Book Of A Thousand Sins*, *His Pain*, *Population Zero* and many others. He is the co-author of *Teratologist* co-written with the king of extreme horror, Edward Lee, *Something Terrible* co-written with his son Sultan Z. White, *Orgy Of Souls* co-written with Maurice Broaddus, *Hero* and *The Killings* both co-written with J.F. Gonzalez, *Poisoning Eros* co-written with Monica J. O'Rourke, among others.

Wrath lives and works in Austin, Texas with his three daughters, Isis, Nala, and Zoe, his son and co-author, Sultan Z. White, and his beautiful wife Tammy.

STEPHANIE M. WYTOVICH is an instructor by day and a horror writer by night. She is the Poetry Editor for Raw Dog Screaming Press, an adjunct at Western Connecticut State University, and a book reviewer for Nameless Magazine. She is a member of the Science Fiction Poetry Association, an active member of the Horror Writers Association, and a graduate of Seton Hill University's MFA program for Writing Popular Fiction. Her Bram Stoker Award-nominated poetry collections, *Hysteria: A Collection of Madness*, *Mourning Jewelry*, *An Exorcism of Angels*, and *Brothel* earned a home with Raw Dog Screaming Press, and her debut novel, *The Eighth*, is simmering in sin with Dark Regions Press. Follow Wytovich at http://www.stephaniewytovich.com/ and on twitter @ JustAfterSunset

THE MOSH PIT

Hardcore Corps of Extremity Explorers

Reader-recommended hardcore and extreme books compiled from Reddit, Goodreads, forums, blogs, Amazon forums, and various other sources.

Anthologies and Magazines:

John Pelan, Editor: *Darkside: Horror for the Next Millenium*

Paul M. Sammons, Editor: *Splatterpunks: Extreme Horror; Splatterpunks II: Over the Edge*

Jim Goforth, Editor: *Rejected for Content*

David C. Hayes & Jack Burton, Editors: *D.O.A. Extreme Horror Anthology*

Jack Bantry, Editor: *Splatterpunk Zine*

Collaborations:

Blake Crouch & Jack Kilborn/J.A. Konrath: *Serial Killers Uncut*

John Skipp & Craig Spector: *The Light at the End*

Randy Chandler & t. Winter-Damon: *Duet for the Devil*

Eric Enck & Adam Huber: *Snuff*

Novels:

Clive Barker: *Books of Blood*

Poppy Z. Brite: *Exquisite Corpse*

Simon Clark: *Blood Crazy*

Tim Curran: *Cannibal Corpse; Devil Next Door*

Nick Cutter: *The Deep; The Troop; Little Heaven*

Samuel R. Delany: *Hogg*

Robert Devereaux: *Deadweight; Slaughterhouse High*

Aaron Dries: *The Fallen Boys; House of Sighs*

Bret Easton Ellis: *American Psycho*

John Everson: Siren; *The 13th; Sacrifice*

Ray Garton: *Shackled*

Jonny Glynn: *The Seven Days of Peter Crumb*

J.F. Gonzalez: *Survivor; The Beloved*

Ryan Harding: *Genital Grinder*

Charlee Jacob: *Season of the Witch; Haunter; This Symbiotic Fascination; Dread in the Beast*

Mendal W. Johnson: *Let's Go Play at the Adams*

Brian Keene: *The Rising; Jack's Magic Beans; Kill Whitey; Take The Long Way Home; Urban Gothic*

Ronald Kelly: *The Sick Stuff*

Jack Ketchum: *Off Season; The Girl Next Door*

Jack Kilborn/J.A. Konrath: *Afraid; Endurance; Haunted House*

Kathe Koja: *The Cipher*

Jan Kozlowski: *Die, You Bastard! Die!*

Joe Lansdale: *The Nightrunners; On the Far Side of the Cadillac Desert with Dead Folks*

Richard Laymon: *The Woods Are Dark; Resurrection Dreams; The Cellar*

Edward Lee: *Monstrosity; The Bighead; Header; The Pig; The House; Creekers*

Patrick Lestewka: *The Preserve; The Coliseum*

Cormac McCarthy: *Blood Meridian*

Shane McKenzie: *All You Can Eat; Pus Junkies*

Carlton Mellick III: *Zombies and Shit; Apeshit; Clusterfuck*

Rex Miller: *Slob; Frenzy*

Tim Miller: *Hacked; Hell, Texas*

Mark Mirabello: *The Cannibal Within*

Monica J. O'Rourke: *In the End, Only Darkness; Suffer the Flesh*

Chuck Palahniuk: *Haunted; Snuff*

Mark E. Rogers: *The Dead*

Gord Rollo: *Jigsaw Man*

David J. Schow: *Seeing Red*

Matt Shaw: *The Farm; Porn*

John Shirley: *Cellars; Wetbones*

John Skipp: *Book of the Dead; The Scream*

Michael Slade: *Headhunter; Ghoul; Ripper*

Bryan Smith: *Depraved; The Freakshow; The Killing Kind; House of Blood*

L.L. Soares: *Life Rage*

Lucy Taylor: *Unnatural Acts and Other Stories*

Thomas Tessier: *Finishing Touches*

Ryan C. Thomas: *The Summer I Died*

Tim Waggoner: *Pandora Drive*

Sam West: *Djinn: An Extreme Horror Novel*

Wrath James White: *Succulent Prey; Population Zero; The Resurrectionist; Sloppy Seconds; The Book Of A Thousand Sins*

Barbie Wilde: *The Venus Complex*

COPYRIGHTS CONT'D.

Selected Poems from *Brothel* by Stephanie M. Wytovich, Publisher: Raw Dog Screaming Press (2016)

"Coming of the Darkula" by Andrew Darlington, Publisher: *Literotica: Sci-Fi & Fantasy* (March 2016)

"Little Sister, Little Brother" by Sarah L. Johnson, from *Suicide Stitch: Eleven Stories*, Publisher: EMP Publishing (March 2016)

"Miss_Vertebrae" by Eric LaRocca, from *Rejected for Content 4: Highway to Hell*, Editor: Jim Goforth, Publisher: J. Ellington Ashton Press,Wetworks (July 2016)

"Bed of Crimson Joy" by Jasper Bark, Publisher: KnightWatch Press (July 2016)

"Please Subscribe" by Adam Cesare, from *Splatterpunk's Not Dead*, Editor: Jack Bantry, Publisher: Splatterpunk Zine (September 2016)

"Backne" by Tim Miller, from *A Gathering of Gore*, Publisher: Gut-Wrench Productions (2016)

"The Girl Who Loved Bruce Campbell" by Christa Carmen, Publisher: *Corner Bar Magazine* Vol. 1 #4 (March 2016)

"Implant" by Bryan Smith, from *Seven Deadly Tales of Terror*, Publisher: Bitter Ale Press (May 2016)

"Father of Dread" by Matthew Chabin, from *Cthulhu Lies Dreaming*, Editor: Salome Jones, Publisher: Ghostwoods Books (February 2016)

"On This Side of Bloodletting" by Stephanie M. Wytovich, from *555 Vol. 2: This Head, These Limbs*, Editor: Joseph Bouthiette Jr, Publisher: Carrion Blue (November 2016)

RED ROOM

EXTREME HORROR MAGAZINE

OCTOBER 2017

FICTION BY
JACK KETCHUM
MEG ELISON
TIM CURRAN

FEATURE INTERVIEW
MEG ELISON
AUTHOR OF THE BESTSELLER
THE BOOK OF THE UNNAMED MIDWIFE

REDROOMMAGAZINE.COM

Made in the USA
San Bernardino, CA
05 June 2017